Moonlight Plains

Multi-award-winning author Barbara Hannay is a city-bred girl with a yen for country life. Most of her forty-plus books are set in rural and outback Australia and have been enjoyed by readers around the world. In her own version of life imitating art, Barbara and her husband currently live on a misty hillside in beautiful Far North Queensland where they keep heritage pigs, hens, ducks, turkeys and an untidy but productive garden.

barbarahannay.com

ALSO AVAILABLE FROM PENGUIN BOOKS

BARBARA HANNAY

Moonlight Plains

MICHAEL JOSEPH
an imprint of
PENGUIN BOOKS

MICHAEL JOSEPH

Published by the Penguin Group
Penguin Group (Australia)
707 Collins Street, Melbourne, Victoria 3008, Australia
(a division of Penguin Australia Pty Ltd)
Penguin Group (USA) Inc.
375 Hudson Street, New York, New York 10014, USA
Penguin Group (Canada)
90 Eglinton Avenue East, Suite 700, Toronto, Canada ON M4P 2Y3
(a division of Penguin Canada Books Inc.)
Penguin Books Ltd
80 Strand, London WC2R 0RL England
Penguin Ireland
25 St Stephen's Green, Dublin 2, Ireland
(a division of Penguin Books Ltd)
Penguin Books India Pvt Ltd
11 Community Centre, Panchsheel Park, New Delhi 110 017, India
Penguin Group (NZ)
67 Apollo Drive, Rosedale, Auckland 0632, New Zealand
(a division of Penguin New Zealand Pty Ltd)
Penguin Books (South Africa) (Pty) Ltd
Rosebank Office Park, Block D, 181 Jan Smuts Avenue, Parktown North, Johannesburg 2196,
South Africa
Penguin (Beijing) Ltd
7F, Tower B, Jiaming Center, 27 East Third Ring Road North, Chaoyang District, Beijing 100020,
China

Penguin Books Ltd, Registered Offices: 80 Strand, London WC2R 0RL, England

First published by Penguin Group (Australia), 2014

13 5 7 9 10 8 6 4 2

Text copyright © Barbara Hannay 2014

The moral right of the author has been asserted

Cover design by Nikki Townsend © Penguin Group (Australia)
Text design by Grace West © Penguin Group (Australia)
Cover photograph: girl by Blend Images/Trinette Reed/Getty Images;
girls/grass/hills by Andrej Godjevac/Getty Images; palms by Iakov Kalinin/BIGSTOCK;
house by Dieter Woelfle/Ozstockimages.com
Typeset in 11/17 pt Sabon by Post Pre-press Group, Brisbane, Queensland
Printed and bound in Australia by Griffin Press, an accredited ISO AS/NZS 14001 Environmental
Management Systems printer.

National Library of Australia
Cataloguing-in-Publication data:

Hannay, Barbara, author
Moonlight plains / Barbara Hannay
9781921901928 (paperback)
Man-woman relationship – Fiction
Family secrets – Fiction

A823.4

penguin.com.au

For Elliot

This one was always for you . . .

1

Sally's friends were wrong. She shouldn't have come to the ball. It was a mistake.

But her friends had been so very persuasive.

'You have to get back into the social scene, Sal. You can't go on like this. There's only so much running and swimming and kickboxing a girl can do.'

The messages had been coming at her on all fronts. She should be over her loss by now. Her grief for Josh was a moving and beautiful thing, but two and a half years was long enough.

Even the little old ladies at her grandmother's nursing home had chimed in with their two cents' worth.

'You still have your whole life ahead of you, my dear. You're not Queen Victoria, you know. You can't grieve for your husband forever.'

The only people in Sally's circle who had *not* showered her with advice were her parents. Admittedly, Sally's mother had tried to steer her out of the black morass of her initial grief, but she'd been rebuffed by her only child one time too many. Angela Spence's focus had quickly reverted to her mega-busy job as one of

Townsville's most in-demand lawyers.

And yet it *was* Angela who'd come up with the suggestion that Sally needed a dog. Of course, Angela hadn't visualised an elderly female cattle dog, virtually on death row at the pound. She'd tried to urge her daughter towards a puppy.

'This poor thing only has a few years left in her,' she'd said as they stood in front of the old dog's cage.

But there was something about the cattle dog's wistful look that speared straight to Sally's wounded heart. The poor old girl might be slow and arthritic, but she looked like a creature who needed a companion as much as Sally did.

The dog had arrived at the pound without a name, so Sally called her Jess, and after only a few nights together she and Jess were old friends, as if they both understood and shared the same sadness and loss.

Sally's father had done his best, too. Tom Spence ran a second-hand furniture business, and while he wasn't quite as busy and distracted as her mother, he was far too reserved to discuss deeply emotional issues with his daughter.

Instead, Tom had taken Sally skindiving on the reefs off Magnetic Island, where they'd swum around brain coral as big as a truck and she'd rediscovered the beauty of blue damsels and rainbow-coloured wrasse, silvery schools of herring and fascinating spotted maroon rays. Together they'd also canoed down the Burdekin, paddling between steep limestone cliffs and drifting lazily around shady bends, making their camp on the riverbank where, in the late afternoon, they listened as a wind rippled through the river gums, as if someone had rolled out an invisible rug, shaking dead leaves from the treetops.

To her huge surprise, Sally had found she enjoyed these activities now in her twenties almost as much as she had when she was a child. She'd understood that this was her father's gentle way of showing her that it was possible to enjoy Life After Josh.

But while her parents had been gentle, Sally's girlfriends had been persistently vocal. They'd coaxed her steadily and with such rowdy enthusiasm that eventually she'd started to feel the tiniest glimmer of hope.

At first it was scary to sense even the slightest change in herself. She'd become used to the awful emptiness that had dulled her for the past two and a half years, but now the lethargy shifted ever so slightly.

'I don't know what you expect of me,' she'd warned her friends as they gathered for Friday drinks in their favourite Palmer Street wine bar. 'I couldn't possibly face the nightclub scene again. And I don't want any of your matchmaking, thanks. Don't bother inviting me to dinners and parties where you've already lined up some poor guy to be nice to me.'

Her best friend Megan had pouted at this. 'You're really making this hard, you know, Sal.' Since kindergarten, Megan had always been a girl who needed quick-fix solutions to every problem.

In the end, it was Kitty Mathieson, an old lady at the nursing home, who'd told Sally about the ball. Sally and Jess were making their weekly visit to Sally's nan, who had Alzheimer's.

While Angela Spence only had time for quick visits to the home, mainly fussing with admin over the level of care her mother was receiving, Sally had developed the habit of sitting with her grandmother. Conversation was difficult, so she often read aloud to her.

'Read the one with all the food,' Nan nearly always said, and Sally knew exactly what she meant. She'd lost count of the number of times she'd read about Ratty and Mole and their picnic on the riverbank, but she read their favourite scene from *The Wind in the Willows* yet again. Whenever she looked up from the book, she felt a lump in her throat to see the almost childlike smile on her nan's sweet familiar face as she listened and nodded and patted Jess.

As always, it was quite a lengthy process for Sally and Jess to make their way back through the home from Nan's high-care ward. They had to stop for lots of visits with other residents who also loved to pat Jess's soft coat or to slip her treats.

'Here comes *our dog*,' they would call, gleefully waving.

Sally always made a point of visiting Kitty Mathieson, who saved pieces of biscuit for Jess. While Kitty's mobility was limited and she apparently had a heart condition, her brain was as sharp as a needle and she always had something interesting to discuss.

Today, her eyes held a special sparkle. 'I have something for you, Sally.' With a very shaky hand, she shifted a tea mug on the stand beside her bed and revealed a flyer underneath. 'My daughter dropped this off.'

Sally had a nodding acquaintance with Kitty's daughter, Virginia, a slim, lively woman, around sixty, with greying blonde hair and friendly blue eyes.

'They're having a dance with a wartime theme out at Charters Towers, and Virginia thought I might be interested.' Kitty laughed. 'Not to dance, of course, but I spent time near the Towers during the war.' She pointed with an arthritic finger to a decorative string of American flags on the front of the pamphlet, partly obscured by a tea stain.

'Reviving old memories, Kitty?'

'Actually, I thought *you* might be interested.'

'In a ball at Charters Towers?' Sally tried to hide her dismay.

'It's really just a dance with a wartime theme.'

'How . . . how nice,' Sally said doubtfully.

'Those war years were such a romantic time.' Kitty's normally clouded grey eyes were shining. 'All the men in their snappy uniforms. The wonderful big-band music.'

'I guess you have fond memories.'

For a moment, Kitty seemed lost in those memories, lost in the past, but her smile trembled sadly as if the memories were bitter-sweet. Then, with a little shake, she snapped back to the present, switching her gaze directly to Sally. 'You could write a story about it for one of your magazines.'

'About your love life during the war?'

Kitty made a little huffing sound of impatience. 'About the dance, the old-time music and everything.'

'I suppose I could . . . possibly . . .' Sally wondered if she'd touched a nerve. It almost seemed as though the war might be a sensitive subject for Kitty. She found herself looking hard at the old lady. Her skin was crisscrossed with lines and it looked incredibly fragile, as if to touch it might leave a bruise. Her hair was thin and snow-white, but she wore it swept up into a surprisingly elegant topknot.

Sally tried to imagine how Kitty must have looked seventy years earlier, but it was impossible.

'There'd be plenty of photo opportunities at this ball,' Kitty prompted. 'The uniforms and medals. The forties dresses were very elegant, you know.'

'I guess.' To Sally's surprise, she could *almost* feel a skerrick of interest in the idea. An old-fashioned ball was not her scene, but it could, quite possibly, kill two birds with one stone. She could head off to this dance and prove to her girlfriends that she wasn't a total social drop-out, and if she took her notebook and camera, she could make a start on resurrecting her off-and-on career as a freelance journalist.

After the recent downward trend in the mining industry, her old job as PR rep for an engineering firm had been reduced to two days a week. She'd picked up casual work, subbing and writing advertorials for the local papers, but what she really wanted was to write features. Magazines with a focus on country lifestyles were always looking for good colour stories.

She would go, Sally decided with uncharacteristic impulsive-ness, which was how she found herself, two weeks later, driving a hundred kilometres west on a Friday evening to a ball in Charters Towers, dressed in no less than a precious and fragile 1940s dress of pale-pink georgette that Kitty Mathieson had unearthed and offered to her.

The dress was beautiful, with a band at the hips and triangles on the hem outlined with black beading. Sally hadn't been sure it would fit her, as Kitty was so tiny these days, but to her surprise it was perfect and it made her feel unexpectedly glamorous.

For one night, she would put on a costume and play a new role . . .

It was a good idea in theory. Unfortunately, Sally's newfound bra-vado deserted her almost as soon as she arrived at the ball and saw a room filled with strangers. Admittedly they were happy strangers, many dressed in appropriate 1940s costumes, dancing and swing-ing to the jazzy rhythm of brass band music. But why on earth had she thought she was ready for this? Her first impulse was to turn tail and to drive straight back to Townsville. So much for trying to impress her girlfriends.

She had a job to do, though, and that was easier than trying to make friends with strangers. Needing to look busy, Sally began to take photos of the band as they blasted out a brassy swing tune, and another pic of the little stars-and-stripes pennants strung over the bar. She snapped the middle-aged men dressed in their hired World War II military costumes, and a shot of a cheery, tipsy younger guy in the sailor's cap with *Marine* painted in red letters on his white T-shirt, as well as a trio decked out as short-skirted hatcheck girls.

The ball's organiser was a bustling, rather formidable woman, who reminded Sally of her school headmistress, but at least the woman was happy to provide far more details than were strictly necessary about the planning and execution of this 'exciting evening'.

After that, Sally knew she should try to fit in and chat with the revellers. It wouldn't be too difficult, surely? The band was surprisingly good, and not too loud for conversation right now, as a young man in a sailor suit crooned 'You Made Me Love You'. It wasn't as if there weren't plenty of young people here, all having a good time. And yet . . .

Joining the young people was where Sally bombed.

She knew what she was supposed to do – she should introduce herself, take their photos, make cheerful small talk, including polite questions about their costumes or their elegant forties hairdos, and try to be incredibly interested in their answers. But after one look at the laughing groups who all seemed to know each other, Sally was instantly awkward and shy.

I've lost my mojo.

It was worse than that. The sad truth was, Sally had never been to a mixed social gathering without Josh. That was what happened when you bucked the trend of your generation and fell in love with the only guy you'd ever dated . . . when you married your high school sweetheart.

And when he went and died on you . . . you were left in your late twenties with a huge black hole where your head and your heart used to be . . . and with major, *major* gaps in your social skills.

Embarrassed and very much the wallflower, Sally drifted to one side and while the band switched to the exciting 'Chattanooga Choo Choo', she studied a montage of old black and white photographs. Rows of aircraft were lined up on an airfield in the middle of a paddock and handsome young pilots smiled and laughed at the camera. She looked at their combed-back hairstyles, at their lean, athletic bodies, at their bright, confident smiles and imagined them dancing with lovely girls to this lively music. She wondered how many of these men had survived the war.

Then she stopped herself. She was *not* going to think about death tonight. The thought of any young man killed in the prime of his youth could still reduce her to tears.

Daily, hourly, for the past thirty months, she'd grieved for Josh, but tonight she was supposed to be taking a brave step forward. Quickly she switched her attention to a picture of an older man, frail and stoop-shouldered, sitting in a wheelchair with a tartan rug over his knees. He had rows of medals on his chest and she wondered if he'd been one of those same dashing young pilots. Someone had written names beneath each photo. If she stepped closer she could read them, but she wasn't planning to write about old soldiers.

She sighed. *I might as well just slip away home.*

'You look like you need a drink. Or directions on how to escape from here.'

Sally spun around.

The young man smiling at her was not in vintage fancy dress. He was wearing modern-day dark trousers and a smoothly tapered white shirt that showed off his wide shoulders and narrow hips. Already he'd loosened his collar and tie and hooked his suit coat over his shoulder. He might have been posing for a 'cool dude' commercial, except there was something very natural and easy and not at all *posing* about him.

'I've watched you prowling around,' he said.

'And here I was trying to be invisible.'

He smiled. 'I can't imagine why.'

Their gazes connected.

He was tall, with sun-flecked, light-brown hair and an indefinable air of the outdoors. Not handsome exactly, but his face had a kind of ruggedness that was manly without being tough. His eyes held smiling warmth. Almost certainly he was a country boy. A man of the land.

Not my type.

Just the same . . . Sally realised she was smiling at him.

Whoa, girl. Careful.

Granted, she'd caved in to her friends' pressure and come to this ball, but she'd come as an observer, not as a participant. Accepting a drink from a charming guy might seem innocent enough, but it started the ball rolling, so to speak, and awoke possible expectations that Sally had no intention of fulfilling.

Then again, as everyone had lectured her over and over, she had a long and lonely life ahead of her. If she didn't start somewhere . . .

'You're right,' she said, quickly, before she could change her mind. 'I could do with a drink. I'd love a glass of —' She'd been about to ask for anything white, but she said impulsively, 'I think I'd like bubbles, thanks.'

'Champagne it is.' He extended his hand. 'The name's Luke. Luke Fairburn.'

'Pleased to meet you, Luke. Sally Piper.'

His handshake was firm, his palm slightly rough. Sally suspected that he had calluses, presumably from hard outdoor work, and the thought fascinated her more than it should have. Actually, everything about him was . . .

Attractive?

Intriguing?

It felt mad to think that way. Wrong. Of course it had to be wrong. She should be terrified, and yet for some reason she couldn't explain, meeting Luke Fairburn felt . . . ever so slightly . . . okay. Maybe even more than slightly okay.

Sally found herself watching him as he headed to the bar and she realised she wasn't the only female with eyes on this guy. A young woman in killer heels and a super-short, tight, black, contemporary dress spotted Luke, peeled away from her group of friends, and sidled up to him at the bar. With a look-at-me flick of her long blonde hair, she began an animated conversation with him.

It was pretty clear she was flirting her head off, but while Luke didn't rebuff her, his body language wasn't exactly welcoming, which pleased Sally rather more than it should have.

Of course Sally quickly switched her attention back to the photographs so he didn't catch her spying.

Moments later, he returned with her drink.

'I'm guessing you're not a local,' he said.

'Not quite,' Sally agreed. 'I'm from Townsville.'

Luke acknowledged this with a nod, dropped his gaze to her hand. She'd taken off her rings so she wouldn't have to explain about Josh, but she hoped he hadn't seen the faint telltale mark. Her ring finger felt naked and exposed. She was so used to wearing the rings, even flashing them at times, to keep guys at bay.

Now, though, Luke let out a little huff of breath that might have been relief. He smiled. 'I probably should've asked you to dance before I grabbed these drinks. That dress looks like it's designed for dancing.'

Turning, Sally watched the couples on the dance floor swishing through an old-fashioned number with proper steps, not the usual nightclub shuffle. Many of them had obviously learned these old dances and they were swinging and spinning like professionals. 'I'm not sure I'd know how,' she confessed. 'My dress might be from the forties, but I'm afraid my feet aren't.'

She wouldn't admit it, but her high heels were already killing her. It was ages since she'd worn them. She couldn't actually remember the last time.

'Must admit I wouldn't know which foot to put in front of the other.' Luke grinned again and gestured to her dress. 'But this is amazing. Did you hire it?'

'No. It's the real thing. It belongs to one of my grandmother's friends. She actually wore it during the war.'

'Wow. Must be one sexy grandmother.'

His compliment made Sally's cheeks heat. They were smiling at each other. Again.

2

Sally Piper had blown Luke away, bowled him over, knocked him for six. From his first sight of her in the old-fashioned pink dress that skimmed and hugged her body in *all* the right places, Luke knew he was grinning like a shot fox.

He supposed he should be cautious. He was already dodging the attentions of Kylie, the girl from the local hardware store who'd just cornered him at the bar.

But hell, he might have taken Kylie out once, but he hadn't come to this ball as her escort. He was here because he owed his grandmother a favour; more than one, actually.

Now that he'd met Sally, Luke felt as if his indebtedness had trebled. Sally was beautiful – *a stunner* – with red hair – no, he couldn't call it red. Auburn was the word, wasn't it? And she had the fair skin that went with auburn hair, so soft and smooth a guy could only wonder what it felt like to touch.

By contrast to her pale skin, her eyes were dark, a warm nut-brown. Unsettling . . . which was weird given that he was normally relaxed and confident around women.

They found a small table with two chairs in a reasonably quiet corner of the dance hall. Sally took a sip of her champagne. 'That's lovely. Fabulous, thanks.'

'So . . .' Luke schooled himself to sound calm and casual. 'I take it you're here on your own?'

'I am, yes. And you?'

'The same.' He smiled. 'I've been trying to decide if you're here for business or pleasure.'

'Bit of both. I guess you saw me taking notes?'

'And photographs.'

Sally nodded. 'I'm hoping to do a small story for one of the country style magazines.'

'You're a journalist?'

'Freelance.' Quickly she added, 'What about you?'

'Builder.'

'Really?' Those brown eyes of hers widened with surprise.

'Wrong answer?'

'No. Sorry.' She gave a small laugh. 'It's just that I had you pegged as a man of the land; a cattleman, I guess.'

Luke smiled. 'I've done my share of cattle work. My family have cattle properties and that's all I did until a couple of years ago. Actually, I'm still running a few head where I am now, but on a much smaller scale.'

'Where's that? Somewhere near here?'

'Moonlight Plains. It's my grandmother's property, about forty k's out of town. I'm here tonight because there are a few broken scraps of an old American plane from the war in one of the paddocks.'

He waved a hand to encompass the decorative flags, the band, the photographs. 'The ball's organisers are treating the paddock like it's a sacred site. They want to take some people out there tomorrow.'

'That's interesting. So you're here as a VIP guest?'

'Something like that.'

A slight pause followed, but before Luke could come up with a question about Sally, she fired another of her own. 'So . . . what are you building?'

'I'm renovating, actually. Fixing up the old homestead.'

'On your own?'

He knew his smile was less assured. This was his first solo job as a fully qualified builder. 'Seemed like a good idea at the time, but I may yet live to regret it. It's a huge job.'

'You're enjoying the work though?'

Luke dropped his gaze to his beer. He remembered the first time he'd gone back to Moonlight Plains, fighting his way through waist-high grass to the front steps, to find a sagging building filled with cobwebs and mouse droppings. And yet . . .

He could hardly confess his love affair with a house to this girl. How could he explain the wonder of it? Discovering a broken-down thing of beauty and absorbing the abandonment, sensing the haunting memories of the people who'd lived there? Being gripped by the need to restore and rebuild?

'Sorry,' Sally said quickly. 'That's the journalist in me, asking too many questions. Tell me to shut up.'

'Nah, it's cool.'

'I must admit I've always thought it would be fun to do up an old house. I'm sure renovations are much more interesting and creative than building a brand-new square brick box.'

'Won't argue with that.'

'But there must be a lot of challenges.'

Sure. Clearing the ceilings of a dozen carpet pythons, for starters. Luke gave a slight shake of his head as he wondered how interested Sally really was. 'You sound like you're still in journalist mode.'

'I know. Sorry, but I'm genuinely intrigued. Truly.'

She looked so earnest and . . . *keen*. Luke felt his throat constrict. Hell. He had to be careful. He had a long job ahead of him and the last thing he needed was to lose his head over a chick from Townsville. He'd already made one mistake, allowing himself to be sidetracked by Jana, a German backpacker he'd met at a B&S ball, but she'd moved on now and he needed a clear run on this renovation.

Sally tipped her head to one side, her autumn curls slipping softly with the movement, and she eyed him quizzically. 'You know, I can imagine doing a kind of *Grand Designs* story on you. Following your progress on the house.'

'For one of your magazines?'

'Yes. Why not?'

Luke swallowed. He imagined seeing this girl again over the coming months, sharing his precarious dreams with her. 'Are you serious?'

For a moment, Sally seemed distracted by a group behind him. Turning to glance over his shoulder, Luke saw Kylie from the hardware store, watching the two of them with a venomous glare.

Damn. He thought she'd got the message when he'd spoken to her at the bar.

He returned his attention to Sally, repeating his question. 'Are you serious about the article?'

'I'm serious about doing the story. I can't promise that I'll be able to sell it to a national publication, but I'd have a darned good go.'

'You haven't even seen the house.'

'That's true.' Her smile was complicated – boldly challenging, yet shy.

'Would you like to see it?'

'I'd love to. When?'

'First thing tomorrow morning? Are you staying in town?'

Sally nodded. 'I've booked a motel room.'

Luke glanced out the window to the moon-silvered lawns and tennis courts that belonged to this hall, and he drew a deep breath.

His sudden difficulty breathing was crazy. About as crazy as his next suggestion. 'It's two days off full moon and the homestead looks amazing in the moonlight. We could always escape out there now.'

3

Boston, 2010

Dearest Kitty,

Here I go again. After all these years, almost seventy of them, still revisiting lost dreams. Often my recollections are happy ones with you, but there are times when unsettling memories of the war take over, usually when I'm desperate for sleep.

Now, with yet another generation in harm's way, they're working on treatments for post-traumatic stress. I have my own answer. Remembering you and everything we shared blocks the dark memories, and writing it down helps to package my feelings safely and neatly.

There's only one problem with this. I now have a carton filled with my ramblings, like the X-Files at the Pentagon or Pandora's box in a hidden cave . . . never to be opened.

Fortunately, I haven't been troubled for many months, but last night I was in a jammed cockpit again and it wouldn't open and I could smell fire. I woke in a sweat and, as always, I took a while to recover. I forced myself to remember happier times.

I remembered you.

Once again you saved me, Kitty.

When I finally slept, I dreamed I was back at the homestead, walking up the path between the old rose gardens. I could see the house perfectly, big and rambling and built of timber with verandahs all around.

The front door with its beautiful stained-glass panels opened to my touch and I went in, down the dark central hallway, past the row of pegs with your uncle's WWI greatcoat, past the lounge room with the Beale piano.

I found you in the kitchen at the back of the house. This was unusual. Most times, when I dream about you, you're magically, impossibly here in America. Sometimes, you're getting along famously with my family, which is also impossible. They don't even know about you, and never will.

But last night it was so good to be in Australia with you, my darling girl. You were sitting at the kitchen table shelling peas, your hands quick and graceful and mesmerising. The sunlight fell on your hair, warming it to a rich honey glow. You were wearing a blue floral dress with a scalloped neckline, so pretty, and you looked up at me and smiled that slightly crooked smile of yours. You were so beautiful my heart swelled with happiness.

Then, in that mysterious way of dreams, we were in the big old metal bed on the island. It was morning and you were in my arms; early light filtered past the corrugated-iron push-out windows. We made love while the pale-green light cast wonderful patterns across the bed.

Next, you were in front of the faded mirror, trying on my leather flight jacket. It kept slipping from your bare shoulders. You were laughing as you snapped salutes at your reflection . . . and I just stared at your beauty and soaked up your joy, your womanly promise of life . . .

These are the best memories, Kitty. These are the memories that have kept me going all these years, the memories that sustain me now when I'm just a silly, sad old fool.

Winter's hanging on too long this year and thoughts of you keep me warm.

All my love,

Ed

4

Sally knew she should reject Luke Fairburn's suggestion. She couldn't believe she was hesitating, that she could actually contemplate saying yes, even for a moment.

How could she possibly go off with a guy she'd just met? Into the bush in the middle of the night?

It was crazy.

Admittedly, Luke had assured her it wasn't far to the homestead.

'I can have you back at your motel before the ute turns into a pumpkin.'

It was the sort of thing her friends did all the time, but Sally wasn't a risk-taker. Never had been, and if losing Josh had taught her anything, it was that life was unpredictable. Danger and heartbreak lurked in the happiest moments. She wouldn't shorten her odds by taking unnecessary risks.

And yet . . . she was truly interested in old houses. It had actually been a bone of contention with Josh; one of the few things they hadn't agreed on. He'd wanted their first home to be an ultra-modern, minimalist apartment, while Sally had had her heart set on a Queenslander cottage that they could do up together. She'd pictured the two of them painting walls, puttying window frames, rejuvenating old furniture, and she'd been disappointed that Josh was so against that idea.

After he died, she'd almost used the insurance money to buy a house, but she'd been so conscious of Josh's negativity that she'd held off.

Tonight, though, she had to admit that it wasn't only the idea of the house that intrigued her . . . There was an unreal quality to the whole evening: being away from Townsville at an old-fashioned dance in a borrowed dress from another era . . . It was almost like stepping into a dream . . .

Strange things happened in dreams . . . and Luke Fairburn's open and friendly smile invited her to trust him.

Except that already he was shaking his head. 'Okay, that was damn clumsy. Come and see my house in the moonlight. That's not my style. Corniest pickup line ever.'

'Well, it almost worked.'

Luke frowned.

A giddy little laugh escaped Sally. 'I was about to say yes.'

His eyes narrowed momentarily, but then he relaxed into another warm smile. 'Well, there you go. That's fantastic.'

Now she'd done it. Just like that, she'd thrown away her lifebelt. Anyone would think she'd drunk six glasses of champagne instead of one.

A pulse in Sally's throat hammered frantically to life and she dropped her gaze as she hastily considered her options. It wasn't too late. She could still drive back to Townsville, or she could retreat to the safety of the motel room she'd booked. Or she could accept the surprisingly attractive prospect of driving in the moonlight with a friendly and rather gorgeous guy to see an old homestead.

After hiding and playing it safe for so long, the simple act of coming to this ball had felt like a bold step. But it had been liberating, too, and now Sally was seriously tempted to take another, bolder step.

There was something about Luke Fairburn, something beyond his physical appeal. It wasn't just the appreciation that shone in his eyes when he looked at her. His eyes were green, she'd realised, a remarkable, fascinating shade – but she'd also sensed an inner decency in him that made her feel safe.

Safe *and* excited.

It was an intoxicating combination.

'Will anyone mind if you leave early?' she asked him.

'I've chatted with the historical committee, but I don't have any official duties, so I doubt anyone will really notice.'

'Not even that girl who's been giving us the death stare?'

'No way,' Luke said gruffly, but he *did* look slightly embarrassed. 'I hardly know her.'

They both looked around then, at the dancers, at the band and at the groups of people absorbed in conversation and laughter. The scowling girl seemed to have disappeared.

'We're not needed here, are we?' Sally said.

Luke shook his head and his green eyes sparkled. 'So, let's go.'

Not giving herself time for further doubts, she offered him a brave smile. 'Let's.'

She could almost hear her friends cheering.

Outside, the night air was decidedly crisp and Sally shivered. She'd forgotten that temperatures were cooler away from the coast, and she hadn't brought anything warm.

'Here.' Luke slipped his coat over her shoulders.

His gallantry was unexpected but reassuring and she was

grateful for the warmth of the smooth silky lining as it settled sensu-ously against her skin. 'Thanks.'

She was a tad nervous, though, as she climbed into Luke's ute and they zoomed off. She felt for the reassurance of her mobile phone in her handbag, clicked it on to check that she still had reception.

There was a text message from Megan.

So how's the ball, Cinders? Any princes? Hot cowboys?

Sally smiled and typed a quick reply.

1 or 2.

Almost immediately, an answer appeared.

Enjoy. ☺

Dragging a shaky breath, Sally dropped the phone into her bag.

'Your phone should work out at the homestead,' Luke commented.

'Oh . . . that's good.' Had he guessed she was nervous?

'There's a spot near the front steps that gets good reception, but walk a few paces and you often drop out.'

Right. Okay. She told herself to relax. *Enjoy.*

They kept conversation light, mostly about their favourite bands and TV shows, and Sally's relaxation held until Luke turned the ute off the main road onto a rutted and bumpy dirt track flanked on either side by dark spooky clumps of rubber vine and tall skinny gum trees.

'This is really in the bush.' So different from the seaside suburbs of Townsville where she'd always lived. Her voice squeaked a little.

'Not far now. The track's rough because it hasn't been used much and I still have to get it graded.'

Sally had forgotten that a house on a large cattle property was unlikely to be positioned right next to the main road in full view of passing traffic. Now, as the truck plunged deeper into the dark bush, she squashed thoughts of axe murderers, but she wished Luke's face wasn't in shadow. She needed to check out his smile again.

Slices of countryside appeared momentarily in the bright head-lights. Weathered timber fence posts, tree trunks and silvery grass flashed to brief life before the black night reclaimed them. A small furry animal scampered across the track. Every so often, the almost full moon appeared, sailing serenely through the gaps in the trees.

Sally hadn't been in the bush at night since the canoe trip with her dad almost a year ago, and now, despite her nervousness, she couldn't help feeling a slight sense of adventure.

'I should warn you not to expect too much,' Luke said as he slowed to take a bend. 'The old manager wasn't interested in the homestead. He preferred to live in an air-conditioned donga.'

'You mean like one of those prefab places they use on mining sites?'

'That's right. So the house isn't over-the-top grand. It's just —'

He left the sentence dangling as he steered the ute around a bumpy corner, and then the bush fell away, revealing paddocks that stretched flat and pale to a distant rise where the white timber home-stead stood, faintly glowing.

Luke slowed to a halt and cut the headlights.

'So there she is,' he said quietly. 'Moonlight Plains homestead.'

The old house looked exactly right for this setting, a classic Queenslander – a simple, large rectangle with deep verandahs all round and a peaked iron roof sweeping low, like a hat brim. The build-ing was dilapidated, of course. Even from this distance Sally could see the sagging wooden shutters and broken verandah railings. She guessed the paint would be shabby and peeling, the iron roof rusted.

Somehow, the house's neglected state reminded her of her dog, Jess. She smiled. 'It's the kind of house that deserves to be loved.'

Luke nodded. 'Yeah. That's exactly how I feel.'

She was touched by the depth of emotion in his voice.

I get it, she wanted to tell him. I do understand.

'It's such a simple design,' he said. 'No frills or fuss, but for me this house still has a certain elegance about her. I love the pitch of her roof line. I reckon she has a touch of class.'

He might have been describing a woman and, watching his manly profile outlined by moonlight, Sally felt an edgy excitement dance down her spine. She'd never been totally alone like this with a guy who wasn't Josh, and it was ages since she'd felt this jangling awareness, this growing curiosity and low buzzing inside her.

She wished she knew what Luke was thinking and feeling right now, and to her mild alarm, she realised she hoped he was thinking about *her* rather than the homestead.

'So that's the long-distance view,' he said as he flicked the truck's lights back on. 'Now for the close-up.'

Sally was very self-conscious as he drove across the paddocks, and the buzzing inside her grew more insistent.

To distract herself, she asked quickly, 'So has this been in your family for a long time?'

'My grandparents took it over after the war, but the property's not very big, so later they expanded and bought another place further west. This is good country for fattening, though, so my uncles nearly always have some of their cattle here, especially if there are droughts out west.'

By now they were pulling up near the homestead's front steps. 'Don't forget this is a building site,' Luke warned as she climbed out of the ute in her spindly heels.

The night was exceptionally quiet. There wasn't a sound except the soft trilling of crickets in nearby trees.

'You'll have to be careful. Some sections of the verandah aren't safe.'

The bright moon illuminated the timber verandah and Sally saw a roped-off section down one side.

'Stick close to me.' With casual confidence, Luke reached for her hand.

Such a simple, innocent, practical gesture . . . but Sally was super-aware of their skin contact, of their palms connecting, of the tingling warmth that spread up her arm as he guided her carefully up the stairs and along the verandah. Their shoulders brushed, and then their hips, and each time she felt an electrifying flash.

She was conscious of every millimetre of her skin under the borrowed dress, and she couldn't believe how quickly this had happened. For the first time in a very long time she didn't want to think about the past. She didn't want to mourn.

She realised now, incredibly, that she wanted Luke to touch her. This was why she'd come here. It had been so long . . . and her body had developed a mind of its own . . .

After two and a half years of loneliness, she longed for the comfort of a hug, for strong masculine arms around her, hungry lips on hers.

With a flick of a switch from Luke, the verandah was bathed in yellow light, revealing a workbench at one end with a power saw on it, and beside it a large toolbox holding hammers, screwdrivers, chisels and other gear. Sawdust and fine curls of pale-gold timber lay on the floor beneath the bench. Sally caught the scent of new wood and felt a rush of excitement that astonished her. Josh had never owned so much as a hammer.

'So basically, I've had to start by pulling the place apart.' Luke spoke calmly enough, but he was still holding Sally's hand. 'I began with a grand vision of the end result, but right now I'm in the demolition phase and it feels like I'm destroying it. It's a damn —'

He stopped and seemed to forget what else he wanted to say as he stared at her, and she stared at him.

She saw the movement of his throat as he swallowed, saw how tense he was. She held her breath as thrilling expectation sent her pulse racing. The emotion in his eyes made her limbs feel boneless.

'Truth is,' he said, pulling his gaze from her, 'all I have to show you is an empty old house with an internal wall and some cupboards ripped out. No real changes. No furniture to speak of.'

Sally smiled. He was as nervous and uncertain as she was, and the knowledge brought her a new sense of calmness. 'So . . . you're camping here?'

'More or less.'

'Well, we've come all this way, Luke, so you'd better show me around.'

For a long moment he just looked at her as if he was trying to make up his mind about something, and then he gave a smiling shrug. 'Sure.' He grinned. He had the cutest sparkling-eyed grin. 'I think I've cleared most of the cobwebs.'

He waved a hand towards the open front door with its multicoloured stained-glass panels. 'So it's a standard design. Hallway down the middle. Lounge and dining room on one side, bedrooms on the other, kitchen at the back.'

'Laundry outside?'

'Yeah, but I'm thinking about bringing it into the house, next to a bathroom.'

And some woman in the future will love you for that, Sally thought.

She noticed, with interest, a pile of books in one corner. At a glance they seemed mostly to do with architecture.

They moved through the front doorway into a hall with tongue and groove timber walls and exposed timber floorboards.

'Oh, I love the timber archway.' Sally pointed to a decorative arch halfway down the hall.

'There's a better one in here.' Luke steered her through another doorway where a larger, gracefully curved timber arch divided the empty lounge and dining rooms.

'Yes, lovely,' Sally agreed. 'I can picture it with fresh white paint and pots of ferns on those built-in plant stands.'

He laughed. 'I might have to consult you on the interior décor.'

She thought of the piles and piles of decorating magazines she'd collected but never put to use, and felt a little shiver of excitement. *We'll see.*

Once again, she was incredibly conscious of Luke, of his broad shoulders and deep chest, his suntanned skin, his capable hands . . .

Carefully they continued, making their way around a ladder that disappeared through a hole in the ceiling where timber panels had been removed. The doors to the other rooms, presumably bedrooms, were closed and Luke didn't offer to open them, so they arrived next at the kitchen.

A small, rusty fridge stood in one corner and a very basic sink was positioned beneath the bank of windows. In stark contrast to the orderliness of the toolboxes she'd seen elsewhere the sink was filled with a clutter of unwashed plates and mugs.

A couple of crates on the floor held bottles of sauce and tins of basics like tomato soup and baked beans. A two-burner stove plate was propped on another box that was turned on its side and there was also a camp table and a metal folding chair.

Standing in the middle of the room, all big shoulders and boyish smile, Luke shoved his hands in his trouser pockets as he looked about him. 'Believe it or not, this is going to be a showpiece one day.'

'Of course it is.'

His smile tilted. 'So . . . would you like a drink? I'm afraid it'll have to be beer or beer.'

Sally gave a soft laugh. She wasn't much of a beer drinker. 'I'd love a beer.'

'Great. Take the weight off.' Quickly, he grabbed a tea towel. 'Hang on.' With a flick of the towel he dusted off the metal seat. 'Can't spoil that borrowed finery.'

*

Luke watched as Sally sat down, watched the way his dark coat fell apart to reveal her pale-pink dress, watched her graceful movements as she crossed her slim legs.

For a moment he was transfixed and he just stood there, drinking in the sight of her. So perfect in his shabby, inadequate kitchen.

Then he remembered he was supposed to be getting their drinks. Shit, did he have a clean glass?

He wished he was calmer. Anyone would think he'd never hit on a girl before, but there was something about Sally that messed with his head. Half a dozen times already – in the ute, on the verandah, in the hallway – he'd nearly given in to his desire to kiss her, but for some reason he didn't quite understand, he knew he wanted to get this right. *Had* to get this right. Sally was different, so perfect in every way, he needed to lift his act.

To his relief, he found a clean glass and poured her beer, and it didn't froth too much or run down the sides.

Sally smiled as he handed it to her, and her dark eyes were warm and eloquent, almost as if she was sending him a silent message. He just hoped he was reading that message correctly.

'So,' she said, looking about her and pointing to the recessed section of the kitchen that was clad with ripple iron, 'is that where the wood stove used to be?'

Luke nodded. 'I'm thinking of turning it into —'

'Let me guess,' she interrupted eagerly. 'A walk-in pantry?'

'Yeah, that's one possibility.'

Her eyes were shining. 'That would be fabulous.' She took a sip of beer and set the glass on the table. 'Have you thought about the cupboards and benchtops yet?'

'Not really. I've a long way to go before I get to those details. I'm still working on the roof.'

Sally nodded, looking about her.

'You know,' she said next, and Luke half-expected her to offer a few cupboard suggestions. 'I came out this way last year with my father. We canoed down the Burdekin from Big Bend to the bridge at Macrossan.'

This was a surprise. 'Did you enjoy it?'

'I did. It was so quiet and peaceful on the river, but there was also a section with canyons and rapids. It's fantastic country.'

It wasn't every city girl who liked the bush.

'We saw so many birds. Dad caught fish. I took photographs.' Smiling, she asked, 'So do you know this area well? Did you grow up around here?'

'Further north,' he said. 'Almost a day's drive. Up in the Gulf on Mullinjim Station. My sister Bella's running the show now.'

When he saw Sally's raised eyebrows, he added, 'With the help of her husband, Gabe. And then there's another sister, my half-sister Zoe and her husband. They're on a neighbouring property.'

'Quite a family concern then?' Sally was clearly intrigued. 'Have your parents . . . retired?'

'My mum's in Townsville. She moved there after my father died.' Luke swallowed quickly as he said this. 'About a year ago.'

'I'm so sorry.'

Luke nodded and a small silence fell, and he was grateful that Sally didn't push him for details. There were still times when he found himself reliving the shock of his father's fatal heart attack. The news had come when he'd been driving back from Mullinjim to a job at Charters Towers, and the painful memory could still catch him out.

But when he glanced at Sally, he saw that her shoulders had drooped and she was staring forlornly at a spot on the floor. She looked so sad he felt a stab of fear. Had he roused bad memories for her as well? It was time to change the subject fast. His mind raced, searching for an interesting topic to put her at ease.

She gave a little shake and took a delicate sip of her beer, but she didn't seem to be enjoying the drink. She probably wasn't a beer drinker and had only accepted it to be polite.

Then she lifted her gaze and her cheeks were slightly flushed, and he thought how much the colour suited her.

'This isn't right, Luke,' she said, frowning. 'I feel wrong sitting here when you don't have a seat.'

'I'm fine,' he said, but he knew it was awkward. He should at least have two chairs. Jana had said as much, but that had been different. He'd made do with sitting on a crate, because he'd known she would soon be leaving.

'I'll make sure this setup's better when you come back to do your story,' he said now.

With an enigmatic smile, Sally stood again, leaving the barely touched beer on the table. She looked back down the hallway to the closed doors. 'So what's in these rooms?' Already she was heading towards them.

Luke dragged a quick breath as he followed her. She had to know they were bedrooms. 'Just . . . my gear.'

She turned back to him, her eyes bright and ever so slightly teasing, her cheeks a deeper pink than ever. 'Where do you sleep?'

His heart was hammering now. This was it. Miraculously, even though he'd told her he wasn't trying to pick her up . . . she'd known all along that he was doing exactly that. And here she was . . . asking the way . . . to his bedroom. His bedroom, which was as spartan as the kitchen.

Just his luck to find the perfect girl and have nothing more seductive to offer her than a swag on the floor. Sally was a city girl. She might have enjoyed a canoe trip on the Burdekin, but little giveaways like the pale perfection of her skin and her neatly painted fingernails shouted loud and clear that she was still a smooth city chick.

'It's a bit of a mess in there,' he warned, stepping between her and the closed door.

'I've never fancied neat freaks.' Sally smiled up at him, robbing him of breath.

Seemed she fancied him. This was going to happen.

'All night I've been wanting to tell you how gorgeous you are – the most beautiful girl I've ever met.'

With a soft smile, she stepped closer and lifted her face to his.

I wonder . . .

Lying in her nursing home bed, Kitty Mathieson couldn't sleep. She knew it was silly to pin too many hopes on what might be happening in Charters Towers, but she'd been picturing the scene at the ball . . . Sally Piper arriving in the pink georgette dress she'd lent her . . .

She wondered if her grandson Luke had gone to the ball as well. She knew he'd been invited.

She would give anything to be there, a fly on the wall, listening to the band play Benny Goodman and watching the dancing couples. Closing her eyes, Kitty could hear the music, faint at first, but coming to her more strongly, bright and brassy, stirring memories . . .

As the music swelled, the fates of Sally and her grandson were forgotten as she found herself slipping back . . .

She was nineteen again, in that frantic February when the war arrived on her doorstep.

5

Townsville, February 1942

The smells of sweat and fear mingled with train smoke as Kitty pushed her way through the anxious crowds on the station platform. The scene was depressingly familiar. Distraught mothers tried to calm crying babies, hassled porters yelled, 'Make way!' as they pushed trolleys piled dangerously high with suitcases and boxes, while bewildered children clutched prized possessions – a teddy bear, a doll, a wooden truck. It had been like this every night for the past week, as Kitty farewelled friends and neighbours. Everyone was leaving Townsville now that Darwin had been bombed. They were getting out of the north while they could. Any day now, the full-scale Japanese invasion would begin.

'I feel as if we're abandoning you,' Kitty's neighbour Jean said as she bundled her children into their carriage and kissed Kitty goodbye. 'I wish you could come with us.'

'Don't worry about me. I'll be fine.'

Kitty had said this to other friends on other nights. What else could she say? She wasn't especially brave. She was as scared as anyone else. The spectre of the Japanese terrified her.

She'd heard the stories about what they would do, but her

grandfather had refused to leave. As head churchwarden, he took his responsibilities to the remaining parishioners very seriously.

'If it comes to the worst,' she said now, 'the government will evacuate us.'

'Let's hope so.' Jean sounded doubtful and looked awkward, her fashionably painted dark-red lips drawing in tightly as she dropped her gaze.

There'd been horrifying rumours that the government intended to pull out of northern Australia. Apparently, it wasn't possible to defend the entire coastline, and everything north of Brisbane was to be abandoned to the Japs in the same way that Prime Minister Curtin and his cabinet had abandoned Rabaul in New Guinea. Bert Hammond, who lived in Kitty's street, had heard it from someone who worked in the government.

Kitty consoled herself that the Americans had already started to arrive. She'd seen their landing barges on the beach, their noisy convoys of trucks, their sunglasses and spiky haircuts, the money they readily flashed around. They were so smartly dressed and efficient. Surely they would make a difference?

'I know you'll be fine. You're a sensible girl,' Jean said. 'But I wish you were a little older.'

Kitty lifted her chin. 'I'm almost twenty.'

Jean smiled and lowered her voice so her children couldn't hear her. 'I'll tell you one thing, Kitty Martin. You're too pretty by half. Don't go making eyes at those Americans, or you'll be asking for trouble.'

Kitty wrinkled her nose. 'Now you're talking like my grandfather. If I believe him, the Americans are a greater threat to Australian girls than the Japanese are.'

'That's a bit rich.' Jean smiled ruefully, and she might have said more, but the guard was calling, 'All aboard.' It was time to settle her children.

Almost immediately, a shrill whistle blew and Kitty and the others on the platform began to wave.

From the carriage windows people called tearful farewells.

'Goodbye!'

'Stay safe!'

Arms waved madly as the train pulled slowly out of the station.

A hand tapped Kitty on the shoulder and she jumped.

'Gosh, Andy!'

Andy Mathieson lived in the street behind her and she'd known him for years, but it was a surprise to see him in uniform midweek. Like most of the boys his age, he'd joined the local militia, training on weekends down at the army reserve at Kissing Point, but here he was now, with his slouch hat turned up at the side and a stripe on his shoulder.

'I've signed up with the regulars,' he said with a shy smile. 'I convinced my parents I have to do my bit.

'Gosh,' Kitty said again, softly. In all the confusion and tension of the past week she hadn't heard the news.

'Mum said I might find you here, Kit.'

'Were you looking for me?'

Andy nodded. 'I'm heading off tomorrow morning.' Now his Adam's apple worked overtime. 'I wanted to make sure I said goodbye.'

'Oh, Andy.' She tried, unsuccessfully, to smile. 'The only thing I seem to say lately is goodbye.'

'Well, I can't miss out then.' He squared his shoulders. He was a tall fellow, nice enough looking – lanky-limbed and sandy-haired, with friendly blue eyes. 'Can I walk you home?'

The earnest way he asked this was a surprise. They'd known each other for almost ten years, since she'd first come to live with her grandparents, and they'd walked home from the pictures once or twice, casually, as friends, but Kitty sensed this was different somehow.

Of course it would be, wouldn't it? Everything was different now. 'That would be nice,' she said cheerfully. 'Thank you.'

As they left through the station's rather grand, white-tiled entrance, the warm tropical night pressed around them, close and humid. Outside, new rows of evacuees were lining up, ready for the next train in two hours' time. They looked tired and nervous, as if they feared something might go wrong and stop them from leaving.

Opposite the station, a slice of Castle Hill's rusty-pink rock face was caught in the beam of a searchlight. Andy took Kitty's hand and, because she couldn't think of a good reason not to, she let him hold it. She was wearing lace cotton gloves, and she could feel an unsettling heat coming from him through the open-weave fabric.

'So what happens after tomorrow?' she asked. 'Do you have to do more training?'

'I go to Enoggera first. After that —' Andy gave a carefully nonchalant shrug. 'I'll be a real digger. Who knows where I'll end up?'

Indeed. Who knew? There was talk of men being needed in Malaya. Kitty tried to put herself in her friend's shoes and she felt a hot surge of fear. But then she couldn't help wondering if staying at home and waiting to be invaded might be almost as bad as heading off to fight.

'I'm planning to write to you, Kitty.'

She struggled to hide her surprise. Quite good friends at times, she and Andy weren't sweethearts. Recently they'd played tennis together, and once or twice Andy had taken her to the pictures, and they'd danced at church socials.

But she'd danced with other fellows too. Kitty liked boys, as a general rule, and she was popular, although her grandfather's stern eye rather cramped her style.

'You won't have time to write to me,' she suggested. 'You'll be too busy writing to your family.'

'I want to write to you too.'

'Well, if you have time, I'd love to hear from you,' she assured him as they headed along Flinders Street, where the shop windows were full of the war, filled with posters for war loans, V for Victory flags and displays of the gear needed for air raids.

In a few short weeks, their sleepy tropical town had become a garrison. The post office clock tower had been dismantled so Japanese pilots couldn't use it to navigate. The graceful palm trees and pretty gardens in the centre of Flinders Street had been dug up and filled with sandbags and ugly concrete air-raid shelters.

'What do you think about all this talk of a Brisbane line?' Kitty asked. 'Will the government really abandon us up here?'

'Nah, I reckon it's tommy rot.' Andy shook his head, full of new importance and superior knowledge. 'You watch. Townsville will be an important Allied base. It'll have to be defended at all cost.'

'My grandfather's not so sure. He says Curtin and the politicians abandoned Rabaul. They didn't evacuate anyone or reinforce the soliders.'

'But Townsville's different and the Yanks are here now.'

'I guess.' His confidence was comforting.

At the top of Denham Street they crested the hill and their suburb lay below them, nestled at the foot of Castle Hill and fringed by the still waters of Cleveland Bay. Offshore, the dark silhouette of Magnetic Island floated in the purple dusk, but the beauty and serenity of the view was marred by three huge steel landing barges moored in the bay, and rolls of ugly barbed wire strung along the beachfront.

Always, everywhere were reminders of the war.

They went down the hill and the delicate scent of frangipani drifted from shadowy gardens. The front verandahs of the houses were dark and secretive – everyone had obeyed the council's instructions to remove their verandah light bulbs – but Kitty was sure she could feel curious eyes watching them as they walked, still holding hands.

At her front gate, Andy gripped her hand more tightly. 'Are your grandparents home tonight?'

She shook her head. 'Grandfather has a churchwardens' meeting and Grandma's there to help with serving supper.'

As she said this, she saw a mysterious tilt to Andy's smile and she wondered if she'd been foolish to be quite so forthcoming. 'But I suppose they *might* finish early. They *could* be home any minute.'

She pulled her hand from Andy's, pushed the squeaky front gate open and hurried through, but before she could close it, he followed her. He'd taken his hat off and his blue eyes flashed with a determined brightness that was just a little alarming.

At the bottom of her front steps Kitty stopped with her hands clasped tightly in front of her. 'What time does your train leave in the morning?'

'Half past ten.'

Another goodbye. 'I – I'll make sure I'm there.'

Andy looped the strap of his hat over the stair post and then, without warning, gripped her elbows and mounted the first step, drawing her to him. 'Just in case you can't make it tomorrow morning, why don't we say goodbye now?'

'Well, all right, but I promise I'll be there.'

He climbed two more steps, pulling Kitty with him. 'I want to say goodbye properly, Kit.'

Her insides jumped, partly with alarm, partly with excitement. With grandparents as strict as hers, her experience of kissing boys was sadly limited. There'd been one or two boys who'd stolen kisses at dances, but they'd been rather furtive and not exactly passionate. Andy had only kissed her once before and that had been years ago when a group of them played spin the bottle down behind the sand dunes. The bottle she'd spun had actually been pointing at Donny

Roper, but Andy had elbowed Donny out of the way.

Now they reached the darkness of the verandah and his grip tightened.

'It might be ages before I see you again,' he said.

That was true enough. The thought of his heading off into unknown horror made Kitty soft with sympathy, and she was caught off guard when he pulled her roughly against him and pressed his mouth over hers.

It was strange to be held so tightly. The buckle of his belt pressed into her stomach. His lips were cool and hard and tasted of cigarettes overlaid by peppermint. But it was rather exciting in a strange way. Not wonderful exactly, not romantic, but exciting nevertheless.

'Oh, Kitty.' Andy sounded out of breath.

She stood quite still, glad of the darkness, not sure what to say, wishing that she wanted this as much as he seemed to.

His lips found hers again, more gently this time, and it was quite nice, really. But then his tongue pushed between her lips and he squeezed her breast.

'Andy!' She struggled to be free of him. 'What do you think you're doing?'

'You know what I'm doing.'

'But you can't. Not that.'

He caught her hands, gripped them so tightly she couldn't move. 'You don't understand, Kitty. I *really* like you. I've never been game to tell you before, but I'm crazy about you. And – and I'm going away tomorrow. If I'm going to fight for my country, I should be brave enough to tell my girl how I feel.'

His girl?

It was oddly flattering. And very confusing. She wasn't his girl.

'I don't know when I'll see you again.'

Kitty knew he meant *if*. He didn't know *if* he would ever see her again. Poor fellow. He was the same age as she was – they'd been to the same primary school and shared endless sessions of backyard cricket and swimming in the rock pool at the end of the Strand, Sunday school picnics and church socials.

Years ago, in grade seven, Andy had thrown prickly burrs in her hair and the other girls had said it meant he liked her. If she was honest, she'd always known he was a bit keen on her. Now he was heading off for war and he was trying to hide how scared he was.

Kitty understood that too. They were all scared these days.

Her throat hurt, as if she'd swallowed a fishbone, and tears burned her eyes. 'You'll be fine, Andy. You'll come home. And now that the Americans are here, the war will be over before you can say Bob's your uncle.'

'Kitty.' There was a sob in his voice as he slipped his arms about her waist and pulled her harder against him. She could feel him shaking. 'We've got to do this.' His voice was hoarse and urgent. 'I'm going away and we've got to. Everybody's doing it.'

She stiffened with shock. 'But —'

He was holding her so tightly now, pressing hot kisses into her neck and using his body to shepherd her back into the darkness, towards the daybed at the end of the latticed verandah.

Kitty knew what he'd said was true. Well, maybe not everybody was *doing it*, but Val Keaton had confided that she'd let her boyfriend go *all the way* with her before he left for the front, and she'd hinted she wasn't the only one who'd been so daring.

Kitty had always planned to 'save herself' until she was married. She wanted the first time she made love to be romantic and beautiful, but already, the arrival of war had muddied her thinking, smudged the lines around ideas that had always been sharp and clear before.

All around them, the world was changing. The air-raid shelters and the new displays in the shop fronts, the landing barges in the bay were outwards signs of the war, but she'd already sensed the changes taking place in people's heads and hearts too.

'You're my girl, Kitty.'

I'm not, she almost told him. *I'm not anybody's girl.* They were friends. Old friends, yes. Mates, chums, but they were not lovers. Once, when Andy had tried to cuddle up to her at the theatre, she'd dug him in the ribs with her elbow and told him not to be silly.

But now . . .

The poor fellow was going off to fight for King and country.

He might die.

Heaven help her, Kitty could actually imagine him being shot. To her horror, she could picture it in vivid detail. She could see the sudden, wide-eyed shock in his eyes; see his sandy head flung back, his mouth gaping in a silent scream, his lanky body crumpling.

In a rush of sympathy she wound her arms around his neck and she smelled the oil he'd combed into his hair.

Emboldened, he lunged across the last bit of verandah, taking her with him, making her stumble into the gloom in the corner, till the backs of her knees bumped the cane daybed where her grandmother took her afternoon naps.

Andy kissed her so passionately now she couldn't breathe. Her legs caved beneath the pressure of his weight and a heartbeat later she was on her back, with Andy on top of her.

She felt a flare of panic, but then, unexpectedly, she knew she wasn't going to put up a fight, and a strangely cool resignation settled over her.

When his hand slipped beneath her skirt and skimmed her thighs then closed on the elastic of her bloomers, she told herself that many, many girls had done this sort of thing in wartime. It was probably sentimental and selfish to cling to romantic dreams when young men were sacrificing their lives and the whole world was falling apart.

She tried to think sensibly. 'Andy, have you got something?'

'What?'

'Protection?'

'Yeah. French letter.' He sounded scared.

'So you planned this?'

'Course.'

'Do you know how to use it?'

Instead of answering, he kissed her and thrust against her, grinding his hips, and Kitty closed her eyes and told herself over and over that this was terribly important to him.

He was trembling and breathless as he fumbled with his clothing and she with hers, and she felt like crying when she felt him, hard yet silken, shove blindly between her legs. Was this how it was supposed to be?

She was grateful for the darkness. It helped her to distance herself from her body. Kitty held her breath, waiting for the pain she knew must come, but then without warning, his violent movements ceased and he collapsed on top of her. Her relief was mingled with surprise and mild disappointment. Had they really done it?

Was that all it was? So desperate and awkward?

She was sure it was supposed to hurt more than that. Had he actually been properly all the way inside her?

She had no chance to find answers to these questions. Beyond the verandah, the front gate squeaked.

'My grandparents!' Kitty hissed. 'Get off! Quick!'

Andy swore softly and Kitty's heart galloped as she pushed him roughly away and grabbed at her bloomers, yanking them up her legs.

Already footsteps were coming up the concrete path. Frantically, she smoothed her skirt and fastened her blouse. Beside her, Andy, in a panic, fumbled with his trousers and with his belt.

The footsteps reached the front steps.

'What in heaven's name?'

Her grandfather's tall frame loomed towards them, topped by a shock of silver hair.

Andy groaned and turned away, trying to hide the front of his trousers and the belt buckle still hanging loose.

With a cry of outrage, her grandfather grabbed Andy by the shoulder.

'You bastard, Mathieson!'

Kitty had never heard her grandfather use such bad language. To her horror, he put his foot in Andy's back, and propelled him forward. Andy stumbled, almost lost his balance, and had to grab the railing to stop himself from falling.

'Get out of here,' her grandfather snarled.

'Alex!' Her grandmother's voice came from the dark near the steps. Kitty had forgotten she was there too. 'Alex, please. What would Reverend Johnson think if he heard you?'

Andy stood his ground, shoulders squared. 'You don't understand, Mr Martin. It's okay. We're getting married.'

Kitty stifled a gasp. This was a nightmare spinning out of control.

'Kitty's my girl,' Andy insisted. 'She and I – we're getting married.'

'The only thing you're getting is out of my house. Don't you ever show your face here again.'

Andy had the sense to give up. Kitty was grateful for the dark, so she couldn't see the look on his face, but she heard the heavy tread of his boots descending the steps.

She had no time to work out whether she felt sad or mad. Her grandfather turned his attention to her and she braced herself for the full force of his venom.

She expected shouting and righteous outrage, but when he spoke, his voice was menacingly quiet.

'You didn't resist,' he told her coldly.

'But I —'

'You're a daughter of Eve. You've shamed us, girl. You've shamed your family and you've shamed yourself in the eyes of the Lord.'

'I'm sorry, Grandfather.'

'Sorry? Is that all you can say?'

It was all she dared to say. He wouldn't listen to excuses and she wasn't about to lay blame. How could she explain the muddled thinking that had led her to give in to her friend?

'How could you shame us, Kitty? After everything your grand-mother and I have done for you?'

His words seared her, and she remembered the first time she'd met her stern North Queensland grandparents when they'd come to collect her from the children's home in Sydney. Her parents had both died of tuberculosis and these people were her rescuers! How she'd loved them – and despite their strict ways, they'd always been caring and kind. For the past ten years she'd been happy.

There was the sound of a key in the lock. Her grandmother was opening the front door. Grandma turned on the hall light and it spilled over her, revealing to Kitty her crimped grey hair, her aging, pale face and wide, worried blue eyes.

'Come inside, Alex,' she said in her quiet, no-nonsense Scottish accent. 'You don't want to share this with the whole street.'

Grandfather's narrowed eyes glinted as he glared at Kitty. 'I'll have no temptress in this house.'

There was a shocked gasp from the hallway and her grandmother hurried forward and pulled at her husband's coat sleeve. 'For heaven's sake, Alex, you can't throw our granddaughter into the street.'

He blinked at his wife, taking in her words, then drew himself up tall, hooked his thumbs beneath the lapels of his coat. 'Maybe not tonight, but the girl needs to be put away from temptation. And in his own time, God will punish her for this.'

6

Sally slept and dreamed of Josh.

They were together on Magnetic Island, on the Forts Walk, one of their favourite tracks, which wound through bushland and pockets of rainforest. Every so often the track offered spectacular views of the blue and white bays and the Coral Sea below, dazzling in the sunlight.

Sally was trying to dawdle, giving herself a chance to look up into the gum trees for the koalas that frequented this track, but Josh was a fitness fiend, always wanting to go faster. If he'd been with his football mates, he'd have tried to run the whole way.

So they compromised, dawdling at times and then breaking into a jog, and then stopping in the gentle winter sunlight to admire the best of the sea views.

High on the ridge above Radical Bay, Josh stood behind Sally, slipped his arms around her and nuzzled her neck, giving her shivers of deliciousness.

Loving the moment, she nestled into his warmth, relishing the firmness of his strong chest as she gazed down at the tall hoop pines and the huge, smooth rocks that studded the headlands at either end of the bay.

'Would you like to see the Greek islands?' she asked him. 'They're probably as pretty as this, but there'd be lots of lovely tavernas and gorgeous cafes along the way.'

When Josh didn't answer, she turned to him. 'Earth to Josh? I was asking if you'd like to go to Greece.'

'I can't,' he said simply.

Sally blinked at him in surprise. 'Really? Why not?'

Josh was dark enough to look as if he had Greek heritage – black hair and eyes and lovely olive skin. Fancifully, she imagined some long-held family secret that prevented him from ever going to the country of his forefathers. But Josh was looking at her so sadly that she felt an icy chill.

'I can't go with you, Sally.' He looked far more serious than her casual suggestion warranted.

'Josh, what's wrong? I don't understand.'

To her horror, Josh was starting to fade before her very eyes. As they stood there on the rocky outcrop looking out at the bay, with the sun shining on their backs and a gentle sea breeze wafting pine scents over them, her husband grew fainter and fainter.

'Josh!' she cried in panic, but now he was no more than a ghostly outline. 'Josh!'

She woke, gasping, to find herself lying in a strange room, and cruel reality crashed over her. A soft moan escaped. Josh was gone.

Dead.

The horror of it seized Sally, sickened her. Once again she had to face the awful truth. She'd lost Josh forever. He was never coming back.

Now, with the dream and the regret so fresh and raw, she looked around her, appalled to find herself at Moonlight Plains, in Luke Fairburn's bedroom, in his swag on the floor.

She'd slept with another man. For the first time in her life, she'd slept with a man who wasn't Josh.

Silver moonlight had given way to the creamy blue of early morning and Luke was already out of bed. The smell of frying bacon drifted from the kitchen. On the wall in front of Sally, Kitty Mathieson's pink dress hung from a coat hanger on a hook, and Sally remembered taking it off very carefully last night. Luke's hired suit was on another hanger beside a shelf that held his other roughly folded clothes – signs that commonsense had prevailed before the longing and passion had overtaken them.

Sally winced now, as she remembered how that longing and passion had played out.

What have I done?

She couldn't shake off the dream and the happiness of being with Josh. For precious moments, he'd been so real, so gorgeous. She'd been able to touch him, to smell him, and she'd been euphoric, buoyed by an over-the-top joyousness and sense of wellbeing, as happy as she'd been on the night of the surprise birthday party she'd organised for him, when she and their friends had hidden in the flat, waiting in happy expectation for his knock on the front door.

Instead two sombre policemen had arrived to tell her about Josh's accident. 'Mrs Piper? Mrs Joshua Piper?'

Once again, Sally was gripped by the horror of losing her husband, and remorse clung to her like wet clothing, making her feel terrible about last night . . . as if she'd sinned.

It was so hard to believe she'd let it happen.

Clearly, all the loneliness and the isolation of the past thirty months, all the suppressed longing had been ticking inside her like an unexploded grenade. And last night it had seemed as if the whole world was waiting for her to take a step . . . and that step had taken her into Luke's arms . . . his bed . . .

She couldn't have been luckier, really. He'd been lovely.

More than lovely. He'd swept her away and lit flames of longing that had taken her by surprise. She'd gone a little wild, she remembered now, blushing.

But thinking about it so soon after her dream, her guilt came back tenfold. Now she felt as if she should apologise to Josh.

Her social experiment – primarily to please her friends – had gone too far. Way too far. How could she have behaved like that, as if . . .

As if she was available?

Luke turned from the frying pan and sent Sally a smile as she came into the kitchen. He looked as attractive as ever with his rumpled, sun-bronzed hair and the whole cowboy thing happening – those shoulders stretching the shoulder seams of his checked cotton shirt, his faded low-slung jeans.

'Morning,' he said, still smiling.

'Good morning, Luke. I borrowed some of your clothes. I hope that's okay.'

'Absolutely.'

His amused glance took in the crumpled cotton shirt she'd found on the shelf in his room and a pair of his track pants that she'd rolled over at her waist and up at the ankles.

'Those old clothes have never looked so good,' he said.

Sally wasn't sure how to react to his compliment so she paid attention to the bacon and eggs in the pan. 'This smells great.' Quickly, she added, 'You were up early.'

He shrugged. 'I've got those history buffs coming out here this morning.'

'Oh, yes, of course. To see where the plane crashed.' She frowned. 'Is there still time to drop me back in town?'

'Of course. No problem.' He snagged a bright-red enamel mug from the dish drainer. 'Tea?'

'Lovely.'

'How do you have it?'

Every time he looked at her, his eyes flashed, sending her happy messages she didn't want to read.

'White with one,' she said rather tightly.

A small silence fell as Luke poured the tea.

'I'll do the milk and sugar if you like.'

'Sure.' He handed her the mug. 'Sally, I'm not quite sure how to put this, but last night . . .'

She nodded quickly, dropping her gaze again as heat rushed into her cheeks. 'It was amazing, Luke.'

It was a mistake to look up at him and see that shining light in his eyes, to see hope, admiration and desire. The warmth of his smile sent a panicky chill snaking through her.

This was going to be as bad as she'd feared. She'd been reckless and selfish with a really, *really* nice guy and she'd given him the wrong impression.

She had to get things right, had to set Luke straight immediately. It was only fair. She spoke quickly, before her courage failed. 'I'm sorry . . . but don't expect too much from me, Luke.'

Several beats passed before he spoke. 'What's that supposed to mean?'

Sally's chest tightened. Now his expression was wary and she couldn't blame him. She swallowed nervously. 'I'm afraid . . . I'm not really . . . available.'

He stared at her, his green eyes serious. He gave a bewildered shake of his head. 'What is this? Some kind of a joke? You're not – you're not telling me you're married?'

'No, there's no one else, not now. But I *was* married.' She looked down at her tightly clasped hands. 'My husband died, you see, and – and I'm afraid I'm not available *emotionally*.'

The bacon sizzled and spat in the pan as Luke stood there, clearly stunned, and Sally remembered the way she'd more or less led him to the bedroom last night.

How could she have been so thoughtless?

It felt like an age before he spoke. 'So what was that last night?' A cool edge had crept into his voice. 'Diversion therapy?'

'No, it was . . .' Sally stopped. She felt wretched, unwilling to hand out compliments and a rejection in the same breath. 'I'm sorry. I really am.'

Luke was staring out through the window now. 'I'm not the first, though, am I? Since your husband died, I mean. Someone like you, unattached, would have offers from all kinds of guys.'

'No. God, no.' It was so hard to talk about this. 'You're the first, Luke.'

To her dismay, a red flush stained his neck as he continued to stare out the window. His eyes were narrowed, his expression tense.

Sally felt worse than ever. How could she explain this without making it worse? 'I thought I was ready.'

The silence that followed this was excruciating, but then an acrid smell tainted the air. The bacon and eggs were burning.

'Shit.' Luke whirled around and grabbed the pan's handle, pulling it off the flame. Tight-lipped, he used an egg flip to free the blackening edges that had stuck to the pan. 'This breakfast is stuffed.'

'It's fine.' Sally hoped he couldn't guess how close to tears she was. 'I like my bacon crispy.'

With a grim-faced shrug Luke silently served up the brittle bacon and rubbery eggs, setting her plate on the table and indicating that she should take the only chair.

'Thanks.'

He perched on a metal esky, balancing his plate on a solid,

jeans-clad thigh, and scowled as he speared a curling piece of bacon. 'How long since . . . since your husband died?'

'Two and a half years.'

Surprise flared in his eyes.

'I know that sounds like a long time,' she said. 'I know I have to get over it.'

'It wouldn't be easy.' Luke kept his focus on cutting his food.

Sally tried to explain. 'I thought – I suppose I assumed that last night was casual.'

'Yeah, well, obviously it was.'

She knew Luke was trying to sound as if he didn't care, but his gaze was hard now, even though he countered it with an offhand shrug.

Their conversation lapsed as they finished their food and scraped the inedible bits into the bin.

'Let me wash up,' she offered.

He shook his head. 'Leave the plates in the sink. We need to get cracking.'

'Oh, yes. Before the visitors arrive?'

'Yeah.'

She supposed he was relieved to have an excuse to be rid of her quickly and, less than ten minutes later, she was climbing into his ute, once again wearing Kitty's dress.

Through the windscreen, she looked up at the homestead. It seemed shabbier in the daylight, with peeling paint and broken guttering and a whole section of the verandah railing missing. But the house still had the strong pleasing lines that would respond well to a makeover.

'You'll make this place fabulous,' she told Luke as they drove off.

'That's the plan,' he responded grimly.

Conversation was clearly going to be awkward. She looked out across the paddocks bordered by bushland. 'Where's the wrecked plane? Can you see the pieces from here?'

'Not any more. Those trees are in the way. And it's only a couple of bits of twisted metal.'

But at least the plane provided an opportunity for a less troubled conversation on the journey into town, so Sally decided to pursue it. 'Do you know much about the crash? It seems strange that an American plane ended up all the way out here.'

'Apparently there were stacks of crashes all over North Queensland during the war.'

'I wonder why. There wasn't fighting here, was there?'

Luke didn't respond at first as he steered the ute down the bumpy, rutted track, but then he must have decided it was better to talk than to spend the entire journey in uncomfortable silence.

'According the story my family tells, the guy who crashed here was flying back from New Guinea.' He rounded a bend and their last view of the homestead disappeared. 'There was a big storm, apparently, practically a cyclone, and the Yanks were blown off course. They were running out of fuel, so they took a chance on landing here.'

'But they crashed.'

'At least one of them crashed and his plane burned.'

'And your family rescued the pilot?'

'I guess. I'm a bit hazy on the details. My grandmother was living here at the time. She was sent out here from Townsville to housekeep for her great-uncle.'

To Sally's surprise, Luke sent her a quick grin, and it was the relaxed, almost cheeky grin that had been so appealing last night when they met. 'My mother reckons Gran was sent out here to keep her away from the Americans.'

'Why? Because the flashy and handsome American airmen might lead her astray?'

'Something like that.'

'But instead the Americans came to your grandmother.'

Smiling at the irony, Sally looked down at the dress she was wearing. She wondered about Kitty Mathieson and whether she had ever danced with an American airman.

'Was there a romance?' she asked.

'Doubt it.' Luke's hands tightened on the steering wheel. 'I certainly haven't heard anything.'

'That's a pity. A wartime romance would have been a nice touch for my story.'

He frowned. 'The magazine story you wanted to write – about the homestead?'

'Yes . . .' she said, feeling uncertain.

'So you're still planning to write it?'

'Well, yes, if you're keen. I'd love to record your progress with the renovations.'

'You'd come out here . . . we'd see each other on a regular basis and we'd just pretend last night never happened?'

'Well . . . I . . .'

Luke was shaking his head. 'Sorry. I think you'd better scrap that plan.'

7

Moonlight Plains, 1942

Kitty had just lugged the late-afternoon milk pail up the stairs and into the kitchen when she heard the low drone of aeroplanes.

She was used to the sound of Allied planes flying high up, but these were coming her way, and they were so low and menacing she was sure they *had* to be Japs. She froze, her heart thrashing like the pistons on a locomotive. The war wasn't supposed to reach her all the way out here.

For six weeks now, she'd been at Moonlight Plains, her recently widowed great-uncle's property west of Charters Towers. She'd been keeping his house, cooking his meals, weeding his vegetables and milking his two dairy cows, such very different work from her old job on the haberdashery counter at Carroll's in Townsville.

Her grandfather had supposedly sent her here to keep her out of harm's way, but they both knew it was her punishment. Admittedly her ruddy-faced, stout and elderly great-uncle needed Kitty's help. He'd let everything go since his wife died last year.

Aunt Lil's beautiful garden had quickly deteriorated over the long hot summer and the lovely old house had all but disappeared beneath layers of dust. The only thing her great-uncle seemed to care about was his cattle. But although there was plenty to keep Kitty busy, and she knew Uncle Jim valued her help, she still felt like a prisoner, banished into the never-never.

If she was still in Townsville, she could be helping the war effort. Women were needed for all sorts of work, now that the men were away.

She threw a frantic glance to the timber-framed casement windows, but they were covered in brown paper, her great-uncle's version of blackout curtains, so she couldn't see a thing outside – not a hint of sky, or gum trees, or paddocks.

Shaking, she put the milk pail down. It spilled, but that hardly mattered if these were Jap planes and she was about to die.

A loud snarl of engines almost overhead sent her diving beneath the kitchen table. She was sure her world was going to end. The very last sound she would hear was the deafening explosion of a Japanese bomb as it plunged through the homestead's iron roof.

She tried to pray. *Our Father, who art in heaven . . . Gentle Jesus . . . Thy rod and staff shall comfort me . . .*

It was no good; her mind kept slipping from the task. Despite her grandfather's best efforts, she'd never been very good at prayers and now she was going to die like all those poor people in Darwin. At least those people had been together.

Kitty felt very alone as she cowered beneath the table. Uncle Jim had left two days earlier, after an official order came through to destock. For once, he'd agreed with the government. He'd be damned if he'd let the Japs get their stinking hands on his prime Hereford beef, so he was driving his cattle to the saleyards.

Now the noisy thumping of Kitty's heart was almost as loud as the roar of the aircraft. She cringed, tense as a shotgun trigger, chin tucked, eyes closed, arms tightly locked around her knees.

The lord is my shepherd; I shall not want. He maketh me to lie down in green pastures . . .

Above her, a droning engine hiccupped, and she heard a sickening whine. A hair-raising screech of ripping metal. And —

Crrrump!

The shocking, thudding crash was so close that the homestead's walls and windows rattled.

Hands clamped over her ears, Kitty braced for the final explosion. The end of her world.

She tried to remember the rest of the psalm. *He leadeth me beside the still waters.*

Not daring to breathe, she waited.

And waited.

Eventually she had to breathe and when she took her hands from her ears, she heard . . . *nothing . . .*

Not a sound. Not even a distant thrum of additional planes. The bush had returned to its everyday, comforting silence.

Cautiously incredulous, Kitty uncurled. She'd been in a tight ball for so long that her stomach muscles and her knees complained as she eased out from beneath the table and tiptoed to the window, pushing it open to peer into the purple-grey dusk.

She half-expected to see flames, but the paddocks and the bush looked much as they always had. She pushed the casement as wide open as she could and leaned out. A fine mist of rain drizzled onto her face. It had been raining on and off for days and she smelled wet earth, wet grass, wet eucalyptus leaves. She smelled the sweet scent of the mock orange bushes growing in tubs on either side of the stairs and the lilies that had grown from bulbs sent out from Scotland by Aunty Lil's family. Right until she'd died, Aunty Lil had kept them alive with water from the washing copper.

There was no sign of a plane. But Kitty knew that a plane had crashed out there, somewhere on Moonlight Plains land . . . which meant . . .

Oh, help. It meant the enemy was out there. A pilot, at least, and probably crew. Japanese airmen, who might be dead, or injured, or worse – *alive*.

Enemy invaders, living and breathing or mildly injured, could, at this very moment, be creeping towards the homestead.

Night was closing in.

And Kitty was alone.

At the thought of those menacing, evil shadows creeping towards her, she threw a hasty glance at her great-uncle's shotgun hanging on the wall. Her stomach lurched at the thought of using it, but she might not have a choice.

Then, with something of a shock, a new thought struck. *Could they be our planes?*

Could an Australian pilot have crashed?

It was such a comforting idea that she felt a burst of courage and she pictured herself rushing out into the rainy evening and rescuing brave Australian airmen.

But her bravado vanished almost as quickly as it flared. It was much more likely that the airmen were Japs, and she'd heard shocking, terrifying stories about what they did, especially to women.

Now, fear – real, scalding fear – exploded in her chest. A moan burst from her, and she gulped it down as she struggled with her conscience.

The appalling thing was, she had no choice but to go out there. She would never forgive herself if good Aussie men died, or lay in the rain in agony, simply because she was a coward. If there was a tiny chance that the airmen were Australian, she really should go.

Oh, help. She wasn't brave enough, was she? Her instinct was to dive back under the table and stay there. But cowering in the house and letting the Japs find her was possibly even more dangerous. She would have a better chance of hiding in the bush.

With that thought, Kitty felt a new sense of purpose, a realisation that this was her chance to show her mettle, to prove to herself and to her grandfather that she wasn't the weak, spineless girl he believed her to be. After all, there was no hiding from this war, and when the time came, everyone had to be brave. Now it was her turn. She had to find out who she was dealing with, and if it was Japs she'd have to head for the bush and just keep going, even if it took days. That was what her great-uncle would do.

She would take a lantern, but she wouldn't light it yet. She didn't want to give herself away.

I'll have to take the shotgun, too.

Nervously, she lifted the weapon from the wall. Just the feel of the gun's smooth timber stock and cold metal barrel brought back the fiasco of two weeks ago, when Uncle Jim had insisted on showing her how to shoot.

'There'll be times when you're here on your own,' he'd said. 'And you might find a brown snake in the dairy, or a damned dingo sneaking after the chooks. You can't just throw a stick at them, lass. You have to know how to shoot.'

But Kitty had been a terrible shot and the horrible bruising recoil and deafening noise had terrified her. She'd been in tears afterwards.

There was no time for tears now, though, as she took cartridges from a drawer in the kitchen dresser, then opened the breach and loaded the gun.

That done, she pulled a heavy, brown potato sack from a hook near the door and slipped one corner over her head to make a rain hood. It was scratchy and damp and smelled musty, but beggars couldn't be choosers and it would keep most of the rain off.

Carrying the shotgun and unlit lantern, she opened the back door and went cautiously down the wooden steps, glad there was still enough light for her to see her way.

At a guess, the plane was somewhere just beyond the home paddock. Diagonal streaks of rain slanted through the slim white trunks of gum trees, and their drooping leaves were silhouetted against a gun-metal sky. This paddock hadn't been grazed for weeks and the sodden, knee-high grass dragged at her trousers as she followed a barbwire fence till she came to the gate leading to the next paddock.

Heart thumping, she stopped, and with the shotgun under her arm, fumbled with the gate's wire fastening. A shout sounded close by and her heart leapt so high she almost dropped the gun.

Should she answer? Or should she hide?

There was no time to waste and she tried to think calmly. Would a stalking enemy call out?

Surely not. Gripping the shotgun more resolutely, she pushed the gate open. The hinges creaked alarmingly and her heart threatened to burst clear through her ribcage.

Carefully, fearfully, she crept forward. It was almost dark now, but ahead loomed the unmistakable shape of a silver-grey plane at an awkward angle. It didn't look too badly damaged, but its nose had ploughed into the earth and its tail was in the air.

Kitty prayed. She prayed especially that it wasn't a Jap plane. She'd seen photos of their fighter planes in the newspapers and she knew they had the red circle of the rising sun on their sides. This plane had a clear white star.

Not Japanese.

Thank you, God.

Almost giddy with relief, Kitty hurried forward. 'Hello?' she called. 'Is anyone there?'

A dark figure emerged from the grove of trees behind the plane, and a deep voice answered in an accent Kitty recognised from countless movies.

'Quick, over here. I need some help, buddy.'

An American.

Oh, my goodness.

Now that she knew she was safe, Kitty quickly lit the lantern and lifted it high. The man was tall and dressed in a dark leather flying jacket. A flying helmet and goggles dangled from his left hand and he was loosening the knot of a white silk scarf at his neck.

She had never actually met an American before and she could feel her mouth gaping.

She caught the keen glance in his dark eyes and the silky gleam of his jet-black hair, not yet flattened by the drizzling rain. He didn't merely sound like a hero in an American movie, he had the handsome looks of a film star too. He was, as her girlfriends would say, *a real dish*.

But this was no time for girlish flutters. It wasn't even a time for introductions.

'I'm glad you've brought a lantern,' he said in a brisk, no-nonsense voice. 'I've been trying to find my buddy. He ditched close by here.'

'I heard a crash.'

'Yeah. He could be injured.'

Without another word, the American dived back into the trees and Kitty plunged after him, doing her best to dodge saplings while she held the lantern high.

'He's over this way somewhere,' the American said. 'He didn't make it to the open field, and I think his wing might have clipped a tree. We were losing daylight fast. Lift that light a little higher, will you?'

This man was clearly used to giving orders and being instantly obeyed. Lifting the lantern as instructed, Kitty pushed the potato sack back from her face so she could see better.

The airman stopped in his tracks, staring at her, his gaze taking in her trousers, her gun. His dark eyes widened with surprise and then dismay.

'What's the matter?' Kitty asked.

'You're a girl?'

He seemed so stunned she almost giggled. 'Yes, I'm afraid I am.'

To his credit, he recovered quickly. 'Forgive me, madam. I thought you were a boy. No offence.'

'None taken.'

He slanted an approving smile her way and as his gaze rested on her for a moment longer, she had the distinct impression that under other circumstances he might have said something charming, even flirtatious.

Instead he said, 'Where are your menfolk?'

'I – er – they're away.'

Kitty wondered what her grandfather would think if he could see her now. After her reckless behaviour with Andy Mathieson she'd been banished from Townsville to be kept clear of American servicemen.

Now, despite her grandfather's efforts, the Americans had arrived on her doorstep. Seemed there was no avoiding them.

The pilot held out his hand. 'The name's Ed Langley. United States Army Air Force.'

His hand was warm and strong as he gripped Kitty's.

'Pleased to meet you, Captain Langley.'

'Please, call me Ed.'

'All right. I'm Kitty Martin.'

'I'm in your debt, Miss Martin.'

It was her turn to smile. 'Please . . . call me Kitty.'

Momentary warmth glowed in his dark-brown eyes before he remembered his mission and hurried forward again.

'Are we anywhere near Townsville?' Ed shot the question over his shoulder.

'Not really. You're about eighty miles to the west.'

He made a low sound that might have been a curse. Just then, in the darkness ahead of them, Kitty's lantern caught another gleam of metal.

The second plane was spreadeagled on its stomach in the middle of a small clearing. It had lost a wing and it looked defeated, like a slain silvery monster.

The sight of it made her throat sore.

'Keep the lantern back, well out of the way,' Ed warned.'

Kitty smelled the pungent odour of petrol, and she set the lantern down, but followed at a careful distance as Ed continued forward.

In no time, he was wrestling with the metal door above the gaping hole where the wing had been.

'Is there any way I can help?'

'This goddamned cockpit hatch is stuck. Bobby should have ejected it,' he grunted. 'I'll need something to lever it open.'

'A piece of timber? Like a tree branch?'

'That might do the trick.' Ed shot an assessing glance at the surrounding gum trees. 'An axe would be handy.'

Kitty smiled. This was one problem she could solve. Now she was grateful for her great-uncle's lesson about the power of shotguns at close range. She would put it to good use.

Holding the barrel close to the base of a sapling's trunk, just as her great-uncle had demonstrated, she closed her eyes and pulled the butt hard into her shoulder, then she fired a blast and the young tree fell instantly.

'Nice work, Annie Oakley,' Ed drawled close behind her, and without wasting a moment, he grabbed the sapling and hurried with it to the plane.

By the time Kitty caught up with him, he was already prising it beneath the cockpit's latch.

'Keep back!' he ordered her. 'We were low on fuel, but there's still a good chance this could go up with a bang.'

Kitty stepped away smartly, watching Ed work. Perhaps she should have prayed again, but she was too fascinated. Too scared.

Ed's face pulled into a grimace as he used the broken sapling to lever the door free. It took several tries. One end of the sapling snapped, but Ed persevered and it eventually worked, thank heavens. As soon as he'd yanked the door aside, Ed leaned into the cockpit and swiftly grabbed the pilot beneath his armpits and hauled his limp body out.

Kitty caught a glimpse of the other man's flying goggles and his broad nose. Long arms. Loose, floppy legs.

'Is – is he alive?'

'Not sure,' was the grim reply. 'Would you mind grabbing his legs, so I can get him clear of this plane?'

Ed had barely said this before a terrible *whoomp* exploded behind him and a red ball of fire leapt high, lighting up the darkness.

He yelled and jumped clear, dragging the man with him. Somehow – later, she was never sure how – Kitty managed to grab the injured pilot's ankles. She was surprised by the weight of him and she was decidedly shaky as they lugged him away from the burning wreckage to a safe piece of cleared ground.

Behind them, the fire spread quickly through the plane, but Ed paid scant attention to the garish flames leaping high into the night sky. He was too concerned about his companion.

By now a strange white glow from the fire lit up the night and Kitty watched as Ed knelt and gently removed his comrade's goggles and leather flying helmet. Ed's forehead was creased by a deep frown as he loosened the silk scarf at the airman's throat and pressed long, supple fingers to the side of his neck.

'Can you feel a pulse?' She had to ask.

'Just. I'm no medic, but I'm sure it's too faint.'

Kitty leaned closer, and to her horror, she saw dried blood staining the corner of the unconscious airman's mouth.

'Does that mean he has internal injuries?' she asked, pointing.

Ed let out a heavy sigh. 'I think so. He needs a doctor. A hospital.'

Her heart sank. They hadn't a hope of getting him to hospital, but how on earth could they help him on their own, all the way out here?

'We should at least get him out of this rain and up to the house,' she suggested, but she didn't add that there would be next to no help at the homestead, apart from a rudimentary first aid box.

'How far is it to the house?'

She made a rough guess. 'A few hundred yards.'

'Right.' Ed stood. 'Normally, I'd sling him over my shoulder, but if he has internal injuries it might do him more harm than good.' He looked back at the burning plane, eyes narrowed thoughtfully. 'If Bobby lost a wing smashing through here, it can't be too far away. You wait with him and I'll see if I can find it. We can use it as a stretcher to carry him.'

'All right.'

Unexpectedly, Ed smiled at her. His smile was tinged with fatigue and worry, but gosh, she couldn't help noticing how young and handsome he was.

His gaze dropped to the man on the ground and his smile faded, his voice softened. 'This is my good friend and comrade, Lieutenant Robert Kowalski. He likes to be called Bobby.'

Kitty gulped. She was sure Bobby seemed too still.

A moment later, Ed was gone, hurrying away into the night.

Kitty knelt beside Bobby Kowalski. He had a nice face, with a broad, flattish nose, fair eyebrows and eyelashes and widely set cheekbones. His lips were very pale, too pale, and the bright streak of blood looked garish by comparison. He looked young, maybe not quite twenty.

To her surprise, his eyes slowly opened.

'Hello,' Kitty said softly, kneeling closer.

His pale-blue eyes accentuated his youth. He stared at her, then he turned and frowned at the burning plane, then back at her again. Fear crept into his eyes.

'Don't be frightened, Bobby. Ed's here. You're going to be okay.'

Her reassurance was useless. As Bobby continued to stare at

her, his eyes widened with terror.

'Don't be frightened,' she said again, wishing there was something she could do.

But he looked more terrified than ever. Terrified of *her*.

Perhaps she looked weird with the potato sack over her head. Kitty quickly slipped it off and shook her hair free. The sacking was standard wet-weather gear out here, but in the dark it probably made her look more like the Grim Reaper. *Poor man*.

Bobby's relief was instant.

She took his hand and offered him a smile. 'I'm Kitty,' she told him.

He nodded and a slight movement of his lips might almost have been a greeting.

'It's so nice to see you awake,' she said next.

His Adam's apple jerked. 'Where's Ed?'

'Not far away.' Kitty pointed to the blackness beyond the plane. 'He's fetching something to make a stretcher, so we can carry you up to the homestead.'

'You don't have to carry me. You can't. You're a girl.' Bobby tried to sit up, but he'd barely lifted his shoulders before he moaned and grimaced horribly, then coughed.

Alarmed, Kitty pushed him gently back. 'Shh. Don't move. Ed will be back any moment now.'

Sure enough, Ed was already hurrying towards them, bringing what looked like a sheet of roofing iron across his shoulders.

'This might work,' he said, but he didn't sound confident as he laid it on the ground. 'It's part of the tail section.'

Bobby fainted while they were carefully lifting him onto the makeshift stretcher.

Kitty drew a deep breath. She knew it wasn't going to be easy, keeping Bobby balanced on the metal stretcher as they made their way through the rain-drenched scrub. She wouldn't be able to carry the gun or lantern, so she set them under a tree. She'd come back for them later.

'Ready?' called Ed.

'Yes.'

'We'll lift on the count of three. Okay?'

'Okay.'

'One . . . two . . . three . . .'

Carrying the stretcher was indeed as difficult as she feared, especially during the first part of their journey, where they had to weave their way through the scrub with night closing in and the rain still falling. When they reached the open paddock, they set Bobby down for a short breather before going on.

The hardest part was lifting Bobby off the tail to carry him through the back doorway. When Ed took his shoulders, Bobby groaned again, horribly, but at last they were safely in the kitchen.

8

It was only when they got back to the house and Kitty lit another lantern that she saw how pale and exhausted Ed looked.

She realised then that she had no idea how long the Americans had been flying, or what kind of ordeal they'd been through before they were forced to land at Moonlight Plains. Ed showed no concern for himself, though. His focus was entirely on Bobby as he knelt beside his friend, his face taut with worry.

Kitty took off her sacking cape, glad to be rid of it, and hung it on the hook behind the back door.

Turning, she caught Ed watching her, his dark eyes intent, and she wished she was wearing something a good deal more fetching than a rumpled cotton smock, tucked into a pair of damp and mud-streaked men's trousers cinched at her waist with a piece of rope.

Almost immediately, she was ashamed of herself for even caring how she looked in these circumstances.

She stepped forward as Ed unzipped Bobby's jacket.

'No obvious signs of injury,' he said, frowning, then he shook his head. 'But he's out to it again and that can't be good.'

His expression remained grim as he opened Bobby's shirt. Kitty stepped closer, appalled by the sight of a huge purple bruise that covered the entire left side of Bobby's chest. She couldn't hold back a horrified gasp.

'I've got to get help,' Ed said, clearly as shocked as she was. 'I'll need to use your phone.'

Kitty winced. 'I'm sorry. We don't have a phone.'

For uncomfortable seconds Ed stared at her in disbelief. 'Damn,' he muttered softly.

She couldn't blame him for cursing. Their situation was dire.

Ed looked around him at the simple kitchen with its plain wooden dresser, scrubbed pine table and its old-fashioned wood stove in a ripple-iron alcove. He glanced at the lantern she'd lit and then at the timber ceiling, bare of light bulbs. 'You don't even have electricity?'

'No.'

'How do you communicate? Is there some kind of radio?'

Kitty shook her head. 'I'm sorry. It's very isolated here.'

'What about your men?' he demanded impatiently. 'When are they coming back?'

She wished with all her heart that she could offer him more hope. 'There's only Uncle Jim. Most of the other men from this district are fighting or they've gone to help the war effort, working in the railways or in offices.'

Then, apologetically, she had to add, 'I'm afraid my great-uncle won't be back for another two days.' As she said this, the rain began to fall more heavily than ever, drumming on the iron roof. 'He might take even longer if the creeks come up.' She hated to add to Ed's troubles, but he needed the full picture. 'This is still the wet season.'

It was more like the middle of a nightmare for Ed and Bobby, she suspected.

'Okay,' Ed said with weary resignation. 'What about transport, then? Do you have a vehicle?'

Kitty swallowed nervously. 'There's a truck, but no fuel.'

Now Ed didn't hold back on a heavy sigh. 'How can I get gas then?'

'My great-uncle's hoping to bring petrol back from Charters Towers.'

'He's hoping? Goddamn. I can't believe we ended up so far off course.' Ed looked down at Bobby, lying at his feet, ran a despairing hand through his hair. 'I have to get a doctor. I have to find a phone. There has to be someone around here who can help. What about your neighbours?'

The nearest neighbours were twenty miles away. Kitty looked down at her hands, wishing she could offer more help. Then she threw a frantic glance at the papered windows. 'I guess you could hitch a horse to the sulky, if it's in working order. Can you handle one? I can't.'

Ed smiled and shook his head. 'Sorry, I'm a city guy. I barely know one end of a horse from the other. I'd be better off on foot.'

'But it's such a dark night and you don't know the way.'

'I don't have any choice,' Ed said after only the slightest hesitation. 'Do you know if your neighbours have a telephone?'

'I – I'm really not sure. I'm so sorry. I'd like to be more help, but I've only been living out here a few weeks.'

'Where were you before that?'

'Townsville. With my grandparents.'

To her surprise, the grimness in Ed's dark eyes softened. As he rose from his post beside Bobby, he actually smiled at her. 'You've been incredibly brave tonight, Kitty. You came out in the rain to search for us. With a shotgun, no less. Heaven knows what you expected to find.'

She remembered how scared she'd been when she thought the airmen were Japs. But now, with another glance at Bobby, a new fear replaced the old. If Ed left to search for help she'd be alone with

Bobby. She'd be responsible for him, and she couldn't imagine how she could possibly save him. She was an inept city girl, so unprepared for this emergency.

A suffocating pressure filled her chest. She went to the window to push it further open, peering out, taking deep, necessary breaths of fresh air. 'There's no signs out there, Ed. Not even a proper road. Just a dirt track – a couple of wheel ruts in the bush. And it'll be wet and muddy. I hope you don't get lost.'

'It's a risk I'll have to take. I *have* to try. It's what Bobby would do, if our positions were reversed.'

Kitty nodded. She understood – Ed would never forgive himself if he didn't try. 'Will you help me to get Bobby into bed before you leave?'

'Of course.'

'I'll get the room ready.'

She wished there was time to make up the bed with good sheets, but her great-uncle had never been well off, and ever since Aunty Lil had died last year, he'd lapsed into living rough, with little pride or care.

She'd done everything she could to make the place clean and welcoming, but there was no way she could disguise the rustic mattresses made from wool bags cut down to size and filled with corn husks that rustled every time anyone rolled over.

She'd seen the fine quality of the Americans' uniforms and by comparison, these beds were embarrassingly rough, but the good linen and quilts were still packed away in the linen cupboard, wrapped in brown paper and kept 'for guests'.

At least the pillows were soft. Aunty Lil had made them from white flour bags filled with chicken feathers, using only the breast feathers and the soft down from beneath the wings.

Quickly now, Kitty smoothed out the old patched and darned sheets. She tucked the bottom sheet firmly beneath the mattress, spread out the top sheet and a blanket and folded them down, then plumped up the pillows.

'Bobby will be more comfortable in a bed,' she said when she returned to Ed.

He nodded wearily, and once again ran long, tanned fingers through his hair as the muscles in his throat worked. 'Thanks.'

His voice was rough and Kitty knew he was dreadfully upset about Bobby. It was more than possible that Bobby was dying, and there was so little they could do to help him. It was terrible to feel useless.

She'd never seen anyone close to death before and her stomach knotted at the thought of being left alone with Bobby for long, lonely hours. What if Ed couldn't get help? What if he couldn't get back?

It didn't help to dwell on such things. After all, this was another chance to prove to her grandfather that she was not simply a wicked girl with deplorable morals.

Ed removed Bobby's boots, scarf and jacket and unbuckled his belt and slipped it free from his trousers.

'Should we change him into pyjamas?' Kitty asked.

'Later maybe. For the time being, I don't want to move him any more than we have to.'

Mindful of Bobby's dangerously bruised chest, they lifted him extra-gently, with Ed supporting his head and shoulders while Kitty supported his knees.

Very, very carefully they made their way down the hall, through the narrow bedroom doorway, then lowered him onto the bed.

'I don't like the sound of his breathing,' Ed said.

'Perhaps we should prop him up a little. I'll get another pillow.'

Without waiting for his reply, Kitty dashed to her great-uncle's bedroom, and returned with the extra pillow. She found Ed sitting on the edge of the bed, looking down at Bobby's still face with a look of bleak despair.

'I can't get to him to speak to me,' he said. 'But I don't like to shake him.'

Fear eddied through her and her throat filled with an aching lump.

Pasting on a brave smile and holding up the extra pillow, she tried to sound cheery. 'Let's see if this helps. You lift Bobby's shoulders and I'll rearrange the pillows.'

As they did this, Ed's arms brushed hers. More than once. And she was dismayed by the flashes that zapped her skin. To make things worse, a bright blush flamed in her cheeks.

How ridiculous to react this way to the first American she met. Perhaps her grandfather was right.

When Bobby was settled, Kitty spoke rather brusquely, not daring to make eye contact. 'I'll get you something to keep the rain off.'

The rain was fairly thundering on the iron roof now. In the hallway, she stopped at the coat rack. 'Here, take this,' she said, lifting down a heavy khaki greatcoat with brass buttons.

'It looks like military issue.'

'Yes. It's Uncle Jim's. He wore it in the last war. In France.'

Ed frowned. 'You sure he won't mind my using it?'

'Course he won't. If he was here, he'd insist.'

On their way through the kitchen Kitty stopped. 'You should take some food.'

'No, it's okay. I need to get going.'

'Just a few Anzacs,' she insisted, overriding his protests and reaching for the biscuit tin. 'You don't know how long you'll be.'

Quickly, she put the biscuits in a brown paper bag along with a banana, and filled a canvas water bag. 'This isn't very flash but it should keep you going.'

'Okay. Thanks.'

She went with him to the back door. The rain was sheeting down.

'Please be careful,' she told Ed. 'We had floods back in February, and the creek can come up again without much warning. There's no bridge, just a ford over the shallowest part. Just remember, follow the track to where it meets a formed road and then turn left. You'll see the entrance to the neighbours' about five miles down that road.'

She didn't like to add to Ed's troubles, but she knew that he might get across the creek and then find he wasn't able to get back, leaving her alone with Bobby.

But she also knew that if he stayed, Bobby would almost certainly die. It was an agonising dilemma, but there was only one possible response.

9

Townsville, 2013

Kitty was overjoyed when the firm footsteps in the nursing home corridor proved to be her grandson's. Luke came striding into her room, greeting her with a broad grin, and as he leaned down to kiss her he brought a hint of the fresh and sun-drenched outdoors, a scent that she'd missed terribly since she'd moved to the home.

'How wonderful to see you, Luke.'

What a handsome fellow he was, so tall and strapping and golden. Such a nice style of young man, with his blue and white–striped shirt tucked into surprisingly respectable blue jeans.

Kitty knew she wasn't supposed to have a favourite grandchild – of course, she loved all eleven of them, and she didn't have a favourite, really. But from an early age this sunny-natured boy had stolen a good-sized chunk of her heart.

'How are you, Gran?' he asked as he pulled a chair closer to her bed.

Feeble was the word that first sprang to Kitty's mind. She felt especially frail now beside Luke's athletic and vibrant youthfulness, but she was sure he didn't need to hear the dreary truth.

'I'm not bad for an old girl.' She smiled at him. 'And what brings you to Townsville?'

'I came to collect some gear – some trusses I ordered and cyclone bolts.'

'For the homestead?'

'Yes.'

'Don't they have what you need in the Charters Towers hardware store?'

Luke shrugged and looked momentarily caught out. 'There's more choice in the stores here.'

Kitty was too pleased to see him to quibble. 'So how's everything coming along? Are you happy with your progress?'

His smile tilted. 'It's steady, steady, I guess. But it's a big job.' A fleeting shadow flickered in his clear green eyes.

'It's certainly a big job to tackle on your own,' Kitty agreed.

She felt a measure of responsibility regarding this project, as she'd been the prime mover in starting the restoration. Some folk might suggest she'd been manipulative, but Luke had been between building jobs and was looking for a venture that would hone his newly acquired skills, and she'd discovered a strong desire to see the homestead renovated before it ended up as part of her estate.

Luke had been dubious, though, when she'd first raised the subject.

'Do you reckon it's worth doing up?' he'd asked. 'If you're planning to sell, most cattlemen are more interested in the land. They'd live in a tin shed if the land was good.'

'Their wives might have something to say about that,' Kitty had promptly responded. 'And I just don't like the idea of passing on a house in such a dilapidated state. I know your grandfather would have hated to see the place like it is now. He took such pride in it.'

'That's true,' Luke had admitted solemnly.

Kitty had known the mention of her husband would do the trick. Luke had always been especially close to his grandfather. As a little boy he'd loved to follow him around his workshop. But she'd felt a little guilty, too.

'You'll make sure you get help if you need it, won't you, Luke?' she said now.

'Yes, Gran, don't fret. I'll get there.' His big brown hand covered hers, giving it a gentle squeeze. 'By the way, I brought you something.' Undoing the button-down flap, he reached into his shirt pocket. 'I found this when I was lifting a few floorboards.'

In the centre of his palm lay a silver coin. 'It's American. A dollar.'

'Oh, my heavens.' Kitty's heart took a fearful leap that sent her sinking dizzily against her pillows. She had to close her eyes and take a steadying breath.

'Gran, are you okay?'

The dizziness passed, thank goodness, and she managed to smile again to allay Luke's fears. 'Sorry, darling. Just one of my silly little flutters.' She shot a nervous glance at the coin he held.

It couldn't be, surely . . .

'Here.' Luke pressed the dollar into her thin, withered palm. 'You take it, so you can see it properly.'

The coin was still warm from his touch, but Kitty felt a distinct chill as she saw the American eagle on one side and then turned it over to find the shining head of Liberty on the other.

After all this time . . .

'It says *In God We Trust*,' Luke told her, his eyes flashing with enthusiasm. 'And the year's 1923. That makes it ninety years old. Same age as you.'

'Yes,' Kitty said softly.

There could be no doubt then . . .

Against her will, she was remembering . . .

She was back in the past . . . at Bobby Kowalski's bedside . . . seeing Bobby's face on the day he showed her this very coin, his eyes vivid blue against the deathly pallor of his skin.

'I suppose it must have come from one of those American airmen,' Luke said, oblivious to her distress. 'From during the war.'

'Yes, I think it must have.' Kitty's voice was faint, while her heart took off again at a dangerous gallop. 'How – how on earth did you find it?'

'It was the weirdest thing. I just saw it perched on a support beam under the floor. It was covered in dust and I almost knocked it flying with my jemmy. At first I wasn't even going to pick it up, but then curiosity got the better of me.'

'I wonder how it ended up on a beam.'

'Must have fallen through a crack in the floorboards, I guess.'

Yes, it's the only explanation.

'I can't believe it's been there all this time.' Kitty was pleased her voice was steadier now. 'More than seventy years.'

'Yeah, I know. It blows my mind.' Luke was grinning happily, proud of his discovery. 'You met those American pilots, didn't you?'

'I did, yes.' The memories were rushing back, roaring towards Kitty like a tidal wave, threatening to drown her. 'I – I knew them briefly.'

'That's what I thought, so I wanted *you* to have the dollar.'

'That's very thoughtful, dear.'

Unfortunately, Kitty wasn't sure she wanted the coin. For decades, she'd worked hard to keep the memories of that tumultuous time buried. For the sake of her sanity . . . and for the sake of her marriage . . . .

Now she had an uncanny presentiment that this was just the start, the pulled thread that might dangerously unravel everything . . .

Her past might catch up with her after all.

Of course, there'd always been a risk when she asked Luke to restore the homestead that questions about the war might be raised, but she'd been confident that her grandson's eyes were on the future, not the past. Now Kitty was extremely grateful that Luke showed no inclination to ply her with questions about the Americans.

'So, tell me,' she said briskly, as she set the dollar on the dresser beside her, 'I want to hear all about that commemorative ball you went to in Charters Towers.'

Luke's cheerful face was pulled into a dismissive scowl. 'Not much to tell.'

'Does that mean you didn't enjoy it?'

'It was okay,' he said, without enthusiasm.

How very disappointing. Kitty had been pinning foolish hopes . . . and yet Luke was as unforthcoming as Sally Piper had been.

When Sally had returned the pink dress, Kitty had asked her about the ball, but while Sally had been politely complimentary about the band music and the efforts of the ball's committee, she apparently couldn't remember whether she'd met Luke.

It was all very frustrating. Kitty knew she was probably pouting, but that was too bad.

'I was hoping you'd have a lovely time,' she told Luke sadly. 'Actually, it was silly of me, I suppose, but I was nursing a hope that you might meet a young friend of mine. A lovely young woman who comes here to visit her grandmother.'

Luke's eyes narrowed warily. 'Someone from Townsville?'

'Yes. I even lent her a dress. I know that sounds hard to believe, but it was a genuine relic from the 1940s. Your mother dug it out for me and washed it and ironed it beautifully. It was in surprisingly good condition.'

'What's the girl's name?' Luke asked, so cautiously he might have been a detective interviewing a murder suspect.

'Sally. Sally Piper.'

Kitty had never thought of her grandson as mulish, so she was surprised to see the sudden hardness in his face and the way his jaw jutted with deliberate obstinacy. He was still scowling as he sat straighter in his chair and looked away to a corner of the room. 'I think I might have met her. Briefly.'

Kitty's spirits sank further. There could only be two ways to read this. If Luke had met Sally, the meeting had either not gone well, or there'd been no spark at all. Whichever was correct, the result was disappointing.

But Kitty had never been one to give up easily, and she couldn't resist putting in a good word for Sally now. 'I'm sure you'd remember Sally if you'd met her, Luke. She's such a lovely girl, and so kind to her grandmother. She comes in here at least once a week, sometimes more often, and she always brings her dog with her. We all love —'

She was interrupted by raised voices outside.

It was noisy old Bill Gooden from down the hall calling out in his great booming voice, 'Here she comes! Here comes our dog!'

Kitty couldn't have been more delighted. 'Well, can you believe it? I mention Sally and her dog and that's probably them now.' She waved her hand, hurrying Luke. 'Quickly, scoot out there and ask her to come in. Otherwise we won't see her till she's finished reading to Dulcie and that can take ages. You might be gone by then.'

'Gran, I don't think —'

'Oh, go on, Luke. Don't be such a spoilsport.'

With evident reluctance, her grandson rose, but instead of obeying her, he stood looking down at her with his hands resting lightly on his lean hips, a canny knowingness gleaming in his eyes.

'You wouldn't be trying to play matchmaker, would you, Gran?'

Stifling a gasp, Kitty managed, miraculously, to keep a straight face. 'Heavens no, Luke. Give me some credit. I know better than to pull something like that.'

He paused for a longer moment, apparently assessing her answer, and somehow Kitty managed not to squirm.

'Let me just warn you, dearest grandmother: don't bother.' He said this quietly but with surprising firmness. 'I'm quite capable of finding my own girlfriends, thank you.'

10

Sally came to a shocked halt when a tall, masculine figure stepped into the hallway, almost blocking her path.

'Luke? What – what are you doing here?'

'Visiting my grandmother.'

'Oh, yes, of course – Kitty Mathieson.' Sally felt ridiculously flustered and breathless. She pressed her hand to her chest. 'She – Kitty mentioned you. Sorry. I got such a surprise to see you. I'm used to frail old men with walking frames.'

Luke nodded without smiling.

'It – it's such a coincidence that Kitty's your grandmother.'

'It is, isn't it?' He stood tall, with his hands in his jeans pockets, the stance making his shoulders look broader than ever.

Awkwardness reigned as they eyed each other.

It was so weird seeing him in this atmosphere; he looked even more attractive than Sally had remembered.

'How are you, Sally?' he asked at last, quietly and without warmth.

'I – I'm fine, thanks.' It was a lame thing to say, but Sally couldn't get her brain into gear.

Then Jess padded forward, tail wagging madly, and she looked up at Luke with eager hazel eyes, as if she'd found her new best friend.

'Hello there, old blue dog.' His voice was friendly enough now.

'She didn't have a name when I got her, so I called her Jess. She just looked like a Jess, like a farm girl.'

'Hi, Jess.' Luke smiled down at the dog, but he made no attempt to pat her and very quickly he shifted his gaze back to Sally. 'Gran's just been telling me about your dog, but I imagined something cute and silky.'

'Like a handbag?'

He almost smiled. 'Yeah, I guess. I certainly didn't expect a cattle dog.'

'I know. I didn't actually plan to get such an outdoor breed, not when I live in a flat, but Jess's very elderly. A happy retiree. I don't think she minds that she can't chase cattle any more.'

'I'm sure you're right. She'd prefer sleeping in the sun.'

'Exactly.' It was much easier to talk about her dog. 'I found her at the pound and she had such sad eyes, I couldn't resist her. She was on death row, only a few days away from being put down.'

'She's a very lucky dog then.'

Luke gave Jess an ear scratch, which she loved, and then he looked about him, watching a wizened old man shuffle down the long linoleum corridor. He glanced at the open doorways that offered glimpses of frail old men and women in their beds. 'I'm surprised they let you bring a dog in here.'

'I was surprised, too. But the staff encouraged me, actually, and everyone here seems to welcome Jess with open arms. They all spoil her. Kitty, your grandmother, loves her.'

'Yes, so she told me.' Luke gave a stiff nod to the nearby doorway. 'Speaking of Kitty, she sent me out here to ambush you.'

'Oh?' Sally wondered how Luke felt about that.

'Apparently, she's very keen for us to meet,' he said, lowering his voice, but still managing to inject a note of sarcasm.

'I see.' Sally fiddled with the leather loop on Jess's lead. 'So you didn't set her straight and tell her we've already met?'

Luke looked annoyed by her question. 'No, not really, and I take it you haven't either.'

'No.' Sally had been worried that Kitty would somehow find out the truth that she'd jumped into bed with her grandson and had a lovely time, and then told him thanks, but no thanks.

How could she explain such wanton behaviour to a ninety-year-old? She couldn't properly explain it to herself. It didn't help that she kept remembering the night she'd spent with Luke.

Over the past fortnight, she'd remembered it rather too often, reliving the surprising excitement and pleasure of being with a sexy new man, and remembering how at ease and happy he'd made her feel. So different from the way she and Josh had been at first.

Starting out so young, they'd taken years to discover the best ways to please each other, whereas Luke had either amazing instincts or loads of experience. From the moment their lips met, every kiss, every touch, every move had been incredibly right. Blissful . . .

But beyond all that . . . she'd been thinking about the home-stead too, and how much she would have enjoyed writing its story. Projects that captured her imagination had been thin on the ground lately and since Josh's death, she'd been struggling with her career – along with every other aspect of her life.

More than once, she'd wished that she hadn't been quite so hasty in telling Luke they had no future.

But those moments of regret had been balanced by even bleaker moments when her grief for Josh had reclaimed her, holding her down in its dark, relentless grip. On those days she'd known that she'd done the right thing; she simply wasn't ready for another relationship.

'So,' Luke said, frowning as he watched her, 'do you have time to see Gran now?' He managed to sound as if he couldn't care less about her answer.

A hunched old lady shuffled past them, walking with a wheeler. 'Hello, Sally!'

Sally nodded to her. 'Hello, Alice. How are you today?'

'Hunky-dory,' the old woman replied with a twinkling smile before she moved on.

Sally turned back to Luke, who was standing waiting, perfectly still and patient, his hands in his pockets, his eyes watchful but unfriendly: the complete antithesis of the lovely, warm guy she'd met at the ball.

'I'd be happy to see Kitty, Luke, but I don't want to cause any more awkwardness.'

He nodded. 'I'll make excuses for you then, shall I?'

It was goodbye. Luke Fairburn wasn't going to be messed around again.

And that was fair enough. Sally knew this dismissal was what she deserved. More than that, it was sensible. She just wished she didn't feel quite so bad about it.

'Then again,' he said, 'you'd make an old lady very happy if you came in now. You shouldn't let what's happened between us inter-fere in your friendship with Kitty.'

'No, no . . . of course not.'

'Your visits mean a lot to her, Sally.' His voice was less gruff, almost conciliatory; the light in his eyes a shade warmer.

Sally was surprised by the change, but it was all the encour-agement she needed. Really, there was no question, was there? Of course she would go in to see Kitty, but nerves knotted her stomach as she and Luke went in together.

'Oh, lovely!' Kitty seemed excited to see them. 'So, do you remember Luke now, Sally?'

Sally prayed that she wasn't blushing. 'Yes, of course.'

She shot a quick glance towards Luke, but his expression was bland, giving nothing away.

'Luke, there are dog biscuits in the drawer here.' Kitty tapped the dresser with a bony finger.

Clearly pleased to have a task, Luke found the biscuits, fed one to Jess and spent a few moments engaged in small talk with the dog, giving her another ear scruff. Then, as if feeling a need to orchestrate the scene, he picked up a coin from the dresser and held it out to Sally.

'I brought this to show Gran,' he said. 'I found it out at the homestead I'm renovating.'

'Is it American?' Sally turned it over. 'Wow, yes, a dollar from 1923. What a find!'

To Sally's surprise, Kitty seemed unhappy and retreated into her pillows.

'There were American pilots at the homestead during the war years,' Luke said, his eyes warning Sally not to give their game away.

'But that's not nearly as interesting as the fact that Luke's restoring the homestead to its former glory,' interposed Kitty.

'How fabulous.' Sally hoped she sounded suitably surprised. 'I love old houses.' Still fingering the coin, she said, 'And an old place like that is bound to have so many stories.'

'Except there's not much point in digging up the past,' Kitty responded dourly. 'I'm more interested in the future, and seeing the homestead looking its best again.'

'Well, yes, that's important too.' Sally found herself walking a diplomatic line. 'And I'm sure Luke will do a great job.' She dropped her gaze. If she wasn't careful Kitty would catch her sneaking extra peeks at Luke.

Luckily, the coin fascinated her. The head of Liberty was beautiful, and she was intrigued to think it was so old. Ninety years.

'The old stories *are* fascinating,' she couldn't help commenting as she handed the dollar back to Luke.

'Gran was at Moonlight Plains during the war when the airmen crashed there.' Luke tossed the coin a little way into the air and caught it.

'Now *that* would make a great story.' Sally was surprised that Luke didn't glare at her for saying this. After all, he'd been quite definite he wanted her to drop her story ideas.

Kitty was shaking her head. 'Don't bother with the war, Sally. There were so many plane crashes in North Queensland back then. Two more won't make much of a story. I'd rather see you write something about Luke's renovations.'

This was getting tricky. Sally deliberately avoided eye contact with Luke.

'Maybe you should come out and see the place some time,' he said casually.

Zap!

Sally stared at him. It was quite possible she was gaping as flashes of shock zigzagged under her skin. His suggestion was so totally unexpected it caught her wrong-footed. She tried to cover her shock with a smile, but it was a very shaky attempt.

Kitty, on the other hand, was beaming. 'What an excellent idea. You'd love Moonlight Plains, Sally. And you could take Jess. She'd love it out there too.'

A cautious glance in Luke's direction showed that his face was deadpan.

'Think about it, anyway,' he said casually, with the hint of a shrug.

It was clear he was opening a door, a very surprising but enticing door . . . Sally couldn't be sure if he was just being friendly or if he'd changed his mind about the story. Or was there more to it, some other clue she hadn't picked up?

'I'll certainly give it some thought,' she said.

Luke was watching her carefully now, as carefully as she was watching him, and she wondered what sort of messages their searching glances were sending to his inquisitive grandmother.

'You must take Luke's phone number,' Kitty enthused. 'Luke, write it down for her.'

'No need. Here's my phone.' Sally whipped it from her shoulder bag and handed it to Luke, making only the briefest eye contact.

It was impossible to read his thoughts as he keyed in his number, but she knew it was likely that this whole exercise was nothing more than a charade to keep his grandmother off his back.

One thing was certain – she wouldn't return to Moonlight Plains unless she and Luke laid down some crystal-clear ground rules.

Kitty lay with her eyes closed. Sally had left to visit her grandmother in the secure wing and Luke had said his goodbyes, and Kitty was exhausted.

She'd put far too much energy into willing those two young people together, but now that she'd achieved her long-cherished hope, she was afraid it might backfire on her. Sally seemed as interested in the war story as she did in Luke's restoration, and the girl's curiosity plus her journalist's instincts could stir things up . . . things that Kitty wanted to leave buried and forgotten . . .

I'll have to play my cards close to my chest . . .

As she at last drifted off to sleep, however, it wasn't Luke and Sally who floated into her vision. It was Ed . . . and Bobby Kowalski . . .

11

Moonlight Plains, 1942

After Ed left the homestead, heading off with a lantern to light his way through the pitch-black, rain-lashed night, Kitty had to keep busy. She lit a fi re in the kitchen stove and hung the airmen's flying jackets over the backs of two wooden chairs to dry. She set their neatly folded helmets and goggles on the dresser, then decided to heat water.

She wasn't at all sure about the dos and don'ts of caring for injuries like Bobby's, but she would try to give him a few sips of well-sugared tea. And perhaps a little arrowroot biscuit soaked in water.

She had left a kerosene lamp burning low on the dressing table in the bedroom, and when she returned, she was very surprised to find Bobby awake.

'Hey there, sleepy head,' she said.

Bobby stared at her for a long moment and then his mouth twisted in a lopsided grin. 'I don't know how I got here, but I guess I should move over, and make room for you.'

'Don't you dare move,' Kitty chided gently. 'You've hurt your chest, and I want you to lie very still while I clean you up.'

Setting a cup of tea and a bowl of warm water on the marble-topped bedside table, she sprinkled a washcloth with drops of lavender, then soaked it and wrung out the excess. Gently, she bathed Bobby's face and neck, taking great care not to put any pressure on his bruised chest.

'Thanks, angel,' he murmured, letting his eyes drift shut again.

'My name's Kitty,' she said, not sure that Bobby should be talking about angels at such a time.

He gave a slight shake of his head. 'I wanna call you Angel.'

Kitty let this slide. 'I thought you might be thirsty. Would you like a little tea?' She picked up the cup.

His blue eyes opened to a squint and he frowned at the teacup in her hands.

'I know you Americans prefer coffee, but I'm afraid we don't have any. This is nice, hot tea – well, not too hot – with plenty of sugar to give you strength. Let's give it a try.'

She dipped a spoon into the cup and held it to Bobby's lips, tilting it carefully, hoping she didn't make him cough. She was sure it would be agony for him to cough.

Obediently, he swallowed the tea, but after only a few sips, he was exhausted from the effort and sank back against the pillows with his eyes closed. His lips were very pale and faint beads of sweat gleamed on his forehead.

Alarmed, Kitty set the cup back on the bedside table.

'Are you feeling too hot? Or too cold?' she asked softly.

Bobby gave a faint shake of his head.

'Please, tell me if there's anything I can do for you.'

'Just stay with me, Angel.'

There was an old bentwood chair in the corner. Until now, Kitty had only ever flung clothes over it, but she drew it close to the bed and sat down. Outside, the rain continued to fall, drumming on the iron roof in a monotonous downpour, and she wondered how far

Ed had walked. Had he managed to get across the creek yet?

As if Bobby could read her mind, he said, 'Where's Ed?'

'He's gone to fetch a doctor.'

'So you've a vehicle?'

'No, he's on foot.'

'But hell, it's too far. There aren't any houses for miles around.' Even though his eyes were still closed, Bobby's forehead was furrowed in a deep frown. 'We could see that from the air.'

'Yes, well . . .' Kitty knew she wouldn't help Bobby by casting doubt on Ed's efforts.

'S'pose he's managed to blame himself for the crash,' Bobby said next. 'Wasn't his fault. He can't take the blame just because he outranks me.' Now he began to pick at his bedclothes with anxious, stabbing motions. 'We ran into a storm and it drove us inland and then we ran out of fuel.'

Kitty was alarmed by Bobby's agitation. It couldn't be good for him. His voice was getting hoarse and she was terrified he'd make himself cough if he talked too much.

'Don't worry. You're safe now. I'm sure Ed will get help.'

'Of course – he's the prince,' Bobby said next.

'A prince?'

'That's his nickname. The prince. Born to lead.'

She patted his hand. 'Shh . . . don't try to talk. You need to rest.'

'No, but it's true,' Bobby insisted. 'Ed's a Boston blueblood. Family goes back to the *Mayflower*. Rich as Croesus.'

'Shh, Bobby. Please, rest now.'

In spite of the rain, it was a warm night, but Bobby's skin was cold and clammy. Kitty wondered which was more dangerous – being cold or burning up. She collected another blanket from the cupboard in the hall and tucked it around him. He seemed to be asleep, so she sat again, quietly watching and worrying, listening to the rain.

She thought about what he'd said about Ed. A Boston blueblood.

It fitted with his handsome, film-star looks. She thought about the strange turn her life had taken, bringing her out here to Moonlight Plains, which was such a different world from the suburbs of Townsville. Arriving here, she'd found the house a mess and her Aunt Lil's beautiful garden flattened by the February rains, even heavier than the rain falling now. Vegetables had been rotten on their stems, their leaves yellowed and blotched with mould.

She thought about Andy Mathieson and their fumbling farewell on the verandah. Back in Townsville, giving in to Andy on that final night had felt so grown up. But now, just a matter of weeks later, she felt years older.

This evening, she felt as if she'd had to mature by decades in just a matter of hours. And when she looked at Bobby's almost colourless face, she feared her most difficult challenge lay ahead.

She hoped Andy was okay. She imagined he was probably embarrassed about his rushed and unromantic farewell and she knew he'd be worried about her. Now, with six weeks' distance from that alarming night, she could think about Andy more calmly.

She found herself remembering snippets of their past, like the time Andy first invited her over to his house to see the bantam chicks he'd raised. Such tiny, fluffy little balls they'd been, and he'd handled them so gently as he'd offered her one to hold. She'd been entranced, just as her grandmother had been a few years later when Andy had volunteered to mend the heirloom rocking chair.

'It's English oak,' Andy had said. 'That's hard to come by, Mrs M, but I think I know where I can get hold of a piece.'

He'd fixed the chair as good as new and her grandmother had been overjoyed. Recalling those happier times now, Kitty hated to think he might be somewhere in Malaya . . . dangerously wounded like Bobby . . . lying among strangers.

'Angel?'

Bobby's soft voice broke into her thoughts.

'You ever go to church?' he asked without opening his eyes.

'Yes,' Kitty told him. 'Before I came to live here, I went to church all the time with my grandparents.'

'You like to sing?'

'Um . . . I do, yes.'

'I knew it. You got such a sweet voice. I bet you sing like Deanna Durbin.'

Bobby seemed to fall asleep again then, and after a bit Kitty got up and tiptoed across the bare floorboards. Carefully, she opened the wardrobe and took out clean clothes, went to the kitchen and bathed in a dish at the sink and changed her clothes. She felt much better once she was clean and had changed into a dress. She thought about making a sandwich, but she would check on Bobby first.

As she entered the bedroom, a floorboard creaked.

Bobby stirred. 'Angel,' he murmured.

'How are you?'

Instead of answering, he asked a question. 'You know any nice hymns?'

Kitty gulped. 'I – I guess.' She came up beside the bed again.

'Can you sing something now?'

Although Kitty loved to sing – in fact, she was actually a little vain about her voice – she didn't like the track of Bobby's thoughts. First angels and now hymns. Had he decided he was dying?

'You're going to be all right, Bobby. Are you sure you want a hymn?'

There was no response at first, but then he gave a slight shake of his head. 'Just something . . . nice . . . reminds me of home.'

Home. Where was his home? Kitty didn't want to ask him. He'd been talking too much already.

'What about "Summertime"?' She hummed the opening bars of the popular song from *Porgy and Bess*. 'It's not a hymn. I suppose it's more of a lullaby, but I've always thought it was very soothing.'

Eyes closed, Bobby smiled. 'Yeah, sing that. That's real nice.'

So Kitty sang. She was sure Bobby slept through most of it, but if her songs worked like lullabies, all the better. She sang 'Summertime' and 'Spring in My Heart' and 'Home, Sweet Home'.

She was holding Bobby's hand and singing 'Danny Boy', crooning the words as softly and sweetly as she could, when she heard a noise that sounded very much like the squeak of the back door. And then footsteps.

A moment later, Ed appeared in the doorway. He'd taken off his boots, but he was still wearing the army greatcoat, which was dark with rain. His hair was plastered to his skull. He stood for a moment staring at Kitty, his expression a disturbing mix of delight and sorrow.

'What happened?' she called softly. 'Was the creek up?'

'Yeah, practically breaking its banks.' Ed ruffled his hand through his damp hair as if trying to dry it. 'I didn't have a hope of getting across. Nearly drowned myself trying. Just as you predicted.'

'I'm sorry.'

'Yeah, so am I.' He cocked his head, gesturing for Kitty to come out into the hallway. He was obviously agitated, so she quickly joined him. 'How long will this damn rain last?'

'I – I'm not sure.'

Ed grimaced. 'I've got to get help for Bobby. I've got to get a message to the base at Townsville or the Breddan airstrip at Charters Towers.'

'I know. I'm sorry, but I don't have any answers, Ed.'

He stared at her for a long moment, his dark eyes tense and troubled, and then he seemed to accept the situation and he cracked a rueful smile. 'That was very pretty singing, Kitty.'

She couldn't believe she was blushing. Quickly, she lifted her shoulders in an embarrassed shrug. 'Bobby asked me to sing.'

'Good for him.' Moving into the bedroom now, with Kitty

close behind, Ed looked down at Bobby's sleeping face. 'How's my buddy?'

'Much the same.' She gave a sad shake of her head. 'Although I'm scared he might be a bit worse.'

There was a frightening bluish tinge to Bobby's lips now and when she slipped her hand in his, he gave no sign that he noticed.

Carefully, Ed lifted the sheet back and then Bobby's shirt. The bruise was darker and meaner looking than before, and Bobby's breathing was shallow and rapid.

Ed sighed heavily and closed his eyes. Next moment, he grasped at the iron bed-end and swung dizzily as if he was overcome by exhaustion or despair, or both.

'I think you'd better come through to the kitchen, Ed.' Kitty was on her feet, watching him with concern. 'You need to get something in your stomach. I don't want two crocks on my hands.'

In the kitchen, she went to the stove where the large black kettle was heating.

'You'll probably want to wash first.'

'Thanks,' said Ed. 'That'd be great. After the dip in the creek I'm disgustingly muddy.'

'The bathroom's off the back landing. I got it ready in case you came back.'

He cracked a wry grin. 'Oh, ye of little faith. You knew I'd be back, didn't you?'

'I hoped you'd get through.'

'I wonder if I could prevail on you for some spare clothes,' Ed asked. 'My uniform's saturated. I left it hanging out on the verandah.'

'Oh, so that means —'

'I'm naked under this greatcoat, yes.'

His smile was handsome, almost devilish, and of course Kitty blushed.

'I'll get you some of Uncle Jim's things,' she said, already hurrying away, flustered by the thought of his naked body. 'They'll be big around the waist, but your belt should pull them in.'

She returned quickly with a flannelette shirt and an old pair of trousers. 'Will these do? Or – or would you like underwear?'

'These are fine, thanks, Kitty. Fabulous.'

'And take this lantern to the bathroom with you,' she said. 'You'll have to fill the basin with warm water from this kettle. I'm afraid there's no actual bath or shower.' The only shower was an outdoor affair under the tank stand.

Ed gave a polite dip of his head as he accepted the clothes and the kettle, but weariness seemed to cling to him as he went through to the primitive bathroom. Kitty wondered if he minded the shabbiness of the chipped enamel basin, or the spotty old mirror. If he was as rich as Bobby had said, he must be used to much finer things.

At least the basin had a pretty trim of green leaves and rosebuds, and she'd set a fresh rectangle of bright-yellow soap in the white porcelain dish. *And* she'd given Ed the biggest and fluffiest bath towel. No way was she giving one of Uncle Jim's threadbare, holey towels to an American pilot who looked like a film star and was the next best thing to a prince.

Supper was the reheated remains of the last of the corned beef with a few boiled potatoes and beans on the side. Thanks to her greatuncle's dairy cows, there was enough milk and butter to make an onion sauce to add a bit of flavour.

'Wow, this looks swell,' Ed said when he came into the kitchen and saw the meal. His dark eyes seemed to shine with genuine appreciation. 'You're going to join me, aren't you, Kitty?'

'I'll go back and sit with Bobby while you eat,' she said.

'But you need to eat too.'

'I can have my dinner later.'

Ed pointed to the chair opposite him. 'Come on, keep me company.' Once again, he sounded as if he was used to giving orders.

'Let me just check on him quickly.'

She was back a moment later. 'No real change,' she said sadly as she took her seat.

Ed's face was sombre. 'If only there was something we could do for him.'

'It's awful to feel helpless,' she agreed as she helped herself to a modest serving. She was too tense to feel very hungry.

They ate in silence for a bit.

'Thanks for this. Thanks for *everything* you've done, Kitty. You've been wonderful, you know. Coming out in the rain and finding us, putting us up here. Taking care of Bobby.'

'It's all part of the war effort, isn't it?' After all, if she'd still been in Townsville, she would have joined the VADs, or the Red Cross, or both for that matter.

Ed's smile didn't quite reach his dark eyes as their gazes met across the table.

'You've been brave and kind, Kitty. Don't underestimate yourself.'

The tenderness in his expression touched Kitty deeply, as if a small gong had been struck inside her, filling her with unexpected happiness.

Good heavens. She couldn't have a crush on this man. She couldn't be so foolish. And yet . . .

'I'm worried about Bobby,' she said quickly, desperate to get her thoughts back on a safe track. 'Do you think he's getting worse?'

Ed sighed. 'I studied law at Harvard, not medicine, so I can only guess, but I'm pretty darn sure Bobby needs the expertise of a surgeon.'

'I was afraid of that.'

Ed let out another heavier sigh. 'Damn rain.'

'We'll just have to try to keep him comfortable.'

'Yeah.'

The weight of their inadequacy seemed to hover over them as they ate.

'Do you know Bobby very well?' Kitty asked.

'Reasonably well, I guess. I only met him a couple of months ago, but we've been pretty much in each other's pockets since then.'

'Is he from Boston like you?'

Ed looked surprised.

'Bobby told me you're from Boston.'

'Yeah, well, Bobby's a farm boy from Minnesota. He's an only child with older parents.'

Imagining how distraught Bobby's parents would be if they knew he'd been injured, Kitty felt her eyes fill with hot tears. She blinked furiously.

'Hey,' Ed said gently, offering her a cheering smile. 'Bobby's great talent has been making us laugh. I remember the first day I met him at Lawrence Field in Virginia. We were both lined up for a medical and the doc was a particularly nasty jerk with no sense of humour. It was a freezing cold morning and he enjoyed making us strip down to our shorts. Didn't even bother to warm up his stethoscope. But Bobby was cracking jokes the whole time, making us all laugh when we were supposed to cough.' Still smiling at the memory, Ed shook his head. 'Cheesed the doc off no end.'

Kitty managed to smile. 'We call cheeky guys like that larrikins.'

'Larrikins? That's a great word. That's what Bobby is. A larrikin.'

Remembering Bobby's talk of angels and hymns, Kitty was struggling not to cry again.

12

Boston, 2013

Late on a Sunday afternoon, the inner Boston condo was bathed in shadows and only the softest dusky light filtered through the tall elegant windows that looked down to the Charles River.

When Laura Langley Fox let herself in, she still half-expected to find her father sitting there in his favourite chair, reading or watching a Red Sox game on TV. But, of course, it was almost a month now since his funeral.

Laura shivered. Sunday evenings were always depressing. There was nothing to look forward to but the start of another working week, and on this particular Sunday afternoon she felt especially tired. She'd spent the weekend grading her seniors' art history papers and then telephoning both her daughters, and she'd travelled in via the subway from West Roxbury to continue clearing and sorting her father's belongings. The unhappy task had been left solely to her. Neither of her brothers had lifted a finger.

It had been a different story ten years ago, when her older brother Edward Langley Junior had been only too happy to help their father move out of his dignified, bow-fronted home on Mount Vernon Street. Now, Edward and his wife Sarah-Jane were firmly ensconced in the Beacon Hill house that had been in the Langley family since the mid-nineteenth century. Ed Junior, usually to be seen in a square-shouldered tweed jacket and plain Oxford shirt, was so caught up with charities, concerts and parties these days that he simply hadn't time to help Laura.

Her younger brother Charlie had a different excuse, but the result was the same. He'd raced back to his beloved war zones the very day after the funeral.

If Laura was the family's failure – and that was how she'd felt ever since her divorce – Charlie was the family's escapee. She'd watched her brother's almost nightly reports from Syria or Egypt or Afghanistan and decided he was hiding from his grief behind other people's catastrophes.

It was probably for the best. Charlie was softer than he liked to let on and if he'd been here, he would have hated the emotional knife twist of going through their father's things, sifting through his life, a task their father had spared them when their mother died. Now it hurt to come face to face with the reality that a living, warm, vital and intelligent man had been reduced to rooms full of things.

There was one heartening fact: Laura's task at the condo was almost done. She'd already sent most of the furniture and kitchen items to charity shops and she'd sorted through her father's clothing, weeping copious tears over his favourite old beige elbow-patch cardigan that he'd worn when he was relaxing at home, still with a roll of cool mints in the right-hand pocket.

She'd taken it to her place, folding it carefully and wrapping it in tissue paper, then placing it with due reverence in the bottom of her chest of drawers, along with the family christening gown, her mother's Bible and a folder of her own artwork from her college days.

Of course, she'd taken the photo albums home as well, weeping again as she carefully turned the pages of black and white prints of her parents' beautiful wedding in the Church of the Advent and their glamorous honeymoon in Paris.

Predictably, these photos had been followed by pages devoted to Laura and her brothers. Ed Junior, with dark bangs flopping forward and the Langley sculpted cheekbones, looked serious and self-important at a surprisingly early age. Laura, the only daughter, had almost always been dressed in stiff frills and ruffles that she'd never found comfortable, invariably with a ribbon pinned into her wiry, mousey hair that was neither blonde like her mother's nor dark like her father's. Charlie had been cute and handsome from birth.

And there were photos of various family birthday parties and Christmases and of vacations in the snow or at the beach. For Laura, they woke countless memories . . .

Skating on the smooth, perfect ice, making snowmen with her brothers, and her frustration when she couldn't make them look perfect like the ones on Christmas cards. Standing with her toes digging into the damp sand at the edge of the sea, waiting impatiently for her turn to be taken out on her father's strong shoulders into the huge, exciting waves. Being tucked into bed and listening to her father's deep, expressive voice as he read her favourite stories aloud.

But it was the photos of her parents that held her attention the longest and brought back the strongest memories. Through a mist of nostalgic tears, Laura had stared wistfully at their smiling faces and at the unmistakable evidence of their very deep and abiding love.

She'd recalled how their father had cared for their mom with such amazing devotion during her final illness. And she remembered the many occasions in her childhood when she'd sat at the top of the stairs in the Beacon Hill house, watching her parents leave for a night at the theatre. Her mom in midnight-blue silk with diamonds at her throat and ears. Her father in tails, looking like Prince Charming as he helped his wife into her fur coat.

Laura remembered the way he smiled at Mom as if she were

his princess, how he drew her into his arms and kissed the graceful white curve of her neck instead of her mouth, because he wasn't allowed to smudge her lipstick. Laughing, they would leave through the front door in a flurry of snowflakes . . . like beautiful creatures from a fairytale.

She remembered the everyday moments too, when her parents' eyes would meet across the dinner table, smiling with happy secrets, momentarily cut off from the children and in a world of their own. Their love had sustained them through fifty years of marriage and it had filtered through to their children, providing the adhesive that held the family together.

Now, however, with her father's death five years after their mother's, Laura felt as if she and her brothers were drifting apart – three separate vessels sailing in three vast and very different oceans.

Perhaps she was oversensitive after the breakdown of her own marriage, but this new sense of solitude made her anxious, especially since both her daughters were now living on the west coast.

She was feeling especially low and vulnerable this evening as she started on the biggest task of all – clearing her father's study.

It had been her father's favourite room, with his beloved mahogany desk and pale-green fitted carpets and white-painted floor-to-ceiling bookshelves built around tall elegant windows that looked down to the Charles River. Books, books and more books.

Much to his family's dismay, Ed Langley had given up law after the war and had turned to history. He once told Laura he'd hoped that studying the past would help him to make some kind of sense of the crazy maelstrom he'd just lived through.

Quite a few of his history books had already been removed, in line with directions in his will that they be donated to the History Department at Boston University where he'd taught for forty years.

There were other history books Laura was sure Charlie would like, if he ever settled down in one place. Then there were all the

other books, the novels, the travel books, the ones on philosophy
and music. Laura would take the volumes of art history, but just
looking at the rest of the crammed shelves and imagining the task
ahead exhausted her.

Come to think of it, sorting the books was too big a task to begin
on a Sunday evening . . . She would take a look at some of the paper-
work instead . . .

Laura eyed a row of large cardboard boxes on the bottom
shelf of the bookcase behind the desk, some of which were clearly
labelled, others left plain. Her father had mentioned several times
that he planned to dump most of this. It was one of those jobs he
probably would have attended to if he hadn't died so suddenly.

She picked up the nearest box. It was rather shabby and grey
and fortunately not too heavy, and she lifted the lid, surprised to discover sheets of handwriting. Her father's handwriting.

In recent years, he'd rarely written by hand. All his correspond-
ence had come via his PC.

These papers looked like letters, and the top one was to a woman.
Dearest Kitty . . .

Laura frowned. She couldn't remember anyone by that name in
her father's circle. There were a couple of Kates, but no one called
Kitty. Who was this person? An old relative? There was no date on
the letter.

Quickly she flicked through other pages. *Dearest Kitty . . .*

Dearest Kitty . . .

Dearest Kitty . . .

Nervous now, Laura sank into a chair and fearfully turned back
to the top sheet. She would have to read this letter properly.

Dearest Kitty,
I heard a woman singing 'Danny Boy' on the radio tonight
and my thoughts rushed straight back to you.

Oh my God. After reading two lines, Laura was scared. This did *not* look good. As far as she could tell, the box held loads of letters written to a strange woman . . . For some very weird reason the letters hadn't been posted, but even from this first sentence, the tone was clearly *intimate* . . .

Confused and shaking, Laura forced herself to read on.

I remembered the night I came back to the homestead after I'd been almost washed away and drowned trying to cross that damned creek.

I was cold and wringing wet as I came into the house by the back door. I remember a pretty lamp with a ruby glass bowl sitting on the scrubbed pine table and the big blackened stove giving out gentle heat.

Then I heard you singing.

Even now, goosebumps prickle my skin when I recall your lovely voice. Honestly, Kitty, I don't think you ever knew how good you were.

I'd heard enough top-class singers to recognise your talent. My mother was an amateur violinist and a great music lover and supporter. When I was a youngster, I went with her to classical music concerts at the Boston Symphony and to the Lyric Opera. I heard a wide range of highly trained voices, all of them beautiful, but not once was I moved to tears the way I was that night by a girl singing sweetly to the accompaniment of rain on an iron roof.

I knew you were singing for Bobby and I was so touched I nearly broke down completely.

What happened to your singing, Kitty? What happened to you?

Do you ever think about that night? It's so clear in my mind. I came down the hallway to the room where we'd put Bobby to bed, and I stopped in the doorway.

There was a lamp on the dresser, casting a warm circle
of light over the bed and over Bobby and you. Bobby was so
very still I couldn't tell if he was asleep or unconscious and he
looked very pale, much as he had before I left.

You'd changed out of your mannish shirt and trousers
into a pretty blue floral dress, and you were sitting on a chair
beside the bed, leaning forward, with your elbows resting on
the mattress, watching Bobby, while you held his hand. Such a
sight – Bobby's big, work-toughened, farm-boy hand clasped
innocently in yours.

I could only see your profile, but I knew you were smiling
as you sang, and your hair gleamed bright and coppery in the
lamplight.

So beautiful . . .

Where are you now, Kitty?

I long to find you, and yet I know that seeing you again
would only break my heart.

Take care. Sweet dreams.

Ed

Laura was shaking by the time she'd finished reading this.

I know that seeing you again would only break my heart.

So many questions screamed in her head. What was this letter
about? Who the hell were Kitty and Bobby? When had this happened?
Her father had recalled this night in such vivid, intimate detail.

But he couldn't have had an affair. There hadn't been another
woman in his life. There simply wasn't. It was inconceivable.

Shaken to her very core, Laura forced herself to read another letter. And then another . . .

Half an hour passed . . . and then an hour. Often, she read with
a trembling hand pressed to her mouth. At other times she could
barely read the words through her tears. Page by page, she pieced

together a story – an old story from long ago, a story that had taken place in Australia in 1942, during the war . . .

By the time she finished reading she was shivering and aching. The room was completely dark and she was sitting in a small island of light from the desk lamp.

Some of the more hurtful words her father had written were by now burned onto her brain.

Kitty, I hope you are at least as happy as I am with my good, intelligent and eminently suitable wife, who is the most wonderful mother to our three very different but quite amazing children.

How could he describe their mother as *good, intelligent and eminently suitable*? Laura was appalled. Her father hadn't said his wife was beautiful or beloved, but *eminently suitable*?

How could he say that?

How *dare* he?

Shocked and hurt, Laura could draw absolutely no comfort from the fact that her father had met this Kitty person in a foreign country years before he'd met her mother and that he'd apparently had no further contact with the woman.

How could this possibly console her when he'd never forgotten the Australian girl? Never let her go? Clearly, he'd never got over his *Dearest Kitty*, and Laura couldn't bear it.

The bitter knowledge brought her world collapsing all around her. Everything she'd ever believed about her family and herself was imploding. There were cracks in the perfect image that had been her parents' love, and she no longer knew the father she'd adored for almost fifty years.

She wasn't sure she could ever forgive him.

13

Moonlight Plains, 2013

All morning, Luke was on high alert, ready for the first sound of a vehicle, or the first cloud of dust that would signal Sally's arrival.

She was due around noon and he was totally cool about her visit. At least, he'd assured her he was cool when she'd phoned a few days after their meeting at the nursing home.

'Are you sure you're happy to go ahead with this story, Luke? I couldn't tell if you were serious the other day, or just keeping your grandmother onside.'

'If you're still keen to write the piece, then you're welcome,' he'd countered.

He could hardly admit that his invitation had been completely impulsive. He'd already made one error of judgement by driving all the way to Townsville on the pretext that the stores there were bigger and better, when in reality, he'd chosen to avoid the increasingly annoying invitations from Kylie at the local hardware store.

Served him right that he'd run straight into a Sally-sized complication.

All it had taken was a glimpse of Sally's candle-flame hair and delicate air and he hadn't been able to think straight. Now he was setting himself up for another round of self-torture – being alone with her and knowing he had no choice but to respect her grief and keep his distance.

Luke was genuinely sorry that she was suffering. He couldn't imagine how hard it must have been for her to lose her husband. So the sane thing would have been to back right away from her, give her all the time and space she needed.

Instead he'd invited her right back to the scene of her Major Mistake.

Of course, they would both make sure that the mistake wasn't repeated, but he was nervous when he turned off the noisy Lucas Mill he'd been using to saw planks and heard the sound of an approaching vehicle.

His chest tightened as Sally's car appeared. It was a neat little city sedan in peacock-blue and it looked like a shiny jewel as she pulled up beside his dusty ute. Jess leapt out the minute Sally's door opened and took off, racing across the dirt, tail wagging like a windscreen wiper on top speed.

Sally was laughing as she climbed out, laughing and heart-stoppingly lovely in green patterned jeans and a coffee-coloured top that made her skin look soft and sensuous.

Luke's smile was strained as they said 'Hi', both careful to make sure no touching was involved.

At least the dog's overjoyed exploration of fence posts and grass clumps provided a helpful distraction. 'I think Jess's in her second childhood,' Sally said.

'She'll find so many smells out here that she probably remembers. Kangaroos, bandicoots, cattle . . .'

'I guess.' Sally stood for a moment, shading her eyes as she watched her dog running in ecstatic circles. 'Wow,' she said. 'I didn't take much notice of the garden last time I was here. You've been mowing.'

'Thought I'd better try to get the grass back to something closer to lawn.'

'It must have been lovely once, Is that a pond over there?'

'Used to be a lily pond. Apparently my grandfather built it for Kitty.'

Sally smiled. 'How romantic.'

Then she looked as if she wished she hadn't said that.

'Do you need a hand carrying anything?' Luke said to cover the awkwardness.

'Um, if you could grab the esky, that'd be great, thanks.'

Sally had insisted on bringing lunch. 'I hope you like chicken salad,' she said, lifting the lid to reveal a cling wrap–covered glass bowl filled with dainty pieces of chicken and avocado and cherry tomato halves.

Girl tucker, Luke thought, swallowing a wry grin as he took the esky. 'Looks terrific.' He could probably do with a break from corned beef and pickle sandwiches.

Slinging a large canvas bag over her shoulder, Sally looked up at the house. 'How's it coming along?'

'I'm making progress, but you won't notice any big changes yet. I've been mainly tackling the structural work – strengthening the roof beams and the foundations.'

Sally nodded. 'I guess that's very important.' Then she drew such a deep breath that Luke wondered if she might be nervous too.

She looked back again at the sweeping paddocks, the stands of gum trees and the overarching blue sky. 'Jess's not the only one who likes the smells out here. There's a lovely timbery scent.'

'I've been milling cypress this morning.' He pointed to the sawn timber.

'Of course. It smells fabulous.'

Luke couldn't help smiling back at her. He was partial to the smell of cypress, too. There were days when he could quite happily live in a cloud of that woodsy scent. But there was absolutely no point in getting excited about the first tiny thing they had in common.

'Well, I guess we should get down to business,' he said.

Determined to be sensible and professional, they'd settled on a lunchtime slot for the interview so they didn't lose too big a chunk from their working day. They called to the dog and settled her on the verandah with a chewy treat and a bowl of water before they went inside.

Sally made a show of great interest in the new roof beams as they made their way to the kitchen, which now boasted *two* chairs, plus an extra camp table.

'I hope you don't mind,' she said reaching into the bulging shoulder bag. 'I'm certainly not trying to tell you how to do your job, but I brought a few decorating magazines and brochures from a paint company. I'm afraid I couldn't help myself. I love dreaming about houses and stuff, and I've been collecting these for ages.'

'Okay. Thanks.' Luke thumbed through a magazine with beautiful colour photos of country-style interiors – a simple table topped by an urn of flowers set beside a gauzily curtained window, a spacious white kitchen with views of grazing sheep.

He had a pretty clear vision of what he wanted for this house, but it occurred to him now that it would be all kinds of fun to go through his ideas with Sally, tossing around options.

'Anyway, lunch first,' she said, becoming businesslike. 'I just need to add a dressing to the salad.'

'Would it be impolite to slap a few rounds of bread on the table?' Luke asked as he watched her toss her dainty concoction with salad tongs.

'No need.' Sally shot him a triumphant grin as she produced

bread rolls wrapped in a tea towel. 'Fresh from the bakery.' As they made themselves comfortable at the camp table and Luke took his first mouthful, he forgot his hankering for corned beef and pickle sandwiches. Sally had sprinkled the salad with toasted nuts and, combined with the dressing, the flavours were amazing.

'I think you could convert me to chick food,' he admitted as he tucked in.

'Chook food?'

'*Chick* food. Girl food.' He gave a guilty grin. 'Bit of a joke in my family. The guys think every meal should be mostly meat, while the girls seem to love salad. But don't get me wrong. This is great tucker! I'm loving it.'

'That's a relief.'

Sally was smiling again but there was still an awkward awareness between them. It wasn't easy to pretend that the amazing night in the swag hadn't happened.

Luke eyed the notebook and pen she'd set beside her on the table. 'So how does this work . . . your job as a freelance journalist? Is it tricky, having to chase stories all the time?'

'It can be. Luckily, it's not my only source of income. I'm actually juggling a few jobs at the moment.'

'A few?' Luke frowned as it occurred to him that she might be a widow with money worries. 'What sort of jobs?'

'Oh, nothing backbreaking. I work a few days a week as a marketer for a big engineering firm – or at least, it used to be big before the downturn in mining. I was originally full-time, but when they had to reduce staff, I was offered a choice – redundancy, or a part-time job in the head office in Brisbane.'

'How'd you feel about Brisbane?'

Sally shrugged and looked down at her plate. 'I couldn't really consider it. Not when Josh's job was in Townsville.'

Oh, yeah . . . Josh . . . the husband . . .

Luke fought off an inappropriate desire to envy the poor bastard.

'Then, when Josh died . . . unexpectedly . . . '

There was an uneasy pause while she pulled her bun apart.

Luke cleared his throat. 'Was there an accident?'

'Yes. A car accident.' Sally concentrated on spreading a piece of avocado from her salad onto a corner of the bun. 'The company decided to keep me on after all. I don't know, I guess they felt sorry for me. But they could only offer me two days a week, so I do casual work for the Townsville newspapers as well. Subbing, advertising features.' She pulled a face. 'It's all pretty boring, to be honest. That's why I really want to do a lot more freelance work. Interesting feature stories.'

'Like this one?'

'Yes.' Her eyes were alight with enthusiasm. 'By the way, I pitched this idea to *My Country Home*, and they're interested. I can't believe it. I'm so excited. This could be my big break!'

Her bright smile caught Luke like a lasso. Damn it, he almost leapt out of his chair and swept her into his arms.

'Only too glad to help,' he said instead.

But what he really should have told her was: *Sorry, this story is a bad idea. This interview is a really bad idea.*

He was practically jumping out of his skin with lust.

'I'll make us some coffee, he muttered, leaping to his feet and grabbing the kettle. 'And feel free to fire away with your questions.'

A spurt of excitement fluttered through Sally as she opened her notebook to a clean page and picked up her pen. She loved gathering material and making notes and looking for leads. At this point, every story brimmed with possibilities.

'I think I'd like to start with talking about you,' she said. 'The human angle. I can focus on other details later.'

'So . . . what do you want to know?'

Luke's smile had a cute little-boy quality and Sally was momentarily distracted.

'Um . . . ' Hastily, she dropped her gaze to her as-yet empty page. 'Number one, I guess, is why this project's important to you.'

'Well, you already know about the family connection.'

'Yes, but do you have a more personal interest?'

Luke nodded. 'I guess I'm trying to prove something. I've worked for other builders and I helped a mate to knock up an extension. But that's way out where my family lives in the Gulf Country. This is my first chance to work solo, and on a homestead that isn't too isolated.'

'Does that mean you're hoping more people will see this? You'd like it to showcase your work?'

Luke nodded. 'If all goes well.'

'And it will.'

Their gazes connected and Sally quickly looked down at her notes again. 'Can you remember when you first became interested in building and carpentry?'

He seemed to give this some thought as he set two mugs on the counter and spooned in instant coffee, and she found herself leaning forward, genuinely curious.

'I guess I've always had a go at making things,' he said. 'Even as a little kid, I was always building stuff. Tree houses, forts, go-karts, even laying boxes for our hens.'

He gave a small, self-deprecating shrug. 'Most of the early stuff was pretty shonky. My granddad – Andy – was a builder and he used to lecture me. You know, the usual things . . . if a job's worth doing, it's worth doing well, et cetera.'

'From what I've seen of your work, the message must have sunk in.'

The compliment was spontaneous, but as soon as she said it,

Sally was conscious of a new level of awareness between them.

'Well, sure,' Luke said, frowning. 'There's no value in just knocking something together and tarting it up with a coat of paint. You've got make sure you get it right the first time. You need to make something that'll last.'

She was scribbling madly to get everything down, but she couldn't help thinking as she did so that there was something very appealing about a man who wanted to make things to last.

Her mind flashed to Josh, her cute, dreamy, romantic Josh, who'd never wanted to plan for their future and who certainly hadn't wanted to talk about houses. Looking back, Sally had to admit there'd always been a Peter Pan quality about him, almost as if he'd been avoiding growing up.

Sometimes she wondered why he'd been prepared to get married. In her darkest moments, she worried that he'd plunged into marriage to secure his place in the law firm where her mother was a partner.

'Do you take your coffee the same as your tea?' Luke asked. 'White with one?'

Sally murmured her thanks, and as Luke brought their mugs over and sat down again he looked *almost* at ease, with an ankle propped on a knee.

'My granddad used to be pretty tough on me, making sure I got things right,' Luke said, looking down at the mug in his hands. 'I thought I'd never live up to his standards. But then —' Luke swallowed. 'When he died, he left me his toolbox. It's no big deal, but . . . '

Across the table, their gazes met and something in the green depths of Luke's eyes made Sally's heart stumble.

'So, what's the next question?' he asked quietly.

She felt as if he'd opened a door, showing her something deeply important to him, and it took her a shade too long to gather her wits. 'Okay . . . let's see . . .' She hoped that the warmth in her cheeks didn't show. 'I guess I'd like to hear about the renovations. Have there been any surprises so far?'

'You mean apart from the snakes?'

'Eww.' Sally shuddered. 'What sort of snakes?'

'Carpet pythons. Brown tree snakes. And I found a family of tiny bats about the size of your thumb coming out of some pipes.'

'I guess they'd be cute.' Sally glanced at the prepared questions in her notes. 'I imagine . . . when you're working with your hands and working with timber, it must be quite a sensory experience.'

Why on earth had she thought *that* was a good topic?

'I – I mean . . . we've already talked about the scent of the newly sawn cypress. Is – is there anything else . . . about working with your han— with timber, that is?'

Crikey, she was making a hash of this.

Leaning back in his chair, Luke rubbed at the grainy shadow on his jaw and Sally found herself mesmerised by his broad hand. Everything about him was so *very* masculine.

Stop it. Don't stare.

'Working with my hands . . .' Luke looked mildly amused. 'There's the texture of fine-grained wood, of course. You can't help but love that. So smooth when you run your palm over it.'

And don't think about his hands touching anything except timber . . .

'And there's a certain exhilaration from the physical work,' he went on. 'You know . . . lifting things . . .'

I'll have to get a photo of that. Now she was imagining Luke with a low-slung toolbelt around his hips, showing off his broad shoulders and muscular biceps as he hefted a piece of roofing timber.

There was something primal about a builder, wasn't there? Perhaps it was the earthy caveman-provider thing.

Or perhaps I'm getting carried away . . .

It would be unforgivable to fall for Luke Fairburn after she'd already, so definitely, warned him off.

'Okay,' Sally said quickly, vowing to be sensible immediately. 'I should probably take a look at the house now and get a few shots.'

But walking around the homestead with Luke while she admired new roof trusses and strengthened window frames was almost as tricky as chatting to Luke in the kitchen. Sally willed her attention to the wall he'd knocked down.

When he showed her gorgeous stained-glass panels for the front door, which needed re-leading, she offered to take them back to Townsville, and Luke accepted gratefully. But the whole time they were talking about the house, she was plagued by a crazy level of excitement that she couldn't shake off. Taking photos of Luke was precarious, too. Every time she looked up from her viewfinder she caught him watching her with a shimmering cheekiness that stole her breath.

This meeting was turning out to be as difficult as she'd feared it might be. There was too much sizzle in the air. Too many memories of that night in his swag. She should *not* have jumped at Luke's invitation to come here.

'I'd better get going,' she said finally, glancing at the time on her phone. 'I have another meeting this afternoon.'

She suspected Luke guessed she was making an excuse, but he would probably be relieved to see her leave. Without delay, she collected her things and stuffed them into her bag. Luke wrapped the glass panels in old pieces of tarpaulin and carried them out to the boot of her car. Sally called to Jess and bundled her into the back seat.

'Thanks for lunch,' Luke said, as she stood beside the open driver's door.

'Thanks for sparing me your time. I'm going to do some research on Moonlight Plains now, so I can balance the modern story with a little history.'

He nodded. 'Good luck. I'll be interested to hear what you find.'

'I'll let you know.'

He looked down at the ground and kicked at a stone with his boot.

This farewell was as tense as the last one. Perhaps he was remembering it.

'Thanks for the magazines,' he said, not meeting her gaze. 'I'll check them out. I'm sure I'll get a few good ideas.'

'Keep them as long as you like.'

Sally slipped her keys into the ignition, but she didn't climb in behind the wheel. She turned back to Luke and she couldn't help it, she had to ask. 'There's something that's been bugging me, Luke. I should have asked you on the phone, or when I arrived.'

He scowled at a point beyond her right shoulder. 'What's that?'

'Why did you change your mind about doing this story?'

It was impossible to miss the way he stiffened. He looked unhappier than ever, which should *not* have sent Sally's heart thumping, and it certainly shouldn't have made her want to reach out. To touch him. To give him a hug.

'Just go,' he said tightly. 'Go now.' Plunging his hands into the back pockets of his jeans, he glared at her. 'Go quickly, Sally, before I do something we'll both regret.'

'I – I don't understand.'

Stupid, stupid thing to say.

Luke's scowl was ferocious. 'You'd understand if I kissed you senseless.'

14

'Laura, I hear you, honey. I understand how your father's letters have rocked you. And I hesitate to say this – so please don't jump on me – but don't you think you might be overreacting . . . just a teensy bit?'

Laura stared at her best friend in disbelief. 'Overreacting?' She felt so let down she actually thought she might cry.

She'd been so looking forward to this after-school get-together. She and Amy had shared many of their deepest secrets sitting right here in these upholstered club chairs in a secluded corner of the Sugar Bowl, their favourite coffee shop in Dorchester.

Laura had been sure that Amy, out of everyone she knew, would understand her latest dilemma. After all, they'd been best friends since college. They'd been bridesmaids at their respective weddings and as newlyweds they'd bought houses in the same suburb of West Roxbury. As young moms, they'd cooked casseroles for each other when their kids were sick and they'd cheered for each other's children on the athletics track and at swim meets.

For many years, their families had enjoyed weekly backyard barbecues. They'd even taken a couple of shared vacations in the days before Laura's husband Terry lost his battle with his gambling addiction.

Later, throughout the bitter process of Laura's divorce, Amy had been her mainstay as well as her shoulder to cry on. So of course Amy was the first person Laura had turned to after she found the box of her father's letters.

She'd been sublimely confident that her friend would understand, and now she couldn't quite believe her ears. An overreaction? Really?

The accusation stung like a slap.

'Of course I'm not overreacting.' Laura was so disappointed she was tempted to leap to her feet and walk out.

'Laura, honey.' Reaching over the small table that separated them, Amy rubbed Laura's arm. 'I'm sure it was a shock to find out that your father has been writing all these letters to a strange woman.' She spoke in her most soothing tones. 'I understand that. But I think you should try to find the positives in this.'

'You see positives?'

'Well, to begin with, your father never posted the letters.'

Laura knew this was true. Her father had actually stated this fact in one of his letters, almost as if he was afraid that someone in the family would find them, as if he expected them to be found . . .

'But that's not the point,' she protested.

Amy overrode her. 'And it sounds as if this romance happened way back – years before he met your mom.'

'But he *never* stopped missing this Kitty woman. That's what eats at me. Surely you can see that, Amy? I can't bear to think that all the time he was married to my mother, all the years he lived with us, my father was simply playing the role of the perfect family man while he couldn't let go of this other woman. It was almost like she had a spell over him.'

Laura's voice was shaking. She couldn't help it. 'I – I think he still loved her. He must have, and I can't stand that. I can't stand knowing that she had such a big impact. Such a lasting impact.'

Amy nodded. 'I know, I know. It's a bit weird and it must be hard for you.' Her eyes narrowed in thought as she picked up her coffee spoon and stirred her second cup of French vanilla. 'I'm wondering, though . . .'

Laura sighed, not sure she wanted to hear what her friend was wondering.

'Can you remember your first boyfriend?' Amy asked abruptly.

'What's that got to do with —'

'Can you? Come on. Have a try.'

Almost against her will, Laura's brain zapped straight to high school and Harry Bradshaw. She could see Harry clearly. In history class. On the football field. On prom night. His curling mop of rusty hair, his deep-blue eyes and cheeky smile. Without warning, a fleeting memory of their first kiss flashed to life. She could actually feel his lips on hers and the recollection was so poignant and sweet she almost smiled.

She managed to squash the impulse just in time.

'I might be able to remember him,' she said rather haughtily. 'But I hardly ever think about him.'

'But it might have been different if you'd met him in a foreign country while you were caught up in the middle of a war.'

That scenario was so impossible Laura couldn't even begin to imagine it. Annoyed, she took a sip of her dark roast decaf.

'We've never lived through a world war,' Amy persisted. 'We have no idea what it was like for our fathers, fighting in the Pacific. Didn't you say your dad crashed his plane somewhere in the Australian outback?'

'Yes, in North Queensland.'

'How difficult would that have been? He was so young and no doubt scared. I don't think we should judge them.'

'Well, I certainly don't need a lecture,' Laura sniffed. She was an artist and she liked to think she had a lively and sensitive imagination, but even if she could put herself in her father's shoes, she couldn't excuse him for the letters. There'd been dozens of them over the years and Amy was simply trying to whitewash a deeply shocking situation.

'I thought you'd see it from my point of view, not theirs,' she said tightly. 'I thought you'd understand how hurt I feel.' *As though my very foundations have crumbled. As though I'm no longer sure about anything in my life.*

That was the worst of it. Everything Laura had ever believed about herself was now in question. She was besieged by doubts about her father, about the depth of happiness in her parents' marriage, even about the honesty of the family life that had moulded her.

And the loneliness of her knowledge ate at her, too. She'd guarantee that no one in the family knew her father had felt this way about a woman in Australia.

'I'm trying to understand, Laura,' Amy said now. 'But honestly, honey, be careful. You don't want to make too big a deal about this.'

Amy reached across again, and squeezed Laura's unyielding hand. 'You're going to make yourself sick if you worry too much about these letters. You've been through such a tough time with the divorce and with both the girls getting jobs so far away.'

Before Laura could protest, Amy grinned. 'Perhaps you should try for a little perspective, hon. It's not as if your father was Tony Soprano and you've just found out he was Mafia.'

'Now you're trivialising this.'

Laura couldn't laugh. She was disappointed in her friend. Bitterly disappointed. 'You didn't know my dad the way I did. He was so —'

Perfect. She couldn't say that, but in her eyes, her father had been as heroic as Atticus Finch.

'He always claimed the moral high ground,' she said instead. 'And for him to keep up this writing . . . was a kind of infidelity.'

'I'm sorry.' Amy sounded surprisingly contrite. 'I tend to forget that your family has a pedigree.'

Laura inwardly flinched at this. For years now, she'd been confident she'd shaken off any shadow of Boston snobbery. Marrying Terry Fox had felt like a gesture of bohemian defiance. She'd grown up knowing that her parents expected her to marry from within their closely conservative and wealthy circle, just as they had done and their parents and grandparents before them.

Laura, however, had been intent on freeing herself from the shackles of the Brahman conservatism that her family's circle revered. Her reckless choice of a husband had received her younger brother Charlie's blessing, at least. He'd been as enthusiastic as she was about throwing off the past.

Of course, her marriage had proved to be a huge mistake, which she now regretted, far too late.

She'd never questioned whether her parents had once felt the same urge to rebel against the pressures of their ridiculously outdated *Mayflower* connections. If Edward or Rose Langley had ever experienced regrets, they'd hidden them well.

Nevertheless, her friend Amy had, perhaps inadvertently, given her something to think about.

Two days later, driving to school in the middle of the early-morning rush hour, Laura was still chewing over this puzzle when she arrived at a possible solution, or at least a step in what might be the right direction. She could send out a feeler: a letter to Australia.

It was unlikely that Kitty Martin was still alive and living at Moonlight Plains, but perhaps whoever lived there now would know something about her. Laura wondered if she could even include a copy of one of her father's letters. Something safe, very carefully selected . . .

By the time she reached school, the idea had taken hold. She would send her letter off into the unknown, rather like a scientific space probe. She might never hear anything from it again, or it just might solve the riddle that her father had left behind.

15

'Okay,' Sally's best friend Megan began in her habitually hearty voice. 'Let's see if I'm picking up the right info here.' Megan started to tick off points on her fingers. 'You met a hot guy at the Charters Towers ball. You're doing a story about a homestead he's renovating. And by a lucky coincidence you're also great mates with his granny.'

Dismayed, Sally came to a complete standstill. Luke had been on her mind far too often, of course. She'd reached the point where he invaded her thoughts so frequently that now her friend's reasonable questions during a sunset walk along the beach with their dogs felt like some kind of trap, like an interrogation behind enemy lines.

'Why would you string together those three random items?' Sally tried to sound justifiably self-righteous.

Megan laughed. 'Maybe because they all have a common denominator called Luke Fairburn?' She gave an exaggerated eye-roll. 'I'm simply stitching together what you've already told me over the past few weeks.'

'I never told you Luke Fairburn was hot.'

'No, but you've let his name slip more than once and coming from you that's a *huge* deal, Sal. Don't forget how well I know you, girlfriend.'

Too true.

Sally knew she was lucky to have a friend like Megan. Not only had they known each other forever, but Megan's boyfriend Barney was an electrician working on a fly-in fly-out job at one of the mines, which meant Megan was often a singleton like Sally and they could hang out together.

Now a brisk sea breeze blew across the bay and whipped at Sally's hair as she frantically scrolled back through her recent conversations with her oldest and closest friend. She thought she'd been super-careful, answering Megan's probing interrogations without giving away a single vital clue about Luke.

'I'm right, aren't I?' Megan prompted smugly.

'No, you're way off.' Annoyed, Sally bent down, picked up a stick and called to their dogs racing up the beach ahead of them. 'Here, Indigo! Here, Jess! Fetch!'

She tossed the stick high and the dogs went crazy.

But Megan wouldn't be put off. 'So, what are you trying to suggest, Sal? That this Luke guy is ugly? Or a figment of my imagination?'

Sally sighed. 'You've certainly embellished him with your fertile imagination. I'm simply writing a story about a homestead near Charters Towers.'

'And Luke Fairburn happens to be working on the homestead?'

'Yes,' Sally snapped. She certainly wouldn't tell Megan there was a very good chance she'd have to drop the story because the vibes between them were just too awkward.

'But he also has a granny at the same nursing home as *yours*?'

'It's not as if there's a huge choice of nursing homes around here. It's no big deal.'

'Okay, okay.'

A testy silence fell as the girls walked on towards Pallarenda, their bare feet sinking into the warm, damp sand while the waters of Rowes Bay kept up a slow and lazy *slap, slap, slap* . . .

It was a beautiful afternoon. A fringe of palms and she-oaks shielded the beach from the road and the sky was softening from blue to mauve. Children played on swings in a nearby park. Cyclists whizzed along a bike track. Sally and Megan and their dogs had the sandy beach almost to themselves, and it was too lovely and tranquil to spoil with uncomfortable conversations.

'But you *did* meet Luke at the ball?' Megan slid this question in slyly, just as Sally was beginning to relax.

Sally choked back a groan. If she got too angry, Megan was sure to smell a rat. 'I met him briefly,' she said, keeping her voice carefully calm.

'And he *is* hot-looking.'

At this, Sally did groan. She couldn't help it. 'I've never said a thing about his looks. To be honest, I haven't really taken much notice.'

Megan snorted. 'Come on, Sal. A crocodile wouldn't swallow that.'

Hastily, Sally switched her gaze out to sea. It would be disastrous to catch her friend's eye while she lied about Luke. 'He's not my type.'

'What type is he then?'

The dangerous type, who can make a girl swoon just by threatening to kiss her.

Sally forced a shrug. 'Oh, you know – rural.'

'Ahh . . . the outdoorsy and athletic, horse-whispering type?'

'I guess.' Sally concentrated on the view out to sea where the soft hills of Magnetic Island rose from the still waters of the bay, while further to the north she could just make out the faint outline of Palm

Island. The whole scene was bathed in the lilac and pink streaks of the sunset. It was beautiful, and it should have been soothing.

'It's on, isn't it?' Megan said softly. 'You and Luke. Sal, you know I'd keep it to myself. And you know, if it's true, I couldn't be happier.'

'Will you shut the fuck up?'

Megan gasped.

Looked hurt.

Sally gasped too. 'Sorry,' she said quickly, but it was too late and she felt bad.

Megan was understandably quiet as they walked on, her shoulders hunched and her mouth set in a downward curve. When Indigo brought the stick up to them again, it was Megan who threw it for the dogs, while Sally continued to worry.

The problem was . . . and it was a pretty *major* problem . . . she found talking about Luke way too stressful. She'd been stressed ever since she left him at Moonlight Plains. She knew she should forget him, once and for all – and she knew he would understand if he never heard from her again.

She just wished she wasn't haunted by the smoulder in his eyes when he'd talked about kissing her. She'd been dreaming about him practically every night.

It was crazy. And it was pathetic to be so attracted to the first man she'd met socially since she lost Josh. She was supposed to be playing the field. She wasn't yet thirty and she should be sampling all the guys she'd missed when she rushed into marriage the first time.

Why didn't the prospect of variety hold more appeal?

'Sal?' Megan was watching her now with concern. 'I'm sorry if I pissed you off.'

'Oh, you know me,' Sally tired to reassure her. 'Touchy as a thin-skinned toad.'

Megan slanted her a small smile. 'I guess I was getting carried away, hoping that maybe things were happening for you at last.'

Deep down, Sally knew that she'd been excited about meeting Luke for the very same reason. She was excited about finding an attractive guy and yet scared that her seesawing emotions would sabotage *any* new relationship.

Truth was, she was behaving like a freaking yo-yo.

And Luke deserved better.

She felt Megan's hand on her arm. Next moment her friend was pulling her close.

'You poor thing,' Megan murmured, giving Sally a warm hug. 'Here's me probing your old wounds and carrying on like a teenage matchmaker.'

'But I shouldn't be so prickly.'

Sally knew what her problem was. She knew what was nagging at her – something she'd been nursing to herself ever since Josh's death, something she'd never told Megan.

It was possibly the real reason she was so tense, the reason she couldn't let go of the past, couldn't move on the way everyone urged her to.

'Look,' she said, feeling scared. 'There's – there's something I should probably explain.'

Megan turned to Sally, her angular face instantly curious, yet justifiably wary.

Sally stopped walking. This wasn't going to be easy. 'Maybe we should sit down.'

Her friend's eyes widened with surprise. 'Okay.'

The dogs also looked puzzled when their mistresses settled on the sand, but their confusion didn't last long. Soon they were off, chasing seagulls.

'Okay,' Sally began, her heart hammering madly. 'The thing is —' She had to stop and swallow the lump that now jammed her throat. 'It's something that happened on the morning after Josh's accident.'

Megan was silent now, waiting while the water slapped gently against the sand, and Sally found herself reliving that dreaded Saturday morning when she'd woken in her bedroom at the flat, drowsy from the sleeping pill her mother had given her.

For a moment she hadn't been worried about the vacant space beside her in the bed. Still half-asleep, she hadn't remembered the accident. She'd assumed Josh was jogging out to Pallarenda as he did most Saturday mornings.

Then the truth had hit, cruelly, with sledgehammer force.

Josh. Dead. Gone. Forever.

She'd crawled back under the covers and stayed there, but although she'd made sure the bedroom windows were closed, she could still hear the snarl of her neighbour's lawnmower, and the chirrups of children playing in a nearby backyard.

She'd drawn the curtains, but bright strips of light blazed along the fabric's edge, as if the sun was trying to taunt her.

The world beyond her bedroom had carried on as it always did on Saturday mornings, as if nothing cataclysmic had happened. But Sally had remained numb, isolated by her grief, her mind locked in a cycle of terror that had started when she'd opened the door to the grim-faced policemen.

In the depths of despairing grief, she'd relived the horror of going to the hospital with Megan and Josh's mate, Toby, as well as her parents.

Josh's father had got there just ahead of them and he'd looked as if he'd aged ten years. He'd told them that formal identification was needed, and Sally had insisted that she must go in.

'Sally, it doesn't have to be you.' Her mother's voice had been gentle, but with a warning edge.

'I can do this.' Sally had been so sure she could. And she'd been sure that she had to. In a bizarre way she'd thought she was prepared, as a huge fan of forensic investigation on TV.

She'd been okay until she saw the sign over the door. The single shocking word *Morgue* had been too much and her legs had given way.

Josh's father had gone in instead and he'd returned white-faced.

You made the right decision, his eyes had told her.

Why? How did Josh look?

Sally hadn't been able to ask those questions, but they'd haunted her ever since.

As had the accident, which had never made sense. A single vehicle? Really? The police had mentioned road curves, distractions, speed . . . They'd investigated the crash, of course, but they hadn't come to any conclusive decisions.

But what had haunted Sally most was not her unanswered questions. Her most persistent worry had come that Saturday morning when her mother, who'd stayed overnight on the uncomfortable sofa bed, had knocked on her bedroom door, bringing her a cup of tea.

'My mum put this proposition to me,' Sally told Megan now as they sat together on the dusk-shadowed beach. 'On the morning after the accident.'

She could remember it so clearly, recalling every detail, even the way the mattress dipped slightly as her mother sat next to her and handed her the steaming mug.

At first, they hadn't said anything as they sipped. It was as if they'd both reached the conclusion that words couldn't help.

But then the roar and rattle of the mower next door had stopped abruptly and in the sudden, almost startling silence her mother had spoken.

'Sally.' Her mother's voice had been tight and careful. 'I've been ringing people from work . . . There's been a suggestion, Sally . . . something I think you should consider.'

Remembering now, Sally leaned forward, wrapping her arms

tightly around her bent knees, and she stared at the distant horizon where the darkening sea met the darkening sky. The temperature was dropping and she should tell Megan quickly or it would be dark.

'Mum wanted me to save Josh's sperm,' she said.

Beside her, she felt Megan shiver. 'Wow.'

'I didn't want to have to think about it.' Sally felt the hot prickle of tears in her eyes. 'All I could think of was Josh lying lifeless on a cold slab of stainless steel and a malicious-looking doctor hovering over him with gloved hands and a scalpel.'

Just thinking about it again now, her chest ached, and she couldn't hold back her tears.

'That would have been a very difficult decision,' Megan said gently.

'It was terrible.' Sally swiped at her eyes. 'And it was so weird to hear my mum talking about my husband's sperm. I found it icky, to be honest.'

'No doubt,' Megan agreed with gratifying fervour. 'If it had been my mum talking about Barney, I would have been grossed out.'

'But I let her talk me into it,' Sally said. 'I had to make the decision really quickly. There was only a twenty-four-hour window. I didn't want to think about my future. It was too soon. I was numb and I just wanted to stay numb. But Mum was very persuasive.'

'That's why she's such a good lawyer.'

'Yeah. She reminded me that Josh was an organ donor, and that other people were going to benefit from his death, so I should save this one vital part of him.'

'Okay . . .' Megan said slowly and cautiously.

'For a while there, I really liked the idea,' Sally said. 'I missed Josh *so* much, and I started to think about a little baby with Josh's dark glossy hair and olive complexion, his cute smile . . .'

In the distance their dogs barked at another seagull.

Another sigh escaped Sally. She picked up a broken piece of coral and tossed it out into the water, where pieces of seaweed floated in the shallows like lacy scarves.

'The problem was,' she continued, 'I wasn't sure that Josh really wanted kids. I'd only asked him about it once or twice, but he always changed the subject pretty quickly.'

'Well, yeah, that's not so surprising. You were both young and Josh was focused on making money and having a good time.'

Sally nodded. 'Anyway, eventually, I decided to have the sperm destroyed.' She didn't want to tell Megan that she'd made the decision after her night with Luke. Her friend would read far too much significance into that.

Nevertheless, she'd come away from Moonlight Plains with the strong feeling that there was something wrong about hanging on to her dead husband's sperm. After all, everyone had been telling her to stop looking to the past for happiness, so she'd made the decision quickly and acted on it the very next day.

'But ever since I've felt so bloody guilty,' she said, and without warning, the stress of her confession overwhelmed her. She crumpled, weeping hard, pressing her face into her knees, trying to stem the tears that would not be stemmed.

It was quite a while before she felt Megan's hand on her shoulder.

'Sorry,' she sniffed, rubbing at her damp face.

'No need to apologise, hon. That's heavy shit you've had to deal with.'

Sally found a tissue in her pocket and blew her nose.

'But I don't think you should feel guilty, Sal. It might have been different if Josh had actually talked about wanting to be a father.'

Sally managed a shaky smile. 'And I can't pretend I was keen to be a single mother.'

'I reckon it's time to stop feeling guilty,' Megan said.

Sally drew a deep breath of sea air. 'I'm glad I told you. I feel better just getting it off my chest.' Slipping her arm around Megan's shoulders, she gave her a one-armed hug. 'Thanks.'

After a bit Megan asked cautiously, 'So . . . have you thought about what you do want for the future?'

Slowly, Sally nodded. 'I want to get my life back. I want to stop feeling as if I've fallen off the merry-go-round and can't get back on.'

'And you won't bite my head off next time I mention another guy?'

Sally let out a huff that was almost a laugh. 'How about a deal? If anything exciting happens, you'll be the first to know. I promise.'

Megan grinned. 'I'll hold you to that.'

Reaching for another piece of driftwood, Sally tossed it up the beach, calling to the dogs. Indigo, Megan's young and bouncy black lab, reached it first, but elderly Jess was soon trying to wrestle it from him.

'Look at them,' Sally said, and both girls were smiling as they ran to sort out their dogs.

16

Sally felt calm and surprisingly cleansed as she walked to her flat after Megan drove off. It wasn't far, just a block back from the beach, and still the flat she'd lived in with Josh. She supposed her inability to leave was part of her general inability to move on, but she also loved living so close to the sea. The sea and the bush both had strong appeal for her.

She fed Jess in the laundry and watered her pot plants, mostly herbs that she kept by the back door, then went inside to take a shower.

Refreshed, she raided her freezer and found a container of left-over risotto that she set in the microwave to defrost. Luke would probably call risotto girl food, she thought, and was promptly mad with herself for thinking about him. Yet again.

There was a half a bottle of white wine in the fridge and she poured herself a glass and carried it through to the spare bed-room, which she used as her study. Her notebook was lying on the desk beside her laptop, still open at the notes she'd made about Moonlight Plains' history. Even though she wasn't sure she'd con-tinue with the story, she'd done a little research at James Cook Uni as well as at the city library. She'd traced back to the mid-nineteenth century, to the time after explorer Ludwig Leichhardt's expedition when early settlers had moved up from Bowen to try grazing sheep near Charters Towers.

Now, she flipped through a page or two as she took a sip of wine. The more she'd found out about this story, the more interested she'd become. She knew she could do a good job, and this evening, she felt a renewed sense of purpose.

The early history of the Moonlight Plains homestead was also linked to the gold rush days when cattle had found a ready local market and prices were really high. That era was interesting enough on its own, but if she added in the World War II connection and the hunky young builder descendent who was currently renovating the house, she had a really good colour story.

It could even be her big break, a golden chance to achieve her dream to go beyond freelance and become a commissioned writer for a quality magazine.

She really wanted to write this.

Of course, her chances of completing this story would be a thousand times more straightforward if she and Luke Fairburn hadn't slept together on the night after the ball. She'd made the classic mistake of mixing business with pleasure, and now, if she wanted to go ahead, she really needed to sort something out with Luke. Really, she should phone him. Clear the air. Get that night behind them, once and for all.

Or was it all too messy?

Should she just forget about it?

She glanced again at her notes and thought how excited she'd been as she made them.

No, do it. You know you want to.

Now.

Just do it.

She was ridiculously nervous as she keyed in Luke's number.

The phone rang for ages and she was bracing herself to leave a message when Luke answered at the last minute.

'Hello?' He sounded distant, possibly annoyed.

'Hi, Luke, it's Sally.' At least she managed to sound calm.

'Sally, how are you?' He was mega-polite.

'Fine, thanks.' She hurried on quickly to cover her nerves. 'I should have rung you earlier to let you know I delivered your stained glass safely.'

'Thanks. I appreciate that.'

'Actually, they made quite a fuss at the shop. They said it was some of the oldest glass they'd seen in North Queensland. The glazier reckons it must have been brought out from England.'

'That's interesting.'

'I thought so too. And I think it would be really interesting to try to find out more about it.'

'I guess.'

A small silence limped by.

'Luke, I —'

'Listen,' he jumped in. 'What I said last week was probably out of line. I didn't mean to make you uncomfortable. I know how much you want to write this story and if I'm honest, I might benefit from it as well, so I don't want to make it hard for you.' He was talking fast, as if he needed the conversation to be over. 'But it's not easy to pretend that night didn't happen, is it?'

'No.' Sally drew a sharp breath as she recalled her uninhibited response to Luke's lovemaking. She couldn't deny that she'd been partly responsible for what happened that night. It wasn't as if Luke had coerced her.

She heard a soft sound as he inhaled.

'But it was a mistake,' he said next. 'That's what you decided, right?'

Sally winced.

When she'd woken on the morning after the ball, her head had been filled with dreams of Josh and she'd been beyond shocked to find herself in another man's bed. Of course, she'd been consumed by guilt and regret. But now . . . now she was shocked by how genuinely conflicted she felt.

Yes, she wanted the Moonlight Plains story. Yes, she liked Luke. And yes, she was attracted to him, disturbingly so. But despite this evening's helpful conversation with Megan, she couldn't pretend that her emotions weren't still all over the place.

Luke was an open, straightforward kind of guy and the last thing Sally wanted was to stuff up his life with the messy war zone that was currently her heart.

'Look, I know your situation,' Luke said, coming to her rescue when she didn't answer. 'I can't imagine how hard it must have been to lose your husband, and I shouldn't have spoken to you the way I did.'

'Well . . . thanks.' Sally hoped she sounded as grateful as she felt. Luke was a really nice guy, and he was taking the trouble to look at this situation from her point of view. 'But you should tell me straight, Luke, if you'd rather I dropped the story.'

'I don't want you to,' he said without hesitation. 'Not unless you do.'

'No, I'm keen. I've done more research and I think the story has a lot of potential.'

'Good, that's great.'

Was she imagining the relief in his voice?

'Actually, your windows will be ready next week,' she went on. 'I could bring them out, if you like and – and make a progress check.'

'Which day next week?'

'Thursday?'

There was a sound that might have been a sigh.

'I'm going to be busy on Thursday. My Uncle Jim is buying a pen of young steers at next week's sales. The family tends to share this place and my uncle lives in Brisbane, so he's organised to have the cattle trucked here on Wednesday afternoon. I was planning to brand and ear-tag on Thursday.'

Sally found herself fantasising about watching Luke do his cowboy routine.

'That would be amazing to see,' she said boldly.

'You think so?'

'Absolutely, Luke. If I got shots of you working with cattle as well as on the house, it would round off the whole picture perfectly.'

She hoped she didn't sound too enthusiastic.

'Right,' he finally replied. 'But you'd need to get here pretty early.'

'Not a problem.' Sally saw her reflection in her laptop's screen. She was grinning.

Luke was frowning as he disconnected – frowning in spite of the excitement drumming through him, frowning because he'd just invited a major complication back into his life.

He'd been certain that he'd seen the last of Sally Piper after he'd threatened to kiss her. Kiss her senseless, no less. He couldn't believe he'd done that. Couldn't believe he'd been so crass. Clearly, his brains had taken a bloody hike.

Trouble was, he'd been acting crazily ever since he'd met Sally. For her, that first night after the ball had been a casual fling, which was fair enough, but for some reason Luke couldn't pin down, he hadn't been happy with that.

His reaction hadn't made sense then and it still didn't. Until now, his track record with girls had been nothing but casual. He'd always preferred to be a moving target, to hook up with girls who were passing through – free-spirited backpackers like Jana, girls he'd met at rodeos, at parties.

Hell, he'd been the King of Casual.

Sure, he was quick off the mark with girls, but he was never looking far into the future, despite what others in his family might hope.

Now he was intent on breaking into a new career. At this stage he had no idea where his next job might take him, so why the hell would he eat his heart out over a grieving widow who'd seen him as a momentary diversion?

Luke didn't like the way Sally had got under his skin. He didn't like the way he could so easily and so often recall every detail of her delicate profile, or the shape of her mouth, or the charming picture she'd made sitting in his messy kitchen with her auburn hair and her dark-brown eyes alight with enthusiasm.

For the homestead.

The homestead, dickhead.

Your project. Not you.

Still frowning, Luke stared at the view through the window where biscuit-coloured paddocks shimmered with silver beneath a rising moon. This was his dream, to be working at restoring a beautiful rural property – and not just any property, but the place where his grandparents had come after the war to start a new life as cattle graziers.

Luke had very happy memories of long-ago summers when he'd come here to family gatherings at Christmas and followed his grandfather around his workshop like an adoring puppy, watching his broad capable hands at work . . . the mix of concentration and delight in the old guy's keen blue eyes as he'd hammered and sawn and drilled . . .

There's no point in doing a half-hearted job, Luke. You either put everything into it, or you don't bother.

In those days, Moonlight Plains had seemed perfect to Luke. He'd loved the happily chaotic mealtimes with aunts, uncles and cousins joining his grandparents at long trestle tables on the verandah, and with everyone pitching in to help with the cooking or washing up.

In the long afternoons, they'd played cricket on the lawn, or they'd fished in the river and brought their catch home to barbecue. At night after dinner, the tables had been cleared and stretchers with mosquito nets were set up, so all the kids could sleep on the verandah. It had been so much fun, whispering in the dark with his sister Bella and his cousins, and watching the moon slip across the starlit sky, while cattle chomped and snorted in the distant paddocks, or curlews cried under the trees by the creek.

This old homestead had been the hub that drew their far-flung, big and boisterous family together, and after his grandfather's death the memories had gained leverage, prodding at Luke and firing his dreams, until recently his goals had felt clear and certain, driven by an inner compulsion that he could neither explain nor ignore.

That was why he'd agreed to Sally's story – to raise the property's profile and to help boost his fledgling business as a builder. He had to remember this when Sally turned up next week looking all kinds of wonderful.

It was time for a new strategy.

17

Moonlight Plains, 1942

Dawn light filtered slowly through the papered-over windows, and by the time Kitty woke it was already bright outside. She and Ed were supposed to have taken it in shifts to sit with Bobby. She leapt out of bed in a fright.

Ed had let her sleep right through the night.

Surely that didn't mean . . .?

Surely the worst hadn't happened?

A chilling dread gripped her as she snatched her cotton dressing-gown from the end of her bed and hurried barefoot to the next room. Bobby was still lying there with his eyes closed and Ed was in the chair in the corner. He seemed to be asleep, with his long legs stretched in front of him, his head lolling sideways at an awkward angle. His jaw was covered by a five o'clock shadow, and a wing of dark hair flopped over his brow.

Tiptoeing forward, Kitty touched him on the hand. 'Ed,' she said softly.

His eyes flashed open and then he winced and rubbed at his kinked neck.

'You didn't wake me,' she scolded.

He smiled sleepily up at her, looking more like a film star than ever with the dishevelled fall of hair. 'I couldn't disturb you. You looked too peaceful.'

Her desire to argue this point was overridden by her concern for Bobby. 'How is he?'

Ed sighed. 'Much the same, I think. I'm sure I haven't been asleep for long.' He reached for Bobby's wrist, felt for the pulse, and frowned.

'Not great?' Kitty whispered, reading his face.

He shook his head and with another sigh, he went to the window and pushed it open. 'At least it's stopped raining. I should try that creek again.'

'But you haven't really slept.' Kitty hated the thought of Ed leaving her again. 'And it would be crazy to try if the rain's only just stopped. You'd spend most of the day sitting on the bank waiting for it to go down. Get some rest, Ed. Then let me make breakfast for you.'

'No, don't bother, thanks. I'm not hungry.'

He looked far too pale and drawn.

'Even if it's only half an hour's rest.' Kitty shooed him. 'Go on. Sleep in my bed.'

At this, his mouth quirked in a quarter-smile and his dark eyes glinted, momentarily amused.

Of course Kitty blushed.

'Don't let me sleep too long. Half an hour maximum.'

'All right. I promise.'

As Ed disappeared, Kitty waited with Bobby for a moment or two, then went to the kitchen and started a fire in the stove. She put the kettle on, planning to give Bobby some tea when he woke.

While the water was coming to the boil, she checked her reflection in the spotty bathroom mirror.

She looked like a birch broom in a fit.

Embarrassed that Ed had seen her like this, she quickly washed her face and combed and tidied her hair. She couldn't get fresh clothes from her room without disturbing Ed, so she retied the knot at the waist of her dressing-gown. It would have to do for now.

To her surprise, Bobby was awake when she carried two cups of tea to his room, but his face was so pale and gaunt that his eyes were like pools of blue fire.

'Morning, Angel.'

Just speaking seemed to exhaust him.

'Good morning, Bobby,' she said softly. 'I've brought you some nice, sweet tea.'

She supported him with one arm as she carefully fed him spoon-fuls, but the effort weakened him terribly.

Worried, Kitty sat, watching him as he closed his eyes again and dropped off. She sipped at her own cup of tea and wondered if Ed was already asleep. Wondered how long Bobby could go on like this. Wondered where her great-uncle was. What would Uncle Jim think when he found two strange American airmen in his house?

Without warning, Bobby cried out, 'It's okay, Mom. I'm okay. Don't look so worried.'

Kitty jumped, surprised to find him staring at her strangely. 'Sorry.' She dredged up an answering smile. 'But I'm Kitty – I mean Angel – not your mum.'

Bobby blinked several times, looked around the room and smiled wearily as he recalled where he was. 'I'm going to be okay, you know, Angel.'

'Yes, of course you are.'

'I'll show you why.' Patting his shirtfront, he fumbled with the pocket flap. 'I got my lucky charm in here.'

'Here, let me help you.'

Kitty was pleased the pocket was not on the same side of his chest as the bruise, but she was as gentle as she could be while she undid the button.

Carefully, she slipped her fingers inside. The pocket seemed to be empty. 'What am I looking for?'

'A silver dollar.' Bobby's voice was sleepy and slurred. 'It'll be down the bottom.'

'Oh, yes. Got it.'

She removed the coin and was smiling at the small triumph as she placed it in Bobby's palm.

'It's a beauty, isn't it?' In his pale face, his eyes were glowing. 'A Peace dollar from 1923. The year I was born. My dad set it aside for me. And he gave it to me for good luck when I joined the air force.'

Good luck? Kitty's throat ached with the effort of holding back her tears. 'It's lovely, Bobby.'

'It's my lucky charm.' He rubbed the coin with his thumb and forefinger, feeling the outline of what looked like an engraved eagle on one side and the head of a woman on the other.

'Here, you take it.' He held it out to Kitty. 'Have a feel of it, Angel. It'll bring you luck too.'

Wanting to oblige, Kitty accepted the dollar, but Bobby's hand was shaking and, somehow – she wasn't quite sure how it happened – the coin seemed to bounce on her palm. And then it spilled out. Frantically, she tried to catch it, but to her horror it slipped through her fingers, rolled off the bed and onto the floor.

She heard the *tink* as it hit the bare floorboards and then a rolling sound.

Perhaps it wasn't logical to panic over a dropped coin, but Kitty was terrified. If ever a man needed a lucky charm, Bobby needed this one now. She'd seen the way he looked at the bright shiny dollar. She'd seen the hope in his eyes as he rubbed it with his fingers and she couldn't bear, even for a moment, to have anything dim that hope.

In an instant, she was scrambling on her knees, desperate to return Bobby's charm to him.

But when she looked on the floor, there was no sign of it.

'Can you see it?' he called weakly.

Kitty was struggling not to cry. 'Not yet, but it's here somewhere, Bobby. I know I'll find it.'

'Son of a gun. I might have known,' she heard him say with a sigh.

A coin couldn't have rolled far. It had to be under the bed, or under the mat, the chair, the bedside table . . .

Just the same, Kitty was shivering with a kind of reasonless fear as she searched on her hands and knees. Why couldn't she see that bright circle of silver? Where in heaven's name was it?

It couldn't vanish into thin air. It just couldn't.

The space under the bed was dusty with cobwebs – it was an area she hadn't yet got around to cleaning – but now she slithered desperately on her stomach, searching behind the iron legs, searching every nook and cranny while her panic mounted. It had to be here somewhere. It had to!

'Angel?'

'It's okay, Bobby.' She tried to sound confident as she called from the floor beneath him. 'It's got to be down here somewhere. I'll have it in a jiffy.'

'Don't worry, sweetheart. I guess my luck ran out when I crashed.'

'No!' Kitty was so panicked she shouted at him. 'Don't say that. Your luck hasn't run out at all. Ed's going to find a doctor and the dollar's here. I've almost found it.'

But no matter how carefully she searched, the dollar wasn't under the bed, or the mat, or the bedside table, or the wardrobe in the corner. A malevolent force was at play, it seemed, and the coin had mysteriously disappeared.

Kitty couldn't bear it. Bobby clung to life by such a fragile thread and she and Ed were powerless to help him. For all she knew,

Bobby's faith in the lucky charm might have been the only thing keeping him alive.

Fighting tears, she clambered out from under the bed, banging her head on the way. She dashed at the tears with the heels of her hands, grateful that Bobby didn't see them. His eyes were once again closed.

'I'll get Ed to help me find your dollar,' she told him.

He didn't answer. He showed no sign that he heard.

In the next room, Ed was sound asleep and Kitty felt terrible about waking him. He couldn't have had more than ten minutes with his eyes closed, but she felt compelled to ask for his help. They *had* to find the coin.

She hadn't thought she was superstitious – her grandfather had never allowed a breath of superstitious talk in his house – but Bobby truly believed his dollar was lucky, which meant he needed it almost as much as he needed the attention of a doctor.

'Ed,' she said softly as she touched him on the shoulder.

'What?' He sprang up instantly, his eyes wild in his unshaven face. 'What is it?'

When Kitty tried to explain she felt foolish. She knew Ed would think she was.

'I'm sorry,' she said. 'I – we've lost Bobby's lucky charm. He had a dollar —'

'Yeah,' Ed interrupted impatiently. 'His father gave it to him.'

'Yes, and Bobby wanted to show it to me, but his hands were shaky and somehow it fell to the floor, and I've searched everywhere, but I can't find it.'

Ed had thrown off the covers and he was sitting on the edge of the bed now, brushing back the long wing of hair with his fingers.

'I know it's not really a proper reason to wake you, but the dollar means so much to Bobby.' Kitty's voice was shaky as tears threatened again.

So much had happened since yesterday afternoon. Aeons seemed to have passed since she'd first heard the drone of approaching plane engines. Now she was beginning to feel the strain.

'I've tried to find it.' She stifled a sob and wished she was stronger. For Bobby's sake, she had to be stronger. 'I've looked everywhere, Ed. I thought maybe another pair of eyes . . .'

'Sure.' Ed was on his feet now, already on his way across the room.

But even with the two of them searching, there was no sign of the dollar.

'It must have slipped through a crack,' Ed said finally, as he got to his feet once more.

'I suppose I could try to crawl under the house.' Kitty said this almost to herself, but she knew there would be spiders and possibly snakes under there, as well as puddles after all the rain. Was she brave enough?

Ed didn't take her up on the offer. He was standing by Bobby's bed now, his face filled with sorrow as he looked down at him. 'Hey, Bobby,' he said gently.

There was no response and Ed once again reached for Bobby's wrist. 'Hey, buddy.'

Kitty held her breath as she watched the growing concern in Ed's eyes. This time she didn't dare to ask.

Ed's expression was distraught as he released Bobby's limp wrist and felt for a pulse in his neck.

A beat later, he turned to Kitty, his face a picture of horrified despair. 'I can't find anything.'

No.

'I – I think he's gone.'

'No, Ed. He can't be.'

'There's no pulse.'

'But what about his breathing? Isn't he breathing?'

Ed leaned down with his ear close to Bobby's mouth. 'I can't hear anything. I can't feel any breath.'

Terror filled Kitty's chest, rising and swirling like a tempest. 'What about a mirror? I'm sure I've seen people do that in a film. They hold up a mirror to the person's mouth.'

There was a hand mirror in her great-uncle's bedroom. It had been her great-aunt's. 'I'll fetch a mirror.'

'Kitty, no, don't —'

She heard the remonstrance in Ed's voice, but she ignored it and charged from the room. The mirror was on the dressing table that stood in a bay window in her great-uncle's bedroom. Such a pretty, feminine mirror, with a silver handle and pink roses painted on its back.

Snatching it up, she rushed back to Bobby.

Ed was standing at the end of his bed.

'Here.' She shoved the mirror into his hand.

'Kitty,' he said gently. 'There's no need.'

'Of course there's a need.' Her voice leapt on a high note of panic.

Ed set the mirror on the bed and took her by the shoulders, gently but firmly. 'Kitty, I'm sorry. Bobby's gone.'

'No.' Vehemently, she shook her head. She wanted to pull herself out of Ed's grasp, wanted to push him away, push his words away. But when she looked up, she saw the fierce pain in Ed's eyes and the silver glitter of tears.

'No,' she whispered. She didn't want to believe it. She *couldn't* believe it. Dropping out of Ed's grasp, she fell to her knees again. 'I'll find the dollar and he'll be all right.'

'Don't,' Ed said gently.

Desperation clawed at her. She had to find the dollar.

'Come here,' Ed said, reaching down to take hold of her elbow.

Now she was crying. 'But we have to find it.'

'Not now.' Gently but deliberately Ed pulled her to her feet.

She shot a furtive glance at the bed where Bobby lay very still with his bright-blue eyes closed. His broad Polish face with its high cheekbones and soft, boyish lips was eerily white.

Ed drew her against him.

She heard his heart pounding beneath her ear. Without warning, her legs gave way and she clutched at his shirt. His arms came round her and she began to weep against his chest, noisily, messily. She was terribly afraid that she might never be able to stop.

18

Kitty was in a low mood on the day she learned about the letter from America. It was one of those days when she longed to be free of the constraints of her ageing body, to be done with over-friendly jolly nurses and the dour fragile inmates of the nursing home, one of those days when she couldn't forget the gloomy fact that she and the other old folk were all here waiting to die.

She knew she should be grateful that she'd lived a long life and that she wasn't like poor Dulcie White, Sally's grandmother, who had no real idea of where she was now or why. She knew that she should remember with gratitude the busy, laughter-filled days of the past when she and Andy had raised their large and lively brood at Moonlight Plains.

Today, however, she felt frustrated by her feebleness and annoyed that she was unable to walk without hanging onto some-one or something, and that she had to eat what was put in front of her, like a helpless child.

When Luke telephoned her with the news about the American let-ter, she was thinking about how nice it would be to just pop off in her sleep as Andy had. It took her a good couple of minutes to understand.

'It's been sent to Kitty Martin, not Mathieson,' Luke said, somewhat bemused. 'And the address is care of Moonlight Plains,'

'Martin was my maiden name,' Kitty managed to tell him. She
spoke calmly enough, but her heart was instantly quaking.

'Would you like me to forward it to you via Mum?' Luke asked.
'Or will I post it straight to the nursing home?'

'Oh, send it here.' Kitty spoke too brusquely, but if her daughter Virginia got wind of this letter she would only ask awkward
questions.

The questions rushing about in Kitty's head were bad enough.

After Luke's call, she was a mass of nerves. She knew in her
bones that the letter was either from Ed, or about Ed.

Deep down, despite the long seventy years of silence, she had
always known that something like this letter would come one day.

Perhaps the feeling had been born of a foolish longing, but she'd
secretly hoped that someday her unvoiced questions would finally
be answered, that at last, she would know what Ed Langley had
done with the rest of his life.

There'd been so many times, despite her surprisingly happy
marriage – probably happier than she'd deserved – when she'd
wondered whether Ed had stayed in Boston, whether he'd married
and fulfilled his family's expectations . . . whether he'd occasionally
remembered her . . . or mentioned her to anyone.

Perhaps it was just as well that she hadn't died yet.

But along with her questions, she'd also harboured fears that Ed
might try to track her down, when she'd decided that their lives after
the war should remain quite separate. Now, it seemed, the day she'd
both longed for and feared had arrived. A letter from America was
about to be delivered. Luke had said the sender's name was Laura
Langley Fox, so there *was* definitely a Langley connection.

Was she Ed's daughter, perhaps?

Did this mean that Ed had died? Or had he died years ago?

So many questions. So many possibilities and memories danced ceaselessly in Kitty's head, and for twenty-four hours she'd waited for the letter's arrival with a mixture of trepidation, curiosity and nervous exhaustion.

Eventually, mid-morning, Marcie, a plump young nurse with mousey hair and a round, freckled face, appeared at Kitty's door waving an envelope.

'Look what's come for you.'

Kitty was out of bed and sitting in a chair by the window. Marcie was all smiles as she bounced into the room.

'Would you like me to slit the envelope open for you, Kitty?'

'Yes, thank you, dear.'

Kitty knew her own arthritic hands weren't up to the task, and her heart had developed an alarming flutter. She tried to take steady, calming breaths as she watched Marcie take a nail file from her hip pocket and slit the fine paper crease. She was grateful that her hands weren't shaking too badly as she accepted the thin blue rectangle.

She saw that the original handwritten address had been crossed out and readdressed in Luke's scrawl.

'So, can you read it okay?' Marcie asked. 'Or would you like me to read it for you?'

Kitty did very little reading these days, mainly because her hands were so painful that she found holding a book difficult. However, she certainly didn't want to share the contents of this letter. 'I'll manage, thank you, dear.'

Marcie decided to refill her water jug and Kitty had to watch her with churning impatience, waiting until she'd left before she took the thin pages from the envelope.

Skipping the address and date, her eyes flew straight to the message.

Dear Ms Martin,
I'm writing on the slim chance that this might find you,
because I wanted to let you know that my father, Edward
Langley, died in March this year.

Oh.

Kitty had almost expected this, but it was still a shock. A shock,
too, to know that Ed had been alive all this time. All these years.

Her shaking hands made the letter hard to read and she had to
steady them in her lap, leaning forward to read on . . .

My father's death was unexpected but quick, for which we
were grateful, and the funeral was held in the church where
he and my mother were married and where my brothers and I
were christened. The service was very well attended.

I believe that you met my father in 1942 when his plane
crashed at Moonlight Plains during the war in the Pacific, and
I understand that the two of you became quite close for a time,
which is why I thought you should know of his passing.

I hope that you have lived a long and fulfilling life, just as
my father has, and that this letter finds you and your family in
good health.

I'm enclosing another letter that I found among my father's
papers. For some reason it was never posted, but I believe it
was written to you.

With my best wishes,
Laura Langley Fox

Another letter?

Kitty was struggling to take in so much news all at once. She
found it hard to believe there was a letter to her from Ed.

She needed several deep breaths before she dared to turn the page. Her mind had already flashed back to the past, bringing memories of being nineteen again, at Moonlight Plains . . . making her fearful way across a rain-drenched paddock towards a crashed plane . . . and then, in the gathering dusk, a dark-haired man as handsome as a film star . . .

Oh, dear.

She had to take off her glasses and reach for a tissue to dab at her streaming eyes. She was trembling with both fear and hope as she finally set the sodden tissue aside and began to read Ed's letter.

Boston, 1969

Dearest Kitty,

We had a family photograph taken last week to mark our twentieth wedding anniversary. Today several copies arrived for our inspection, and looking at them I think Rose and I are weathering pretty well. Of course our three children, two sons and a daughter, look vibrant and are bouncing with good health.

Actually, I don't suppose Ed Junior thinks of himself as a child any more. He's eighteen – old enough to go to war.

He has no idea what that might mean, does he, Kitty?

If I'd retained the faith of my forefathers, I would pray each night that my son isn't caught up in the new war in Vietnam. But I fear I lost my faith during our war. I can no longer believe in the power of prayer or divine intervention. I've turned to philosophy and existentialism instead.

Your grandfather would roll in his grave, wouldn't he, Kitty?

See how much about you I remember?

Now, looking at this family photo, I can't help wondering how you look now. Have the decades been kind to you? Have you been happy? Do you have a son or sons? Do you fear for them?

Regrettably, I have moments, now and then, when I can't recall your face. I panic then, Kitty, but the harder I try, the more your loveliness eludes me. I hate those moments.

Usually, to my intense relief, an image of you eventually slides back into focus and once again you're with me.

In my memory, you are still nineteen and your hair is long and wavy, the colour of rich, dark honey. Your skin is fair and finely textured, with a soft delicate bloom unmarred by make-up. There's a little bump on the bridge of your nose that stops you from being too perfectly pretty. Instead you are my Kitty, which is so much better. And then there's that rather determined set to your chin, my dear, and your eyes so very bright and sparkling grey.

I've got you right, haven't I, Kitty?

Ah, well . . .

I hope you're happy. In fact I hope you're at least as happy as I am. It's a huge relief to be able to tell you that I am, in all honesty, happy.

I send you my love, Kitty, and every good wish.

Ed

For the longest time Kitty simply sat, staring at the letter.

It was incredible to receive words from Ed after all this time. Wonderful words. Words written by his hand. Words that brought inevitable sorrow and longing, but also, thank heavens, brought peace to her heart.

She knew she would read this page again, but for now she just wanted to sit here in the sunlight, while she waited for her clamouring heartbeat to steady, and while she thought about the letter and the ways her world had shifted in just a few short minutes.

It was amazing to know after so long that Ed had remembered her and thought about her often, just as she'd remembered him . . .

And it was reassuring to know that he'd been happily married with a family – his wife Rose and his sons and a daughter. At least, Ed had said he was happy at the time of writing, and Kitty was pleased and relieved to know that. She'd been happy, too . . . She wished she could tell Ed that.

Do you have a son or sons? Do you fear for them?

That question had given her pause, but he'd been referring to the Vietnam War, of course – Aussies and Yanks fighting alongside each other once more – and naturally, both Kitty and Andy had been fearful, especially when the birthday ballot for National Service had been introduced.

Miraculously, none of their boys had been drawn in the ballot, and after Andy's own wartime experiences, he certainly hadn't encouraged them to become professional soldiers . . .

So that was one fear Kitty had been spared.

If she could reply to Ed's letter, she'd tell him about Andy and the simple pleasures that had enriched her life – about her family and the excited anticipation with which she'd approached her pregnancies, the joy she'd experienced in caring for her children when they were little, and then later, the fun of sharing the life on the land with them.

It hadn't all been a bed of roses, of course. There'd been long days of horseriding and cattle work as well as housework, and worrying times with drought and floods, and her children's inevitable illnesses and accidents. But there'd been wonderful times of relaxation and laughter, too: campfires on the riverbank, birthday parties on the verandah, the excitement of visitors or trips into town.

She would tell him proudly about her daughter Virginia's happy marriage to Peter Fairburn from Mullinjim Station, and then she would surprise him with the list of her strapping sons.

Her eldest son, Jim, named after her great-uncle at Moonlight Plains, was a lawyer in Brisbane these days, although he still retained an interest in the family's cattle business.

Her next two sons, Robert and Andrew, were running their respective cattle properties at Richmond and Julia Creek. Kitty hadn't been too disappointed when her younger sons rejected life on the land, like their older brother Jim. And of course she would tell Ed about the twins, who'd come last, as a total surprise – an accident, a happy one, of course.

Kitty hadn't been too disappointed when her youngest sons both rejected life on the land. She would have enjoyed telling Ed that Ian was now a very successful chef in Sydney, while Mitch was living in London of all places, an accomplished photographer with one of the city's top newspapers.

Six children . . . who would have thought?

Again she looked down at Ed's letter and let out a long, surprisingly satisfied sigh. She'd been worried that he might bring a long-held fear to the surface, but now she knew these pages held no threat.

Her hands were no longer shaking as she folded the thin sheets and slipped them back inside the envelope. She knew now that she would read Ed's letter over and over, and each time it would bring her fresh peace and only the most tender of regrets . . .

19

'I don't know how to lay out a body.'

If Kitty had felt inadequate when Bobby was injured, she was completely at a loss in the face of his death. She was stunned, left feeling empty and useless, and sad, so darned sad.

She'd never seen anyone die. She'd been ten when her parents had died of tuberculosis, and they'd both been in hospital for weeks beforehand, so she'd witnessed very little of their illness. In the nine years since then, she'd rarely attended a funeral.

'Don't worry,' Ed told her. 'This isn't your responsibility. I'll have to bury him here, Kitty. Later, people from my unit will come out and move him to our military cemetery in Townsville.' His jaw tightened and pain crept into his eyes.

Kitty nodded, not wanting to speak for fear she'd start sobbing again.

'When this damn war's over, Uncle Sam will take him home,' Ed said dully.

She tried to imagine how Bobby's family would react when the news finally reached them. It was too sad to contemplate. She'd only known him for a day, and yet she felt as if she'd lost a good friend.

She insisted on washing his face, hands and feet and combing his short fair hair. These simple tasks were both terrifying and consoling. When they were over, she fetched one of her great-aunt's mended sheets to wrap him in. Then they closed the bedroom door.

Now the long day stretched in front of them.

Needing to keep busy, they went out into the hot, bright morning and Kitty showed Ed the toolshed, where the picks and shovels were stored. She stood nervously twisting her hands as he set to work digging a shallow grave.

It was almost a relief to remember that Dolly was waiting to be milked. Having spent six weeks at Moonlight Plains, Kitty had finally got the hang of milking, and today there was something almost soothing about the everyday task of brushing Dolly's flanks and washing her teats to make sure that no sand or loose hair fell into the shiny clean pail.

She was putting the milk away in the kitchen when Ed returned from his digging. While he washed his hands and face, she made another pot of tea and set it on the table with a plate of sandwiches – homemade bread and cheese – plus the last bottle of her great-aunt's pickled chokos from the pantry. She hoped her great-uncle wouldn't mind about that.

'I thought you might be hungry,' she said, wondering whether people from Boston ever ate such rustic meals. She was sure she'd read in a novel that Bostonians dined on creamed oysters and coffee.

'I feel almost ashamed to admit to hunger today, but this looks wonderful, thanks.' It was impossible to miss the sadness in Ed's eyes and the slant of his mouth, but he showed no qualms about spreading thick dollops of the yellow pickle onto the cheese, and he wasted no time in tucking in.

Kitty agreed that it seemed wrong to be hungry, but she definitely felt better after some food . . . until a new worry loomed.

'Ed, you're not going to leave today, are you?' she asked as she gathered up their plates. 'Even if the creek's gone down, you should stay for another night. I don't think I could cope with being left alone here now . . . with Bobby.'

Ed looked up at her, his dark eyes gentle with sympathy.

Kitty strengthened her plea. 'Could you possibly stay until my great-uncle gets back?'

'When's he due back?'

'Tomorrow.'

'Then that's fine. I can certainly stay overnight.' Ed rose, almost as if he was standing to attention, and then he gave the slightest hint of a bow as he smiled at Kitty. 'It would be my very pleasant duty.'

In that moment, he looked every inch the tall, handsome prince that Bobby had claimed him to be.

They planned to bury Bobby in the cool of the afternoon, which meant there were still hours and hours to fill. While Ed went back across the paddocks to inspect his plane, Kitty cleaned the few dishes they'd used at lunch, then she washed Ed's flight suit and hung it out to dry, before going to the chicken coop to collect the day's eggs.

Ed was gone a good long while; he was frowning and looked angry when he returned.

'How's your plane?' Kitty asked.

'It's fine. A couple of knocks but the undercarriage is okay.'

'But you're angry.'

'Sure, I am. I could have taken off if only I'd had the damn fuel. There's enough cleared ground.'

With surprising force, he slammed his fist into a verandah post. 'I can't believe we survived dogfights with the Nips in New Guinea and then flew back into this fiasco. It's crazy.'

'Bobby was worried you'd blame yourself.'

'Of course I blame my—' Ed turned to frown at her. 'What did Bobby say?'

'He said you'd blame yourself, but he insisted that the crash wasn't your fault.'

Ed sighed. 'Of course it was. I was responsible.'

'You ran into a tropical storm and were driven inland, Ed. Then you ran out of fuel. How is that your fault?'

'There were *six* Airacobras caught in that storm but we lost visual contact. I'm not sure what happened to all of them. Some probably landed on a beach up on Cape York. But I was pigheaded. I decided to push on. I thought I had just enough fuel to reach Townsville and Bobby —' His face twisted in a grimace of pain. 'And Bobby stuck with me. I failed my first real test of leadership,' he said with a sad shake of his head.

If Kitty had been braver she might have given Ed a hug. He probably wasn't accustomed to battling with feelings of guilt and failure.

'I – I guess these things happen in war,' she said gently.

Ed stiffened. 'Yes, of course.'

She wondered if he was thinking, as she was, that the war might get a lot worse before it was over.

But then her own feelings of guilt came back in a rush. 'I lost Bobby's lucky dollar.'

The very thought of the bright shiny coin made her cringe. One minute Bobby had been showing it to her, proud as punch and the next —

It was too awful to remember scrambling on the floor, desperately searching for the coin.

Don't worry, sweetheart. I guess my luck ran out.

'Kitty, you know you can't blame yourself for that. It was a fluke. A freak.'

'But if I'd looked under the house, I might have found it.' Her face crumpled as she remembered the desperation of that search.

'I was too scared of snakes.'

'And so you should be,' Ed said, watching her with the glimmer of a smile.

A shiver-sweet smile that arrowed straight to Kitty's heart.

The afternoon dragged on. Kitty told Ed he should rest, but she wasn't surprised when he turned this down. She knew they were both too tense and miserable to relax. Ed's cotton-drill flight suit was almost dry and she brought it inside to iron.

'You don't have to do that,' Ed said when he found her setting up the ironing board, balanced between the backs of two kitchen chairs.

'I want to,' Kitty said.

'But I might be wading through that creek again tomorrow morning.'

'The creeks can go down very quickly once the rain stops. We may as well have you looking like an airman and not like a no-hoper.'

'It seems like too much trouble.'

He looked slightly worried as he watched her use a thick pot holder to lift the iron from the wood stove where it was heating. Kitty wondered if he'd ever seen his mother do any ironing or laundry work.

'It's no trouble at all,' she said breezily. 'But I'm afraid I didn't use any starch.'

'I'll forgive you.' With his arms folded across his chest, Ed leaned a bulky shoulder against one of the kitchen cupboards and stood, watching her, his mouth tilted in a wry smile, as she ironed.

Naturally, his attention made her self-conscious, but she could hardly tell him to go away, and she turned a simple task into something of an ordeal, ironing in creases and then having to sprinkle warm water and re-iron the creases out. And twice she almost burned her hand, despite the pot holder.

Eventually the sun began to sink towards the western treeline and it was time to bury Bobby.

As Kitty helped Ed to carry him in the carefully wrapped sheet, she was reminded of their journey the previous night when they'd carried Bobby from the plane. Had it really only been yesterday? She remembered the hours she had spent sitting alone with him, singing to him, hoping . . .

Just stay with me, Angel . . .

How vain she'd been, imagining that her singing might save him.

Now she was acutely aware that this Australian bush was foreign to Bobby. His home was in Minnesota and Ed had told her that it snowed there, so it seemed wrong that he should be laid to rest in this hot, red dirt surrounded by khaki gum trees. She wanted to shoo away the nonchalant, pink-breasted galahs that fed noisily nearby on grass seeds, and she wanted to frighten off the curious kangaroos that watched, ears twitching, from the shade of wattle clumps.

She was determined that she wouldn't cry again, even though hot tears stung her eyes and burned her throat. She wanted to be strong, wanted to show Ed she was not a weakling.

She managed pretty well until she tried to sing the Twenty-Third Psalm, but from the first words – *The Lord is my shepherd* – her voice faltered, and when she got to *Yea, though I walk in death's dark vale*, she couldn't go on.

She simply couldn't.

'Hey, it's okay.' Ed slipped an arm around her shaking shoulders.

'I'm s-sorry,' she whispered, struggling to hold back her tears. 'I – I c-couldn't even s-sing a psalm for him.'

'You've been magnificent, Kitty. You sang for Bobby last night when he needed it most, and that was wonderful. Way more important.'

He said this so sincerely that she could almost believe him.

*

They sat on the verandah, watching the last of the sunlight. Kitty lit pieces of dried cow dung in a tin saucer to keep the mosquitoes away. Ed had changed into the freshly ironed flight suit for the burial, and now he lowered his long frame into a cane chair and smoked a cigarette.

'You must be terribly tired by now,' she said. 'I slept last night, but I still feel exhausted.'

'I'm not surprised. You've been through quite an ordeal.'

'But I haven't, really. Not compared with those poor people in London who've had to deal with the Blitz.'

Ed shot her a questioning look. 'Sure, the Londoners have been brave, but you're a girl on your own in the middle of nowhere.'

It was true that a lot had happened. She thought about it now, remembering her fear when she first heard the approaching aeroplanes, then meeting Ed and Bobby, Bobby's initial terror when he saw her with the potato sack over her head, the hours she'd sat with him . . .

Just stay with me, Angel . . .

'I can't stop thinking about him,' she said softly.

'Yeah, I'm the same.'

'He was only nineteen, the same age as me.'

'Yeah.' After a small silence, Ed asked, 'You're nineteen?'

'Yes. Why? How old did you think I was?'

'I – I wasn't sure. I'm no expert on women's ages.' The hint of a smile warmed his voice.

'How old are you, Ed?'

'Twenty-one.'

'An old man.'

'One of the oldest in my unit.'

Gosh . . . So many young men, all of them putting their lives on the line. Kitty shivered and tears brimmed again. She sniffed, hoping the tears wouldn't fall.

'Do you believe in heaven?' she asked after a bit.

'Do you?' Ed countered.

'I don't know.' Kitty had been having trouble with the concepts of God and heaven even before the war began. Now, she found it really hard to understand how the Great War, the war to end all wars, had finished just five years before she was born and yet here they were, at war again. What kind of God allowed the people he loved to annihilate themselves like this, over and over?

'My grandfather would have a fit if he heard me say this,' she said, 'but I can't help thinking that death might be a bit like before we're born, when we know nothing . . . when we have no consciousness.'

Ed's eyebrows rose. 'You could be right. But even before we were conceived, I guess we were still an idea, a prospect, a possible dream in our parents' heads.'

'Probably.' She realised that Ed was smiling and she wondered if he was amused by her simplistic attempt to ponder one of life's greatest mysteries, but she found herself smiling back at him. 'And after we die, we go back to being an idea in people's memories.'

Their smiles held for a moment, but then they sobered. Kitty thought again about Bobby.

'You know . . . he only had seven hours of flying lessons before they packed him into that plane,' Ed said.

'Seven? Seven *hours*?' It seemed impossible to Kitty. 'What about you? Don't tell me that's all you've had too.'

Ed shook his head. 'I joined up last year and so I had several months of training.' He drew on his cigarette, then let out a heavy, smoky sigh. 'Damn it. I don't know if Bobby even kissed a girl.'

'Oh, he has,' Kitty said.

Ed shot her a look of sharp interest. 'Did he kiss you?'

'No. Don't be silly.'

'But he talked about girls?'

'Not really,' Kitty admitted. But she couldn't help remembering how Bobby had cheekily offered to make room in the bed for her, despite his terrible injuries, and how easily the nickname Angel had come to him. She was quite sure that he would have flirted with her if he'd been well enough.

'He didn't need to tell me,' she said rather brashly. 'A girl knows these things.'

'Does she, now?'

The mild amusement in Ed's eyes made Kitty feel foolish, as if he'd caught her out pretending to have a vast knowledge of men and kissing. In reality, she'd only ever kissed Andy and that last time had been so rushed and furtive she could scarcely remember it.

And yet now, just *talking* to Ed about this subject felt dangerous and exciting, as if she was a moth fluttering too close to a flame.

'I need another cigarette.' Ed was frowning as he reached into his pocket.

Kitty watched his handsome profile, admiring the way his lips held the cigarette at a jaunty angle as he struck the match. She watched the dark wing of his hair shining in the last of the daylight as he dipped his head to hold the cigarette's tip to the flame. He looked so sophisticated.

'Can I have a puff?' she asked.

If Ed was surprised, he quickly covered it. 'Sure.'

Kitty took the cigarette, carefully holding it between two fingers, and took a little puff, pleased that she didn't cough.

'You don't need to share. Have one,' Ed said, casually flipping the soft packet of cigarettes towards her.

'No, I'm fine, thanks.' She'd begun to feel woozy almost straight away. 'That puff was lovely though.'

Perhaps it was just as well that the cicadas started to trill then, signalling nightfall. She and Ed went inside and lit lamps, and as there were plenty of eggs, Kitty made an omelette for their supper.

They ate in the kitchen once again and she allowed herself only *one* fanciful moment in which she pretended that Ed was her man and that they ate alone like this, just the two of them, all the time.

Then she was shocked by her silliness. She really was *the dizzy limit*, as her grandmother had told her many, many times.

To remind herself that Ed was way out of her league, she said, 'Bobby told me that you're a Boston blueblood. What does that mean?'

Ed gave a smiling roll of his eyes. 'It means very little, to be honest.'

Not satisfied, Kitty pushed. 'Bobby didn't seem to think so.'

He shrugged. 'Well . . . it means I come from a family with very high expectations.'

'Oh.' Was that all? She felt quite disappointed.

'And it means I heard plenty of paternal lectures in my childhood,' Ed expanded.

Thinking of her grandfather, Kitty was instantly sympathetic. 'Lectures about religion?'

He laughed. 'About religion, about money, about sober habits and the importance of family. My family is terribly snobby, I'm afraid.'

'And rich?'

'Well, yes. But don't worry – this war is knocking any snobbery out of me fast.'

'So what did your family say when you joined up?'

Ed drew a sharp breath. 'My mother spent a week in bed with a migraine. And my father . . . was at a loss at first. After that, he was angry. I was in the middle of a law degree at Harvard and he couldn't understand how I could give that up. He decided I was simply looking for adventure.'

'Were you?'

Ed stared at her for a moment and then his eyes twinkled.

'Partly.' He put down his fork and leaned back in his chair, looking around him at the simple homestead kitchen with its wood stove and kerosene refrigerator, the gentle lamplight.

'I felt as if I'd been living in a gilded cage,' he said. 'So yeah, I admit I probably joined up initially to escape the pressure and expectations. But the thing is, I've already learned so much – important things – mixing with men from all over, and from all walks of life.'

'What sorts of things?' Kitty asked, fascinated.

'Well . . .' In the ruby glow of the lamp Ed shifted the salt and pepper shakers as if they were chess pieces. 'I've found that the most unlikely people have the qualities I most admire,' he said quietly. 'Not cleverness or wealth or authority, but things like tolerance, kindness, courage . . .'

Across the table his dark eyes met Kitty's and he smiled again. 'Who would have thought I'd find all that in a young girl in the Aussie outback?'

After their simple supper, Ed insisted on helping with the washing up.

Kitty protested. 'I know you're exhausted.' He'd had next to no sleep last night and the day had been gruelling.

She was pleased when he acquiesced and left her to the dishes. 'If you're not ready for sleep, go into the lounge room,' she said. 'There's a lamp in there and matches to light it. Have a smoke, or you can read a newspaper if you like, although they're a couple of weeks old.'

A neighbour had dropped the newspapers off with their mail after he'd been to town. But perhaps she shouldn't have mentioned them. They only carried bad news. The Japanese had landed at Hollandia in New Guinea and two British cruisers – HMS *Cornwall* and HMS *Dorsetshire* – had been sunk off the coast of Ceylon.

She finished the dishes, which didn't take long, then went into the lounge room and found Ed asleep in her great-uncle's armchair.

His cigarette had burned down and was in danger of singeing his fingers, so she carefully removed it and stubbed it out in the ashtray. Then she stood looking down at the handsome stranger who'd arrived in her life only twenty-four hours ago. So lean and dark and princely.

She imagined bending down and kissing him while he slept. Like Sleeping Beauty in reverse, she thought, and sharp tingles rushed painfully over her skin.

She remembered a new song she'd heard on the wireless just before she left Townsville: Peggy Lee, with Benny Goodman's orchestra, singing 'I Got It Bad'.

20

Moonlight Plains, 2013

Sally couldn't quite believe the excitement that buzzed through her as she drove to Moonlight Plains, conscientiously early, on the following Thursday morning.

Ever since her beachside confession to Megan she'd felt unexpectedly liberated and unfettered by the guilt that had plagued her for over two years. Perhaps she really might be ready to move on at last.

In fact, as her little car ate up the kilometres between Townsville and Charters Towers, she thought there was every chance that if Luke mentioned kissing her again, she would suggest less talk and more action.

Her excitement was at a rolling boil when she arrived and saw Luke coming down the front steps, crossing the lawn to greet her with his easy, long-legged stride.

'Hi there,' she called with a smile and a wave.

'Morning.'

Almost immediately, she sensed that something was different. Instead of Luke's usual cheeky smile, his expression was cool – polite, but with a new, unmistakable sense of distance.

'You didn't bring Jess,' he said, frowning at her car's empty back seat.

'I thought she might get too excited when she saw the cattle. I was worried I wouldn't know how to handle her.'

His response was an unconcerned shrug, but Sally felt as if she'd made a mistake already.

It wasn't a promising start.

She'd gone to a lot of trouble to prepare for this visit, not only double-checking the history of Moonlight Plains, but taking care with her wardrobe as well. She'd dressed for the stockyards in jeans and a long-sleeved cotton shirt. Primarily, she'd hoped to look less citified, and if Luke asked her to help, she wanted to be ready. She'd even borrowed riding boots and an akubra from a girlfriend.

Admittedly, she knew zilch about branding and ear-tagging cattle, and now, one glance at Luke showed her that her clothes weren't right after all. They were far too neat and new-looking, like something out of an RM Williams catalogue, compared with Luke's authentically battered and faded jeans and his ripped and paint-spattered shirt.

As for his boots, they had the kind of creased and scuffed and covered-in-dust look that only a decade of living in the bush could achieve.

The result was inexplicably eye-catching.

Pity about his mood.

'Ready?' he asked when Sally was barely out of her car, and without another word he turned and headed for his ute.

'Don't you want to see your stained glass?' Sally called after him.

'Sorry, we need to get going,' he replied over his shoulder. 'I'll take a look at it later.'

It was a quarter to eight. Sally had left home at six-thirty and she was sure Luke had told her that any time between seven and eight would be fine. 'Am I late?' she called after him.

'No, but I want to get started. Everything's set up.'

Puzzled, but having no choice, she grabbed her camera and note-book and hurried after him. By the time she scrambled into the ute, he'd already started the motor and, as she pulled the door shut, he shoved the gear into first and took off.

All right. I get the message.

She took a deep breath and told herself to calm down as Luke steered the ute over a rutted track through paddocks of pale-brown grass that shimmered prettily in the early sunlight. Ahead, through the windscreen, the sky was already a bright summer-blue and it stretched overhead as clean and fresh as a newly washed tablecloth hung out to dry.

'It's a gorgeous morning.'

Luke nodded but made no further comment.

Sally considered attempting further conversation, but it was pretty clear that this new, gruff Luke wouldn't bother with a response, so she opted to remain silent.

At least it wasn't far to the stockyards, which consisted, as far as Sally could see, of a pen of steers and a complicated network of tim-ber and metal fences.

When Luke pulled to a halt, she decided this wasn't the prudent moment to confess that she was a tiny bit scared of snorting, wild-eyed cows, and that she didn't like the way they looked at her, not to mention what they might do with their horns and hooves.

She decided instead to road-test her new courage.

'So what can I do to help?' she asked, casting a scant eye at the pen of cattle and the mass of sleek hides and hooves.

Luke was watching her coolly from beneath the shabby brim of his akubra and he took his time to answer. 'I think you'd better stick to taking pictures.'

Sally supposed she should feel relieved, but the new aloofness in his manner made her feel foolish. Inadequate, a useless city chick.

'You should stay well out of the way,' Luke added. 'Don't want you getting hurt.'

She couldn't deny this was probably sensible, but she was subdued as she slung her camera strap around her neck and perched on a timber railing to watch while Luke set to work. It was hard work, she quickly realised. Damn hard.

To begin with, Luke had to cajole a steer out of the pen and into a race that led to the steel crush. Then he had to get swiftly to the crush and work levers so the beast was held still, before he performed at least four tasks in smooth and incredibly dexterous sequence.

In no time, Sally was quite mesmerised by the way he moved so fluidly back and forth.

Now she understood what he'd meant when he said he had everything set up. There was a pistol-like dispenser that he used to squirt anti-tick spray down a steer's back, and when this was done, he grabbed a plastic bag of vaccine with a syringe attached and gave the beast a quick jab. After hanging the vaccination gear back on a peg, he moved quickly to the front of the crush to attach a plastic tag to the steer's ear with something that looked like a stapler. Finally, he wielded the red-hot branding iron, applying it swiftly and precisely to the steer's shoulder before flipping a lever and releasing the somewhat stunned animal into freedom.

Then it was time to start all over again.

Sally had expected to feel masses of sympathy for the poor cattle, but she had to admit they didn't appear traumatised. In fact they seemed to recover quite quickly and were soon calmly munching the hay that Luke had strewn around the perimeter of the new holding yard.

But while the cattle gained a share of her attention and sympathy . . . if she was honest, she was mostly ogling Luke.

Actually, she was so busy watching him that she almost forgot to take photos. She was a bit ashamed about that, but surely any girl would find it hard to ignore his almost effortless grace and athleticism.

No wonder he was fit.

Now Sally understood how he was able to lift heavy timber beams as if they weighed no more than matchsticks.

Of course, it wasn't long before she felt bad about sitting on the fence, an idle spectator, while Luke worked his guts out.

'Hey,' she called to him as he hurried past to usher yet another steer down the race. 'I think it's time I helped.'

Luke turned, frowning, tilting his akubra to block the sun's glare and appraising her with a narrowed gaze.

Clearly he was considering her usefulness and Sally lifted her chin and tried to look confident. And competent.

'Look, it's okay, thanks,' he said. 'You stay there where you're safe.'

'No, Luke. No way!' Annoyed, Sally jumped down from the railing, hastily looping her camera strap around a fence post. 'I've been watching you, and I can see what happens. I'm sure I can at least work that gate and shoo the cattle while you get on with the business end.'

He stood a little longer, work-toughened hands poised lightly on his hips, his eyes still wary, his jaw set.

Sally was sure he was about to shake his head, but when he looked at her again, his expression was slightly less fierce.

'Okay. Let me show you what to do,' he said quietly.

Sally's heartbeat took off at a gallop, but she flashed him a smile. After all, the steers were only half-grown, weren't they? They couldn't do too much harm.

Perhaps it was her smile that did the trick. The chill that she'd sensed in Luke ever since she'd arrived seemed to thaw a tad and his green eyes sparked with the ghost of an answering smile.

'Come on,' he said, giving a nod towards the pen.

Feeling braver than a gladiator entering the Colosseum, Sally followed him, carefully avoiding cowpats.

'You need to approach the animal from the side,' he explained. 'So it separates from the mob.'

He handed her a long piece of plastic pipe that had been propped in a corner. 'You can use this. Give the steer a tap on the back if you need to. The important thing is to make sure you're always behind the cattle. Always.'

'Got it.'

'That's important, Sal. Never get in front of them.'

'I'll remember.'

He looked worried again.

Sally waved her hand. 'Go on. I'll be okay. At least they're not very big and they don't have horns.'

'I'll stay here with you while you send the first one down.'

Leaning against a fence with his elbows propped on the top rail, he left Sally alone facing the mob.

Her heart was thumping as she took a minuscule step towards the nearest steer, which, although half-grown, seemed huge and menacing now.

'Off you go,' she told him.

The steer stared back at her blankly.

'Come on,' she urged. 'It's your turn. Luke won't hurt you too much.'

Still the animal didn't budge, and she shot a despairing glance over to Luke, watching her at the fence, his eyes squinting against the glare.

'Get in a bit closer,' he called.

Right.

Sally took another step and made a shooing gesture, and the

steer lurched away, obviously frightened, dashing towards the opening to the race.

Thank God.

'Way to go!' Luke cheered, but immediately he was racing after the steer to attend to the branding.

Sally felt ridiculously pleased with herself.

She was still basking in the giddy joy of her success when Luke called, 'Next!'

Yikes. She was supposed to have had another steer ready and waiting.

Nine steers later, she was well into the swing of things. She'd worked out how to approach an animal so it moved forward straight away, and it was pretty easy once she got over her fear. She found it rather satisfying to come to grips with something so completely outside her experience.

It was quite an adventure, really.

'Thanks for your help.' Luke was smiling when they were finished. In fact, he'd sent her a few tummy-tumbling smiles during their teamwork.

'You did well,' he said.

'You think so?' His praise shouldn't have mattered but it did.

'Sure. You were a great help. I reckon you're a natural.'

This time his smile was full-on, making the skin around his eyes crinkle. His teeth flashed white in his tanned and dusty face. Sally was relieved that they seemed to be friends again.

As he got busy packing up his gear and stowing it in the back of the ute, she checked the photos she'd taken, mostly close-ups of Luke caught in action, muscles straining, his face, shaded by his akubra, deep in concentration. She remembered how he'd looked on the night she met him at the Charters Towers ball, all handsome and spruce and dashing in a suit.

Today's scenario couldn't have been more different – out here

beneath the blazing North Queensland sun with the scent of eau de
cattle in the air – and yet Sally felt the same unmistakable sizzle.

It set her blood singing and robbed her of breath.

'I could do with a swim,' Luke said when the ute was loaded.

Sally laughed. She was covered in dust and her sweat had combined with the dust to make grime. 'I'd give anything for a swim.'

'Let's go then. Just a quick dip in the river to cool off before we
go back to the house.'

'But I didn't bring my bathers.'

'Swim in your undies.'

Lightning flashed through her.

'You're in the bush,' Luke said. 'Out here we hardly ever swim
in togs.'

She tried to recall which undies she was wearing. A sports bra
and floral knickers, if she remembered rightly. *Not too shabby.*

'Look, if you're concerned . . .' Luke's gaze was now fixed on the
distant horizon. 'You don't have to worry, Sally. I meant it when I
apologised for what I said last time. Nothing like that will happen
again.'

'Of course. I know.' How hopeless she was to feel disappointed.

'We've got an agreement, okay?' He turned back to her, his gaze
steady. 'The only agenda for us now is your magazine story.'

'Yes.' Sally couldn't believe the ridiculous regret that eddied
through her. She knew she should be grateful that Luke had sensibly
and thoughtfully set the record straight.

She tried to dig up a smile, but couldn't find one. 'Do you swim
in the river?'

'Yes. It's not far.'

'Is it safe?'

'Of course. You can swim, can't you?'

'Sure.' She loved swimming, actually.

'Then come on. Let's go.'

The section of river that Luke drove to was particularly beautiful. The edge of the water was shaded by magnificent river gums and creamy-trunked paperbarks, while direct sunlight dazzled the middle of the river. On the far side a sandy beach stretched, with another line of trees standing guard on the opposite bank.

The water came sweeping across from this other side, sparkling and clear, running shallow over gravel and sand until it pitched down into a deeper pool that was dammed about one hundred metres downstream by a rocky bar. It formed a perfect, naturally designed swimming hole that just called for anyone to jump in.

As the ute stopped in a clearing, a group of wallabies loped away like moving shadows and, out on the river, a flock of black ducks took off with a *thump, thump, thump* of their wings.

Luke jumped out and pulled off his shirt, revealing a broad golden chest and back, rippling and male.

Sally didn't hang around to watch him strip down to his boxers. She ducked behind a clump of bushes to strip and by the time she emerged, wearing just her bra and knickers, Luke was already in the water.

He turned over, floating on his back, and waved as she made her way, self-consciously, down the grassy bank.

'What about crocodiles?' she called to him.

'Not this far inland. There could be freshwater crocs, but they only eat fish, and they're rare as hen's teeth up this way.'

Sally's father had told her the same thing when she'd canoed with him last year, but she wasn't completely reassured. Actually, she no longer felt as hot and grimy as she had before and she almost changed her mind. Then again, she'd always hated watching people who dithered on the water's edge, so she slipped in quickly, not allowing herself a second thought.

The water was deliciously cool and inviting and she decided to stop worrying and enjoy herself. When she touched the bottom, she felt soft gravelly sand. 'This is glorious, Luke.'

But she was rendered breathless by the sudden dark intensity of his gaze. A quick downwards glance showed her that her wet bra was damn near transparent, but before she could duck safely below the surface, Luke abruptly pushed off and started to churn down the waterhole, swimming furious laps.

The only agenda for us now is your magazine story.

Right. Okay. After accepting that worthy speech, she could hardly tell Luke that she wouldn't mind a little playful flirtation.

She swam out to the middle and floated on her back, looking up at the pristine sky and the graceful weeping branches of the paperbark trees reaching almost to the water.

From this angle she could see debris caught high in the forks of some of the trees – sticks and broken branches and even a gnarled old fence post with a piece of barbed wire still attached. They'd obviously been washed there during the floods in previous years. Now they were a reminder that the river wasn't always as peaceful and benign as it was today.

The debris could almost be a metaphor for her life, she decided. The floods had caused havoc and grief in the same way as Josh's death had brought her pain and heartbreak, and yet the river had reverted to a life-giving stream, and lately she'd felt as if she was coming back to life, too. She'd been left with scars, but these days she found herself thinking more and more about a happier future.

It felt good to think positively at last.

She joined Luke in swimming laps, not trying to race, but just taking easy, smooth strokes through the cool green water. Eventually, they swam over to a shelf of water-sculpted limestone.

The rock was smooth and warm from the sun, and just the right height for resting their arms and warming their backs while they dangled their legs in the cool water.

It was incredibly relaxing, although it would have been even *more* relaxing if Sally hadn't been so super-aware of Luke's smooth golden skin stretched over sigh-worthy muscles.

'Eek!' she cried. 'Something's nibbling at my toes.'

'Rainbow fish.' Luke was grinning. 'The bush version of a pedicure.'

'That's getting a little too close to nature for my liking.'

'Time to get out?'

'Sure.'

Leaving the river brought its own dangers, however. As they climbed onto the rock shelf to dry off in the sun, Sally knew Luke was surreptitiously checking her out, and a quick downwards glance showed her that her wet bra was still quite revealing. In return, she had heaps of trouble keeping her eyes off him.

Their unmistakable tension pointed to a flaw or two in the new, agenda-free status that Luke had proposed, and it was both a disappointment and a relief to finally get dressed again and drive back to the homestead.

'So would you like to see the glass panels now?' Sally asked when Luke had stowed his gear.

'Absolutely. How did they turn out?'

Flipping her car boot open, she peeled back the sheeting from the top panel. 'What do you reckon?'

'It looks great.'

Luke carefully lifted the bright rectangle of glass and held it up to the light. The design was a simple pattern of circles and diamonds but the colours were dazzling and jewel-like in the sun – pink, green, aqua, gold and a brilliant, rich cobalt-blue.

'They've done a good job with the lead work,' he said.

'Yes, I can't wait to see these set back in the door.'

'I should be able to get onto that this week.' Luke smiled at her.

'Thanks for carting these back and forth, Sal. I really appreciate it. You've saved me stacks of time.'

'No worries. My pleasure.'

Their polite, businesslike exchange was eminently sensible, but Sally mourned the loss of the sizzle that had scorched between them during her previous visits.

I can't complain. I told him this was what I wanted.

She vowed to squash any lusty thoughts as they carried the panels into the house and laid them carefully, still wrapped, in a safe corner.

'So what do you think of the progress?'

They were in the front living room and Sally turned, looking around her, past a trestle strung between ladders, to the back of the house.

'Oh, wow! You've taken out the kitchen wall.'

The big timber archway still divided the lounge and dining rooms, but she could see all the way to the back wall of the house.

'I've been studying those magazines of yours and I decided to open everything up, to make the main living space into one big area.'

'It's fantastic. It feels huge now. With the high ceilings, it's enormous.' Sally hurried to the kitchen area and looked back. 'Wow! Anyone working in the kitchen can look right through the whole space to the French doors and the verandah and beyond. The view seems endless now. I can't believe what a difference it makes.'

'The floor's box wood so it should come up nicely.'

'Yes, lovely. What about the walls? Have you decided on a colour?'

'I'm thinking I might stick to white. A pure semi-gloss white for the ceiling and trims and something a bit softer, more of an antique white for the walls.'

Sally was grinning as she looked around, imagining the final result. 'It's going to be gorgeous. Honestly, it'll be amazing, Luke. Really modern without spoiling the traditional Queenslander feel.'

He looked quietly chuffed and she would have loved to rush over to him and plant a congratulatory kiss on his cheek.

'Think of the parties you could throw here,' she said instead. 'All this space inside, and then the verandahs, spilling out into the garden.'

'It's hardly a garden.'

'Well, it will be a garden one day.'

Luke lifted an eyebrow. 'Do you like throwing parties?'

'Love it.'

Oh, God. As soon as she said that, Sally's mind zapped to the last party she'd thrown, the one party that she could never forget: the evening when all her friends were excitedly hiding in the flat, waiting for Josh to arrive.

Once again, she felt the rush of terror that had arrived with the police on her doorstep.

'Sally, are you okay?'

'Sorry.' She gave a little shake, trying to black out the memory – for now at least – and she flashed Luke an extra-bright smile. 'To be honest, I do like throwing parties, as long as I don't have to do all the cooking.'

But although Luke nodded, acknowledging her response, he'd apparently opted to change the subject. Crossing to a small workbench, he picked up a magazine – one of the ones Sally had left with him.

'The tricky part for me is trying to decide on the kitchen.'

He flicked the magazine open at a well-thumbed page showing an attractive country-style kitchen with a traditional freestanding dresser painted white, and open shelves displaying an arrangement of bottles and decanters and all kinds of kitchen odds and ends. In front of the dresser there was an ancient, slightly battered, solid timber table and an eclectic collection of unpainted timber chairs.

'That has a nice nostalgic feel,' Sally said. 'I think it would work really well here. My dad deals in antiques. If you like, I could get him to look out for a really lovely dresser.'

'That could be handy,' Luke agreed. 'But see what you think of this one.' He flipped to a double-page spread of a stunning, sleek and very modern kitchen with fitted cupboards. Everything was gleaming white and streamlined with acres of pale stone benchtops.

'Oh, yum.' Sally widened her eyes as she considered Luke's dilemma. 'Now that is rave-worthy.'

She glanced up at him, caught his bright gaze fixed on her. Flustered, she looked down quickly to the magazine and hoped her cheeks weren't flaming like distress beacons.

'Or there's another option,' Luke said in his slow, easy drawl, putting the magazine aside. 'It's a compromise, I guess, but I was thinking of an island bench like that modern one, sheeted with tongue and groove panelling like the walls here. I'd probably paint it the same off-white as the walls and maybe give the cupboards the same treatment.'

'With open shelves on the wall to give it that country feel,' Sally added with a grin.

'I hadn't thought of that, but it would work, wouldn't it?'

'I think it would be perfect.' Sally restrained from dancing a little jig, but she was genuinely excited. 'A lovely modern kitchen, but still totally in tune with this old homestead. Wow, I can just picture it, Luke – maybe with thick, honey-toned timber benchtops rather than stone.'

He grinned. 'Perhaps I should show you my ideas for the bathrooms while you're here.'

'Absolutely. Lead the way.'

It was fun, way too much fun. Sally had never before enjoyed these kinds of conversations with a male. Josh had always seemed to resent any talk about houses or interior décor.

'I have no idea about that stuff,' he used to say, almost as if he felt it would somehow diminish his masculinity. 'I'll trust your judgement, Sal.'

It had meant there were no arguments, of course, but Sally had found it rather lonely trawling around furniture stores on her own and having to choose items like sofas and bedside lamps without any consultation.

And here was Luke going through the same solitary process.

'You've been working so hard on the house,' she commented as they left the bathroom. 'And now you also have these extra cattle to look after for your uncle. It's a lot to take on.'

Luke shrugged. 'I'm getting loads of experience, having to fig-ure everything out for myself.'

'But it must be lonely working out here on your own.'

They were standing in the hallway now and wariness crept back into Luke's eyes.

'I'll have company soon,' he said. 'A plumber and a tiler for the bathrooms.'

But Sally was thinking of the long, lonely nights. She'd experi-enced enough of them to know how hard they could be. 'You don't even have a dog to keep you company.'

A dark colour stained Luke's neck and for the longest moment he stood very still, watching her, his expression stern and impossi-ble to read.

Her stomach tightened. She'd probably put her foot in it well and truly. Everything had been okay when they were talking about the house . . . but this was too personal. They were supposed to have set all this kind of awkwardness behind them.

'Stuff it,' Luke muttered abruptly, almost under his breath, and he reached above him and gripped a lintel bridging the hallway.

With his arms extended, he leaned towards Sally, his eyes lit by a surprisingly fierce glow. 'This isn't working, is it?'

'I – I – what isn't?'

'You know what I'm talking about . . . us.'

21

Us . . .

The tiny word, so loaded with meaning, sent a shiver through Sally . . . a mix of nerves and gathering excitement.

'We need a little honesty here.' Luke eyed her sternly. 'We've never really talked about that night, have we?'

'After the ball?'

'Exactly.' He let go of the lintel and his hands swung down to rest lightly on his hips. 'You said it was casual, which was fair enough, until you told me you were a widow and it was all a big mistake.'

'Not – not a mistake, exactly.'

Luke's gaze was fixed on her now, not missing a millisecond of her reaction. 'But it *was* casual?' he clarified.

Slowly, Sally nodded.

'Casual usually means occasional . . . now and again.'

'Now and —' She swallowed quickly. 'What are you suggesting?'

It was a foolish question. She knew exactly what he was suggesting, and the knowledge sent heat rioting through her, kickstarting her heart, scrambling her thoughts.

While she was coming undone, however, Luke seemed more at

ease. He leaned a bulky shoulder against a doorframe. 'I'm suggesting that you and I can keep everything cool and super-casual, and
repeat that night on a casual, *occasional* basis.'

Sounds perfect, she wanted to say, but her voice didn't seem to
be working. She tried again, but she was still forming the words
when Luke stepped closer, set a hand beneath her chin, lifted her
face . . .

For an exquisite second their gazes met and she read the silent,
heated message in his eyes. Gently, he lifted a strand of hair that had
fallen over her face and then he brushed his lips over hers, ever so
softly, teasing her mouth with the briefest and sweetest caress.

'We can start with a casual kiss,' he murmured.

'Mmm . . .' was all she could manage. She was already melting,
swaying towards him.

Fortunately, his arms came around her at just the right moment
and she sank against him, taking pleasure in his muscled strength
and catching the scent of the outdoors on his skin.

When their lips met again, he reached for her hips and pulled her
against him, heat seeking heat.

Ohhh.

She'd forgotten how dead sexy his body was, how amazing his
kisses felt and tasted. When she slipped her arms around his neck,
he deepened his kiss by slow degrees and longing coiled and spi-
ralled inside her.

I've missed this . . .

She'd missed the excitement and the comfort, the closeness and
the tenderness and even the wildness . . . and she'd missed Luke,
who was in so many ways her ideal lover, easygoing and sexy, tender
and passionate – the perfect combo.

All she wanted was to glory in his kisses, to revel in his touch
and in his sexy confidence. She wanted to burn off the doubts and
the questions and to simply feel and respond, as now, trailing kisses

over her neck, he began to undo the buttons on her shirt.

Against her warming skin, he murmured, 'Just a little casual undressing . . .'

And if there had ever been a reason to stop him, she could no longer remember what it was. When he slipped her shirt from her shoulders, she was aching with need, arching into him, sighing with pleasure as his hands cupped her breasts.

She wanted this man – needed him . . . and as he steered her in a lazy, shuffling twostep towards the open doorway of the bedroom, she was already lost in a mist of longing. No matter how he whistled, she would dance to his tune.

The swag was still that – just a swag, little more than a slim mattress on a bare wood floor in the puddle of sunlight from an uncurtained window, but luckily Sally didn't seem to be fussy.

Take it slowly, man, Luke warned himself.

Not so easy, given that he'd been going quietly insane since her arrival this morning. Every time he'd caught her smiling at him he'd felt his heart turn over. And now . . .

Now Luke believed in miracles, for here was Sally in his bed, wriggling out of her jeans, flashing her long, slender legs, as pale as the moon.

She was smiling at him as she kicked her jeans free and rolled towards him, a heart-stopping picture of pink, white and auburn perfection.

Almost too perfect to touch . . . but he managed . . .

Take it easy, he warned himself again, as he let his hand glide from the smooth curve of her hip to the silky dip of her waist and then, tracing upwards, to the soft swell of her breast.

'Have you any idea how gorgeous you are?' His voice was rough around the edges.

She went pink. 'Have you?'

Choking back a laugh, he kissed her shoulder, her neck, her chin, her mouth, nipping gently at her soft lower lip. 'You taste gorgeous, too.'

Playful now, she rubbed her nose against his. 'Must be the river water I swallowed.'

'You know I nearly drowned in that damn river. I was going so crazy with wanting you.'

'Poor Luke.' She grazed her teeth along his jaw and sent his blood pounding. 'Do you remember what you said about kissing me senseless?'

'How could I forget?'

'That wouldn't be casual exactly.'

'Maybe senseless was taking it a bit far.'

'Let's find out.'

As he kissed her now, he wondered, momentarily, about her dead husband and the hundreds of times they must have made love. But as his lips found her breasts she made a soft sound of yearning and any thoughts about her past quickly melted in the fever of here and now.

Take it easy, man . . .

But Sally was impatient.

In no time their kisses and caresses grew hotter and bolder and she went a little wild beneath his touch, responding with writhing excitement to his every stroke, to every lavished intimacy.

She made him feel like a god.

'Luke!' The cry broke from her as she bucked and trembled and then lay still, while her heart raced beneath him.

But within moments, she was kissing him again, running her hands over his bare chest.

'Hey, slow down. I'm in charge today.' Smiling, he reached for her seeking hands and lifted them above her head, pinning them there as he kissed her.

She didn't try to argue and as their kisses gave way to a needier urgency, she clung to him, wrapping her legs around him and lifting her hips, urgently, sweetly beseeching . . .

Of course, there was nothing casual about the finale as their bodies locked together, building, building, until it seemed impossible to go higher . . . and yet he took them to the very brink . . . to the peak, to the ultimate, heart-stopping starburst.

'That was . . .' Sally began and then stopped, partly because she was still panting for breath, but also because she couldn't quite find the right word. *Nice* was far too bland. *Amazing* could sound a bit over the top, as if her past experiences were somehow lacking. *Moving* might make her sound like a nervy type.

In the end, it didn't matter, because Luke turned to her with a smile and said, 'Yeah, it was, wasn't it?'

She loved that he understood.

22

Moonlight Plains, 1942

Kitty stood on the homestead's front steps and refused to cry as she watched Ed's figure growing smaller and smaller.

At one point he turned and waved his hand high over his head and she caught the flash of his smile. A moment later he was gone.

She knew she would never see him again and perhaps her reaction was melodramatic, but she was quite sure she could actually feel her heart breaking.

Fortunately, she was soon distracted by her great-uncle's return from Charters Towers. He arrived on horseback very soon after Ed left – in fact, he'd actually crossed paths with Ed and so he'd heard the whole story of the crash on his property and Bobby's death, and he'd already ridden past Bobby's grave.

'I offered Captain Langley one of my horses,' Jim Martin told her. 'But he said he couldn't ride. He only knew how to fly.'

Kitty's mouth twisted as she attempted to smile. 'He's from the city. From Boston. He knows nothing about horses.'

'At least he has a sense of humour.'

Kitty wished she'd seen more of the humorous side of Ed. There hadn't been much chance for it during their short acquaintance.

'But will he be all right?' she asked.

Her great-uncle nodded. 'He was almost at our neighbours'. They've got a truck and petrol and I know they'll take him into town to phone.'

Apparently, Ed had also sung Kitty's praises, but that hadn't stopped her great-uncle from worrying about her.

'I should never have left you alone,' he said, over and over, as she poured him a huge mug of strong, sweet tea and assured him for the umpteenth time that she hadn't come to any harm.

'I was only scared at first until I knew they were Americans.'

'But you thought they might have been Japs?'

'I wasn't sure.'

'Oh, Kitty.'

'And of course, it was just awful when Bobby died.' Talking about it still hurt. 'With the creeks up, there was nothing we could do. We felt so helpless.' She dashed at her tears with a corner of her apron.

Uncle Jim looked grave. 'War and death go hand in hand, I'm afraid, but that's for bloody soldiers to deal with, not a young girl like you.'

'I was never in any danger really.'

'I can see that, lass, but still . . . alone with strangers . . .' Worry hovered like a shadowing hawk in her great-uncle's light-blue eyes.

Kitty guessed the real cause of his concern. 'The Americans were perfect gentlemen, so you don't need to worry on that score.'

A faint smile came and went. 'Well, I'm not going to doubt your word, lass. I certainly don't want to carry on like that drongo brother of mine.' He gave an angry shake of his head. 'Alex should never have sent you out here. What was he thinking, sending a young lass out into the bush in the middle of a war?'

'He was thinking of you,' Kitty reminded him. 'He knew you were here on your own and you needed help with the housework.'

'Like hell he was thinking of me. His head was full of fire and brimstone and he was gripped by the damn-fool notion that you needed to be protected from the Yanks.'

Kitty was grateful that her great-uncle had never been fully informed about the embarrassing circumstances that had led to her banishment. No doubt her grandfather had been too mortified to share the details of her shameful fall from grace.

Now, Jim shook his head again and rocked back in his chair. Then, to her surprise, he slapped at his thigh and chuckled. 'I suppose I can laugh about it now. Here you are, supposed to be safe in the back of beyond, like someone out of the Dark Ages, a princess locked in a tower.' His amusement bubbled over and he let out a great guffaw. 'And the Yanks turned up on our bloomin' doorstep anyhow.'

Kitty wished she could laugh. But now that Ed had gone she felt as if she was dangling by a very thin thread. She'd grown up in a dreadful rush during the past two days. She'd learned painful truths about the fragility of life, and she very much feared that she'd fallen in love.

Both experiences had left her with an aching heart.

'By the way, we have mail,' Jim announced as he reached a beefy hand into his trouser pocket and pulled out a fistful of envelopes. 'I collected these while I was in the Towers.' He frowned as he sorted through the envelopes. 'There are some here for you.'

'I hope there's a letter from Grandma.' Kitty was dying for news from Townsville.

'Yes, there's one here from Nell. And . . .' Jim glanced at Kitty and raised a bushy white eyebrow. 'You know anyone in the military? This one here's been censored.'

Kitty's eyes flew to the envelopes he handed her. She didn't recognise the handwriting, but she supposed it might be from Andy Mathieson. He'd promised to write.

The envelope was stamped *Passed by Censor* and there were extra initials scratched beside the stamp.

Curious, she opened it quickly.

Darling Kitty,

I'm sorry I can't tell you much about what's been happening to me, or where I am; the unit censor will just cut it all out.

But I can tell you I'm fit (fighting fit, ha ha) and the food, particularly during our intense training, has been pretty good, probably better than you and my family are having at home.

I told you I would write and I would love to get letters from you as well. Please don't worry if my letters are few and far between. I think of you all the time, Kitty. I carry a photo of you in my top pocket. It's a group photo taken at that picnic down on the Strand last winter. We're sitting next to each other and you're smiling and happy and you look so beautiful.

I'm glad I've known you for such a long time. It means I have so many memories of you to carry in my heart. Can you guess one of the standout memories for me? You're going to laugh.

It was the day we rode our bikes out to the Town Common and I showed you how to trap nutmeg finches. You were intrigued by the whole process, but when you realised I planned to keep the birds you were so angry you tried to hit me. Do you remember how you begged me to set them free?

I knew then that I could never deliberately upset you, Kitty.

Don't expect me home on leave for some time, but as soon as I get back I'm going to have a serious talk with your grandfather. I hope he hasn't been too rough on you, Kitty. I should have made sure he understood before I left.

In the meantime,

I send you all my love,

Andy

'I hope it's not bad news.' Her great-uncle was watching her through narrowed eyes.

'Um . . . no, not at all. It's just from a fellow who lives near us in Townsville. In the next street. An old school friend. He – he signed up just before I left.'

But Kitty was struggling to hide her dismay. During her recent encounter with Ed she'd almost forgotten about Andy. Even though her time with Ed had been so brief, he'd distracted her completely.

Filled your head with nonsense, her grandmother would probably say.

She'd certainly been awakened to entirely new possibilities. Or perhaps she'd been starstruck.

Whatever happened, he's gone. I'll have to forget him now.

Was that possible?

Hastily, she slipped Andy's note into its envelope and turned her attention to the next letter, which, she was relieved to see, was addressed in her grandmother's beautiful script. She'd missed her grandparents, despite their strict ways. She'd especially missed her grandmother, and she knew her grandmother would be missing her.

Just as Kitty had hoped, this letter was crowded with news about Townsville and the impact of the war.

You wouldn't recognise this sleepy town now, her grandmother wrote. *There are tents everywhere, out along the old stock route to the north where there used to be nothing but chinee apple and straggly bush, and all these flash new aircraft runways.*

'Goodness,' Kitty said, as she read a little further. 'Grandma and Grandfather have been evacuated.'

'Really?' Jim was frowning. 'Where to?'

'Hermit Park.' It was a suburb on the other side of town. 'Apparently, they're evacuating all the elderly people from North Ward and South Townsville.'

'Those suburbs are probably too exposed, too close to the sea.'

'Yes, I suppose so. Now Grandma and Grandfather are living in a house with a family of four. They're called the Robinsons.'

'Could be a bit crowded.'

'Yes, it probably is.' Kitty gave a rueful smile. 'I hope Grandfather doesn't try to organise the Robinsons too much. He can be rather bossy.'

'And how.'

'Grandma says Mr Robinson works for the railway.' Kitty read the next part of the letter aloud. '*Mr Robinson is very efficient and organised. He keeps a bucket of sand and a spade at both the front and back door, ready to put out incendiary bombs. Meanwhile, I've been helping Mrs Robinson to make sugarbag poultices. We've filled them with sand and we're supposed to use them like a body shield when we approach a bomb and then throw them on the bomb to extinguish it.*'

Kitty looked up from her letter. 'Gosh, it all sounds very dangerous, doesn't it?'

'Just taking precautions, lass. There's been no bombing yet and probably won't be.'

'*Mr Robinson has also dug an air-raid shelter in the backyard,*' Kitty read on. '*It's big enough to take all six of us at a squash, but it filled up with water during the storms last week, and now we have a problem with mosquitoes. Mr Robinson has also painted the ends of all the garden beds white, so we don't trip over them during the blackouts.*'

She shot her great-uncle a smile. 'I think Grandfather may have met his match in Mr Robinson. He does sound organised.'

'Yes.' Jim was smiling, too. 'It certainly sounds as if Alex and Nell are in good hands.'

'That's nice to know, isn't it?' But Kitty couldn't help feeling left out and useless, stuck here in the bush, away from all the excitement. She longed to be part of the action, especially when her grandmother also reminded her, rather pointedly, that the women were needed for all sorts of work now that the men were away.

Kitty knew that if she'd stayed in Townsville, she would have been doing real war work. Perhaps she should have stood up to her grandfather, but she'd felt too guilty to plead her case eloquently after she'd been caught on the verandah with Andy.

'Grandma sends you her love,' she said to Uncle Jim, as she finished the letter. As she folded it again, her thoughts lingered on Townsville, wondering what her friends might be up to.

She was still thinking about this when she opened the third envelope. Idly curious about who else might write to her, she glanced to the bottom of the page. It was from Andy's *father*.

This was a surprise.

Why would he write? Had her grandfather spoken to him? Would this letter brand her as a scarlet woman?

Fearful now, Kitty scanned the page quickly.

Dear Kitty,

I know Andy was planning to write to you, but I'm afraid our family needs to share some bad news. Our wonderful boy is missing in action.

We are trying to be as brave as he is, Kitty, but it's very hard on all of us. Andy's mother asked me to contact you. She's not up to writing just now.

Things don't look good, but we are living in high hopes that he will be found alive and well.

The message from the army could only tell us that he is missing, and that's the only thing we know for sure. His unit was operating somewhere in the islands. A troop barge was sunk by Jap planes and Andy was not among those who were rescued.

We're grateful that the message just said Missing in

Action . . . *It did not include* Presumed Killed.

I was in the last war and I'm being honest in holding out hope, but I know you will join us in our prayers for our son to come home to us.

Yours respectfully,

Donald Mathieson

Kitty wasn't sure how long she sat there, staring at Mr Mathieson's letter.

Poor Andy. He'd only just joined up. He couldn't possibly be dead, surely? She should have been thinking about him more, worrying about him. Tears prickled her eyes and her throat.

'What is it, lass? Bad news?'

'My – my friend, the one in the army.' She lifted up Andy's envelope with its censored stamp. 'He's missing already. Missing in action. The boat he was on was sunk by the Japs.'

'I'm sorry to hear that.' Her great-uncle frowned. 'But don't fret too much, Kitty. People go missing in war, and it's hard to keep track of everyone. There's always a chance he'll turn up.'

'I hope so.'

But what if the Japs find him first?

She wouldn't think about that. It was too awful to contemplate.

At least neither her great-uncle nor Andy's father seemed to be panicking, and they'd both been in the last war, fighting in Europe.

But it was frustrating to sit here in the quiet homestead kitchen, miles and miles away from home, knowing that everyone in Townsville was doing his or her bit for the war effort. Poor Andy might even have given his life.

Kitty knew that if she had to stay here much longer she would be bored. She missed being able to look out of a window and see a neighbour hanging washing on the line, or children building a cubbyhouse, their father arriving home from work.

Uncle Jim was watching her closely. 'You wish you could go back, don't you, lass?'

Kitty realised she was still sitting with Mr Mathieson's letter lying open in her lap. She looked across the kitchen table to where her great-uncle sat, puffing quietly on his pipe. He had the same craggy profile as her grandfather, but his eyes and mouth were gentler than his brother's. She'd grown rather fond of him over the past few weeks. 'I'd feel bad about leaving you alone.'

'Don't worry about me. I was fine before you came and I'll be fine after you leave. I've always been a bit of a loner.'

'I must admit, I'd like to finish my Voluntary Aid Detachment training.' Actually, she'd read in the paper that the Military Board had approved call-up of voluntary aids to work as part of the Army Medical Service.

Uncle Jim nodded. 'That's much more sensible than fussing around here and getting under my feet. Let *me* deal with Alex if he tries to make a fuss.'

23

'Hi, Gran, how are you?'

'Oh, you know, Luke . . . still here.'

Luke winced at the familiar response. When he rang his grand-mother with updates on the homestead's progress, she invariably expressed surprise or even disappointment that she'd woken to find she was still alive. He couldn't imagine what it must be like to live to ninety. He hoped she wasn't depressed.

'Well, I've a suggestion that might cheer you up.'

'Yes, dear? What is it?'

'I'm thinking about throwing a big party when the homestead's finished.'

'A party?'

'Yeah, a kind of celebration for family and friends, but I'm think-ing of possibly widening the circle and raising money for the bush fire brigade as well. It could be a good way of showing off the house, a chance to spread the word. Kill two birds with one stone.'

'I see . . .' His grandmother sounded dubious.

'Even if we don't make it too grand, it would be fun to have a family get-together – the uncles and their lot, Mum, Bella and Gabe, Zoe and Mac and their little guy – and you, of course. It's been a while since we all got together.'

'Does this mean the renovations are almost finished?'

'Well, there's still a way to go in the kitchen, but they're certainly getting closer. And it takes time to plan these things. I thought maybe Zoe could help with the catering.'

'I was wondering who would help you. I haven't met Zoe, but I think Virginia mentioned that she used to be a professional chef.'

'Yes, she's brilliant.'

'Then she'll be a great asset, if she's free. But I don't think you've had much experience at throwing parties, have you, Luke?'

'Well, no,' he admitted. 'I'd definitely need help.'

This was greeted by a rather prolonged silence.

'Gran, are you still there?'

'Yes, yes . . .'

'So you like the idea?'

'It's a lovely idea, Luke. I guess I'm just a little surprised that you came up with it.'

Luke could feel the back of his neck burn. This hadn't been his idea, of course. It was Sally's brainchild, hatched yesterday afternoon as they'd lain together, lazy and happy after making love, talking about the homestead and its possibilities, which was still a safer topic than talking about themselves.

'I *have* talked it over with Sally Piper,' he said carefully. 'She paid another visit to get more pics and info for her story.'

'Ahhh . . .'

His grandmother's tone was hard to read and Luke decided it was safer to drop Sally from their conversation.

'I've been meaning to ask if you got that letter I forwarded from America,' he said instead.

'Oh, yes, I did, thanks.'

'Does it mention anything about the airmen who were here during the war?'

The small sound on the end of the line might well have been a sigh.

'Yes, Laura certainly mentioned *one* of the airmen,' his grandmother said after a pause. 'She's his daughter. She wrote to tell me that her father had died.'

'Hey, that's great. Well, it's not great that he died, but it's great that she's a rellie. I was thinking, if she was connected, why not send her an invitation?'

'An invitation?'

'To the party.'

'Oh, Luke, for heaven's sake. Why on earth would you ask *her*?'

'It's worth a try, isn't it, Gran? I mean, if we're throwing a party for the homestead, why not invite anyone with a connection? Think how cool it would be if she actually came all the way from America.'

'It's highly unlikely.'

'Yeah, I know it's a long shot, but I'd be happy to write to her. I kept a copy of her address.'

'Oh.'

This unmistakable lack of enthusiasm was puzzling. Luke had expected that his grandmother would be fascinated to meet this woman and swap memories about her father.

'I'm sure you're right. She probably won't be able to come,' he said in his most placating tone. 'But I may as well give it a go, don't you think?'

Sally closed the book on another chapter of *Seven Little Australians*.

'So, Nan,' she said, taking her grandmother's scrawny hand and giving it a gentle squeeze, 'I have some exciting news. I've met a really nice guy.'

Her grandmother nodded with her habitual sweet smile. 'Josh is a lovely boy.'

'No, this isn't Josh, Nan.' Sally tried to ignore the sudden heaviness in her chest. 'Josh died some time ago. He's gone.'

'Has he, dear? That's terrible for him. I'm so sorry.'

Even though Sally was getting used to this now, she was still saddened by each new sign that her grandmother was losing her mind. It was especially hard when other elderly folk like Kitty Mathieson were still so lucid and switched on.

Eight years ago, her nan had still been living in her little timber cottage in South Townsville with its neat lattice-fronted verandah and an enormous mango tree in the backyard shading innumerable, carefully tended pots of ferns and bromeliads.

Sally used to call in each week to take her grandmother out for shopping and afternoon tea. In those days, Nan had been a canny shopper, always ready and waiting with her carefully prepared list that noted the specials at the supermarket. And she would never forget if a chemist prescription needed to be filled, or if she'd needed to buy a birthday gift for a family member.

But after a stroke – only a little stroke that required a mere two days in hospital – everything had changed.

Sally would arrive for their regular Thursday afternoon outings to find Nan sitting on the verandah just staring into space, having forgotten all about the shopping trip. Then she'd begun to notice that Nan was buying jars of honey and Vegemite every week, stockpiling them in the pantry, while forgetting essentials like toilet paper. She'd broken Sally's heart when she constantly asked about Tom, her husband, who had died several years earlier.

Sally's mother was alarmed when Sally finally convinced her there was a problem.

'I'm sorry, Sally. I feel so guilty. I should have taken more notice, but I've been so busy at work. We'll have to do something. See someone. She can't live on her own like that.'

Sally's mother was always crazily busy at work, so Sally had been happy enough, especially after Josh died, to be the one who sat and held Nan's hand and answered the same question three times in thirty minutes, or listened to her rambling stories.

And today, there was an advantage to having a grandmother with next to no short-term memory. Sally could tell her all about Luke and trust that her story would go no further. It was a relief to be able to talk about him with a goofy smile on her face and without being questioned.

'He's not just good-looking and tall and athletic. He's a really nice guy, Nan. I like being around him. I guess you could say we're friends with benefits,' Sally told her now. 'That's a term you wouldn't have heard of, but it means we can sleep together and enjoy each other without any expectations of long-term commitment. These days, a lot of younger people have that kind of arrangement.'

'Why?' her grandmother demanded, looking stern and disapproving.

Sally gulped. The unexpected challenge had caught her completely wrong-footed. 'Not everyone wants to rush to get married,' she suggested. 'Don't you worry about it, Nan.'

She was a bit ashamed of herself for speaking to her grandmother in such a patronising tone.

Perhaps Nan hadn't liked it either. Her dark and normally clouded and vacant eyes looked surprisingly clear and knowing. 'Tom won't like it,' she said. 'You mark my words.'

Kitty shut her book, took off her glasses and closed her eyes as she rubbed at the bridge of her nose. She'd been trying to read a novel that she'd borrowed from the mobile library van on its weekly visit, but she wasn't making much headway.

Her eyes were troubling her today, but that wasn't really her problem. The book was a large-print edition, a romance by one of her favourite authors, which she could manage quite well when it was resting on her propped knees. Normally she would have filled in an enjoyable morning lost in this story.

Today, however, ever since Luke's phone call, she'd found it almost impossible to concentrate. She couldn't believe Luke planned to invite Ed's daughter to a party at Moonlight Plains.

It was such a surprise, such an unexpected, impossible proposition. And it was just too risky.

The woman wouldn't come, of course. Why on earth would she drop everything in Boston and make the long, tedious flight to Australia, simply to attend a party with a whole lot of strangers? The very thought was absurd.

Then again, Laura Langley Fox *was* an American, and everyone knew that Americans were a law unto themselves. The nightly news and endless Hollywood movies were evidence of that – although Kitty had long ago experienced the mysterious power of Americans firsthand, of course.

Just about everyone who'd lived in Townsville during the war had been charmed by the Yanks. There'd been so many of them, taking over the town, wolf-whistling at the girls, calling them 'honey' and handing out nylons and compliments with equal ease, or throwing loose coins to the kids, as well as lollies – aniseed balls, rainbow balls, Texas bars, Kurls.

The Americans would even pay schoolboys to shine their smart lace-up shoes – paid them with shillings, too, not pennies. And they'd dressed so finely, with brass buttons everywhere on their spruce and well-pressed uniforms that were a lighter khaki and a more tailored cut than the Australians'.

Uncle Sam's glamour boys.

The poor Aussie diggers had looked dowdy beside them in their unbecoming, baggy Bombay bloomers and clumpy boots.

It was strange how clear those times were to Kitty now. She found it alarmingly easy to picture hot and dusty Townsville, so bustling and busy in the autumn of 1942 after her return from Moonlight Plains.

24

Townsville, 1942

Townsville was almost unrecognisable when Kitty returned. Castle Hill was the same, of course, still dominating the landscape with its stern pink cliffs bravely facing the sea and the encroaching enemy. And even though it was now the middle of autumn, the tropical sun was still bright and hot in a solid blue sky. But the country town by the sea that Kitty had left behind six weeks ago was now a garrison city, busy and buzzing with men and machinery.

The streets were full of men in khaki. Both the Australian and American military had arrived in droves, doubling and then tripling the population, and in many cases they'd moved into hotels, schools and private homes, including her grandparents' house.

Where bicycles had once been the main mode of transport, the streets now rumbled and rattled with trucks and jeeps, their headlights covered by blackout hoods. Vehicles were always on the go, bringing equipment and supplies from the railway yards and from the harbour, moving troops between the railway station and the camps in outlying suburbs.

And there were guns *everywhere*.

Kitty was rather alarmed to see anti-aircraft guns poking out of the bright-purple bougainvillea that tumbled over the cliffs facing the Strand, or sticking out from the islands of camouflaged sandbags in Strand Park. Guns had even been placed in the suburbs, and the streets in North Ward were now filled with the same ugly barbed-wire entanglements that covered all the beaches.

All over town, soldiers, stripped to the waist, were digging slit trenches. A massive Australian tent hospital had been set up near Cape Pallarenda and Australian casualties were already arriving from New Guinea. The Americans had established their own hospital in Rowes Bay, complete with American nurses with cow-horn hairstyles just like in the films.

At night, more searchlights than ever crisscrossed the sky. If the Japs secured Port Moresby, the whole of North Queensland would be within their bombing range.

But rather than intimidating Kitty, this grim, nervous new world energised her. She accepted the challenge to be braver and more determined, which proved a distinct advantage when she faced her grandfather.

First, she enjoyed a delightful newsy chat with her grandmother over a cuppa in the Robinsons' kitchen in Hermit Park, and then she and her grandfather sat in stiff cane chairs on the front verandah while she outlined her plans.

'I want to be of use in the war effort,' she told him. 'And it's all arranged. I'm going to live with Elsie Gibson and her son Geoff in Mitchell Street. Elsie's husband John is in the islands somewhere. No one knows exactly where, of course.'

Her grandfather couldn't really argue with this *fait accompli*, especially as Elsie Gibson was a parishioner, although Kitty half-expected he might insist that the Gibsons' place was too exposed, being only one block back from the Strand.

'I'll share my coupons and do the washing and ironing for Elsie in return for a bed, and I'll finish my VAD training and work at the

Red Cross.' Kitty lifted her chin. 'And you don't need to worry about any further black marks against my reputation. I've already met two Americans out at Moonlight Plains and they were gentlemen.'

'I suppose that's why they've already set up bordellos behind the Causeway Hotel.' Grandfather's response was grating and pompous, but he didn't put up much of a fight.

Perhaps he'd sensed the change in Kitty. Perhaps he recognised that she was no longer a malleable young girl, but a woman with a new sense of purpose. Or perhaps he was changing too, with the threat of invasion increasing each day as the Japanese fleet headed south.

Kitty soon discovered she'd had it easy at Moonlight Plains. On a cattle property, meat was readily available and daily supplies of fresh milk and eggs were taken for granted. Life in town was much tougher. Almost everything was in short supply. There was no ice or bread. The shopkeepers had stopped making deliveries and civilians could only buy the scrag ends of meat, after waiting in long queues. Watermelons had leapt from two shillings to a pound and potatoes were a luxury of the past.

'Can't remember the last time I tasted a real spud,' Elsie said as she served up their dinner on Kitty's first night in Mitchell Street. A rather scrawny mutton chop sat beside a hefty dollop of mashed potato made from a tin of the dehydrated variety, and there were boiled beans and choko courtesy of Elsie's valiant efforts to grow a veggie garden.

Nearly everyone was trying to grow vegetables, some with more success than others. *Dig for Victory*, the posters urged. A few families kept a cow and quite a few had hens as well, so their homegrown produce could sometimes be exchanged for eggs or half a bucket of milk.

Young Geoff, a cheerful ginger-top of eleven, dutifully recited grace. 'For what we are about to receive may the Lord make us truly thankful.'

'We should also be thanking God for the Yanks' gifts of food,' Elsie remarked to Kitty when he'd finished. 'Don't know where we'd be without them.'

'How do they help with food?' Kitty was eager to learn anything and everything about the Americans.

'Oh, they're wonderful. If you get to know one or two of them, you can mention that you haven't got much of so and so, and next minute they'll be on your doorstep with whatever you need. That's how I got these dehydrated potatoes. They've given me dehydrated onions and tins of peaches too.'

'And packets of chewing gum,' Geoff joined in.

'How handy.' Kitty refrained from asking Elsie how she'd got to know a Yank or two, but of course the question of Ed's whereabouts was practically burning a hole in her brain.

'Our Yanks built our air-raid shelter,' Geoff added self-importantly.

'They did a good job.' Kitty had been impressed by the setup in Elsie's backyard, comprising a large reinforced concrete pipe with big boxes of sand and gravel at either end. One box blocked one end of the pipe completely, while there was just enough room to squeeze behind a second box at the other end. Planks of wood formed seats.

'Art and Bud have moved on though,' Elsie explained. They shipped out last week.'

Again, Kitty wondered where Ed was.

She threw herself conscientiously into her new life, not only starting her VAD training, but taking full charge in Elsie's laundry too. She would boil up the cotton sheets and other whites first, and then dig them out with a stick and rinse them in the big concrete tub with a blue bag in the water. Then she would ease one corner of a sheet or towel into the wringer and roll it through, before pegging the washing on long lines strung across the backyard to dry in the sun. The next day, she would tackle the ironing, and she also practised her first aid bandages on Geoff, who was at a bit of a loose end with the schools still closed.

Together with Elsie, Kitty made pyjamas for the military hospitals, too, and they were quite a team. Kitty cut out the material on the dining room table while Elsie sewed the seams on her treadle machine, before Kitty hand-stitched the buttons and buttonholes.

In her first week back, she also called on Andy's parents . . .

Her stomach was churning as she stood on the footpath in front of the Matheisons' high-set timber house which, like Elsie's and most of the houses in North Ward, was painted with a dark-brown oil stain. Just looking at the familiar house brought back so many memories of Andy. She found herself remembering the time they'd played cricket in the backyard and she'd tried to bat, closing her eyes as she swung and, to her amazement, connecting with the ball. Such a cheer had gone up, until they heard the sound of splintering glass.

Kitty still felt guilty that she'd given in when Andy insisted on taking the blame, but at least she'd been able to raid her moneybox to help him to pay for the damage.

She remembered a special Guy Fawkes Night. Every year, all the kids in their suburb saved up for weeks to buy crackers and let them off out in the street. That particular year, Andy had spent a good chunk of his savings on a Catherine wheel, which normally only the rich kids could afford, and he'd brought it up to Kitty's house. He'd wanted to share it with her. Kitty could recall that hot November night so clearly, with the sharp smell of gunpowder hanging in the air, as she and Andy sat together in the gutter and gazed in awe at the spectacular, high-reaching spirals of purple and gold fire.

She might have stayed there on the footpath, lost in other happy memories, if she hadn't noticed a figure on the verandah, peering out at her through the lattice and no doubt wondering why she was standing there staring.

Trying to ignore the nervous tightness inside her, she pushed the gate open and went up the short path. She was only halfway up the front stairs when the door at the top opened.

'I thought it was you, Kitty.'

Mrs Mathieson looked very thin and strained, and Kitty was sure her hair had become quite a bit greyer.

'How are you?' Kitty asked tentatively.

'Oh, not too bad.' Mrs Mathieson smiled bravely, but then she wiped her hands anxiously on her apron. 'We still haven't heard anything about Andy.'

Kitty let out a huff of relief. That was one difficult question answered. 'No news is good news, surely?'

'I hope so, my dear. It's good to see you back here at any rate. Come on inside and I'll put the kettle on. I've just made a fresh batch of Anzac biscuits.'

The house was filled with their warm, sweet aroma as the two women went inside.

After dinner at Elsie's that night, Kitty wrote to Andy, which was a very difficult task, especially when she had no idea where he was, or if he was hurt, or even if he was still alive.

She told him about her time at Moonlight Plains, not suggesting that it had been banishment, and she told him about Bobby. Andy knew her well, and he, of all people, would understand how upset she'd been, but she wrote to him as a friend, not as a future fiancé. She wrote to Uncle Jim as well, and included all kinds of details that she hoped he would find interesting. She mentioned the food shortages and the reputed American generosity, and how the American Negroes were segregated and living in a big camp out on the edge of the Town Common.

She reported that the harbour was jam-packed with vessels now and that more and more planes seemed to arrive every day, lining up in all the newly built aerodromes, wing tip to wing tip. Everyone was sure something big was brewing.

She asked Uncle Jim about his cattle, about the two dairy cows and how many hens were laying, and whether the magpies still warbled a wake-up call each morning. She also asked if the Americans had arrived to collect Bobby, but she did not ask if Ed had been in the party.

She was quite certain Ed would have been too busy flying in the raids to New Guinea, but she was also shy about drawing any attention to her interest in him.

Since she'd left Moonlight Plains, she'd begun to feel a little foolish about the way she'd fallen so hard and fast for a man she hardly knew, a stranger from another world, and a snobby elitist world by the sound of it.

At other times she was kinder to herself, remembering that in wartime everyone took risks. Life was more precarious and intense in every way and no one dared to look too far into the future.

Meanwhile, the women at the Voluntary Aid Detachment were always chattering about their social lives – the dances at Heatley's or at Garbutt, and the free ice-cream suppers at the Flying Squadron Hall. They, along with Elsie, urged her to come out with them on her nights off.

Kitty could easily imagine the fun of dancing the Pride of Erin and the Gypsy Tap with all these new and exciting men, or jitter-bugging to new songs like 'In the Mood'. Six months ago, she would have jumped at the chance, but now she'd changed.

Her experiences with Andy, with Bobby and with Ed had all left their mark. Within a matter of weeks, she'd lost her virginity, witnessed her first death and unwisely fallen in love. She felt distanced now from her carefree companions, who were all so eager for reckless romantic adventures.

Eventually, however, Kitty made a decision. It was pointless to moon around thinking about a certain airman. She had to get on with life. So she raided her small savings account and bought a dress pattern, a length of pink georgette and some glamorous strings of black beading.

She was nervous about cutting the dress out, hurrying to get it done before teatime when the table would be needed. The skirt had triangles on the hemline and had to be cut perfectly, and she was concentrating hard on her task when a knock sounded at the front door. Geoff was still playing streets away, so he could be no help.

Elsie, who was busy in the kitchen, called, 'Can you get that, Kitty?'

Reluctantly, Kitty removed three pins from her mouth and carefully set down her scissors, mentally reminding herself to cut from the opposite angle into the next peak. She went down the hall and saw an American uniform through the lattice door on the front verandah.

One of Elsie's Yanks.

She opened the door for him.

'Ed!'

25

In his dress uniform Ed looked more splendid than ever.

'Hello, Kitty.'

'How did you find me? I mean – how lovely to see you, but how did you know I was here?' She was surprised she could speak so calmly when her insides were flashing and whizzing like a skyrocket.

Ed smiled. 'Your great-uncle gave me your address.'

'Have you been back to Moonlight Plains?'

'I went to help the boys dismantle my plane and bring it into Charters Towers for reassembly.'

'That sounds complicated.'

'It wasn't really. You'd be surprised.'

'And Bobby?' she asked softly.

Ed nodded. 'He's back here in Townsville.' When he smiled again, his eyes flashed a little too brightly. For a beat, his gaze enveloped Kitty, acknowledging the sad memory that would link them forever.

'You'd better come in,' she said, close to tears.

Ed held up packages. 'I brought a few things I thought might come in handy.'

'Nylons?'

'Yeah.' He grinned. 'Nylons and a tinned ham.'

'Ham! My goodness, what a luxury. How wonderful. Come in quickly and meet Elsie. She's in the kitchen.'

Her legs were shaky as she led Ed down the hallway to the kitchen at the back of the house, where Elsie was checking a shepherd's pie in the oven.

'Look what I found on the doorstep,' Kitty said.

When Elsie turned and saw Ed her jaw dropped. It was hard to tell if she was pink from the heat of the oven or from delight.

'Hello there,' she said, recovering smoothly and flashing Ed a beaming smile.

'This is Ed Langley,' Kitty said. 'Captain Langley. He flies Airacobras.'

'Pleased to meet you, ma'am,' Ed said politely.

'And I'm very pleased to meet you, Ed.' Elsie extended her hand.

'I think I told you about the Americans who landed at Moonlight Plains,' Kitty added.

'Oh, yes, I remember you mentioned *something*.' Elsie sent Kitty a darkly eloquent glance as she fingered the scarf she'd tied around her hair. *You could have warned me.*

'Ed's brought nylons *and* a ham,' Kitty said to placate her.

'Ham!' This brought another pleased smile. 'How thoughtful. You'll have to come back to share it with us.'

'No, no, this is for you. I'm well fed at the camp. Actually . . .' Ed turned to Kitty. 'I know this is short notice, but I was hoping you might be free to come for a walk into town. Maybe a bite to eat at the Bluebird.'

Eating out at a cafe was an unheard-of extravagance. Kitty chose not to catch Elsie's eye. 'Yes, I'm free. I'd love to come.' Again, she managed to sound calm, but her mind was racing, tumbling over itself in her excitement. Ed was here. He'd tracked her down and

asked her out. What did this mean? What should she wear? Oh,
Lord, the dressmaking! She would have to bundle it up and worry
about it tomorrow.

'Can you give me five minutes to get changed?'

They walked over the hill and into town, where the footpaths
were crowded with men in American uniforms strolling arm in arm
with local girls. Kitty felt slightly superior walking beside Ed. He
wasn't just a fellow who'd picked her up at a dance. Their acquaintance went deeper. They'd been through an ordeal together – exciting,
terrifying and desperately sad. And yet it was fun to be as carefree
and smiling as everyone else this evening.

As they squeezed into the only spare booth, the Bluebird Cafe
rang with American voices and with phrases that were strange to
Kitty's ears.

'You're telling me.'

'Yeah, coming right along.'

'Hotsy totsy!'

Someone ordered a lime spider.

'What's a lime spider?' she asked Ed.

He laughed. 'It's just a scoop of vanilla ice-cream in a lime soda.
They're great. You want to try one?'

'It sounds like a dessert.'

'Life's short.' Ed grinned at her. 'Give it a whirl.'

'Why not?' Kitty laughed at her recklessness.

She could see why the girls loved being out with the Americans.
These men not only looked extra-attractive in their beautiful,
smartly ironed uniforms, but they were also generous with their
money, unbelievably courteous, and they carried with them an exciting aura: of coming from another world, a world that local girls had
only ever glimpsed on the cinema screen.

For Kitty, Ed was in a class of his own, of course. She had never
dared to dream that he might come looking for her. It was too good

to be true and their evening out had a magical quality, as if her world had burst from muted sepia into glorious colour.

She and Ed talked nonstop – not about the war, but about the music they liked and the films they'd enjoyed; Ed called them 'flicks'.

Kitty wanted to know more about his family, so he told her about his mother's interest in gardening and music, her passion for growing lilacs, and the classical concerts she'd taken him to.

When Ed asked Kitty what it had been like growing up in Townsville, she gave him the edited highlights: picnics at Black River, day trips to Magnetic Island, the backyard cricket and Guy Fawkes Night.

'Guy Fawkes?'

'Don't you have that in America? Bonfire night? *Remember, remember the fifth of November . . .*'

Ed shook his head.

'I think the original Guy Fawkes tried to blow up the British Houses of Parliament, but these days it's just all about children and crackers,' she said. 'The children buy every kind of cracker they can afford – sparklers, little cheap tom thumbs, skyrockets if they're lucky. The really rich kids have Catherine wheels and, of course, the boys are always desperate for double bungers. We used to let them off out in the street. There were hardly any cars.'

'Sounds a bit like our fourth of July.'

'Yes, probably.'

'What about Magnetic Island?' Ed asked. 'Do you still go over there for day trips?'

'Now and again. It's beautiful. There are all these lovely little bays fringed by enormous boulders, and the water's so blue and clear. Have you been over?'

'Not yet. I'm hoping to.' Ed's dark eyes held an intense light as he smiled. 'Maybe you could come with me, show me all the best places?'

'I – I'd love to.'

Kitty was practically floating as they finished their meal – an expensive, luxuriously juicy steak and fresh salad. Dusk was closing in as they walked down Flinders Street, past the sandbagged doorways and the window displays of air-raid equipment, and the rather grand Town Hall building with its huge V for Victory flag.

They continued on to the Strand on the seafront, skirting the Anzac monument and continuing beneath massive banyan fig trees till they reached the shore.

Despite the ugly network of barbed wire on the beach, the silver sea looked as serene and beautiful as ever. In the darkening sky above Cape Pallarenda, the evening star was already shining and a light breeze blew off the water. And Ed was walking by Kitty's side.

She was sure she'd never felt happier.

At the water's edge Ed picked up a flat stone and skimmed it across the shimmering surface. Then he turned to Kitty, and for the first time he took her hand in his. His hand was warm, his fingers long and strong.

'So I'm thinking that a lovely girl like you must have a sweetheart or two,' he said casually.

Kitty's instinct was to deny this flatly, but then she thought guiltily of Andy, who'd claimed that he was planning to marry her. Even his parents seemed to concede an 'understanding' between her and their son.

She suppressed an urge to sigh. 'There's a boy from here. I've been – been out with him. But now he's missing up in the islands.'

'I'm so sorry, Kitty.' Ed's sympathy was sincere.

'Yes, it's terrible.'

He let her hand go. 'I apologise if I've been presumptuous.'

'You haven't, Ed.' She wanted, desperately, for him to hold her hand again. Even if Andy was still alive, he was so far away he hardly seemed real. And she'd never promised him . . . 'You haven't . . . '

She couldn't find the right word. 'Truly.'

As she said this, Ed was looking clear into her eyes and she willed him to read her silent message: I want to be *your* girl.

His smile was difficult to read, but then he leaned in and kissed her cheek, just the softest touch of his lips to her skin.

And he didn't immediately step away.

Along the beach small waves lapped. In the distance a lone seagull gave a high-pitched crazy cry. Kitty could feel the tension thrumming between them. She wanted him to kiss her. Properly. On the lips.

She lifted her face. Tilted her chin. Just a little closer . . . Moth to the flame. *Ed, please . . .*

She heard the rasp of his indrawn breath.

'We'd better go,' he said and then he took her hand and walked her home.

Ed called again, much to Kitty's joy and relief. Over the weeks that followed, he became a regular visitor at Mitchell Street.

This was a somewhat different Ed from the serious pilot on Moonlight Plains who'd been so focused on trying to save his fellow airman. In Townsville Ed carried a special air of American glamour, with his dark glasses and aftershave – Kitty had eventually learned why he smelled so good. His manners were delightful and he always came with gifts, so he easily charmed Elsie and young Geoff.

The boy was agog to have a real fighter pilot in his home and he would corner the ever-patient Ed with endless questions. Ed couldn't talk about his missions, of course; they were top-secret. But he was happy to tell Geoff all about the US Airacobras and Mitchell bombers and how they compared with the Kittyhawks.

Sometimes he shared a home-cooked meal with them, having invariably supplied the ingredients. He claimed that meals cooked in a military canteen were never as good. He occasionally joined them in a game of cards.

Other times, he and Kitty wandered over the hill to the movies. If it was a matinee they would take young Geoff to the Winter Garden, with its tightly stretched canvas seats. Both Kitty and Geoff were hugely impressed when lower-ranked airmen saluted Ed.

Ed took Kitty to dances and told her that her new pink dress with its smart black trim was beautiful.

'The colour really suits you. It makes you look like a rose.'

But he only ever kissed her on the cheek, or occasionally on her brow, or her chin, or her ear. In every way, he charmed and beguiled Kitty, while living up to the image she had painted of him for her grandfather. To her huge disappointment, he remained a perfect gentleman.

26

The invitation from Australia sat on Laura's desk, unanswered.

When it became too annoying she filed it at the back of the bills waiting to be paid. But then she would come home from school, feeling tired and jaded, or she would finish a phone call with one of her daughters that left her feeling old and unnecessary, and she would find herself taking out the letter again.

Dear Laura,

Thank you for your letter, which I passed on to my grand-mother, Kitty Mathieson. Kitty's in a nursing home now and not really up to corresponding, but I know she was pleased to hear from you.

The families of Americans who were in this area during the war often come back to visit, so please let us know if you're ever planning a trip Down Under and we'll make sure you're welcomed.

Actually, just as a long shot: our family is throwing a party in two months' time to celebrate the renovation of Moonlight Plains homestead, and as you have a family connection to this place, I wanted to extend an invitation.

I know you haven't met any of us, but your father played a famous part in the homestead's history and we'd love you to join us, if that's at all possible. I'm sure we could arrange help with transport or accommodation once you're in Australia, so don't hesitate to ask. It would be great to meet you.

September's usually a pleasant time of year in North Queensland and the Great Barrier Reef is right on our doorstep.

Yours sincerely,
Luke Fairburn

It had been so very unexpected. And unsettling. What did the Australians know about her family connection? What 'famous' part had her father played in the homestead's history? Why had he never talked about it?

Laura wouldn't go, of course, but whenever she reread the handwritten message from Kitty's grandson, her thoughts began to spin.

It was puzzling, even annoying, that she'd never heard anything about her father's war. She and her brothers only knew vaguely that he'd been stationed in Australia, but as far as she could remember, he'd never once told any of them what he'd actually done while he was overseas.

Even in his letters to Kitty, he'd only briefly mentioned the war. His thoughts had mostly been centred on the woman he met. But now that Laura had heard from Luke about other Americans revisiting North Queensland she felt as if she needed the bigger picture.

She dug through the remnants of her father's library again and eventually found a couple of black and white photos slipped carelessly into the back of an album. Her father was standing beside a plane, looking very young and handsome.

By contrast, the plane looked quite threatening, painted khaki with a large white star on its side. It had a most terrifying, tiny and claustrophobic cockpit perched high on its nose. She was shocked to think that her father had actually been up there, locked inside that tiny bubble, flying alone in mortal combat with a foreign enemy, high above the Pacific.

It was hard to reconcile that image with the gentlemanly and thoughtful academic she'd known and loved all her life.

After a little internet research, Laura learned that the plane was an Airacobra and the main task of its pilots in Australia had been to escort the big Mitchell bombers when they attacked their Japanese targets. Apparently, the lighter, more manoeuvrable Airacobras had protected the bigger, heavier bombers from attack by Jap fighter planes called Zeroes.

Airacobras had been involved in regular dogfights with Zeroes, especially in the dangerous cloud-shrouded mountains of Papua New Guinea, the dragon-shaped island that almost touched Australia's northern tip. And there'd been some serious battles in New Guinea, Laura soon discovered – an assault on Rabaul, the Kokoda Trail campaign, the Battle of Buna-Gona.

'Oh, my God, Dad.'

When her brother Charlie came to Boston for an overnight stay before dashing off to cover something incredibly important in Washington, she seized the chance to talk about it.

'I can't believe Dad never told us about his time as a pilot in the war, flying those tiny little planes.'

Along with the brandy she served after dinner, she showed Charlie the photos.

'He would have hated to be a war bore,' Charlie said.

'I know. I guess we should be grateful for that, but still, I wish I'd talked to him, asked a few questions.'

Laura eyed Charlie over her brandy glass. Her baby brother's hairline was receding, much like that of their mother's father, but it suited him, gave him a high-brow air.

'Now that I think about it, I can't believe you didn't plague Dad to tell you all about the war,' she said. 'You're a war correspondent, after all.'

'I did try. He told me a few things.'

'Really?' She sat straighter, suddenly alert. 'About being a fighter pilot?'

'Not about any heroics. I remember he told me that at the start of the war, the Japanese Zero pilots were a lot better trained than the Americans. They'd had more combat experience, and it took our guys a while to get the hang of it.'

'God, Charlie, how scary would that have been?'

Charlie shrugged and looked down at his glass. 'Every war's scary.'

'I guess. I try not to think about it.'

'You're an artist,' her brother said fondly. 'Perhaps it's your task in life to seek beauty.'

Laura smiled. 'While you're a journalist tasked with seeking the truth?' She took a sip of her brandy. 'So what else did Dad tell you?'

'Very little.' Charlie tapped the photo of the plane. 'Our military soon realised that these Airacobras were really built for ground attacks and not for dogfights. These planes were no match for the Zeroes. They were in the process of upgrading pilots like Dad to Lightnings when Dad was shot down in New Guinea.'

At least she'd known that their father was shot down and shipped home. He'd mentioned that briefly in his letters.

Somewhat nervously, Laura asked, 'Did he ever talk to you about any of the Australians he met?'

Charlie gave a slow shake of his head. 'Just that he was keen to listen to any advice they could offer. His squadron flew with the Australians in the early days. The Aussies were just back from

Europe and North Africa and they'd had plenty of experience, so Dad quizzed them whenever he could. He was a bit starry-eyed about meeting one of their aces. Forget the guy's name. I just remember that the main advice was to get plenty of altitude, and come down on the enemy at speed, rather than the other way round.'

Laura shuddered.

'See,' Charlie said, noticing her reaction. 'That's why Dad didn't talk about it.'

'I suppose . . . What about a place called Moonlight Plains?' she asked carefully. 'Did he ever mention that?'

Charlie frowned. 'I don't think so. Why?'

She considered telling him about the letters, but it was already late. He would be up all night reading, and he'd be a mess the next day.

On his next visit, she promised herself.

'I wonder why he was so silent?' she said instead. 'Do – do you think he had something to hide?'

'Seems to me there are two ways men react to their war experiences. They either can't help talking about it all the time, or they clam up completely.'

Or they write about it in letters that they never post, thought Laura.

By the time she had coffee with her friend Amy on the following afternoon, Laura was edging towards a tipping point. 'I think I'm going to have to go over there.'

'To Australia?'

'Yeah.' She'd already told her friend about the letter she'd sent to Kitty. Now she shared the surprising invitation she'd received from Luke Fairburn.

Amy blinked. 'Get outta here!' Then she grinned. 'Of course, you've got to go, Laura. You're sure to have a fabulous time. Besides, you might get a few answers.'

'I'm not sure I want answers.'

Amy lifted her neatly shaped eyebrows as she studied her friend. 'Has it ever occurred to you that your father might have wanted you to go?'

'No. For heaven's sake, what gives you that idea?'

Amy's eyes widened as if the answer was obvious. 'The letters?'

'Excuse me?'

'Laura, your dad was a clever and careful man, yet he left those incriminating letters lying around for you to find. I know he died suddenly, but he was in his nineties, after all – he knew he was taking a risk.'

'I must admit, I *have* asked myself why he wasn't more careful,' Laura confessed. 'Imagine if Mum had found them. It would have been . . .' *Disastrous, a family tragedy, unbearable . . .*

'Perhaps he kept them safely under lock and key while your mother was alive – in his office, at the bank, or with his lawyer . . .'

'That's quite likely, I guess.'

'Listen.' Amy's silver bracelets jangled as she leaned forward and took Laura's hand, giving it a reassuring squeeze. 'If there *are* any answers in Australia, I think you want to find them, honey.'

'But – but what if I don't like them?'

'You're tough. You'll adjust. You'll deal with it and move on.'

Amy made it sound so simple. Perhaps it was.

'I wouldn't know a soul over there,' Laura hedged. 'I'd be nervous.'

'But Australians are supposed to be very casual and friendly.'

She couldn't deny that Luke Fairburn's invitation had sounded both friendly and casual.

'And you're in the perfect position to go,' Amy added.

'You mean I'm divorced and an empty-nester? No ties?'

'Well . . . yes.'

'But I have my job.'

'And you know you're dying for a change.'

This was certainly true. She'd been teaching in the same high school for more than twenty years. *Part of the furniture . . .*

'I don't suppose it's worth going all that way just for a party, but maybe you could make it part of a bigger travel plan.' Amy was warming to her idea now. 'You have a nice inheritance, after all. Spend a smidgen. Buy a round-the-world ticket and go to Italy like you've always wanted to.'

A vision of Florence's domes and rooftops flashed before Laura's eyes, evincing a groan. She'd only ever seen them in photos. 'Don't tempt me with Italy.'

'Why not?'

'My girls —'

'Are living on the west coast and making their own lives.' Amy's eyes were intense now. 'Haven't you earned this, Laura? You put up with that shit of a —'

'Okay!' Laura threw up her hands before her friend let forth with her favourite rant: an extensive list of Laura's ex-husband's crimes. 'I'll give it some thought.'

'Don't think too long.'

She knew this was good advice. If she thought too hard about this, her angst would inevitably strangle her courage, and she would focus on the fear that she might discover more about her father than she wanted to know.

Then again, having read every one of his letters, surely she already knew the worst?

27

Everything changed on the day they went to the island.

Kitty suspected that Ed had done extra duty in order to have a whole day free with her, and she wanted everything to be perfect.

Luckily, the weather was magical on this last weekend in April – still sunny and tropical, but without the energy-sapping humidity of summer. The tang of salt spray filled the air as they sat on the rear deck of the ferry boat *Malanda* and watched the rushing white wake, while Townsville's shoreline slipped further and further behind them.

Everything *was* perfect. The clear, bright blue of the sky above was reflected in the sparkling sea. A brisk breeze blew, and the island lay ahead, green and hilly, with its enticing fringe of pretty bays.

They'd brought a picnic basket and a thermos, swimsuits and towels, and Kitty's stomach tightened with mounting excitement as the mooring ropes were thrown ashore and the boat rocked against the shell-encrusted timbers of Nelly Bay's jetty.

On land they walked in bright sunlight, surrounded by smooth boulders and soaring hoop pines, while below, through the cracks in the jetty's boards, they could see the clear water and colourful fish swimming between clumps of coral.

'We should swim at Arcadia,' Kitty said. 'It's the next bay, and it's like this one only prettier. Just a short walk.'

'Arcadia?' Ed grinned. 'How aptly named.'

When they reached it, he stood for a long moment with a broad, happy smile on his face. He took in a deep breath of pristine air as he surveyed the blue and white curve of the tiny bay, with its fringe of coconut palms and boulder-studded headlands.

'This is paradise,' he said softly.

'You could almost forget there's a war on,' Kitty agreed, even though there were plenty of reminders on the island, with military personnel dashing about in jeeps and heavily armed forts set on the headlands above Florence Bay.

Ed's ebony eyes sparkled, however, and as they walked down to the beach, he slipped his arm casually around her shoulders. She could sense a change in him, as if he'd left his cautious, slightly serious self behind. The island was already working its magic.

Kitty found it rather nerve-racking, though, to emerge from the changing rooms in her swimsuit. She was worried that her costume was too old-fashioned and unflattering, but Ed's admiring smile quickly melted her fears. And as soon as they'd dumped their gear at the base of a coconut palm, they ran together across the warm sand to the cool, startlingly clear water.

Bliss.

I don't do this often enough, Kitty told herself. She'd almost forgotten how wonderfully sensuous it was to dive into the cool, clear sea and to feel the water all over her skin and to roll onto her back and float, gently rocking, looking up at the pines on the headland.

She was constantly aware of Ed, of course. Each time she saw his dark head and bare chest emerge from the water and saw the flash of his smile, she felt a rush of happiness.

He was never far away – and yet it was just when she least

expected it that he caught her hand, pulled her into his arms and kissed her.

Kissed her on the lips, while their semi-naked bodies pressed close.

Kitty thrilled to feel his mouth seeking hers in a cold, salty kiss, and to feel his hard muscled chest, his strong thighs. Lightning jolted through her as she felt his unmistakable arousal.

She was bereft when he released her again, but she caught the burning intensity of the smile he gave her before he dived beneath another rolling green wave.

After their swim, they ate their picnic lunch on the beach. Ed produced a cold roast chicken, an astonishing luxury, and Kitty didn't like to ask how he'd acquired it. Afterwards they lay on the soft grass looking up through graceful palm fronds, listening to the soft rise and fall of the sea and the trilling of cicadas in the nearby shrubbery.

Kitty couldn't stop thinking about Ed's kiss. It was a new obsession to recall the taste of his lips and the sexy shock of his erection pressing against her.

Eventually, keeping her gaze on the sky overhead, she said boldly, 'So now you've kissed me on the lips for the first time.'

When Ed didn't answer, she turned to look at him. Saw his slow smile.

'You did realise it was the first time, didn't you, Ed?'

'Of course.'

'I was beginning to think it might never happen.' Their goodnights at the front gate in Mitchell Street had been so chaste. 'Have you been worried that Geoff might be spying on us from the verandah?'

Ed rolled onto his side, facing her, and lifted his hand to gently stroke her cheek, her neck. His fingers lingered, lightly teasing her collarbone.

'There's a very good reason why I've never kissed you properly,' he said, now tracing the line of her jaw. 'I knew that if I started, I'd never want to stop. I'd need to kiss every enchanting inch of you.'

Kitty shivered. 'I wouldn't mind.'

'Kitty.' His voice held a warning now.

'I'm not a virgin,' she whispered daringly, thinking this might be what had held him back. 'I slept with – with a fellow before he joined up. But it was just, you know, a kind of goodbye.'

'And then your grandfather banished you to Moonlight Plains.'

Kitty gasped. 'How did you know that?'

'So I'm right?' Ed asked now, instead of answering her.

'Yes, but how did you guess?'

'Something your great-uncle implied. That you were sent out there to get away from the American invasion. He thought it was ironic. Reading between the lines, I guessed there might have been a problem in Townsville.'

'So you haven't kissed me because you've wanted to protect me from gossip and from my grandfather's wrath?'

Ed shrugged. Clearly he wasn't going to admit this.

'You're very noble, Ed.'

Now he laughed. 'There's nothing noble about my thoughts.' And she saw an intense look in his eyes that contradicted his laughter.

Picking up a strand of her drying hair, he rubbed it between his fingers, loosening the salty stiffness left by the seawater. 'You know this talk of kissing is playing with fire, Kitty.'

She looked directly into his dark gaze and smiled. 'That's what I was hoping.'

His throat worked nervously as he swallowed.

'Actually . . . I have a key,' he said. 'There's a hut. I believe it's close by, but it's very rustic.'

'How did you get the key?'

'One of the perks of being an officer. Our air force has requisitioned several places on this island.'

Her heart was racing. 'Shouldn't we take a look?'

The hut was indeed rustic. Set back behind a screen of palm trees, casuarinas and bright flowering hibiscuses, its windows were made from corrugated iron that pushed out on timber props.

The floor was bare concrete and the furnishings were simple: a double bed with a faded blue chenille spread, a small cane table and two chairs, a spotted mirror above the table, a cupboard with basic crockery. Another small building at the back housed a shower.

When Ed propped the windows a little way open, dappled green light filtered into the room.

'It's lovely,' Kitty said as she set her picnic basket and beach bag on the floor. 'You can hear the sea from here.'

Ed smiled. 'And the sounds of the parrots and the cicadas.'

'And the geckoes,' she said as he reached for her and nuzzled her bare neck.

'What are geckoes?' he asked, trailing warm kisses along her jaw.

'Funny-looking lizards.' Kitty arched, wanting his lips everywhere.

'Noisy lizards?' He kissed her throat.

'Uh-huh.'

He chuckled. 'I *lurve* the tropics.'

His hands framed her face now and there was no more chuckling or talking as his lips found her lips, gently teasing them apart.

Kitty's eyes widened as she felt his tongue touch hers, but after her momentary surprise, it felt completely natural and perfect. Winding her arms around his neck, she let him take the kiss deeper.

Oh, my, she thought as her skin tightened all over.

Ed was unhurried, almost lazy in the way he kissed her now, but he was most definitely in charge as he slipped his fingers beneath the straps of her swimsuit.

'You must tell me if you want me to stop, Kitty.'

'All right.' She already knew she wouldn't want him to stop.

His dark eyes sought hers. 'I mean it.'

Then he peeled the swimmers down and kissed the tops of her breasts, lighting flames of longing.

'I don't want you to stop,' she whispered, although she gave a small gasp of surprise when he peeled the fabric lower, following with his lips. But then she was seized by curiosity and a new kind of wildness. This was what she wanted – these lightning bolts of desire, his kisses all over. Everywhere . . . *everywhere*.

I'm a changeling, she thought as she quivered and arched. This wanton creature can't really be me.

Once or twice, his kisses were so intimate that she knew she was blushing, and she wondered, Am I supposed to ask him to stop now?

But any possible protests were so hazy and barely formed that they drifted away like smoke on the wind. After all, this was Ed, and he was every kind of wonderful and there was no stopping the blaze that engulfed her.

Kitty felt rather dazed as she lay beside him.

'Hey,' he said gently. 'Are you okay?'

'Yes, of course. Just a little stunned. I had no idea.' She smiled at him shyly. 'I didn't know it could be like that.'

'Neither did I,' Ed said softly.

'But . . . ' Kitty frowned. 'But you knew what to do.' He knew *so* much. Everything.

He smiled and kissed the tip of her nose. 'Doesn't mean it's ever been like that before.'

She tried to take this in as she lay there, feeling like a much more grown-up and womanly version of herself, watching the patterns of light on the walls, while Ed idly played with strands of her hair.

After a bit, she asked, 'What are you thinking about now?'

'About you. About how wrong it would be to take you away from all this.'

His words both thrilled and chilled her. Was he already thinking ahead to the end of the war, to a future in Boston that couldn't include her?

'Perhaps you'll have to stay here then,' she said, half-joking.

'Perhaps I will.' He sounded very pleased with that thought and he was smiling as he began to kiss her again.

Close to dusk, they walked along the beach, hand in hand, their bare feet leaving prints in the shiny wet sand. The ferry had left long ago, packed with tired and sunburned day-trippers, its decks loaded with cases of pineapples from the island's farms. Kitty had felt extremely audacious when she hadn't gone with them.

She and Ed were staying on the island till morning, stealing one glorious, *precious* night from the war.

'Do you remember your parents?' Ed surprised her by asking.

'Yes, of course. I was ten when they died.'

'Do you have happy memories of them?'

'Very happy.' Kitty smiled, remembering the uncomplicated joy of her childhood. The little red-roofed house in Penshurst, her mother singing in the kitchen, her father whistling as he came home from his work in the city. She remembered his nightly ritual, calling, 'Where are my two special girls?' Remembered him swinging her into his arms, holding her on his hip as he kissed her mother, not wanting Kitty to feel left out.

'I knew that my parents loved each other and loved me. There was a lot of laughter in our house,' she said. 'At mealtimes, all the time. That was what I missed most when I moved up here to live with my grandparents. They're not big on laughter.'

The sea and the sky were pearly-grey now, with splashes of pink and mauve from the sunset.

'What about you?' she asked Ed.

'Not much gaiety in our house, I'm afraid.'

'But your parents are happy together, aren't they?'

He gave a soft, huffing sound that wasn't quite a laugh. 'Oh, yes, definitely. In our circles, everyone is happily married. It's the done thing. They're far too refined to fight.'

'But there are no displays of passion?' Kitty asked.

'Absolutely not,' he said glumly. 'That would be undignified.'

'They're not at all like you then.'

That won her another smile.

28

'I'm afraid this is a begging phone call,' Luke told Zoe McKinnon. 'I'm after a little catering advice.'

'Are you catering for another stock camp?'

'Not this time.' Luke smiled, remembering how he'd met Zoe, a fully qualified chef, when he'd hired her as his camp cook for a muster at Mullinjim, the family's station. At the time he'd never dreamed she was his half-sister in search of her family.

'I haven't been within cooee of a stock camp all year,' he said now. 'This is for the bash here at Moonlight Plains.'

'The party to celebrate finishing the homestead makeover? Hey, that's great. We were really excited to get our invitation. So are you nearly finished?'

Luke looked around at the frames for the kitchen cupboards still waiting for doors and bench tops, the holes where the stove and dishwasher were yet to be fitted, the wires hanging from walls awaiting an electrician. From the bathroom across the hall, he heard the sounds of the tiler at work. 'Getting there,' he said.

'I can't wait to see it, Luke. I know it'll be gorgeous. You did such a great job on our place.'

'Well, I assumed most of the family would want to see it, so I decided it was a good excuse to get everyone together. Bella and Gabe. All the uncles. Mum and my grandmother.'

'It'll be fabulous to see everyone. Such a great chance to catch up.' A moment later, Zoe said in a more subdued tone, 'But I can't help thinking how much Peter would have loved this, Luke.'

'Yeah.' Luke sighed. 'We're going to miss him all right.' Zoe hadn't known their father for very long before he died and she'd found his passing especially hard. 'We'll have to raise a glass to him,' Luke said gently.

'Yes. Just a quiet one with your mum and Bella.'

'We'll make sure of it.' Luke blinked, shocked to realise how the loss could still ambush him. Since he'd moved to Moonlight Plains, he'd felt distanced from his family, but a few words from Zoe had instantly reinforced how strong the ties were.

'By the way . . . speaking of families,' he said, brightening, 'I've invited the daughter of one of the Yanks who crashed here during the war.'

'Is she coming out for the party?'

'I'm not sure yet, but I hope so.'

'Wow. That'll put us all on our best behaviour.'

'I guess . . . I s'pose she'll fit in.'

Truth to tell, posting the invitation to the American woman had been quite a wake-up call for Luke. The possibility of her arrival made everything real. Until then, he'd only played along with Sally's brainwave to throw a party, and the actual mechanics of hosting the event had been little more than a vague theory. Now, he had to get cracking with putting it into action.

'Okay.' Zoe sounded gratifyingly businesslike now. 'At least you've given me enough time to plan.'

'I don't expect you to do *everything*.' Zoe and Mac had an ankle-biter now – young Callum, closing in on the terrible twos.

'I was thinking of a barbecue, nothing too flash, or we could throw a beast on a spit.'

'Okay. Sounds good. In either case, you'd really just need fresh salads, crusty bread and some scrumptious desserts.'

'That would be perfect.' Luke laughed. 'You make it sound easy.'

'It will be. Hey, I'm getting excited already, Luke. Does this mean I can throw my weight around in your lovely new kitchen?'

'Absolutely. Feel free.'

'Great. Oh, hang on a sec. Mac's here now, and he's demanding to know what we're talking about.'

Luke could hear her explaining to her husband.

Next, Mac was on the phone. 'Hey, Luke?'

'G'day.'

'I've been meaning to ring you. So you're throwing a big party?'

'Sure,' Luke said with more confidence than he felt. He could already tell from his mate's amused tone that he was in for a ribbing.

'Can't help wondering who put you up to it.'

Luke was glad Sally was safely outside, working in the yard. She'd arrived at Moonlight Plains this morning armed with a rake, gloves and other gardening gear, ready to clean up the disused lily pond. She had visions of it revived and beautiful for the party, stocked with reeds, lilies and fish.

'It just seemed like a good idea,' he said to Mac.

'So let me get this straight. You haven't been on a horse for bloody ages. You spend all your days sawing timber and hammering nails. And now you're moving into big-time catering?'

Luke bit back an urge to tell him to pull his head in. 'It's a family get-together,' he said patiently.

'But if I was a suspicious type, I'd suspect a female's hand in this. I sense a little feminine prompting. Is this another new girl, or someone we've already met?'

Luke gritted his teeth. Until now, he'd been happy with the way

Sally had become more and more involved in his project, ringing him with thoughts about various decorating touches . . .

But now he realised that the party spelled danger, a very real chance that his family would jump to all sorts of wrong conclusions about Sally.

Their 'strictly casual' relationship was going well. Really well. Brilliantly. Sally had become a regular visitor and everything about being with her was way better than Luke had ever dreamed. But it would be ruined if the family got nosy, aided and abetted by his best mate playing the smartarse.

'You're wasting your breath,' he told Mac tiredly, as if bored with this conversation. 'Our entire family has a vested interest in Moonlight Plains and we have to work out what to do with it now. If we're going to have a gathering to discuss its future, we may as well turn it into a bit of a party. It makes sense.'

'Okay. Fair enough. I guess I was just enjoying the idea of a girl behind the scenes.'

'Sorry to disappoint. And for what it's worth —'

'Hey, Luke!' Sally yelled from the front verandah.

Luke spun around.

Sally stood in the doorway, dressed in shorts and muddy work boots, Jess at her side, tail wagging a greeting.

'I was just wondering if you could help me —' She'd raised her voice to reach him, but then she saw the phone in his hand. 'Sorry, I didn't realise you were busy.'

'Who's that?' demanded Mac from the other end of the line.

Luke grimaced. No way would he incriminate Sally. 'The tiler.'

'You have a female tiler?'

'Yeah. What of it?'

There was a snort of laughter. 'Okay, mate.' Mac could barely speak now between chuckles. 'Say no more.'

'Thank Zoe for her offer to help, will you?' Luke responded

tightly. 'I'll get back to her when I have firmer numbers.'

'Sure. And I'll leave you to your lonely, monastic existence. Good for you. All the best.'

Fuck. Luke pressed the button to end the call, pocketed his phone and crossed the bare wooden floors to Sally.

As always, the sight of her cheered him. She'd pulled her hair up into a butterfly clip, but strands had slipped out and now lay in curls at her neck, so bright in contrast to her pale skin. He wanted to hook his finger into a curling fiery wisp, to feel its silky softness.

'Sorry if I interrupted something,' she said.

'Not really.' Luke shrugged the phone call aside. 'Were you looking for help?'

'Yes, please. There's an old concrete pipe in the pond, but it's filled with mud and it's too heavy for me to lift.'

'No worries. I'll take a look at it.'

As they went down the steps, Sally sent him a sideways, searching glance. 'Everything okay, Luke?'

'Sure. Why?'

'I thought you looked a bit pensive.'

He gave a shrug. 'I'm fine. Everything's fine.'

But it wasn't the truth. Mac's teasing was a timely reminder that his family would almost certainly pester him about Sally when they met her at the party. If it was any other girl, he wouldn't care, but Sally was different, still grieving. He would have to warn her, work out a strategy.

Right now, however, he had to deal with the pile of rubbish she'd dragged from the silted pond. 'Bloody hell.'

Along with rocks and rubble and piles of mud, there were filthy beer bottles and cans, an old boot, a rotted wooden crate, and what looked like the bottom section of a metal-mesh garden seat.

'An archaeologist would have a field day with this lot,' Sally said with a laugh.

'It's disgusting. But you've done an amazing job, Sal.'

'Thanks.'

She looked so pleased and pretty, despite the mud smears, that he couldn't resist giving her a kiss. When she melted against him, responding with her usual enthusiasm, their kiss took a lovely long time.

'That's better,' she said, smiling into his eyes. 'You look much happier now.'

Luke kissed her again, couldn't help it. But then he dragged his attention to the almost empty pond. Stepping down onto a muddy island, he tried to lift the concrete pipe. 'That's well and truly stuck. Reckon I'll need a crowbar.'

Sally nodded. 'So maybe I could make a start on clearing all the grass away from the edges.'

'You don't have to. It's a big job.'

'But I want to. I can't wait to get a proper look at all the stonework and paving. I've never done anything like this before and I'm having a ball. Honestly.'

Her warm brown eyes were shining and she looked so genuinely happy Luke felt his throat constrict.

'You know you're one in a million, don't you?'

'Of course,' she said with a cheeky grin and a tempting wiggle of her hips.

Somehow he resisted the overpowering urge to kiss her again. Three kisses within as many minutes might be breaking their 'strictly casual' boundaries.

'I'll get that crowbar and back the ute up so I can cart this mess away,' he said instead.

By the end of the day, the pond and the circle of crazy paving that edged it were cleared. Luke and Sally sat in canvas camp chairs, enjoying a cold drink – beer for Luke and white wine for Sally – as they admired the results of their labours and made plans. They couldn't fill the pond yet; it needed a new liner, which Luke would get from the local hardware store. Meanwhile Sally was going to check out Townsville's nurseries for the most suitable water-loving plants.

'What about fish?' she asked.

'They're easy. I'll catch rainbow fish from the river.'

'So I can dangle my feet in here and have a pedicure?'

'If you like.' Luke shot her a grin. 'And when you're not here the fish can eat the mosquito larvae.'

'Now you've spoiled the romance. So you don't want goldfish?'

He shook his head. 'They'd be a problem if the pond over-flowed in the wet. We wouldn't want goldfish washing down into the creeks.'

'Pity. Goldfish are so pretty.'

'Yeah, but this country already has enough problems with aquar-ium fish escaping into natural waterways.'

Sally pulled a face. 'I didn't know you were a greenie.' But she countered this with another smile. 'Actually, you're right. Goldfish would look out of place here, anyway. They belong in cities.'

So do you, Luke almost said, but he refrained and downed the rest of his beer. Sally was staying the night and there was no sense in spoiling their happy mood with a chilling dose of reality.

Sally watched as Luke stood at the two-burner stove that was perched on the makeshift shelf where the flash new Italian five-burner would eventually sit. He was stirring scrambled eggs with a frown of deep concentration, and she decided he looked incredibly cute in his jeans and ratty old T-shirt, making sure that their break-fast was just right.

She couldn't resist slipping her arms around him from behind and giving him a hug.

These days, just being around Luke made her feel incredibly happy. Last week, she'd even confessed this during another beach walk with Megan, and her friend had been so excited that she'd done cartwheels, literally.

'It's still only casual,' Sally had warned her. 'We're not getting serious.'

Megan, who'd recently announced her engagement to Barney, had rolled her eyes, but at least she hadn't tried to argue.

Now, however, Sally suspected she had a problem. She was beginning to doubt her own hype. Surely, if her interest in Luke was merely casual, she wouldn't be thinking about him constantly. Surely, she shouldn't live for these visits to Moonlight Plains. And most certainly, she shouldn't feel deeply depressed about leaving Luke here and driving back to Townsville.

She wondered if she should raise this with him some time soon. After all, she'd originally gone to great lengths to make it clear they had no long-term future. She'd insisted that their relationship could only ever be casual, and Luke – nice guy that he was – had respected her wishes.

Problem was, she'd been so bossy about this she'd left herself no avenue for learning how Luke honestly felt. He showed all the signs of liking her very much, but he never talked about their future, just took each day as it came. Which was exactly what she'd asked for.

She was still mulling over this catch-22 when he turned from the little stove with a smile of triumph.

'*Voilà!*' He held out two plates of toast topped with perfectly scrambled eggs.

'Sensational,' she told him.

He winked. 'Can you bring the cutlery and cracked pepper?'

'Sure can.'

They'd set the card table and chairs on the verandah where they could dine with a view of the paddocks and the bush while Jess remained close, snoozing in a patch of sunlight.

Sally carefully cut a wedge of toast and egg and took a bite. 'Wow, this is delicious, Luke. Perfect*issimo*.' Playfully, she rubbed her bare foot against his ankle. 'A man of many talents.'

A brief quarter-smile flickered in his face then disappeared almost immediately. To her surprise, he looked unusually serious and his gaze didn't quite meet hers.

Retracting her foot, she cut another corner of egg and toast. Luke was turning pensive again and his thoughtful frown unsettled her more than it should have.

If she probed him about it she'd probably annoy him. He'd been pretty quick yesterday to shrug it off. So she continued to eat, cutting dainty portions, paying careful attention to the paddocks and the flock of cattle egrets that took off, snowy-white against the trees.

But when she heard Luke sigh, a shiver skittered down her spine.

'Listen, Sal,' he said abruptly.

Until now she'd always loved the way he called her Sal. It sounded so relaxed. Easy, yet intimate. Like he was. Like their relationship was.

But now she was nervous.

'We're going to have to be careful about this party.'

So it was *the party* that bothered him. Sally felt a flash of relief. 'Careful?' she queried. 'How?'

Luke shifted uncomfortably. 'The thing is – you wouldn't want my family jumping to conclusions about us, would you?'

'No . . . I guess not.'

His green eyes were fixed on her, heated now, and deadly serious. 'If they think you're my girlfriend, they could get damn annoying. They could pile on the questions.'

After suffering Megan's interrogations, Sally knew exactly what he meant. 'You mean they'll start checking out my ring finger? Asking you if you've set a date for the wedding?'

Luke grimaced. 'Almost as bad as that, yeah.'

She knew she should be pleased that Luke was making every effort to keep their affair free of expectations, exactly as she'd requested. It was illogical now to feel disappointed.

Carefully, she said, 'It shouldn't be too hard to set them straight. I think the older generation accepts that young people in the twenty-first century have different attitudes.'

'Sure.' Luke was still frowning. 'But I wouldn't like things to get awkward for you.'

Sally gave him a reassuring smile. 'I'm sure I'll cope.'

When there was no answering smile from Luke, she forced herself to ask, 'What are you thinking, Luke? Would you rather I stayed away altogether?'

'Hell, no.' Across the table, he reached for her hand. 'I'm just suggesting that we should be careful. We're supposed to be friends. You're the journalist writing about the homestead. Not —'

'Not your lover.'

'Don't get me wrong. I *love* what we have going. I love —' His eyes shimmered as he rubbed his broad thumb over her knuckles. 'I love your spontaneity.' He drew a breath in and out before he went on. 'But if you want to keep my sisters and my mother off the scent, you might have to be cautious. I reckon little things could be giveaways. With the women in my family, even just a look or a smile could be dangerous.'

Sally might have laughed if he hadn't looked so adorable when he was concerned, but she felt a mad urge to tell him she didn't care what the rest of the world thought.

She could hear herself telling him everything. Now. Openly and honestly. How much she liked him, not just in bed, but in so many ways. She'd had a ball getting involved with his project, and she simply liked being around him. He was warm, funny and sexy, and he was also wonderfully steady and reliable. In ways she couldn't really explain, he made her feel centred.

Was this the right time after all? Should she be brave?

She switched her gaze to a point in the distance as she tried to think this through. An admission about her feelings could be quite a game-changer, and right now Luke was up to his eyebrows with last-minute finishes on the house, as well as getting ready for an invasion by his family and friends.

This party was all about the homestead and Luke's hard work. It was about Kitty and her husband and the others who'd played a part in its history.

In the midst of all that, wouldn't it be rather selfish of her to admit to falling in love with Luke? It would be like trying to steal the limelight.

No, she'd travelled a long way to reach this point and she mustn't stuff it up now.

'So do you agree?' Luke asked, watching her.

Now it was Sally who had difficulty smiling. 'Yes, of course I agree,' she said. 'I'd certainly hate to cause any awkwardness.'

'Maybe you should bring a friend or two along to the party with you.'

'As camouflage?'

He smiled. 'It's just a thought.'

What a prize idiot she'd been to imagine that she might co-host this party with Luke. Her task was to mingle with the crowd, to observe and to be virtually invisible.

If it was a week when Barney was out at the mines, she would console herself with Megan's company. If Toby, who'd been Josh's best mate, was available, she might invite him too. She would enjoy bringing them here, and they'd love the experience.

'Do you know anyone with a tent?' Luke asked. 'I'd say most of the guests are going to have to camp out.' He nodded towards the nearest paddock.

Sally cast a dubious eye over the paddock. 'I thought people would stay in motels in town, but I guess if they've been drinking they'd be better off here. They certainly won't all fit into the house, will they?'

'Not a chance. I'll have to get the furniture out of storage and I thought I'd set up bedrooms for my mother and Kitty – and possibly for Zoe and Mac, seeing they have the little guy.'

'And the American woman?'

'Hell, yes. I nearly forgot about her. I offered her accommodation, so I'll have to have something planned in case she accepts. Thanks for the reminder. I think everyone else will have to be in tents.'

'Will they mind?'

Luke smiled as he shook his head. 'That's how it's done in the bush. Some folk will probably just swag down under the stars.'

'Is that what you'll do?'

'Probably.'

She imagined lying under the stars with him. *So* romantic. 'Quite an adventure,' she said sadly, knowing that she'd probably be in a tent with Megan.

29

Things went a little crazy for Luke over the following few weeks as an acceptance from Laura Langley Fox arrived and word of the party spread.

With all kinds of last-minute details to attend to on the house, as well as the expectation that he would keep an eye on the cattle, he resented the extra pressure that came with phone calls from family members.

Yesterday it had been his mother. 'I was speaking to Sheila Douglas and I mentioned the old homestead and how you'd done it up, Luke, and she was *so* interested. She used to go out to Moonlight Plains for parties when she was a girl and she would love to see it again. It would be fine if I invited her to the party, wouldn't it, dear? She wouldn't take up much room.'

Mary Davies from the Historical Society also rang, expressing delight in Luke's achievements. 'Moonlight Plains was such a lovely old homestead,' she said, her voice surprisingly warm and gushing. 'I remember how my mother used to talk so fondly of going out there to play tennis on Sunday afternoons.'

She went on to ask ever so politely if the celebrations would be open to the public. Luke told her no, the party was private, but she was so disappointed he found himself extending an invitation to her committee members and their spouses, and the invitation was, of course, gratefully accepted.

Then Jim Mathieson, his mother's eldest brother, the lawyer from Brisbane who'd bought the steers that Luke had branded, rang to once again express his gratitude and to check that all was well with the cattle.

Luke assured him the cattle were fine and then asked, 'Will you be able to make it up here for the party?'

'Absolutely, Luke. I'll be there with bells on. I've posted my acceptance.' A beat later, Jim added, 'By the way, I hear you've invited Ed Langley's daughter.'

Luke was surprised that Jim knew Laura's father's name. Most of the family just referred to him as the American airman. 'Yes,' he said. 'It should be interesting to meet her.'

'Interesting indeed. I suppose you ran that by your grandmother first?'

Luke frowned, detecting mild reproach in Jim's question. Jim was his grandmother's eldest son, and quite caring despite living at a distance. 'Sure,' he said cautiously. 'I told Gran I was sending an invitation.'

'Was Mum okay with that, Luke? She doesn't usually like to talk about those war years.'

'She didn't object,' Luke countered, feeling a prickle of guilt as he remembered that his grandmother hadn't been over the moon about his proposed invitation.

'That's fine then,' Jim said smoothly. Too smoothly? 'I'll look forward to seeing you in a couple of weeks.'

Luke had little time to ponder this call before another of his uncles rang, from Richmond.

'I'm sure you won't mind, Luke. I've invited my neighbours to our little get-together. They're good folk and they've had a rough trot this past year with bushfires and missed sales and everything, and they could do with a little cheering up.'

What could Luke say but yes?

Of course, he had to make several phone calls back to Zoe with upward adjustments to the numbers expected. Luckily, she took it all in her stride, but she threw her own spanner into the works when she asked Luke if he'd hired a band, or organised one of those portable dance floors.

'Don't worry,' she added quickly. 'Bella and Gabe have put up their hands to take care of that.'

'Do you really think we need a band?' Luke was getting nervous. This party would be bigger than bloody *Ben Hur* if he didn't draw the line somewhere.

'Well, the band come with all their own gear and they would certainly liven things up. We think they would really set the scene.'

They were ganging up on him. 'I guess.'

'Great. Will I tell Bella to go ahead?'

Luke sighed. 'Yeah. Why not?'

'And you know you'll need to order extra tables and chairs from the hire people, don't you?'

'Yep. Already taken care of.' Actually, Sally had looked after that. One of her friends, a guy – Luke had manfully squashed jealous thoughts – was bringing a truck from Townsville with all the gear from the hire company.

'You sound tired, you poor thing,' Zoe said next. 'But don't worry. We'll come early to help.'

'Yeah, thanks. That'd be great.'

As long as he had the damn homestead ready. He let out a frustrated sigh as he disconnected. The plumber had only just arrived to finish work on the guttering, the bathrooms and kitchen, and the electrician was dragging the chain, always claiming that he was caught up, but that Moonlight Plains was next on his job list.

Of course, there'd been yet more phone calls involved in chasing them up. Luke was ready to throw his damn phone into Sally's rejuvenated fishpond.

Sally was a welcome sight when she breezed into Kitty's room with her dog in her wake.

'So would you like to see some photos of the homestead?' she asked as soon as she'd said hello and kissed Kitty's cheek. 'Or would you rather be surprised when you arrive for the party?'

'Oh, I'm too old for surprises.' Kitty fished for the doggie treats she kept in a drawer. 'Here, Jess, good girl.' Then she beckoned to Sally. 'Come and show me what Luke's been up to. He's tried to keep me up to date with phone calls, but it's hard to visualise what's going on.'

She was pleased to have this opportunity to view Sally's photos before she arrived at Moonlight Plains. On the off-chance that she didn't like the renovations, she would at least be mentally prepared and less likely to disappoint Luke with a negative reaction.

Sally had an air of unmistakable excitement as she pulled an album from her shoulder bag and set it in Kitty's lap.

'Goodness. Have you filled a whole album already?'

'It's not completely full.' The girl's fair complexion turned a giveaway shade of pink. 'I had to take lots of shots. I needed plenty to choose from – for the magazine story.'

'Of course.' Kitty hoped her response sounded noncommittal, but she was secretly thrilled that this delightful young woman had developed such a very keen interest in her grandson's project. It was a promising sign, surely?

'They're in chronological order, so you can see the progress,' Sally said, slipping into the chair next to Kitty and crossing her slim, shapely legs.

Ah, the ease with which young people move, Kitty thought wistfully as she struggled to coordinate her arthritic fingers to get the first page open.

Eventually . . . there it was . . .

Oh . . . the nostalgia . . .

In the first photo, the old homestead looked so tired and neglected as it hunkered in a sea of long, brown grass beneath a nailing midday sun. Kitty felt an instant lump in her throat.

'That's the "before" photo,' Sally explained. 'Luke took that before he started any of the work.'

Kitty extended a shaking hand, almost touching the print, tracing the shape of the roofline, the sagging verandah rail. She had stood on those front steps, feeling that her heart would break as she watched Ed walk away from Moonlight Plains. And she'd stood there four years later with Andy and their eldest son on the day they'd moved in to start their new life. A very happy life it had been, too, for which she was endlessly grateful.

'After my husband died, this house was virtually forgotten,' she said. 'The manager we hired didn't want the responsibility that goes with an old house. So the stock was looked after, but the house suffered.'

'I really love these old homes,' Sally said fervently.

'Do you, dear?'

The girl nodded, then looked a trifle embarrassed, as if she'd admitted more than she'd intended to. 'If you turn the page,' she said, adopting a businesslike tone, 'you'll see that Luke had a lot of structural work to do at first.'

Obediently, Kitty turned her attention from the attractive, glowing young face beside her to the pages in her lap. 'Oh, my,' she exclaimed over a photo of a ladder disappearing into a half-demolished ceiling. 'I hate to think what Luke found up there.'

She turned more pages with scenes of devastation rather than restoration. Such a big job this had been for the boy, but Kitty had never doubted he was capable, or that he'd give the task his best shot. He was a very reliable young man. She remembered that he'd been holidaying in New Zealand when his father had his first heart attack, but he'd dashed straight home and had taken over the reins at Mullinjim with extreme competence.

Actually, there were a surprising number of shots of Luke, Kitty noticed, swallowing an urge to smile. Her grandson certainly looked the part with his low-slung toolbelt, battered old jeans and a T-shirt that showed off his muscles as he leaned over a workbench or stretched to reach a high beam.

With an effort, Kitty refrained from commenting on the frequency of these photos, but they were an encouraging sign and they mirrored the pleasing way a mention of Sally had slipped into Luke's conversation almost every time they'd spoken on the phone.

'I brought that stained glass back to Townsville to have it restored,' Sally said as Kitty reached a photograph of the lovely panelled front door with morning sunlight streaming through it.

'I'd forgotten how pretty it is.' Kitty might have lingered over the beautiful door, but her attention was distracted by the next page. She gasped. 'Goodness! He's opened it all up, all the way to the kitchen.'

'Didn't he warn you about that?'

'I knew he'd knocked out a wall or two.'

'Do you like the result?' Sally was leaning forward, watching Kitty intently, her dark-brown eyes round with concern.

'It's very modern. Everything's very clean and white.' Kitty needed a moment to adjust.

'But there's a wonderful feeling of space. Of course, there's no furniture in there yet. That will make a difference.'

'Yes.'

'And Luke kept the beautiful archway between the lounge and the dining room.'

'Yes, yes. Don't be anxious, Sally.' Kitty gave her hand a reassuring pat. 'I'm getting used to it now. The timber floors have come up beautifully, haven't they?'

'They're gorgeous, and the view from the kitchen is superb. And . . .' Sally reached over to turn another page. 'Look at the bathrooms. Luke's done an amazing job. He has a real gift for restoration.'

The girl spoke with such depth of feeling, Kitty couldn't help smiling. *I think she's in love.*

'So do you have everything you need for your story?' Kitty asked when she got to the last photograph.

Sally nodded. 'All I need to wrap it up are a few details from the party.'

'You must be looking forward to it.'

'Yes, sure.'

As Sally said this, however, the happy light in her eyes dimmed.

Kitty needed, quite desperately, to know the reason.

'What's the matter?' she asked a little too sharply.

Sally blinked. 'Nothing. Why?'

'I fancied that you were worried when I mentioned the party.'

'No, I'm not worried. I'm looking forward to it.'

Kitty wasn't entirely convinced but she could hardly argue.

'I'm looking forward to it too,' she said. 'Not only will I get out of this place, but I'll also have fun watching all of you young people having fun. Dancing under the stars.'

'Dancing?' Sally looked more worried than ever.

'Luke tells me he's hired a band *and* a portable dance floor.'

'Has he?'

Good heavens, the girl had gone quite pale. 'I thought you were helping him with the planning.'

'Oh, only a little at the start.' Sally's lips curved in an approximation of a smile. 'Don't forget I'm only a journalist covering the story.'

'But I thought you and Luke were becoming . . . good friends.'

Sally shrugged, dropped her gaze. 'We're friends, sure, but this is a family party. Zoe and Bella are Luke's backup team. I'm just a helper in the background.'

Fiddlesticks, Kitty wanted to snap, but when she saw the look in Sally's eyes she stopped herself just in time.

She'd been worried that this girl might break Luke's heart, but now she was afraid that it might be the other way round.

30

Laura's enthusiasm for Australia went into a sharp decline as soon as she hit the outback. Sydney had been wonderful. Once she'd recovered from her initial jetlag, she'd had a fabulous few days in a harbourside hotel.

She'd found the harbour itself jaw-droppingly beautiful and her artist's eye had hungrily devoured the dazzle of sunlight on water, the visual drama of the opera house, the pleasing curve of the bridge against a clear blue Australian sky. Sydney was different enough from Boston to be exotic, and yet familiar enough for her to feel comfortable and safe.

This trip marked the first time she'd travelled on her own and it had taken a little getting used to, but she'd quickly appreciated how liberating it was to have no one but herself to please. She could sleep in, take a ferry ride to Manly on a whim, spend an entire morning wandering around the historic Rocks district, visit any art gallery she chose without anyone whining at her to hurry up, and she could choose to eat wherever and whatever she liked.

Best of all, being a woman of a certain age, she was more or less invisible. No one stared at her because she was sitting alone in a cafe, and, rather than feeling lonely, Laura found this new independence empowering.

From Sydney she'd flown north to Townsville, where she'd spent a night in another hotel room with another lovely water view. She'd studied the attractively landscaped beachfront and the island floating serenely in the calm tropical waters and tried, unsuccessfully, to imagine what the place had been like in 1942. Then she'd hired a car, a small sedan, and headed somewhat nervously west towards Moonlight Plains.

Laura had never driven off into the unknown before and there was nothing about the landscape she encountered now that made her feel comfortable. She soon realised this had not been her brightest idea. Her notion of the Australian outback had been based almost entirely on vague memories of movies, and she'd expected leafy eucalypt forests or red-dirt plains with dramatic canyons, beautiful waterfalls and pretty lagoons that were home to waterbirds.

Instead, a thin ribbon of blue bitumen stretched across harsh sunburned grazing land with barbed-wire fences, straggly clumps of gum trees and stubbled grass that was nowhere near green. Most disturbing, however, was the lack of stores or villages; there was just the occasional gas station or drab and dusty homestead.

Laura knew it was weak and foolish of her, but she couldn't help wishing she was safely back in Massachusetts with its old stone farmhouses, neat red barns, rolling green fields and orchards.

By the time she passed through the town of Charters Towers, following Luke Fairburn's directions, and continued on through more of the same dry, grey-green bush towards Moonlight Plains, she was very much regretting her decision to embark on this venture.

She supposed that, for some people, this landscape might hold a certain rugged beauty, but right now she found it menacing. Distressingly so.

Why had she ever thought this was a good idea? She didn't even really know what she would say when she met Luke or Kitty. She'd brought gifts – Red Sox jerseys, pretty Yankee candles and finely woven Nantucket baskets – hoping they would be appropriate. Beyond that, she was winging this visit. Now, as a sign pointing off the main road to Moonlight Plains appeared on her right, she felt scarily under-rehearsed.

The track ahead of her was downright creepy, hardly more than wheel ruts in the dirt with rough grass in between that scraped at the belly of her little car. Even though it was still early afternoon, the bush closed in too, with tall skinny gum trees and tangled scrub crowding to the edge of the track and cutting out the sunlight.

Oh, God. Laura had no idea where she was going. She couldn't imagine how her father could have flown all the way out here. And why had Kitty been in such wild country?

What on earth did I think I was going to learn? Surely this is all a terrible mistake.

Apart from Luke's brief letter, which was pleasant enough, Laura had no idea what the contemporary Fairburns or Mathiesons were actually like. They could be hillbillies for all she knew and now, too late, she envisaged being served kangaroo stew or roasted crocodile. She felt sick. Scared.

A moment later she was shaking and dizzy and she had no choice but to stop the car.

In the middle of the narrow track, with no place to turn around, she cut the motor and clung to the steering wheel as her heart pounded and panic took hold.

I can't do this. I was crazy to come here.

Glancing in the rear-view mirror, she saw her white face, the very real fear in her eyes. Madly, she wished she could wind back time, find herself in Boston rewriting the script of her fateful conversation with Amy.

She closed her eyes and tried to breathe deeply and evenly in a bid to calm down.

From somewhere behind her there was a growl of a motor and before she could gather her wits to start up her car, a pickup truck came hurtling around a bend in the track and pulled to an abrupt, noisy halt behind her.

In the mirror, Laura watched the pickup's passenger door open. A young woman jumped out and she caught an impression of long legs in tight jeans, a mane of long tawny hair.

'Hello?' the new arrival called as she came towards Laura.

Her voice sounded friendly enough and Laura gratefully pressed the button to make her window descend.

'Is everything okay?' The girl's smile was as warm as her voice and she was pretty, with a healthy, outdoors glow about her.

Laura said shakily, 'I was looking for Moonlight Plains.'

'Well, you're on the right track.'

'That's good news at least. I was beginning to wonder.'

Now the girl's smile widened. 'You're American!'

'Well, yes.'

Her eyes widened with sudden excitement. 'You must be the pilot's daughter.'

'Yes, that's me.' If Laura had been calmer, she might have been amused to hear herself described that way.

'Oh, wow.' The girl extended her hand through the open window. 'I'm so pleased to meet you. I'm Bella. Bella Mitchell, Kitty Mathieson's granddaughter. I believe Kitty knew your father when he was here.'

'Yes, that seems to be the case.' Laura was scanning the girl's face, wondering if Kitty had looked as pretty as this when his father met her.

'We're over the moon that you've come all this way.'

Really? 'Thank you. I'm Laura. How – how nice to meet you, Bella.'

'Gabe – that's my husband – and I have just been into the Towers for a few extra supplies.' Bella straightened up and looked ahead down the track. 'You haven't too far to go now, but this track's pretty rough, isn't it?'

Laura nodded. 'I – I've never driven on anything like this before.'

'Would you be happier if we led the way?'

Laura imagined trying to move her little car to the side of the narrow track so that the truck could squeeze past her. Surely it was impossible. 'But there's no room.'

'That's okay. These trees are only saplings and Gabe has a bull bar on the front. He can bush-bash.'

Bush-bash? Laura had no idea what this meant.

Bella grinned. 'Just sit tight here till we're ahead of you. And you'll want to keep back out of our dust.' She lifted a hand to wave. 'See you up at the homestead.'

Puzzled, Laura sat tight as instructed, reminding herself that weirder things must have happened to her father when he was out here. Once again, she watched in the rear-view mirror as Bella leapt nimbly up into the truck and spoke to the man behind the wheel. Moments later, the truck turned off the track and into the bush.

Dodging and ducking any larger trees, it simply ploughed through the skinny saplings and scrub, knocking them over like matchsticks and, within minutes, it was bouncing onto the track ahead of her.

Fancy that.

'Welcome to Australia,' Laura murmured, and she realised she was smiling.

Luke had been holding his breath for days. At least that was what it had felt like and yet, incredibly, everything seemed to be coming together now. The house was finished and looking pretty damn good, if he did say so himself. The beds were made up and ready for the house guests. The dance floor and the extra tables, the chairs, glasses and crockery had arrived. Zoe was ensconced in the kitchen with Sally and Sally's friend Megan, who were happy to be kitchen hands.

Of course, whenever Luke thought about Sally, he felt a hitch in his breathing. By far the hardest moment of this entire exercise had been her arrival this morning. It had nearly killed him to stick to the plan to keep their relationship under the radar.

Sally had arrived in a truck with Megan and a guy called Toby, and she'd introduced them as her best friends. Actually, Luke had learned later that they'd been best man and chief bridesmaid at Sally and Josh's wedding, and that in itself had been sobering.

Sal had looked gorgeous, of course, even though she was only wearing jeans and a singlet top. It was torture to greet her politely as she jumped down from the truck, shaking her hand with no more warmth or enthusiasm than he greeted her friends. All he'd wanted to do was to race her off to a secluded corner and haul her in, with her sweet curves hard against him while they lost themselves in a hot, wild kiss.

Unsurprisingly, he'd found himself questioning why he'd deemed it so damned important to throw his family off their scent. His mob had seen him with girls before and Sally's appearance at his side wouldn't have signalled anything serious. So why had he been so anxious to protect her?

The only rational explanation arrived some time later when he saw Sally in the kitchen squeezing lemons for a dessert that Zoe was making. Sally was concentrating hard, frowning as she rotated a lemon this way and that, and for a moment he could see her as a little girl, trying hard to please her teacher or her mother, and his heart swelled so that it seemed to fill his chest. For a moment there he couldn't breathe.

It was then he knew – the way he felt about Sally was totally different from how he'd felt about any other girl he'd dated. And it wasn't just because she was a widow.

She'd got under his skin, into his heart. Damn it, it was possible – *drum roll* – he'd fallen in love.

Right at this moment, with everyone getting ready to party, it was both a happy and a scary discovery.

It didn't help that Sally was playing her part really well. There was no special smile for him. No lingering eye contact. How he missed that sparkle in her lovely dark eyes, the private look just for him.

For the duration of the party, he was condemned to constant awareness of Sally's whereabouts without making any close contact. He was like an amputee who could still feel his missing limb.

And the only person he could blame was himself.

The track widened, opening onto grassland. Ahead of Laura, beyond Bella and Gabe's truck, she saw a paddock where several vehicles were parked and tents were being erected. Beyond that, on a stretch of mowed lawn, stood a scattering of trestle tables and chairs, and what looked like a temporary dance floor. And then, providing a gracious backdrop to the whole inviting scene, the timber homestead gleamed with fresh white paint in the bright outback sun.

So this is it, Dad. I'm here. What now?

What came next for Laura was a warm welcome from a host of friendly strangers. First, Luke, tall and big-shouldered, with laughing green eyes and sun-bleached tips to his light-brown hair, came forward, extending a huge hand.

'Great to meet you at last. We're honoured that you've come such a long way.' He shook her hand firmly without crushing it. 'You must be dying for a cuppa. Come inside and stow your things. Here, let me carry your bags.'

'I feel very privileged,' she said as Luke showed her to a pretty room with a double bed and a long view through French doors across sweeping paddocks. 'Most of your guests seem to be camping outside.'

Luke merely grinned. 'We wouldn't do that to you. The others are used to camping out and they love it.'

Laura met Luke's uncles, aunts, cousins and sisters, and assorted children, all of them pleasant and friendly. Apparently Kitty hadn't arrived yet, she was being driven from Townsville by her daughter, Virginia. Laura found herself waiting on tenterhooks.

Luke was called away to the phone – something to do with a band – and a young woman with glossy dark curls called Zoe asked Laura if she'd prefer tea or coffee. In what seemed like no time Zoe was back on the verandah with a tray laden with a coffee pot, sugar and cream and a small plate piled with squares of perfect-looking shortbread.

'Oh, this is wonderful,' Laura exclaimed, and she meant it sincerely.

On the shady verandah she was able to unwind a little, chatting with Luke's aunts, who explained that they both lived on cattle properties further to the west. She answered their polite enquiries about her journey from Boston and what she hoped to see in Australia, and while they talked, a game started in the paddock – Laura was told it was cricket.

She couldn't make head or tail of the rules, but children and adults and a couple of dogs all played together and they seemed to be having a swell time, with plenty of laughter and lots of shouting when the batter got out, or yells of frustration when the dogs refused to surrender the ball.

Another pickup truck arrived in a swirl of dust, with rolled-up bedding piled in the back. The pickup was called a ute, Laura was told, and the sleeping gear was called a swag. After the party, the young people would probably sleep out in the open under the stars.

Laura wondered what that was like. While it sounded adventurous and fun in theory, she wasn't sure she'd like the reality.

'Don't they worry about snakes?' She had to ask.

But the others simply laughed and shrugged.

'On a cold clear night, there's nothing better,' one of the women, who had to be past fifty, assured her.

Then there was a shout from Luke. 'Gran's almost here!'

To Laura's surprise, everyone reacted. The cricketers, the tent erectors, the people working in the kitchen or setting out chairs all seemed to stop what they were doing and congregate at the front of the house to welcome the vehicle that could now be heard coming down the track.

Laura felt unpleasant flutters in her stomach and chest and she realised she was nervous. This was the famous – or infamous – Kitty, the woman her father had slept with all those years ago, and consequently, could never forget.

She had been going to sit back and watch this family greet their matriarch, but she found herself standing and moving to the verandah railing, as curious as anyone else.

The sudden tension in Luke was unexpected. He'd already received enough compliments about the homestead's restoration to give him a swollen head, so he should have been relaxed and pleased. But it was his grandmother's opinion that mattered most.

She'd lived here the longest, first during the war and then, later, with his grandfather Andy, when they'd started a new life here as cattle graziers. And she was still the nominal owner, although the family's trust was a complicated setup that Luke didn't fully understand.

As his mother's SUV appeared a cheer went up and people started waving. Shading his eyes, Luke could just make out the tiny figure of his grandmother in the front passenger seat. As he walked forward to meet the car, he knew his smile was a little shaky.

His mother climbed out quickly, still as slim and neat and energetic as ever, with hair the colour of dusty wheat. She finally seemed to be settling into her new widowed lifestyle of golf and gardening in Townsville.

'Wow!' she called. 'What a reception.' She kissed Luke and they hugged. 'How are you, darling?'

'I'm fine. How are you? How's Gran?'

'Oh, Gran's in fine fettle. Darling, the house looks amazing. Can you help Gran out of the car? She'll need to take it slowly. Her poor old joints will be stiff after the drive.'

Getting his grandmother from the car was indeed a slow and difficult process. Luke, used to seeing her in the nursing home, was shocked by how tiny and frail she seemed out here in the fresh air and sunshine. He was scared his big hands would bruise her.

'I was going to bring a wheelchair,' his mother said. 'But Mum wouldn't hear of it.'

His gran shook her head fiercely. 'I don't need a wheelchair.'

'We've plenty of chairs and strong arms,' Luke assured her as he helped her to shuffle slowly forward.

When she stopped and gasped after only a few steps, he thought she was out of breath, but then her bony fingers gripped him with surprising intensity. 'Oh, Luke, it's beautiful.'

She was looking at the house, once again strong and sturdy and sporting a new coat of bright-white paint. 'It looks better than ever. You've done a wonderful job.' Her eyes were shining with the glint of tears.

'Wait till you see inside,' someone called.

Luke could feel the knots of tension within him loosen a notch or two.

*

The greetings took a while. Kitty was shown to a chair and made comfortable with cushions, then a cup of tea was placed on a small table at her side. Once she was settled, various family members paid homage – or at least that was how it seemed to Laura watching from the verandah, as grown men, presumably Kitty's sons, kissed her tenderly on the cheek and then crouched in front of her to converse with her at eye level.

She looked sweet, Laura thought. Old and frail and sweet. Her fine white hair had been combed into an elegant chignon and she was wearing a simple dress in a becoming soft-rose shade. *Why was I so worried about this woman? How could she have been a threat to my family?*

'I'm waiting for Kitty to see the fishpond,' said a voice nearby, and Laura turned to see a startlingly pretty young woman with lovely auburn hair. She was addressing her comment to Zoe.

'You should be down there when she does see it.' Zoe gave the girl's elbow a squeeze. 'Come on, we can say hello now. The main family's finished. Time for us extras. You too, Laura,' Zoe added, sending Laura a smile.

'Oh, do you think —'

'Sure. Kitty will be dying to meet you. Come on.'

The pretty redhead was called Sally, Laura soon learned, and it seemed Kitty knew her quite well, greeting her like an old friend.

Kitty's daughter, Virginia, introduced Zoe, with just a hint of awkwardness, as 'my stepdaughter'. There was some shy laughter from Zoe and additional explanation from Virginia, which Laura didn't quite catch.

'And you met Zoe's dear little boy, Callum, earlier,' Virginia was saying. 'With his father, Mac.'

After delighted smiles and hugs for Zoe it was Laura's turn to be introduced to Kitty. An uncomfortable weight in her chest made her feel queasy.

Luke, who'd been hovering in the background, stepped forward. 'Gran, this is Laura Langley Fox, the American pilot's daughter, all the way from Boston.'

'Oh!' There was an awkward moment while Kitty stared at Laura with an expression that was both haunted and dignified, but not exactly friendly.

'I'm so very pleased to meet you, Mrs Mathieson.' Laura hadn't been brought up on Beacon Hill without knowing how to be polite and courteous, and now she laid it on thick.

'You've come all this way,' Kitty said. 'I hope it's worth it.'

'You knew Laura's father, didn't you?' cut in Luke.

Kitty gave a dignified nod. 'Yes, I met your father. There were so many Americans out here during the war. Oh, and thank you for sending his letter. I'm pleased to know your father had a successful and happy life after the war.'

It was like being dropped from a great height, Laura realised later. She'd been so tense about meeting Kitty, so on edge, fearing some kind of emotional outburst. But Kitty was either a wonderful actor, or she was no more emotional about Ed Langley than she was about the weather. She might just as easily have said, 'Oh, yes. It was a very wet year in 1942.'

Had only her father cared? Had the impact of their relationship been all one-sided? *Oh, Dad, thank heavens you never guessed.*

So far, so good, Luke thought as people drifted away to leave his grandmother to enjoy her cup of tea and to catch her breath after so much talking.

Soon he would help her go inside for a rest before the party got properly underway. While she rested in the best bedroom with the beautifully restored bay windows, the afternoon would grow cooler, the shadows would lengthen. He'd turn on the lights that Sally and

Bella had strung between the trees outside and most of the guests would change into their party clobber.

Everything was more or less ready. The drinks were on ice, amazing smells were coming from the kitchen, Mac and Gabe had the barbecue plans all in hand, the band was on its way. Their American guest seemed to be fitting in.

'All good,' he said softly to himself just as another car emerged from the trees.

'Here's Jim,' someone called.

Great. The last of the family had arrived. Now they were only waiting for the extra friends who'd been invited and others like the historical committee.

Luke felt a tug at his elbow.

'Who's that?' Laura asked, pointing a well-manicured finger with dark-maroon nail polish.

'Oh, that's my uncle, Jim Mathieson.'

She gripped his elbow again, more tightly this time. 'Kitty's son?'

'Yes, her eldest.'

'Oh my God.'

Luke frowned at Laura. She was probably around his mother's age, not quite as slim but better preserved, with a fine, almost wrinkle-free complexion and dramatic, thick silver hair, stylishly cut and held back from her face by a black velvet band.

'What's the matter?' he asked, seeing the look on her face as she stared slack-jawed at Jim, who was walking towards them with his easy, long-legged gait. Luke had a particular fondness for his eldest uncle, who was seventy but didn't look it, and still worked part-time, because he liked to keep his hand in.

Now, however, a chill snaked down Luke's spine. 'What's wrong?' he demanded again of Laura.

'He —' She began and then stopped to swallow, as if something had stuck in her throat. 'He looks so familiar, almost exactly like —'

She stopped again and clearly she didn't want to finish her sentence.

Luke was about to ask what Laura's problem was when she clamped a hand over her mouth and her eyes filled with tears.

No. Hell, no. Was she about to ruin everything?

31

Townsville, 1942

'There's no doubt about it,' the stern-faced doctor told Kitty. 'You're most definitely pregnant.'

She was still lying on her back, feeling exposed and embarrassed after his unpleasant probing, and now, in the most matter-of-fact tone possible, he'd confirmed her worst fears. The truth she'd suspected, had known deep down for weeks, was now an Inescapable Fact.

She was having Ed Langley's baby.

Only the tiniest corner of Kitty's heart was thrilled. Just once or twice in the past scary weeks, she'd allowed herself to think that this would be the perfect outcome from their island weekend. In those brief moments, she could almost picture a miniature version of Ed and she would feel a little rush of warm, maternal joy. But almost immediately the fantasy would die and she would come to her senses.

Pregnancy was a disaster. It could bring nothing but shame for her. And for Ed, it would be a huge burden and an extra worry when he was fighting this terrible war, putting his life on the line day after day.

Surely nobody would willingly bring a little baby into the world now, in the middle of all this.

In North Queensland, the past month of May had been the worst yet. The skies over Townsville had thundered with the roar of aircraft, while offshore a great naval battle had been waged in the Coral Sea.

The Prime Minister, Mr Curtin, had warned the country to prepare for the worst and had talked of dire consequences if the Allies were not successful. In Townsville the gossip was rife. Everyone knew they shouldn't listen to rumours, but they were all hearing the same horrific stories from neighbours, from workmates, from men who'd been talking at the pub. The boys in the local battalion had been ordered to sharpen their bayonets and to stand guard facing the sea, ready to fight to the death.

In the midst of all this, Kitty had received no word from Ed. As soon as they'd returned from the island, he'd rushed straight off on another mission and she'd heard nothing since. She had absolutely no idea where he was, or if he was safe.

As the doctor turned away to his desk and told her to get dressed, all she wanted to do was cry. She'd been tense about this for six weeks now and she was ready to burst from the stress of it. But she had to cling to her dignity for a little longer, till she was out of the surgery and past the disapproving eye of the snooty receptionist.

Back at Mitchell Street, Elsie took one look at her and demanded to know what had happened. 'Is it bad news about Ed?'

'No!' Kitty wailed and then burst into tears, finally.

'Oh, love, come here,' Elsie soothed, slipping a motherly arm around her. 'Come to the kitchen and I'll put the kettle on.'

Somehow, Kitty made her stumbling, sobbing way down the hall and almost fell into a chair at the kitchen table, where she slumped forward with her head on her arms and cried her heart out.

The kettle had come to the boil and Elsie was filling the teapot by the time her sobs started to ease.

'I'm sorry,' she whimpered, pulling a handkerchief from her pocket and swiping her eyes and blowing her nose.

Elsie's smile was rather frayed around the edges as she set cups and saucers on the table.

But at least Kitty felt a bit braver now that the crying was out of the way. She took a deep breath. 'I'm pregnant,' she said quickly.

A shocked gasp escaped Elsie and she sat down quickly. 'Oh, Kitty.'

'I'm sorry.' Kitty squared her shoulders. 'If you want me to leave here, I'll go. I'll understand.'

'Oh, don't be silly. Of course I don't want you to leave.'

'But people will talk. There'll be gossip and Geoff might hear it. You know what people are saying about single girls who get themselves pregnant, especially to Yanks.'

'Let them say what they like. I'll handle Geoff.' Calmly, Elsie poured tea into a cup and passed it to Kitty. 'I don't have time for people who stick their beaks into other people's business.' Her expression was quite serious now. 'Anyway, you're going to need someone on your side when your grandfather hears about this.'

'I know.' Kitty winced. All along, her biggest fear had been her grandfather. Oh, dear heaven, how could she ever tell him? She had become the harlot he believed her to be. For him, the shame would be unbearable. She would have to stop going to church.

'Here.' Elsie pushed the bowl of sugar towards Kitty. 'Have some. You need it today.'

'Thanks.' Kitty tried to smile as she helped herself to a precious teaspoon of their sugar ration.

'You must have been so worried,' Elsie said. 'Why didn't you tell me?'

'I – I was hoping it was just stress or an upset tummy or some-thing.' Kitty knew this sounded lame. 'But it shouldn't have happened, you see. We, I mean Ed . . . well, he used, you know . . . protection.'

'Well, unfortunately, those things aren't a hundred per cent reliable.' Watching Kitty over the rim of her teacup, Elsie lifted an eyebrow. 'Geoff's living proof.'

'Geoff? Is he really?'

Elsie nodded. 'John and I had a shotgun wedding, and Geoff was a premmie baby.'

'Gosh.'

Across the table, the two women shared a conspiratorial smile and Kitty felt some of her panic subside.

'Well, if my baby's anywhere near as nice as Geoff,' she said, 'everything should be fine.'

Kitty reminded herself later, however, that there probably wouldn't be any wedding for her. To begin with, she was terribly worried about Ed's silence, but even if he was fine, she was almost certain that he had no plans to marry her.

She kept remembering how Bobby had said he was a blueblood and a prince. And then there'd been little things Ed had said.

I come from a family with very high expectations . . .

In our circles . . .

Even on the island he'd voiced concern about how wrong it would be to take her away from all this. It was pretty clear he could not see her fitting into his life in Boston.

Any way Kitty looked at it, her future was grim, but at least she had a few more weeks before the pregnancy would start to show.

There was still no word from Ed in late July when Townsville was bombed. The wardens had been around making house-to-house inspections of everyone's air-raid equipment, but it had all felt like a great deal of fuss about nothing.

Practice warning sirens had been going off, raising goosebumps on everyone's skin, but after the Allied victory in the Coral Sea, it was hard to believe that the Japs might still arrive.

Young Geoff, however, was positive that 'old Tojo still has big plans for Townsville'. The boy was all eyes and ears these days, part of the network of Townsville boys who'd virtually been adopted as junior mascots by the American units.

But when the rising and falling wail of the siren came on a cold, clear Saturday night, Geoff was sound asleep.

'I'd better wake him,' said Elsie, who found Kitty already up and pulling on her dressing-gown. 'This sounds like the real thing.'

Sure enough, minutes later, there were cries out in the street. 'Air raid! Air raid! The sirens are going.'

From the front verandah, they could see the searchlights reaching upwards from the hill behind them and joining the search beams from the Strand and Kissing Point, the white ladders of light sweeping across the sky.

At any moment Kitty expected to hear explosions, the *whoomp* of falling bombs.

Geoff, shivering in his pyjamas, was agog with excitement. 'I can hear the planes!' he said.

'Where?' demanded Kitty.

'Up high. Listen.'

'Oh, yes. Yes, I can hear them.' Of course, she thought of Ed.

A moment later she heard the rattle of distant machine guns and her heart leapt to her throat. *Wherever you are, Ed, please, please stay safe.*

'Come on. Let's get into the shelter.' At least Elsie was sensible.

It was such a cold night they took extra blankets, along with a torch, a thermos of tea and the emergency biscuit tin. But the moon

was so full and bright they didn't really need the torch as they scur-
ried down the back steps and across the yard, past the banana clump
and Elsie's veggie patch, to the shelter her Yanks had built.

'We won't see anything from in there,' complained Geoff.

'Too bad.' Elsie pushed him in ahead of her.

They spent quite some time cramped and uncomfortable and in
the dark, before they heard the sound of an explosion over near the
wharves.

'It was all a bit of a fizzer,' Geoff complained between yawns the
next day. 'You might as well let me sleep through it next time.'

People at the Red Cross were all abuzz, however. The enemy
planes had flown from Rabaul. Someone had heard bombs drop.

'It was like *swish*, *swoosh*, *thump*, *thump* and then a shattering
blast and the ground shook.'

A couple of girls had been out dancing at the Flying Squadron
Hall and they'd had to dive into slit trenches along with American
airmen.

'We were all singing songs.' They made it sound like a great lark.

'There's a crater the size of a truck over in Oonoonba,' said
someone else. 'The top was blown off a palm tree. Lucky the Japs
were off target.'

At home that night, Geoff reported there was a big row brewing, because the commander of the American anti-aircraft guns had
apparently ordered the crews not to fire at the planes for fear of
exposing their positions to a bigger, second flight of bombers.

'There was no second wave and the Yanks are copping it for not
firing a shot,' Geoff added importantly.

Two nights later there was another raid and the defensive fire
from Townsville was deafening. Silver shafts from dozens of searchlights probed the sky.

Again, Geoff was full of knowledge the next day. 'There was so much ack-ack going up last night that the air force couldn't get a crack at the Japs.'

That night, a third attack was finally met by more determined and organised resistance.

They were all a little blasé by now and Kitty watched with Elsie and Geoff from the front verandah, where they saw the searchlight beams catch the outline of a plane's wing or a tail.

'The Yanks are up there in Airocobras,' Geoff told them self-importantly.

'Shh,' warned Elsie, who must have seen the fear in Kitty's face.

32

'Hello there? Anyone home?'

Kitty was in the dirt-floored laundry under the house when a lilting American voice brought her spinning around.

A young man in an American uniform and dark sunglasses appeared in the doorway. 'Excuse me, ma'am. I was hoping to find Kitty Martin.'

He was a typical Yank with blonde hair cut very short and a round, cheery face, and when he took off his sunglasses his eyes were a surprisingly vivid blue. Kitty had never met him before, but she was sure he had come with news about Ed. Her heart began a fretful pounding.

Somehow, she managed to nod. 'I'm Kitty.'

'That's great. Pleased to meet you.'

She didn't offer her hand – it smelled of the kerosene rag she was using to polish the washing copper.

The man didn't seem to mind, however, and he was smiling as he took a step closer. Surely the news couldn't be too bad if he was smiling?

'My name's Frank Harvey,' he said. 'I have a message from Captain Ed Langley.'

Kitty clutched the rim of the copper for support. 'How – how is

Ed?' she managed. 'Where is he?'

'He's safely back here in Townsville, ma'am. We had him flown back from Port Moresby in a C-47.' Frank Harvey's smile reduced to a look that was closer to sympathy. 'But I'm afraid he's been injured.'

Injured. Kitty couldn't stop her imagination from flashing to horrible images of missing limbs, masses of blood, agonising pain. Her stomach was almost constantly on the edge of nausea these days and now it gave a fearful lurch. She prayed she wouldn't be sick in front of this stranger.

She forced herself to ask, 'How bad is it?'

Frank Harvey made a seesawing action with his hand and then he glanced quickly behind him, apparently fascinated by the line of sheets and towels she'd just pegged out. His gaze took in the rows of beans, newly planted in the veggie plot, the huge mango tree hanging over the fence from the neighbour's.

'Ed has a serious head injury,' he said gently. 'His sight has been affected.'

His sight?

So many times Kitty had worried about Ed, picturing numerous terrible scenarios, but she'd never allowed herself to imagine *this*. She took a deep, very necessary breath. 'Would I be able to see him? Could I visit?'

'Yes, ma'am, you certainly can, and I'd be happy to take you.' Frank Harvey's voice was warm and lilting, his accent quite different from Ed's. 'Are you free to go now?' he asked with a smile. 'I have a jeep handy.'

'Of course.' The ironing could wait, as could all the other questions Kitty was dying to ask. She glanced down at the smelly kerosene rag in her hand, at her patched, hand-knitted cardigan and old, faded dress. 'I just need to get cleaned up and changed. I can be quick. Five minutes?'

'That would be fine. Perfect.'

Perfect? How could anything be perfect if Ed was injured? 'Come upstairs then,' Kitty said. 'Would you like a cup of tea?'

'No, no, I'm fine, thanks.'

Frank followed her up the steep back stairs, ducking his head beneath the dangling leaves of the pawpaw tree that shaded the back porch, then through the kitchen to the lounge room.

'Make yourself comfortable,' Kitty said. 'I'll be back in a flash.'

Flying to the bathroom, she washed her hands and face and under her arms, hastily patted herself dry with a towel, and sprinkled a little talcum powder. In her bedroom, she slipped a green linen dress with a scalloped neckline from its hanger. Ed had particularly liked this dress and her lined tartan jacket went well with it.

But she was dragging a comb through her hair when she remembered – if Ed's sight was affected, it didn't really matter what she wore.

The realisation caught her mid-chest, knocking the air from her. Why hadn't she asked Frank for more details? Was Ed actually *blind*? Might he never see again?

Her mind spun in panic as she pictured his lovely dark eyes . . . sightless. He would never be able to fly again. There were so many things he wouldn't see . . .

She remembered the delight he'd taken in the beauty of the island, but now he might never see the sky or the sea . . . sunsets or gardens . . .

He might never see their baby.

Stay calm.

She couldn't give in to fear now or she would dissolve into a sobbing, useless heap. It wasn't just a matter of pride – she had to stay calm for Ed's sake.

After another deep breath, she picked up her handbag and gloves, straightened her shoulders and went back to the lounge room, where she found Frank Harvey reading one of Geoff's comics. He gave a sheepish smile and dropped the comic book quickly onto the couch before leaping to his feet.

'Wow, that was a mighty quick transformation. All set to go?'

'Yes, thanks.'

With the typical politeness she'd learned to expect from an American, he gave a slight bow of his head as he gestured for her to go ahead of him. His jeep was parked at the end of the street, beyond the barbed-wire entanglements, and as they walked down the footpath together, Kitty knew some of the neighbours were watching from their shuttered verandahs. She ignored them and kept her chin high.

The jeep took off, roaring around the base of Castle Hill, and she had to raise her voice to be heard. 'Can you tell me about Ed's accident? Did you say it happened in New Guinea? Was – was he shot down?'

'More like shot up,' Frank shouted back. 'Ed was about to take off from a forward airstrip when the Nips pulled a surprise attack on the airfield. He was still on the ground when they strafed him.' Frank's customary smile shrank to a grimace now. 'A piece of shrapnel lodged in his head.'

Kitty closed her eyes, too horrified to speak.

When they stopped at an intersection, Frank spoke again. 'Apart from the head wound, Ed's actually not too bad, but I must admit we're worried about the problem with his sight.'

'He – he's not completely blind, is he?'

'I'm afraid he is, ma'am, for the time being, at least. It's hard to know how it'll turn out. He's going home. We know that much.'

Going home.

Kitty went cold. She was pregnant with Ed's baby and he was going home.

Of course, he needed the best medical treatment. But going

home . . . home to Boston . . . to the other side of the world? Home to his rich and highly cultured, strict and snobbish family. Kitty had to bite down hard on her lip to stop herself from weeping.

Despite Elsie's kindness, she'd felt lost and alone ever since her pregnancy was confirmed, but she'd clung to the hope that some day, somehow, she would be able to share her news with Ed. In her fantasy, Ed was delighted and sweet about the baby, vowing that he would move heaven and earth to make sure his future was with her and their child.

But that might not be possible now. Could she tell Ed about the pregnancy when he'd been dealt such a terrible blow?

'We're heading over to Fulham Road,' Frank said as they took off again and he steered the jeep around a machine gun rising from an island of camouflage netting. 'There's a house over thereabouts that's been commandeered as the central sick quarters for all the squadrons based at Garbutt.'

'I think I know the place. It's probably the Fergusons' house.'

'Curra-something House?'

'Currajong House.'

'Yeah, that sounds right.'

Kitty nodded. Mr and Mrs Ferguson, who owned Currajong House, were friends of her grandparents. She'd been incredibly impressed when they offered the use of their beautiful historic home to the parish of St Matthew almost as soon as the war began. Originally, they'd planned to house refugee children, but then, tragically, the ship bringing the children out from London to Australia had been torpedoed by the Germans.

Kitty's grandmother had wept when that news came through.

And now, Ed was being treated there.

She longed to see him, but she was scared. She only hoped she was strong enough. The last thing Ed needed was a hysterical girl sobbing all over him.

She hated this war, hated, hated, *hated* it. It had been going on for such a long time already, claiming and maiming millions of lives in Europe and Asia, and now it was here in the Pacific, casting its poison on people she knew and loved. Andy Mathieson was still missing, poor Bobby had died and now Ed was *blind*.

She wasn't sure how much more she could take, not with the baby as well. It was all too sad and too overwhelming.

However, as Frank pulled up outside the Fergusons' low-set, colonial-style home, now converted to a hospital, she had no choice. She had to be super-strong.

'Last time I was here, Ed was on the verandah,' Frank said as he opened the jeep's door for her. 'The dangerously ill patients are inside the house.'

Then he leaned back against the jeep, and casually lit a cigarette.

'Aren't you coming?' Kitty had been depending on Frank's polite support to at least help her to find Ed.

But he simply smiled at her. 'I figured Captain Langley would like as much privacy as possible.'

'Oh?' Kitty could feel her cheeks heating. She supposed she should be grateful for Frank's discretion, but she couldn't believe how nervous she felt about seeing Ed injured amid a sea of strangers. 'Well, thank you for the lift.'

Frank gave a smiling nod. 'I'll be waiting here, ready to transport you home.'

She was shaky and trembling as she walked the path to the short flight of front steps. There was no reception area, no sign of a friendly nurse who might help her to locate Ed, just rows of men in beds lined along the verandahs, which had been closed in with blinds and flyscreens.

Some of the men were asleep, but many of them turned to stare at Kitty. A few faces broke into broad grins.

'Hello, love,' called a cheeky fellow with a drawling Australian accent. He lifted the sheet that covered him and sent her a wink. 'Have you come to check out my wound?'

'Here's a sight for sore eyes,' said another.

Kitty knew there was no real offence intended by these Aussies. No doubt they expected some banter in return. But she was in no mood to think of a smart remark. Luckily, she was saved when another of the Aussie patients chimed in.

'Don't be fooled by our wounded hero, miss. He probably cut himself opening a tin of bully beef.'

Kitty joined in the laughter, but she had to keep going. She had to find Ed.

After an unsuccessful trip up and down the verandahs, however, she decided that he mustn't be in this ward after all. Perhaps he was now dangerously ill. *Please, God, no.* She would have to find one of the medical staff and ask if Captain Langley been moved.

Then, as she turned to leave the verandah, she caught sight of a man in the far corner. She'd missed him before, perhaps because he was sitting on the side of his bed with his back to her. There was a thick bandage around his head, but she was sure she recognised his dark and shiny hair.

He had to be Ed, but the sight of him sitting there hunched and alone made her chest ache. Despite her vow to be strong, she was already fighting tears as she made her way back between the rows of beds.

'Ed?' she said softly when she reached him.

He tensed instantly and turned to her voice. 'Kitty?'

'Yes.' Her voice was trembling. She was trembling all over. It broke her heart to see Ed sitting there in Red Cross pyjamas, looking completely vulnerable with his eyes bandaged and his dark jaw in need of a shave.

He held out his hand. 'Thanks for coming, Kitty.'

'Try to keep me away.'

She tried to sound cheerful, but a painful brick had lodged in her throat as she looked down at the hand he held out. His hands were long and beautifully shaped – aesthetically pleasing, aristocratic hands, hands that an artist might want to paint. But her head was full of memories of the way he'd touched and caressed her.

Now, when he touched her hand he smiled. 'Can we get rid of the gloves?'

'Of course.' Tears stung her eyes as she slipped them off and then placed her hand into his. He grasped her firmly, wrapping his fingers around hers, so she could feel his skin, warm against hers.

'Sit down,' he said, giving her a slight tug towards the mattress beside him.

'Is it allowed?'

Ed's mouth tilted in another smile. 'Who cares?'

Kitty wanted to smile and cry at once as she sat with her hand still in his. But now, so close, she wanted to curl into his arms, to press her lips to his poor bandaged face. 'I'm so sorry you've been hurt, Ed.'

'Yeah, it's damned frustrating.' He sighed. 'Did Frank tell you there's damage to the optic nerve?'

'He did, yes. And he said they're sending you home.'

His hand tightened around hers. 'There's not much they can do for me here. I just need time to rest and to heal, and they seem to think I'll be better off doing that stateside.'

Kitty clung to the word 'heal'. 'But they think you'll get your sight back?'

'At this stage, there's no guarantee.'

'Oh, Ed.' She was glad he couldn't see the way her face contorted with the effort of holding back her tears. 'Will you be in a hospital over there, or with your family?'

'I'm not sure. A bit of both, I expect.'

His thumb rode over her knuckles, offering her momentary

comfort and reminding her of another time when he'd taken her hand like this . . .

On the island . . . lying in bed in the mauve-tinted shadows of the late afternoon . . . they'd listened to the distant rhythm of the sea and the occasional shriek of a lorikeet, the rustle of palm fronds outside the hut's walls . . . and Ed had lifted her hand to his lips.

He'd kissed each knuckle slowly one by one, as if each little bony bump was precious.

'This one's my favourite,' he said, re-kissing the knuckle of her index finger. 'I'm sure it's the sexiest.'

They'd laughed together at the silliness, and then Ed had paid the same loving attention to her fingertips.

It had been such a simple thing really, the way he'd made love to her hand, and yet Kitty had known in that moment that she would remember it forever.

Do not cry. Whatever he says or does, don't cry. Just don't.

'Kitty, I'm sorry about this.' Ed spoke softly, and she realised then that he hadn't asked her to sit so they were touching. It was so he could talk to her without being overheard. 'There are so many things I want to tell you. So much I want to say that I can't.'

Please, tell me. Don't leave the important things unsaid.

She needed him to talk about their future, after the war. She wanted him to assure her that he would make contact again, that he would come back for her. Send for her.

'You can tell me anything, Ed.'

His throat worked. 'But I can't make any promises. Not when I'm like this.'

She wanted to protest. It doesn't matter, she wanted to assure him, and her throat burned with everything she needed to say. She would still love Ed if he was permanently blind. She would see for both of them.

And yet . . . unbearable as it was, she understood his silence.

He was worried about saddling her with his blindness . . . just as she was worried about saddling him with their baby.

Now she shivered as cold certainty descended like a shroud. Ed was going home and the baby would be her burden. Hers alone. Ed had enough problems. She couldn't load him with another.

The tears she'd been fighting spilled now and she had to blink madly. She'd come here today with so much hope. She'd planned to declare her love for Ed, but now the doubts crowded in. Did she have the right to talk of love? Was she entitled, after such a brief courtship, to lay claim to Captain Ed Langley?

Once again, he tightened his grasp on her hand. 'I want you to know that whatever happens, I'll never forget you, Kitty.'

The finality of this drove ice splinters through her heart. 'Don't talk like that.'

He lifted his hand to her face, traced the shape of her cheek. His fingers found her tears and he gave a soft groan, but he didn't offer the words she longed to hear. Instead, he sat with his lips pressed tightly together, as if he was afraid to speak.

Was he afraid of letting his emotions escape?

A horrible silence crawled by and Kitty was sure she could hear her heart beating in her ears. She thought again about the baby, Ed's baby, *their baby*, curled like a new fern frond deep within her womb.

She tried to picture Ed back in Boston, but the images were hazy. She had no real idea what it was like over there.

She thought about the long, difficult months ahead and the scorn and gossip she would face from certain quarters, as well as her grandfather's wrath.

When Ed's voice broke into her morbid thoughts she jumped.

'Thanks so much for coming,' he said quietly. 'I would have hated to leave without saying goodbye to you.'

So this was it. Goodbye. *The end*.

'Just get better,' she urged in a tight, choked voice.

'I'll do my best.'

Kitty waited for him to add an extra reassurance. When he was better, or when the war was over, he'd come back to find her.

Instead, he put his arms around her and kissed her. To her surprise, instead of clinging to him, she was glad they were sitting and not pressing close. It meant there was no risk of his feeling the little bump.

The important words were left unsaid.

Outside, the sunlight was too bright after the shade on the verandah. Kitty stood on the front steps and found a handkerchief to wipe her eyes and blow her nose. She would fall to pieces when she got back to Mitchell Street, but for now, with Frank Harvey, she had to keep up a brave face.

Frank was waiting by his jeep as promised. 'All good to go?' he asked her kindly.

Kitty nodded. 'Yes, thanks.'

She was glad he didn't try to make conversation as he drove her back to North Ward. No doubt she looked all pale and blotchy and he wasn't sure what to say.

Once again, he parked at the end of Mitchell Street.

'Thanks so much,' Kitty told him. 'It was very kind of you to give up your morning.'

'My pleasure, ma'am. Would you like me to escort you to your door? I'd be only too happy.'

Kitty remembered the eyes spying on them earlier. Frank had probably noticed them too. 'Thanks,' she said, 'but I'll be fine.'

Ever polite, he hurried to open the jeep's door for her.

Kitty held out her hand. 'Thanks again. It was nice to meet you, Frank.' And then, as she stepped away to the kerb, 'I never asked you: is Ed a friend of yours?'

'Well, ma'am, I'm just a corporal and he's a captain, my superior officer, but he's a good'un. I suppose we're about as friendly as our ranks permit.' His mouth tilted in a lopsided grin. 'We call him the prince behind his back.'

Yes, I know, she wanted to say. Bobby Kowalski told me that. She couldn't return his smile. This last revelation only made the gap between her and Ed feel wider than ever. 'What part of America are you from?' she asked.

'I'm from Georgia, ma'am. Clayton County, Georgia.'

'That's not near Boston, is it?'

Frank chuckled. 'Not at all. Georgia's in the south, a long ways south. Have you seen the movie *Gone with the Wind*?'

'Yes, of course. I *loved* it.' After a beat, she frowned. 'It's hotter in the south, isn't it? The climate's more like it is here in North Queensland?'

Frank gave a slow nod. 'Georgia's more like these parts than Boston is, that's for sure.'

Kitty almost wished she hadn't asked. Again she was remembering the conversation with Ed on the island.

What are you thinking about now?

About you. About how wrong it would be to take you away from all this.

33

Moonlight Plains, 2013

I shouldn't have come here. I knew it was a mistake.

The possibility that her trip to Australia could end badly had been gnawing at Laura ever since she'd left Boston, and now that she'd seen Kitty Mathieson's eldest son, she was damn sure she should have stayed safely at home.

As soon as the man unfolded his lanky frame from his vehicle, she was chilled by a sense of foreboding. And that was before she'd taken in details like his silver-flecked dark hair, his handsome face and intelligent dark eyes that were uncannily familiar.

Her first instinct was denial. Her mind must be playing tricks on her. She was on edge, too tense, too invested after trying to read between the lines in her father's letters. This was nothing more than a strange coincidence.

She had to get a grip. And yet . . .

And yet, those eyes, that distinctive profile, the way he held his shoulders . . .

The likeness was so close.

Too close?

Laura was trembling like jello as she watched Kitty's son kiss his mother and his sister, and then several nieces. He could have been close on seventy, although he didn't really seem that old. His manner was very easy and relaxed as he chatted with his brothers and their wives. After what felt like several ice ages, he turned ever so casually to Laura.

This time, Luke didn't rush to introduce her, as he had with other family members.

The man introduced himself. 'Hi, I'm Jim Mathieson. And you must be our special guest from America.'

He politely waited for Laura to offer her hand, and when she did his grasp was warm.

'Laura Langley Fox,' she said in little more than a whisper.

Jim Mathieson nodded. 'I understand you're Ed Langley's daughter?'

'Th-that's right. And I have t-two brothers.' Why on earth had she mentioned her brothers first up? It must have sounded so weird. But it had been a defensive impulse. Now that she was this close there could be no doubt. This man *had* to be *her* father's son.

Oh, Dad, what have I done? I'm so sorry . . .

If she wasn't careful she would blurt out something totally inappropriate. It would be unforgivable to upset this close-knit family when she was their guest.

Jim's dark-eyed gaze held hers for a shade too long, cautiously reckoning . . .

He knows. Oh, God, he knows. Laura's heart leapt into her throat.

Fearfully, she turned to see how Kitty was reacting to this awkward meeting and she discovered that Luke was already shepherding his grandmother out of the way. With a strong arm around her, his shoulders hunched protectively, he was shielding the tiny old lady as he helped her up the steps and into the homestead.

Does Luke know too? Does everyone here know?

They couldn't. Surely someone would have mentioned it before now.

Jim was also watching his mother's departure and he gave a thoughtful frown, before quickly switching his gaze to Laura again and smiling.

'I'd like to speak to you about Ed Langley,' he said quietly. 'Would you mind?'

The trembling started again and at first Laura couldn't squeeze a reply past the painful tightness in her throat.

'I wonder if anyone has shown you where his plane crashed,' Jim said.

'No, not yet.'

She wondered if he was planning to take her aside and clear the air with her. Tell her the truth. Although the thought still scared her – *terrified* her – she desperately needed answers . . .

Laura straightened her shoulders. She sensed an inner strength in this man that she wanted to match. 'I'd really like to see the crash site.'

Jim touched her ever so lightly on the elbow and smiled. It was a charming smile, a little like her brother Charlie's. 'I guess I shouldn't rush straight off,' he said. 'I need to say g'day to a few of the other folk here and you probably haven't met them all yet, but if there's a bit of free time while everyone's still arriving, we could mosey over to the site. It isn't far away.'

'This is just lovely,' Kitty said as she made herself comfortable on the bed with the pretty floral quilt that Sally had ordered online. 'Perfect. Thank you, Luke.'

Luke, setting her pills and a glass of water beside her, felt a surge of relief, until he saw a telling look in his grandmother's eyes that suggested she might have guessed what lay behind his unseemly interest in hurrying her in here to rest.

He swallowed uneasily. He hadn't known what to make of Laura's reaction to Jim's arrival. If he hadn't been standing next to her, he probably wouldn't have noticed the sudden tension that engulfed her, but it was almost as if she'd recognised Jim. Or at least she thought she had. And that could only mean . . .

Luke couldn't let his mind go there, not now, on the brink of hosting his big party. He didn't want to delve into what her reaction might mean, or how it implicated his grandmother.

And yet he couldn't help remembering how tense his grandmother had been whenever the World War II connection came up. He still had no idea why it bothered her, but today, when he'd heard Laura's shocked gasp and had seen where her tense reaction was directed, his first instinct had been to whisk his grandmother away from a scene that was potentially awkward and, quite possibly, disastrous.

'This room is beautiful,' his grandmother said now, looking around at the pale-lemon walls and the white trim in the bay window, the subtle blend of white and cream in the curtains and cushions. 'So fresh and pretty.' Her smile was almost coy. 'Did Sally come up with the colour scheme?'

Luke felt his ears go red. He cleared his throat. 'She – ah – made a few suggestions.'

His grandmother's smile broadened. 'You've done an amazing job, darling. I think the homestead is lovelier now than it ever was. You've brought it up to date and made it very liveable, but you haven't messed with its original character.' She looked around her again, at the ornate ceiling rosette, the carefully restored window seat, the intricate timber carving of the breezeway above the door and her blue eyes sparkled extra brightly. 'Andy would have been so proud of you, Luke.'

At the mention of his grandfather, Luke's throat constricted. Had she any idea how much those words meant to him?

'I – ah – had to put Granddad's tools to good use,' he said

gruffly, backing towards the door. 'You get some rest now, okay? I hope there won't be too much noise outside.'

'I'll be fine, thanks.' Already she was settling into the pillows, stretching her stockinged feet. 'This is lovely.'

Luke was gently closing the door when footsteps sounded in the hallway. He turned to find Sally carrying a basket of cutlery.

He was glad that she had been mixing in well with his family and getting on famously with each and every one of them. His bright idea to pretend they were mere acquaintances seemed to be working. But it was hard, *damned* hard to carry on calmly, as if Sally's auburn-haired, brown-eyed loveliness wasn't driving him wild.

He was continuously conscious of her. All day, his antenna had been constantly tuned to her frequency, and it didn't help that Sally seemed as thrown by his sudden appearance now as he was by hers.

'Hi,' she said almost shyly. Pink stained her cheeks as she held out the basket. 'I was just taking these outside.' Then she gave a shy little laugh. 'As if you couldn't guess.'

'You've been a great help.' Such a lame thing to say.

Neither of them moved and the air between them seemed to thicken and sizzle.

'Is Kitty in there?' Sally lowered her voice as she nodded towards the bedroom door.

'Yeah, she's resting.' Luke swallowed. 'She loves the colour scheme you chose, by the way.'

The pink in Sally's cheeks deepened. 'That's great.'

He wanted to kiss her. Here. Right now. He wanted to grab the cutlery basket and dump it on a bookcase, the floor, anywhere. Wanted to back Sally against the wall, trapping her with his hands as he kissed her . . . tasted her, sucked, nibbled and sipped . . . as he lost himself in her devastating sweetness . . .

She was, apparently, saying something.

Luke blinked. 'Excuse me?'

Sally was watching him closely now and a puzzled frown made a crease between her brows. 'Is everything okay, Luke?'

'Of course. Why?'

'You seem distracted.' She gave a little shrug. 'I was just saying that the plans for the party seem to be going smoothly. As far as the kitchen's concerned, at least, everything's on track.'

'That's great.' With a supreme effort, he collected his wits. 'As I said, you're doing an ace job.'

'Zoe's a cooking sensation. You're going to love the food.'

Stuff the food. Luke needed Sally. Now. In his arms. He took a step towards her.

'Oh, that's where you've got to,' cried a voice behind them. 'I've been looking for you, Luke.'

He spun around to find Bella in the front doorway.

'I think you'd better come,' she called. 'There's been a problem with the band.'

In the year before her divorce, Laura had taken up yoga, hoping that the deep breathing and guided meditations would help her to weather the emotional storms of those tempestuous months. Now, as she walked with Jim Mathieson across a paddock towards her father's crash site on Moonlight Plains, she tried to regenerate those deep and steadying breaths.

'It's not too surprising that Ed and his buddy crashed here,' Jim was telling her. 'We know now that around three hundred Allied planes crashed in North Queensland during the war.'

'Three hundred? I had no idea. What happened? Were they shot down?'

'No, they were straightforward crashes.'

'But that seems incredible. Why were there so many?'

'Take your pick of reasons. This is a big state, so there were vast distances to cover. Throw in bad weather, inexperienced pilots, planes damaged in combat and inadequate radio systems, and there were bound to be casualties.'

They'd reached a barbed-wire fence and beyond it stretched another paddock bordered by a stand of gum trees. Jim used a booted foot to hold down the lowest wire while he lifted the higher ones to make a gap for Laura. 'Can you get through here?'

'Thank you.' She was glad she wasn't wearing a dress as she stooped and climbed gingerly through. 'Can I hold it for you?'

'No need, thanks.' Jim's legs were so long he was able to hold down the top wire and swing over the fence easily.

Laura imagined her father doing that when he was here all those years ago. He and Kitty must have come across this very paddock, carrying Bobby Kowalski.

Her father and Kitty . . .

Laura still wasn't sure she could cope with this.

'This is where your father landed,' Jim said, pointing to a patch of open grassy ground that was dotted with yellow wildflowers and cowpats. 'And Kowalski crashed over there,' he added, indicating the trees.

Laura thought of her father's letters and the terrible guilt he'd carried for years after Bobby Kowalski's death.

I was pig-headed. I decided to push on. I thought I had just enough fuel to reach Townsville.

She tried to picture her father, barely twenty-one, flying his tiny plane back from New Guinea and being blown off course. She could see him landing at dusk in this alien corner of the outback, so far from the base, while his buddy crashed and was mortally wounded and a brave young slip of a girl carried a lantern as she hurried towards them through the darkness . . .

The description from the letters had been like something out of a movie.

'Are you okay, Laura?'

She looked up into Jim Mathieson's handsome face. *So hauntingly familiar . . .*

'I'm worried that I've made a mistake coming here.' She felt as if she was intruding into something very private. Had she the right to pry into seventy-year-old secrets? And yet she felt compelled to speak up. 'I suspect there's more to my father's history than I'd ever dreamed, but I – I don't know if —'

She couldn't finish the sentence. She could very well spoil a happy family occasion with her pesky curiosity.

'I was wondering how much your father told you,' Jim said quietly.

'That's the trouble. He told us nothing. It was almost as if he was never in the war.'

She wouldn't tell Jim about the letters, certainly not yet. But she was shaking now, shaking with emotion, with fear and tension. She pressed three fingers to her trembling lips and drew a deep breath.

Jim was watching her carefully and she thought she caught a flash of sympathy in his eyes.

She felt emboldened to ask, 'Am I right in guessing that you have a story to tell?'

He gave a faint nod. 'I do . . . but I'd only speak up if I thought you wanted to hear it.'

'I – I think I need to hear the truth.' *Even though I might not like it.*

Now Jim smiled, reminding her again of her brother Charlie. Even his choice of dress, a blue shirt with the long sleeves rolled back, combined with pale-cream jeans and well-polished riding boots, reminded her of Charlie's roving reporter garb – a clever mix of casual and smart, ready for action.

'We may as well take a seat.' Already Jim was crossing to a fallen log, giving it a kick, and then breaking off a small branch from a sapling and using its leaves to flick away ants and loose pieces of bark.

He was quite the gentleman. Laura might have smiled if she wasn't so nervous. As they sat together, side by side, Jim leaned forward with his hands loosely clasped and his elbows resting on his knees.

Around them, the grass and the bush buzzed with insects, and Laura reminded herself that she must remember to breathe. It helped that Jim's rather penetrating gaze was now focused on a clump of grass a few feet away.

'My dad – that's Kitty's husband, Andy Mathieson – told me the truth in 1964, on my twenty-first birthday.'

The truth. Laura's stomach churned uncomfortably.

'As you know, in the sixties we weren't considered adults until we hit twenty-one, so in my dad's eyes, that was the day I became a man. He was like the rest of his generation – very conservative, not someone to be challenged by his kids – but around that time, we were having our first real disagreement. I'd done well at school and I'd spent a few years working on the property, but I was keen to go off to Brisbane to university, to study law. He wasn't happy.'

'I guess it would have been expensive to send you off to law school.' It was the only explanation Laura could think of. Why else would his father object? Where she came from, fathers *boasted* about their law graduate sons.

'Well, Dad had made a big shift when Mum inherited Moonlight Plains. He left his work as a carpenter in Townsville to become a cattleman, but he really took to the life, and he raised all of us to be handy bush kids. Riding, cattle work, mending fences, mustering. You name it, we could do it. Then, at my twenty-first, he pulled me aside and asked if I was really sure about giving up the bush for law. I reminded him I'd always loved books. At boarding school I'd loved debates and even a bit of theatre. I wanted something different from cattle and mustering camps.'

Jim kicked at a stone with his boot and Laura studied his profile. His face was a little longer than her father's, his nose sharper, but he had the strong Langley cheekbones.

'I expected Dad to blue about it,' he said. 'But he just nodded and gave me this strange look. And he told me to take a walk with him.'

Laura found herself leaning forward, tense as a tripwire.

'I thought it was a bit weird,' Jim said. 'I wanted to ask him what was going on, but I more or less sensed I should just shut up. Dad said he needed to show me something and he brought me here.'

'To this crash site?' she whispered, fearing what must come next.

Jim nodded, but he kept his gaze fixed dead ahead. 'He put his arm around my shoulders and he pointed to the pieces of charred metal.' Jim's throat worked as he swallowed. 'He said, that's where your mum helped to pull your father's mate out of the wreckage.'

'Oh my God.'

'And he told me that over there a bit was where my father landed.'

So there it was, the brutal truth, spoken so calmly, and now out in the open.

'You – you must have been so shocked,' she said.

'I was. It was a terrible shock, but in some ways it was a relief, too. I'd always felt a bit different. And there was something about the way Dad told me the story, with his arm around me – I don't know – I could feel his love and that helped so much.'

Tears burned in Laura's eyes, but instead of weeping, she felt strangely numb. She supposed her true reaction would come later, but for now, she was pleasantly surprised by her composure.

'I knew it, as soon as I saw you,' she said. 'You're even more like my father than my brothers are.'

A corner of Jim's mouth flickered as he attempted to smile and failed. In the distance, a crow called its universal cry. *Ark, ark, ark.*

Laura shifted her foot away from a line of ants that trailed dangerously close. 'My father was wounded in New Guinea,' she said. 'He was blinded and shipped home to the States. He was lucky and later recovered his sight, but I guess —' She shrugged and then said, softly, 'Jim, I don't think he ever knew about you.'

'I'd say you're probably right.'

'Do you mind?'

He gave his jaw a thoughtful scratch and then offered her a sad, sideways grin. 'On and off, I've been curious, but I can't say I've *really* minded – not till now, at any rate.'

'I'm sorry if I've stirred things up.'

He turned now, letting his dark gaze rest on her, as if he was taking in details. Searching for a deeper connection? 'I'm glad you came. It means a lot to have met you.'

'And I'm glad to meet *you*.' The tears came now and she swiped at them roughly.

In the trees nearby, birds began to squabble. A family of kangaroos hopped quietly out of the shadows and began to nibble at dry stubbled grass. Laura saw them in numbed amazement.

'Are you married?' she found herself asking Jim.

He shook his head. 'Divorced.'

'Oh, really? Me too.'

They shared another shaky smile.

'And yet my parents were very happily married.' She felt it was important to tell him this.

'So were mine,' he said softly.

'So Ed and Kitty were both lucky then.'

'They were either lucky or they worked damn hard at their marriages.'

In a tree nearby, a bird cried a warning note. The kangaroos stopped grazing and went very still, ears pricked. Then they took off, bounding away on their astonishing long, hinged back legs.

'They're so cool,' Laura said.

'Have you seen roos before?'

'No. This is a bonus. But sorry, I distracted you. I don't think you finished your story. I'm curious about Kitty. It must have been so hard for her to be pregnant and alone in the middle of a war.'

'Yes, I'm sure it was. But the way Dad told it, he'd always been sweet on her even when they were young. Then he went off to fight and he was missing in action, and everyone at home thought he was dead. He and two mates spent a couple of months in the jungle behind enemy lines, and he reckoned the only thing that kept him going was the thought of Mum. Apparently, he was mad with himself for not standing up to her grandfather and marrying her before he enlisted.'

'Really?' So Kitty had already been on the brink of an engagement? This was a new twist. And then her father had met young Kitty and swept her off her feet, and vice versa.

'Anyway,' Jim went on, 'Dad was in bad shape by the time he got back to his lines. He was in hospital up there for a while and then shipped back to Townsville for a spot of leave. He said it was fate to be sent straight back home for a second chance with his girl.'

'I'm guessing Kitty was already pregnant by then?'

'She was, yes. Apparently, Dad knew or was told that he wasn't the father, but he told me he hadn't cared. I challenged him on that. Most blokes wouldn't be interested in marrying a woman who was carrying someone else's child. But he reckoned he'd made a pact with God while he was up in the islands. If he survived, he would come back and make sure Kitty understood how much he loved her.'

'Wow.' In a weird kind of way, it was beginning to make sense, the pieces fitting together like patches in a crazy quilt. 'And you learned all this at twenty-one?'

Jim nodded.

'Weren't you upset? Angry?'

'Sure, but then again, not as much as you'd expect. As I said, Dad told his story so calmly and patiently, I felt strangely okay about it. Of course, I wanted to know all about my American father, but he could only tell me that the Yank pilot was injured and sent back to the States. Dad said he was a decent man, but he never knew about me.' Jim shrugged. 'The rest was Mum's business.'

'You must have been curious.'

'Yes, I was, but Dad asked me to promise two things. Not to pester Mum about it and, more importantly, not to go chasing after my American father while Mum was still alive.'

The ants were back, threatening to climb Laura's leg. She moved again, crossing her legs. 'Your father – Andy – must have been incredibly tolerant.'

'I'm not sure tolerant is the right word. That suggests he endured something he wasn't totally happy with, but I never saw any evidence of that. Dad was a good man. We might question his decision, but for him it was the right thing to do. He said you'd have to experience a war to know how it can change your life in ways you'd never imagine.'

Laura thought about her father's letters and the turmoil of thoughts and emotions revealed there that he'd never shared with his family. 'Perhaps that's why my father and your mother both made successes of their marriages,' she said, thinking aloud. 'After living through the war, they knew the true value of peace and – and family.'

'I'm sure it didn't happen overnight, but from my earliest memories my parents seemed to be happy. They were not only good parents, but they also seemed to love each other deeply. It was so obvious to all of us kids.'

'The real thing?' Laura asked softly.

'Well, I reckon it can't be faked. Maybe for a while, but not in the long term. I've worked in family law for long enough to know that, and I've suffered my own failed marriage.' Jim noticed the ants and scowled. 'This isn't such a good seat after all,' he said, jumping to his feet.

Laura stood too, and dusted off her capri pants.

'I guess we should get back.' Jim squinted at the sun, which seemed to be sliding rather quickly now to the west. 'We'll arouse suspicion if we're away too long.'

Once again, he held the wires while Laura climbed through the fence, and together they crossed the paddock.

'So, does anyone here know the truth about my father, other than Kitty and you?' she asked.

Jim shook his head. 'I've kept my word. And I think that keeping it private made us closer – Dad, Mum and me.'

'And I'm guessing that you certainly wouldn't want it out in the open now.'

'Not at this party, hell no.' Jim stopped walking and stood with his hands propped loosely on his hips. 'Look, it's been a secret, Laura, but not a dark secret. I've lived with it for fifty years now and it hasn't been a huge burden. I was happy enough to tell you, because – I don't know – perhaps there's a touch of fate in all this. But I plan to keep my promise and I hope you'll respect that.'

'Of course.' She was still surprised by how calm she felt about this news. Perhaps it was the way Jim had shared it. For some reason she felt lighter. 'What about Kitty? She knows we've met, so she'll be wondering, won't she?'

'Yes, and I don't want to stress her. I suggest we go straight back to the homestead now and put her mind at rest.'

34

The afternoon was sliding towards dusk and Moonlight Plains was coming into its own. The long trestle tables on the lawn were now covered with white cloths and laden with plates, cutlery and rows of shiny wine glasses waiting to be filled.

The coloured paper lanterns that Bella had strung in the trees near the dance floor glowed softly in the purpling light as everyone dispersed to the homestead or to their tents to change into their party clothes.

Sally and Megan were sharing a tent, as predicted, and Sally had barely opened the flap when Megan began firing her questions.

'I thought everything was fine and dandy between you and Luke.'

'It is.'

'Really?' The scepticism in Megan's tone was hard to miss.

'I thought I told you. We're keeping a low profile today, so Luke's family don't get the wrong idea about us.'

Megan's eyebrows took a hike. 'What wrong idea would that be again?'

'Don't be dense, Megs. Luke doesn't want his mother or his

sisters to think we're too serious.'

'But why?'

'Because we're not bloody serious.' Sally snapped this a little more brusquely than she'd intended. Keeping up the pretence
with Luke had been a source of nonstop tension for her today, but
she wasn't prepared to admit it. 'I agreed with Luke. I think it's a
perfectly sensible plan. We don't want everyone jumping to conclusions. It's bad enough having you and my parents watching me like
a hawk.'

At this, Megan pouted, then poked her jaw stubbornly forward.
'Pity,' she said. 'I really like Zoe and Bella. I think the whole family's
nice. And Luke seems like a really great guy.'

He is, Sally wanted to moan. He is, believe me.

'Really nice and extremely hot,' Megan added for good measure.

And that was when Sally almost caved in and admitted that
she was *not* having a good time. Sure, she understood that Luke
had come up with their subterfuge to protect her from his family's
embarrassing assumptions and questions, and that was considerate
of him. But still. *Honestly.* How could she have guessed it would be
so hard to pretend that the two of them weren't an item?

Which begged the question: what *was* their status? Truly?
Friends with benefits? Two casual lovers who hadn't discussed a
future beyond the end of this project?

She had tried not to think too deeply about this. But she was
certainly stewing over it now, as she collected her towel and toilet-
ries and headed for the makeshift shower in a canvas cubicle that
Luke had ingeniously rigged up under a tree for the guests who were
camping. As Megan had never been camping before and she was a
bit anxious about the shower, she'd suggested that Sally try it out
first.

No sooner was Sally inside, however, stripped, clutching a bottle of shower gel in one hand and fiddling with the nozzle above

her head with the other, than her thoughts whizzed straight back to Luke.

So far, today had been totally dismal on the Luke front. Each time his gaze had met hers, he'd swiftly and purposefully switched his attention elsewhere, leaving her with a miserable weight pressing under her ribs.

When she'd run into him in the hallway outside Kitty's bedroom it had been even worse. Their brief conversation had been strained and awkward and deep-down *wrong*. In despair, Sally had nearly hurled the basket of cutlery to the four winds and leapt into Luke's arms in the hope that a display of impromptu passion might have resurrected the guy she knew and loved.

Loved?

This startling thought struck just as the shower water stopped, leaving Sally with a huge unanswered question and an equally huge spread of unrinsed soapsuds that she had to wipe off with her towel. Served her right for not concentrating on the job in hand.

Still, the question remained. Was *love* an appropriate word to describe her feelings for Luke Fairburn?

She'd seen him in a new light today. He'd morphed from a quiet, easygoing and slightly shy cattleman-cum-builder into the confident host of Moonlight Plains, and she'd been impressed by how smoothly he'd balanced the supervision of the final party preparations with greeting people and making them feel welcome. *And* he'd been *incredibly* sweet to his grandmother.

Sally had been genuinely touched when she'd watched the solicitous way Luke took Kitty under his wing, making sure she was comfortable with a cuppa and then helping her into the homestead for a nap before the party.

And when Bella had come running up with the bad news that the band had rolled their car on the last bend before the creek crossing, Luke had been remarkably calm, checking first that there were no serious injuries requiring an ambulance, and then racing off in a truck to rescue them.

There had only been one event that seemed to throw Luke today, and that was the arrival of his uncle Jim from Brisbane. From the moment Jim stepped out of his car, there'd been a strange vibe between him and the American woman, Laura. Luke had noticed and he'd been tense about them too, although Sally had no idea why.

Unfortunately, there was no way she could ask him about it. She was a complete outsider and she wasn't enjoying that status. And yet, ironically, while she and Luke had only exchanged a handful of words all day, let alone kissed or touched, she'd developed a new respect for her supposedly casual boyfriend, a feeling that could not be classified as mere lust or fondness.

'Everything okay in there?' Megan called from outside.

'Oh, yes, sorry. Coming!'

'I was beginning to think you must have drowned.'

Apologetic and slightly flustered, Sally hauled on a beach shirt, thrust her damp feet into thongs and grabbed her belongings.

With her hair still dripping, she stepped outside to find Megan ready to fill the shower bucket with the hose hooked up to a tank on the back of a ute.

'Do you need a hand with that?' Sally asked.

'No, I think I've got the hang of it. Luke's uncle showed me how it works.'

That was another thing, Sally thought as she gave Megan a wave and hurried back to their tent. Her friend's comments about Luke's family were spot-on. They'd both thoroughly enjoyed working with Zoe in the kitchen, and not simply because Zoe was a professional cook and had passed on several great tips. Apart from picking up some gorgeous recipes, like Zoe's watermelon, feta and black olive salad, and her superb flourless chocolate lime cake, it had only taken a matter of moments for both Sally and Megan to feel completely comfortable, as if they were long-time friends of Zoe McKinnon's.

And when they'd met Luke's sister, Bella, she'd been as warm and friendly and as instantly likeable as Zoe, as were their husbands, Gabe and Mac respectively. In no time, Sally had felt totally at ease with the whole Fairburn–Mathieson crowd.

Admittedly, Sally knew she was particularly susceptible to the charms of the big-happy-family scenario. As an only child whose relatives, apart from her parents, all lived far away in southern states, she'd frequently envied other people's large family gatherings. For Sally, there was something magical about their noisy celebrations in suburban backyards, or at the beach, or around barbecues in national parks.

Today, as Luke's sisters and uncles and their assorted extras arrived, piling out of cars and greeting each other with laughter and hugs and family in-jokes, she'd almost felt as if she'd found a tribe she wanted to belong to.

And not one of them had grilled her about Luke.

Luke . . .

Back in her tent, towel-drying her hair and then searching through her backpack for clean knickers and a matching strapless bra, she couldn't keep her mind away from him.

She knew he would soon be getting dressed in another tent nearby and she could so easily picture his naked body . . . his broad shoulders and tapered waist, his toned butt and strong thighs . . . the play of muscles in his back as he raised his arms to haul a clean shirt over his head . . .

Luke, showered, and dressed in crisp, clean clothes, was going to look gorgeous. He would probably smell good too, although she wouldn't get close enough to know. Which left her feeling miserable again as she stepped into the brand-new dress she'd bought for the party.

'Oh, wow!' Megan appeared at the tent door and her jaw

dropped when she saw Sally. 'That dress is sensational. You're going to drive Luke mental.'

The halter-neck dress of copper-toned silk had seemed like a good choice when Sally was trying it on in her favourite Townsville dress shop. The colour suited her perfectly and the style brought out her best features. She'd hoped to tantalise Luke by looking her most alluring, in spite of their charade, but after Megan's reaction, the plan felt a tad childish, even thoughtless.

'It's not too try-hard, is it?' she asked.

'No, it's perfect.' Megan sent her a wry smile. 'That's the problem.'

Sally winced. She hadn't brought an alternative outfit, so, to make amends, she applied only the barest makeup and didn't bother with jewellery. Then she grabbed her camera and hung it, purposefully, around her neck. It was time to get over her downbeat mood and to remember she was here as a journalist and not as *anyone's* girlfriend.

It was almost dark by the time Luke and Gabe had finished helping the harassed band guys to roll their vehicle upright before towing it back to the homestead. Luke was relieved to see for himself that there were no serious injuries, although one of the band members, the lead singer, had hurt his arm. Gabe volunteered to run him into the Towers to have it checked out, but the guy was stubborn, insisting he'd be fine for the evening.

Luke wasn't happy about this, but given the timing, he wasn't going to argue too hard.

As soon as he got back, though, he found one of his cousins from Richmond, a med student home on holidays, who'd come to the party with his physiotherapist girlfriend. Between the two of them, they were able to make the singer comfortable with his arm in a sling. Painkillers would do the rest, and Luke could breathe a little more easily.

With that problem solved, at least temporarily, he headed for the homestead for one last check and found his mother hurrying from the main bathroom with Zoe's youngster, Callum, bundled in a huge, fluffy towel.

'He was playing in the dirt with his Tonka truck and ended up covered from head to toe in red dust,' Virginia told Luke with grandmotherly pride.

The kid, straight out of the bath, had a just-scrubbed glow about him. His dark hair was still damp and his cheeks were pink, and he radiated the amazing cuteness that, as far as Luke could tell, was universal among toddlers.

For an instant Luke couldn't help thinking that he wouldn't mind a kid of his own one day, and slap on the back of that thought flashed an image of Sally with a cute little bundle in her arms.

Jeez, he was losing it.

'How's Gran?' he asked, quickly scratching that errant thought and switching to the business at hand. 'Everything okay with her?'

'As far as I know, Luke. But I must admit it's about forty minutes now since I popped in. I took her another cup of tea, but since then I've been looking after Callum. Zoe's busy getting ready, and Mac's keeping an eye on the barbecue, so I offered to give Callum his bath and his tea and put him to bed. We've set up his portacot in my room.'

'Okay, that's fine. I can make a quick check on Gran. I'll only give you a hoy if she needs you.'

'Thanks, darling. Tell her I'll be along to help her get dressed just as soon as I'm free.'

'Sure.' Luke was already hurrying on to his grandmother's room. The door was closed, so he knocked.

There was no response from inside and he wondered if his grandmother had dropped off to sleep again. He supposed he should check on her, and he was reaching for the doorknob when the door opened.

The last person he'd expected to see was his Uncle Jim.

'Hi,' he said. 'I was – ah – just checking on Gran to see if —' Luke stopped in mid-sentence and totally lost his train of thought.

Laura Langley Fox was sitting on the edge of his grandmother's bed and holding her hand.

What the fuck was *she* doing here? And why was his uncle here too? What was going on? The three of them seemed to be having a private conversation behind closed doors.

Damn it, why?

Fine hairs rose on the back of Luke's neck. He knew this was none of his business, yet he was sure it had to be linked to Laura's dramatic reaction to Jim's arrival.

It was like being thrown from a horse and smashing into the ground, winded. 'I – I didn't realise —'

'No problem,' Jim said with an easy smile. 'Laura and I were about to leave Mum in peace. Your grandmother's keen to get ready for the party.'

Laura was no longer holding his grandmother's hand and she'd risen from the bed. Luke thought she looked rather washed out, but perhaps she was one of those women whose appearance changed dramatically when their make-up wore off.

He switched his attention to his grandmother, but it was hard to tell if she was upset. Just the same, he had the uneasy suspicion that this trio's discussion had involved World War II and Laura's father, the American pilot – subjects his grandmother had always avoided.

Damn. He'd behaved rashly when he sent that invitation without Kitty's permission and now guilt roiled uncomfortably inside him. What problems had he stirred up by inviting the American woman out here?

'We were about to leave anyhow,' Jim said smoothly, and he

held the door open for Laura.

In the doorway, she paused and sent his grandmother a shy smile. 'Thanks, Kitty.'

Thanks for what? Luke wanted to demand.

'We'll see you soon, Luke,' said Jim. 'I'm looking forward to this evening. It's shaping up to be a great party.'

They left, shutting the door behind them. Luke crossed the room towards his grandmother's bed.

'Is everything okay, Gran?'

'Yes, dear.' She looked up at him with wide-eyed innocence. 'Perfectly okay. Why? What's the matter?'

'I know there's something going on. Laura was really upset earlier, when Jim arrived. I – I wasn't sure what to make of it.'

'Oh, you mustn't worry, Luke. It was only a little thing and it's all sorted now.'

Perhaps it was the wary, rather enigmatic smile she gave him, but for some reason Luke couldn't explain, he could not accept this glib dismissal.

He took a step closer to the bed. 'Are you quite sure there isn't something I should know?'

35

Townsville, 1942

'I'm only thinking of you, Kitty. It's for your own good.' Her grand-mother sat stiffly on the edge of the chair in Elsie's lounge room, her distress evident in the pained expression on her face, in her tightly clenched hands, in the quiver of her lower lip. 'I'm sure it's better for the baby, too.'

Kitty stared at her in dismay. 'You can't possibly believe that. How can it be better for a baby to be separated from its mother?'

Kitty couldn't bear this. She'd fully expected her grandfather's outrage when she eventually found the courage to tell him about her pregnancy, but she'd hoped her grandmother would be on her side. Surely another woman, another mother would understand that Kitty already loved her baby completely. At just five months she could feel its movements. Each night she lay in bed, her hands cradling the swell of her stomach, picturing the tiny person inside, loving each tiny flutter and bump.

'Kitty, be reasonable. Any baby would be better off with two parents and the chance to grow up in a proper family. Think, girl. How could you possibly bring up a child on your own?'

'I'd find a way.' Although in truth, she had no idea.

'How can you be so stubborn?' Her grandmother was sitting so far forward now she was almost off the chair. 'It might be different if there was any prospect of the baby's father returning to marry you.' She paused, one eyebrow arched expectantly, waiting for Kitty to respond.

'I told you he was wounded and sent home to the States.'

'And he still doesn't know he made you pregnant?'

'No.'

'And you don't plan to write to him.'

Wearily, Kitty shook her head. She was sure that Ed would have written to her if he was well enough. Clearly he hadn't got his sight back. Nothing had changed. Desperate as her situation was, she knew she must stick to her original decision.

Her grandmother sighed heavily. 'You'd have to work to support yourself, and heaven knows what kind of job you'd get. There aren't many employers who'd take on a woman in your condition. And who would care for the baby while you were working? Kitty, it's impossible. You simply can't have a baby without a husband. And you know it's not right.'

Her grandmother sounded uncomfortable as she said this, and Kitty sensed her grandfather's influence. Now that even his best efforts hadn't stopped her from playing the devil's daughter, her grandfather felt that he'd been vindicated in his decision to send her away from Townsville and the Americans.

Reaching for the cup of tea that Kitty had made, still untouched on the small table beside her, her grandmother said, 'There's clearly only one solution. You should go away. I've made enquiries and there's a good home for unmarried mothers in Rockhampton, or you could even go to Brisbane. Your grandfather and I will pay the costs. They'll look after you there, Kitty. You can have the baby safely, and then come home afterwards . . . No one here need know, and people won't ask too many questions about your absence, not with this war and so many folk coming and going.'

Kitty knew this was the main source of her grandparents' distress. They wanted to make sure no one here knew her terrible secret, wanted her safely out of sight before her pregnancy became too obvious. They probably thought she would give in again, just as she had when her grandfather had sent her off to Moonlight Plains, but they had no idea how much she'd changed.

Loving Ed had changed her. In ways she couldn't explain, he'd given her courage.

Now, she said quietly but firmly, 'I'm sorry, but I don't want to give my baby away.'

'So you'd rather bring shame and scandal on yourself and your family?'

Kitty held her breath. She could never believe that her love for Ed was shameful or scandalous. And now that he was gone to the far side of the world, his baby was especially precious to her. She might never see him again, but his baby would always be a living link to him, and she knew with absolute certainty that she could never give it up.

'I'm sorry, Grandmother. I know this is going to hurt you and Grandfather, but I'm definitely keeping the baby. There's no question.'

'Kitty, you —'

Kitty held up her hand. 'I'm really grateful for everything you've done for me and I truly hate knowing that I'm causing you pain and embarrassment, but I can't give my baby away. I'm sorry. I simply can't.'

Somehow she managed not to cry, or at least not until after her grandmother had left in a cloud of disapproval. Afterwards, the tears came as she damped down a pile of pillowslips and tea towels, ready for ironing. She wept for Ed and her baby and she wept for herself. She had no idea how she was going to manage.

*

It was three weeks later, on a Saturday afternoon, when Elsie tapped on Kitty's bedroom door. 'Are you awake?' she called softly.

Kitty had been lying down, trying to rest. 'Yes,' she said. 'It's too hot to sleep.'

Elsie's smiling face appeared as she pushed the door open. 'Well, shake a leg. You've got a visitor.' Elsie winked. 'A young man.'

Kitty gasped and shot up quickly, her heart hammering. 'Not —'

'No, not Ed, but it's good news. It's Andy Mathieson.'

'Andy?' Kitty's disappointment was only fleeting. This was wonderful news. The last time she'd spoken to the Mathiesons, they'd almost given up hope. 'Tell him I'm coming,' she said, reaching for her hairbrush on the dressing table.

She took only a moment to tidy her hair and slip on her shoes. Crossing her fingers that the loose blouse she was wearing over a gathered cotton skirt would hide the growing signs of her pregnancy, she hurried down the hallway to the lounge room. As she entered, a figure rose from the chair in the corner. A man in uniform, tall, suntanned and gaunt, with his slouch hat hanging from a strap over his shoulder. She knew it was Andy, but my, how he'd changed.

'Andy, how wonderful to see you. Everyone's been so worried about you.' She hurried forward.

'Kitty.' His blue eyes were bright in his brown face and they shimmered with emotion.

She kissed his cheek and he kissed hers. 'We'd almost given up hope,' she said. She found it hard not to stare; he'd changed so much, from a boy to a man, in just a few months. 'How are you?'

He smiled, making deep creases at the corners of his eyes. 'Had some bark knocked off me and a stint in hospital, but I'm just about right now.'

'Your parents must be so thrilled. Heavens, they'll be over the moon.'

'Yeah, they're pretty happy.' He swallowed, smiled shyly. 'It's so good to see you, Kit.'

'And it's good to see you.' She meant it sincerely. She hated to think what he'd been through, but it was lovely to have good news for a change.

Behind them, Elsie made a throat-clearing sound. 'Just wondering if you'd like a cup of tea, Andy?'

'Thanks,' he said politely, 'but I was actually wondering if I could steal Kitty for a bit.'

Elsie grinned. 'Be my guest.'

He turned to Kitty. 'I'm dying for a walk along the Strand. Want to come?'

She only hesitated for a beat. 'Yes, of course. Wait a sec, while I get a hat.'

It was a disgustingly hot and humid afternoon, but a soft breeze on the seafront whispered coolly on their skin as they headed for the park and the shade of the banyan trees. While they walked, black cockatoos squabbled in the sea-almond trees.

Kitty coaxed Andy to tell her a little of what he'd been through. He told her that he and a dozen others from his unit had spent three months in the jungle behind the Japanese lines, living off their wits and the small amounts of food they could find. They'd had to be eternally vigilant, as the Japs were everywhere. Only Andy and two of his mates had survived.

'It was thinking of you that kept me going, Kitty. I was determined to get back to you.'

Kitty drew a deep breath when he said this. She was deeply touched that Andy's feelings for her had given him the will to survive, but knowing this also made her nervous. How could she burst his bubble by telling him about Ed and the baby?

Unfortunately, she had no choice. She'd have to tell him at some point this afternoon. If she said nothing and the news reached him later via rumours, he'd be doubly hurt.

They arrived at a grassy spot under a wide-spreading tree and sat looking out beyond the barbed wire to the smooth blue surface of the bay. Andy lit a cigarette, and as he blew out a thin stream of smoke, Kitty studied his face, noting the changes. All signs of boyishness were gone. His features were now lean and chiselled and she sensed a new determination in the set of his brow and the hardness of his jaw. His eyes no longer sparkled with youthful enthusiasm, but betrayed an unexpected worldliness. She feared they held a knowledge of unspeakable things.

'I'm sorry you've had such a rough time,' she said.

He shrugged. 'Could have been worse.'

'Do you have to go back?'

'Of course.' Grimacing, he flipped the ash from the end of his cigarette.

His khaki sleeves were rolled to the elbow and Kitty could see a scar on his forearm – a pitted indentation, purple and shiny, clearly a wound that was still healing. She sighed and almost told him how much she hated this war, hated that he had to go back to more fighting and danger and horror. But that kind of talk wouldn't help him.

'I loved getting your letter,' she said instead.

'I could hardly say anything in the letter. What you really deserved was an apology.'

'An apology?'

'There was so much I wanted to tell you.' Tension vibrated in his voice now. A smile flickered briefly and then disappeared. 'Every time I think about that night before I left, I cringe. I was bloody hopeless the way I rushed at you, Kit. My only excuse was I was so bloody scared and desperate.'

'I knew that, Andy. I understood.'

He shook his head. 'I was such a ham-fisted fool. And I never got to explain anything to your grandfather.'

'Forget about it now.' Kitty swallowed nervously. If only Andy knew . . . his mistakes were minor compared with hers. 'It's all in the past.'

'The thing is, I want to ask you to marry me.' Now when he looked at her, his eyes flashed with a fierce blue fire. 'That's why I had to get back here. I wasn't letting the Nips get me before I told you how much I love you, Kit. I don't think it's possible to love a girl more than —'

'Oh, Andy.' Kitty had to interrupt him. She couldn't sit here letting him pour out his heart, while she nursed a secret that would shatter his hopes.

But oh, dear Lord, how could she get the words out?

'Kitty, what is it? You're not crying?'

Yes, she was crying, but she couldn't let that stop her. She just had to say it. Had to spit it out. 'Andy, I'm pregnant.'

She saw the shock explode in his face. Then puzzlement as his gaze dropped to her stomach. 'I made you pregnant?'

Kitty swallowed. 'No. An – an American.' Now her face was crumpling, her control disintegrating, while Andy ground out his cigarette and sprang to his feet.

Through tear-blurred eyes she watched him stride away, then come to a halt where the grass met the sand, staring out to sea, his chest heaving as he dragged in air. She covered her face with her hands. Until today she'd merely felt sorry for herself, but now she couldn't have felt more wretched if she'd physically stabbed Andy. He didn't deserve this pain and disappointment.

She hadn't brought a handkerchief and she was dabbing at her wet face with the hem of her skirt when she heard the soft sound of his footsteps. She looked up to see that he'd returned already. His eyes were shiny, but he didn't look angry as he lowered himself to sit beside her. 'So what's the story?' he said tightly. 'Are you going to marry this bloke?'

Kitty shook her head.

'Is he still alive?'

And so she told him. As unemotionally as she could, she gave him the bare bones of her time with Ed, concentrating on their efforts to save Bobby at Moonlight Plains, rather than their romantic weekend on the island. She explained her decision not to tell Ed about the baby.

Throughout her painful narration, Andy listened without interruption.

'So . . . he's a decent bloke, he's back in America and he doesn't know. And you don't want him to know,' he clarified when she was done.

'Yes.'

'That's a rough spot to find yourself in, Kit. What are you going to do?'

'I haven't got it all worked out yet, except I know that I'm not giving the baby up for adoption.'

Andy simply nodded and stared silently into the distance. Further down the beach, a group of servicemen were playing football, and a naval ship chugged across the bay.

'I could be a father for your baby,' he said.

Kitty gulped. Had she known that Andy might say this? Had she secretly hoped? But it wouldn't be fair on him. 'Don't do that to yourself,' she said.

'There's no obligation involved, Kitty. I've already told you I love you and that's not going to change.'

Looking up, she saw unmistakable emotion in his eyes, saw a tenderness in his smile that warmed the icy knot of fear that had lain inside her for weeks now.

'But you've only just got back,' she said. 'You can't make an offer like that without taking time to think it over.'

He shook his head. 'I've had months to think, Kitty. I know what I want.' He was staring out to sea as he said this, but now he turned and held her in his steady gaze. 'Look, I don't expect you to fall out of love with this Yank overnight, but if you let me, I'd promise to look after you and love you. And I'd be happy to help you raise your child.'

'I don't deserve that kind of love.'

'Course you do.' There was a new confidence in Andy's smile as he lifted his hand to gently trace the curve of her cheek. 'Marry me and I'll prove it.'

36

Luke stared at his grandmother, stunned. She'd just confirmed his worst suspicions. His Uncle Jim was the American pilot's son.

'And you were already pregnant with Jim when you married Granddad?'

'Yes, Luke.'

How could she sit there so calmly? Luke was so angry he struggled to breathe.

'So – so Granddad was only ever second best for you?'

'No, it wasn't like that. I —'

Luke gave a groan, cutting her off. Of course it was *like that*. She'd been in love with the American but she'd married his granddad. Un-fucking-believable.

Already he was striding across the room. He was so bloody furious. His grandad had been a *great* guy. Steady, true-blue, brilliant with his hands, always ready with gentle humour. A perfect grandfather, among the best of the bloody best. He'd deserved to be up on a freaking pedestal.

Instead, he'd made do as his wife's second choice.

Fuming, Luke left her room and strode down the hallway towards the verandah. Beyond it he could see the revellers already gathering on the lawn. *Shit.* The last thing he felt like *now* was a party.

He stopped in the doorway, knowing he needed to calm down, saw Sally out on the lawn, busy with her camera.

His gut tightened. She looked divine with her bright hair and her pale slender limbs, wearing a gorgeous silky dress the colour of an autumn leaf.

At some point during these past busy weeks, his feelings for her had grown, put down roots. He cared. Cared deeply, which was why he hadn't wanted the family prying.

But now . . .

Now the reality of his situation with Sally hit him with the force of an A-bomb. History was repeating itself. He would be like his grandfather, always be living in another man's shadow. Once again Luke felt the gut-punching shock of his grandmother's revelation. Hell. This was one aspect of his grandfather's character that he was never going to emulate. Sally's husband would always take first place in her heart and he was damned well *not* going to hang around to be another woman's second best.

But that realisation left him with only one clear option.

Much as he hated the thought, it was time to call it quits. After all, he'd finished the project and Sally had her story.

Luke took a deep breath as he faced the unpalatable truth. For them, this party was the end of the road, and before this night was over, he would have to tell her.

A slim new moon, partnered by the bright evening star, shone in the inky-blue western sky as people emerged from their tents, looking transformed, even glamorous. And as they gathered on the lawn in front of the homestead, the house glowed magnificently with all its lights ablaze, spilling gold into the garden.

For Sally, photographic moments abounded. More vehicles arrived, disgorging locals keen to be part of this exciting event. In a corner of the dance floor, the band had almost finished setting up, and guitarists tested their instruments, an occasional melodic twang bouncing into the night.

Mac McKinnon and a couple of his mates had the barbecues primed and ready. The cousins from Richmond and Julia Creek, who'd been assigned to help as waiters, had started serving wine, as well as cans and bottles of beer from the ice-packed eskies.

As Sally clicked away with her camera, she knew that hardly any of the photos would make it into the magazine, but she wanted to add to the album she'd already started. It would be a great record for Kitty and her family, and she would give a disk of all the photos to Luke.

Speaking of Luke . . . she caught sight of him now, in the front doorway, his face twisted in a dark scowl. She hurried across the lawn and up the few steps.

'Luke, what's the matter?'

His green eyes flared, but then, as if he'd taken a moment to register her presence, he said, 'Hey, Sal. Great dress.'

'Thanks.'

Her delighted relief was only momentary. In no time, Luke appeared distracted again.

She stepped closer. 'Is Kitty all right?'

'Kitty's fine,' he said although his mouth twisted unhappily. 'Actually, she could do with a hand. Do you think you could help her dress?'

'I'd be happy to try.'

'If you don't mind. My mother's busy keeping young Callum out of mischief.'

'Of course. No problem.'

'Right. Thanks. I have to get changed.' He shot this last over his shoulder as he hurried off, down the stairs and across the lawn to the distant tents.

More than a little disappointed, Sally watched him leave. She would have liked the chance to suggest that they should relax and enjoy themselves this evening, drop the silly pretence. She would have to try again later, when Luke would hopefully be in a better mood.

She went into the house and down the hall to the main bedroom, where she knocked and was told to come in. Kitty was sitting in front of the dressing table's winged mirror, her long white hair falling in soft waves to her shoulders as she patted at her neck with a powder-puff.

For a moment, Sally fancied she could see her as a young girl, with lively grey eyes and shiny hair, and with a hint of passion and fearlessness about her. She might have been quite a heartbreaker.

'Luke said you'd like some help with getting ready.'

'How kind of you, Sally.' Kitty turned to look at her properly. 'Oh, my dear, what a wonderful dress. You look beautiful.'

'Thank you.'

'Luke will be stunned when he sees you.'

Sally gave an abrupt little laugh. 'He's seen me already.'

'Oh? I hope he told you how lovely you look.'

'He liked the dress,' Sally assured her, and she almost added that Luke had been very distracted, but she didn't want to burden Kitty with unnecessary worry.

Taking the camera from around her neck, she set it on the window seat. 'Now, how can I help you? Would you like to get dressed before we do your hair?'

'That's a good idea. Virginia hung my outfit on the wardrobe door. I think the creases have dropped out.'

It was quite a slow process, helping the old lady out of the dress she'd been wearing and into a pale-pink two-piece suit with pretty lace inserts.

More than once, Sally found her thoughts slipping back to Luke, wondering what had caused his distracted scowl. It was so unlike him. He was usually so cheerful and in control, and she'd never really seen him looking downbeat. Perhaps he'd had an unpleasant shock.

'Was he very upset?' Kitty asked suddenly.

Sally started. 'Excuse me?'

'Luke.' Kitty was watching her intently, her face serious, almost troubled. 'When you saw him just now, was he very upset?'

Sally tried not to look too surprised, and she secured the button at the waist of Kitty's skirt before she answered. 'He seemed quite distracted.'

Kitty nodded sadly. 'I'm not surprised. Did he tell you why?'

'No, not a word.' Sally's curiosity mounted as she lifted Kitty's jacket from its hanger and began to undo the buttons. She couldn't help asking, 'Do you know what happened?'

Kitty sighed. 'I do. It's my fault, I'm afraid. I told the boy something he didn't want to hear.' Her grey eyes glistened as she offered Sally a sad smile. 'He idolised his grandfather, you see.'

'You mean Andy? Your husband?'

'Yes.'

'Luke told me it's because of Andy that he wanted to become a builder.'

'I know.' Kitty seemed reluctant to say more, but then she must have changed her mind. 'I was in love with another man, during the war,' she said quickly. 'If the circumstances had been different, I probably would have married him.'

Sally needed a moment to take this in. She held out the jacket and Kitty obediently slipped her arms into the sleeves.

'I don't mean to pry,' Sally said as she began to do up the buttons again, 'but was this other man the American pilot?'

'Yes. And I'm afraid it's shocked Luke.'

Sally frowned as she considered this. She knew Luke was quite broadminded and not easily shocked. Then again, his grandfather Andy *had* been his hero.

Kitty sighed as Sally fastened the final button. 'Of all my grand-children, Luke bonded the most with Andy. When he was little, he'd come and spend his holidays with us and I used to call him Andy's shadow. Now, I'm afraid he can't come to terms with the fact that I might not have married Andy if the other romance had worked out. I don't think I've convinced him that I still loved Andy dearly.'

A chill slinked through Sally. She hadn't believed in second chances either. During the long pain-filled years that had followed Josh's death she'd been convinced she could never love again.

And yet, here she was . . . on the very brink of admitting her deepening feelings . . .

'I'm sure Luke will feel differently when he's had a chance to think this over,' she said with more confidence than she felt.

'Yes.' Kitty gave a sigh. 'In time he'll understand.'

Sally smiled. It was time to cheer Kitty up. 'There, see in the mirror? You look lovely,' she said.

'Thank you, dear.' Kitty turned to the dressing table. 'I think I'd like to sit down.'

'Of course.' Concerned, Sally helped her to the seat. 'Would you like a glass of water?'

'No, no. I'm all right now, but I'd love a hand with fixing my hair. My arms just don't seem to have the strength any more.'

'Absolutely. Let's see what we can do.'

Kitty's hair was super-fine and Sally worked carefully, combing it and folding it into an elegant twist, while Kitty, with some diffi-culty because of her arthritic fingers, passed up the bobby pins.

'Pesky things, bobby pins,' Kitty muttered darkly, but when she turned her head to examine her reflection, her face broke into a delighted smile. 'Oh, Sally, that's perfect, thank you.'

'My pleasure. All we need now are these earrings.' She picked up a pair of sparkling droplets from the dressing table and carefully clipped them in place. 'Now get ready for the compliments. You're going to turn heads tonight.'

'Oh, look at that!' Kitty's face shone as she stood on the verandah, using her walking stick for balance while gazing out at the flood-lit garden and the congregation of happy guests. 'Isn't it beautiful, Sally? Oh, my heavens!' She clutched Sally's arm. 'See the pond? It's the old fishpond, isn't it?'

Sally almost danced with excitement. She'd been waiting for hours for Kitty to notice the pond, but the old lady had always been surrounded by her family. Now someone, probably Bella, had lit the floating candles, as well as the lanterns set on the crazy paving. The pond looked gorgeous, even better than Sally had imagined when she'd first started cleaning it up.

'When on earth did Luke find time to clear that mess?' Kitty shot Sally a sharp-eyed smile. 'Did you have a hand in this?'

'I gave him some help,' Sally admitted. 'I thought it was too gorgeous to ignore.'

'Thank you.' Kitty squeezed Sally's hand with surprising strength. 'I'm thrilled. I can't wait to have a closer look.'

'Let me help you down the stairs then.'

There were only a few steps, but Kitty's descent was a necessarily slow and painstaking process, and Sally concentrated hard on supporting her until, eventually, they were on level ground.

People smiled and waved and called greetings, but Kitty wasn't mobbed, so Sally was able to help her over to the pond, which looked really pretty now, filled with fish, waterlilies and reeds, as well as the floating candles. On the paved edges the lovely big urns that Sally had planted with white alyssum, pink petunias and trailing blue eyes provided the perfect finishing touch.

When she helped Kitty onto a cushioned stone seat, the old lady stared at the pond with a trembling smile and eyes shiny with tears.

'You know, Andy built this for me.' Kitty patted the seat beside her, indicating that Sally should sit, which she did. 'It was when Robert, my second baby, was born. I was in the Charters Towers hospital for a week – that's how long they kept us in, in those days – and when I came home, here was this pond, with fish and plants and the paving and this seat. And that bottlebrush tree, planted to give some shade. Andy said, "You've given me such a beautiful gift with this new baby. I wanted to be able to give you something in return."'

Kitty's tears spilled now, and Sally's eyes were also prickling and her throat was tight as she slipped her arm around the old lady's bony shoulders.

'What a beautiful thing to do,' she whispered.

'I know,' Kitty said in a choked voice. 'He had Jim to keep an eye on, and all the cattle work, too, so I don't know how he managed. But how could I not love him? He was so good to me. And he kept the tradition of making something for me with each new baby. Just a little something I thought you'd like, he used to say. He said the same words every time and it became another of those things that couples share.'

Kitty gave a shaky chuckle and she took the handkerchief from her pocket and dabbed at her eyes. 'The gifts kept getting smaller and simpler, because Andy still had to look after the property as well as all the children at home. But he always managed some surprise. A sewing box, a dear little birdhouse to hang outside the kitchen window.'

She gave another, happier chuckle. 'By the time the twins arrived, it was a toy box to store the children's clutter.'

'He sounds like a wonderful man,' Sally said sincerely, and already she could so easily imagine Luke being equally thoughtful and sweet.

'So what do you think of the pond?'

The sudden sound of Luke's voice brought her swinging round. No doubt she'd already been feeling sentimental, but the mere sight of him caused a jolt so strong that her heart bloomed like a rose in a time-lapse sequence.

He'd showered and his hair was still slightly tousled and damp, and he hadn't had time to shave. He was wearing a rumpled, blue and white–striped shirt with cream moleskin trousers and riding boots.

On the night she'd first met him he'd been wearing a suit and she'd thought he looked pretty good, but he was absolutely perfect in these clothes. He'd outshine any city guy in a tuxedo. She knew she was grinning like a loon.

'Luke, the pond's wonderful,' Kitty was saying. 'You've done such a good job. Thank you.'

'It was Sally's idea, and she did most of the hard work.'

'Well, thank you again, Sally.' Kitty gave Sally a hug, and then she lifted her smiling gaze to her grandson. 'I was just telling Sally how your granddad built this pond for me.'

'Oh, right.'

'It's such a romantic story,' Sally added for good measure.

'I'm sure it is.' There was no missing the sceptical note in Luke's voice.

Sally caught Kitty's eye and the old woman gave an ever so slight shake of her head, as if warning her not to push him. Then Sally saw Megan coming down the stairs, her arms filled with salad bowls, and she jumped to her feet.

'I'm supposed to be helping Zoe and Megan to bring out the food. Luke, you can look after Kitty, can't you? I'd better fly.'

37

The party at Moonlight Plains was in full swing beneath a huge and clear outback sky, brilliant with glittering stars.

'I'm sure the old homestead must be very happy tonight,' Mary Davies from the Historical Society told Kitty. 'The house must feel pleased to have so many of your family back under its roof and to be the site of such a wonderful party.'

'I'm sure you're right.' Kitty, having sipped her way through an entire glass of champagne, was feeling much more relaxed and therefore happy to imagine that the old homestead nursed sentiments.

She was thoroughly enjoying the evening. The barbecued steaks and salads were delicious and Zoe's desserts were divine. The band played the right mix of old and new music and people crowded the dance floor almost continuously – couples, children, fathers and daughters, mothers and sons, everyone dancing in whatever style took their fancy.

Kitty was thrilled that, although her busy twin sons were absent, the rest of her family was here. She was especially pleased that Virginia seemed to be enjoying herself, despite her dear husband Peter's absence.

There had been a moment earlier when Kitty noted Luke, Bella and Zoe alone with Virginia and raising their glasses in a quiet toast, and she was almost certain they were honouring Peter's memory.

'They're good people,' she whispered, partly to herself and partly to Andy.

She missed Andy tonight. So much.

She longed to be able to tell him about Luke's beautiful restoration, about Sally's efforts with the fishpond, and the emotional conversation she'd had this evening with Laura and Jim.

Kitty watched Laura and Jim now, happily engaged in conversation with the others. Laura, looking chic in navy silk, seemed very relaxed, which was pleasing.

Kitty decided she was finally comfortable with the choices she and Andy had made all those years ago. At the time, she'd had reservations about her husband's desire to tell Jim the truth, but although the outcome had been very emotional for the three of them, it had also been a release. They'd grown even closer because of the secret they shared, and now she suspected that Jim and Laura would remain in contact. In time they could even develop quite a special bond.

The most difficult moment of her day had involved letting Luke in on their secret. Kitty had seen in his eyes that he'd guessed the truth and it would have been foolish or even harmful to leave him to speculate. Now she had little choice but to trust that in time Luke would come to see his grandfather as an even bigger hero than he'd previously imagined.

Of course, she couldn't think about any of this without also thinking about Ed. And once again, as she had so often over the years, she struggled with nostalgia and guilt. She knew it was unfair never to have told a man he'd fathered a son. And yet . . . the reasons for her silence had always felt justified.

She'd heard nothing from Ed after he left Australia. She'd had no idea if he'd regained his sight. Above and beyond this, she'd been utterly in awe of his reputed life of privilege and high status on the other side of the world. He'd made several veiled references to his parents' snobbery. So how might the Langleys have reacted to an Australian upstart who claimed to be carrying their bastard grandchild?

Of course, it was easy to look back and to see her decisions as mistakes, as Luke no doubt did, but each generation had to be judged by the values of their day and not by its current ways of thinking.

Kitty could see now that if she'd been more sophisticated, she might have made different choices. She might have contacted Ed and braved Boston, or she might have just announced the truth and snubbed her nose at the naysayers.

But when Jim was born in 1943, she hadn't been the slightest bit sophisticated. She'd been sheltered, brought up so very strictly, and Townsville was just a remote northern Australian town. There was nothing glamorous about their war, the less important war at the bottom of the world.

When Andy returned from the islands, after they'd almost given him up for dead, offering unquestioning love and support for both her and her baby, she'd married him in an excess of gratitude. Love had come later, building steadily from a solid base of friendship and respect into something deep and abiding and joyful.

Kitty smiled at the memories. She was content.

Luke was like a man on a mission tonight, although Sally feared that his mission was to avoid her.

Okay, so maybe she was being a tad paranoid. Luke was the host of this party, after all, and he was doing a great job, lending a hand wherever it was needed. He'd helped the guys with the barbecue and helped his cousins with serving the drinks. He'd made sure the band members were fed and had whatever else they needed, and he'd paid an appropriate level of attention to his mother and grandmother, as well as to other family members.

He'd also spent a considerable amount of time fielding questions about the homestead from neighbours and locals, and Sally knew this was necessary too. She couldn't forget that this party had originally been her idea and primarily designed to generate interest in Luke's carpentry skills and the restoration of this lovely old neglected homestead.

So yes, her disappointment was probably unreasonable. Just the same, she couldn't escape the fact that Luke seemed to have time for everyone at this party *except* her. Surely he was taking their camouflage several steps further than necessary? All the same, Sally was also quite certain that Luke was keeping tabs on her. Many times, she'd sensed his keen glance and then discovered him watching her from a distance, although as soon as she looked up or turned and their gazes met, Luke switched his attention elsewhere. And he did this so smoothly that she found herself wondering if she'd imagined his interest.

It was all rather unnerving. Sally almost wished she could retire to bed early as Kitty had. She'd tried to escape to the kitchen, but Virginia and the aunts had shooed her away.

'You girls have been working hard in here all day,' Virginia said. 'Now it's our turn to pull our weight. And anyway, it's mostly only stacking and unstacking the dishwasher.'

In the end, Sally decided she had no alternative but to take action.

She asked Luke to dance with her.

Actually, she thought she handled this manoeuvre rather deftly. She waited till Luke was on his own – the last thing she wanted was to embarrass him in front of his family or friends – and when he was striding across a dark patch of the lawn that wasn't reached by the party lights, she stepped out of the shadows.

To her relief he stopped. 'Hey, Sally, how are you? Enjoying the party?'

'It's fabulous.' She raised her voice to reach him above the sudden burst of laughter from a group of young revellers telling jokes. 'You've been the perfect host.' She reached out, letting her fingertips lightly brush his hand. 'Can you spare me a moment?'

Perhaps it was just as well that his face was in shadow, so she couldn't see his reaction.

'I was hoping you might dance with me,' she said in the lightest, most jovial tone she could manage.

Luke hesitated, as Sally had guessed he would, but she was ready for that.

'Just one dance, Luke. No one will think anything of it.'

'Of course,' he replied. 'Okay, let's dance now.'

But when he stepped into the light, Sally saw deep emotion shining in his eyes and his mouth was twisted in a sad smile that frightened her.

They didn't hold hands as they walked to the dance floor, but Luke was sure everyone's eyes were on them.

Too bad. It was perfectly in order for him to dance with a guest, although the fact that the guest in question happened to be the most gorgeous girl here tonight was bound to hold their attention. Luke just hoped the band kept playing something lively that was easy to dance to without too much touching.

Unfortunately, the band did not oblige.

Almost as soon as he and Sally hit the dance floor the music switched to something slow and moody. And as the lead singer crooned the haunting melody, Sally looked up at Luke, her dark eyes revealing a mix of caution and tenderness, and his heart took a downwards spill. This was going to be torture.

Torture to take Sally's hand in his and to place his right hand in the small of her back, where the warmth of her skin reached him through the thin silk of her dress. Torture to feel the slimness of her waist and the fullness of her breasts as she swayed towards him. Torture to have her body so tantalisingly close and to breathe in the scent of her perfume, to feel her hair brush softly against his jaw.

He was *so* tempted to gather her in, to hold her closer still, with her curves pressed against him. So tempted to touch his lips to her brow, to bury his face in her bright, glossy hair.

His body was throbbing with desire and his heart was set to explode with emotion. Both were major problems now that he knew he had to let Sally go.

He had to. There was no sense in delaying the inevitable, but it meant this was their last dance, his last chance to hold her.

So sad . . .

So tempting . . .

But most of all, so damn sad.

When the dance bracket ended, Sally forced herself to slip out of Luke's arms. Dancing with him had been blissful. Reassuring, too, to have him holding her so close, but she didn't want to push her luck. Another dance would be certain to start tongues wagging, and she didn't want to stir curiosity now when Luke had taken such pains to protect her.

'Thanks,' she said, giving him her warmest smile before she took a step back. 'That should be enough to keep me going for the time being.'

His eyes seemed to burn as he looked at her, letting his gaze travel over her from head to toe with an expression that was both so hungry and so bleak that she wanted to leap into his arms and smother him with kisses. Or weep.

Luckily, she did neither. She stuck gamely to their plan, and with a little shrug, she took another step away.

Squeezing her cheek muscles to make sure that her smile held, she sent him a final wave, held her head high and walked back to rejoin Megan, who was chatting with Zoe and Bella and their husbands.

A small silence fell over the little group when she reached them, and she took a deep breath, bracing herself for questions or dry cracks about her choice of dancing partner. But the others were either too polite, or they'd been warned by Megan to skip that particular subject.

There was a little throat-clearing, a couple of dropped gazes and a mildly awkward gap in the conversation until Megan said brightly, 'Hey, Sal, what are you drinking?'

And so the party continued.

In the past Sally had been quite the party girl, staying up as late as anyone, but tonight she was grateful for a midnight curfew, at least for the area around the homestead.

By a quarter to twelve, many of the locals had already left, and quite a few guests had headed for bed, either in the homestead or in their tents. Luke had rounded up the younger players who wanted to party on and sent them off to build a campfire.

'I've slashed an area in the bottom paddock,' he told them. 'And there's a stack of fallen timber you can use.'

Zoe and Bella and their husbands were heading for bed now and Sally knew there was no point in hanging around. She would see no more of Luke tonight.

'We should probably hit the sack, too,' she told Megan.

'Hang on – I think someone wants to say goodnight,' Megan muttered, giving Sally a dig in the ribs with her elbow.

Following Megan's gaze, Sally discovered Luke heading straight for them.

Her reaction was totally over the top, but she couldn't help it. Her heart set up a frantic tattoo as he spoke politely to both of them and thanked them for their wonderful help.

After that, Sally fully expected to be bade a dismissive goodnight, so Luke's next, casually delivered words were a complete surprise.

'Sal, can I have a word?'

38

Megan, with a surreptitious wink, promptly vamoosed, and Sally gave Luke a broad grin. 'Sure, I'd *love* a word. I've been hanging out all day for the chance to chat.'

She was so relieved that he'd come to see her at last, and of course it made sense that he'd waited till they could be alone.

It was still a beautiful night, and so quiet now that the music had stopped. The house was in darkness and, apart from the occasional flash of a torch beam, the rows of tents were in darkness too. The strings of coloured lanterns had been turned off, but in the distance the beginnings of the campfire glowed, and when Sally looked up to the sky she could see the Southern Cross and the Milky Way and the breathtaking dazzle of myriad stars.

'Maybe we should take a seat,' Luke said.

A seat? She hadn't exactly considered what might happen next, but she was a tad disappointed. Taking a seat sounded more like an interview than a romantic tryst.

'Where would you like to sit?' she asked.

Luke pointed to the stone seat near the fishpond, which looked prettier than ever in the gentle starlight. 'That do?'

'I guess.' With a half-hearted shrug she walked across the grass with him and they sat, together, but apart – Luke with his long legs stretched out in front and crossed at the ankles, with his hands on the seat on either side of him.

When Sally stole a glance, she saw that he was frowning again and his jaw was grimly taut.

Was he still upset about his grandfather? She wondered if she should pass on what Kitty had told her about this fishpond and Andy's thoughtful, loving gifts. But what she really wanted was to rekindle the magic of being alone with Luke. His devastating kisses. His hands all over her.

'I thought it would be easier to talk now than tomorrow morning,' he said.

'Well, yes, I guess breakfast will be busy.'

'It'll be mayhem.'

There was a soft splash in the pond and a circle of small ripples, but Sally couldn't see what had caused it.

'You should be very happy with how the party turned out,' she said.

'Yeah, it went well.'

'And everyone *loves* what you've done with the homestead, Luke.'

He nodded. 'Tomorrow we'll have a family conference to work out the future of Moonlight Plains.'

'Oh? Do you think the family might want to sell it?'

'That's the plan.'

She knew she had no right to feel disappointed, but her trips out here had become incredibly important to her. She hadn't merely chronicled Luke's progress or shared his bed – she'd also shared his plans and dreams. Plans and dreams for the homestead, that was; they'd never really talked about *their* future.

For casual lovers, the future was an out-of-bounds topic.

'I'm fairly certain Jim's going to offer to buy us out,' Luke said. 'He reckons he'd like to retire here. He loves the house. It was his childhood home, it's close to town, and the property's small enough to run with a part-time manager.'

'Well, I'm sure you'd all love to see Moonlight Plains stay in the family.'

'Yeah. I don't think anyone will object.'

Which begged the question Sally forced herself to ask. 'So, what will you do next?'

Luke half-turned to her, without quite meeting her gaze. 'I'm already getting job offers.'

'That – that's fabulous.'

'First up, Robert, my uncle, wants me to build a couple of tourist cabins on his property near Richmond. He gets a lot of gold fossickers out there and people hunting for dinosaur fossils.'

'Cabins would be . . . great.' Sally managed to sound happy despite the uncertainty that worried her now.

'Robert's keen for me to start pretty much straight away.'

'Uh-huh.' She tried to swallow the obstruction in her throat. 'I guess that means that I – ah – probably won't see much of you then.'

'No.' Luke's hands gripped the edge of the seat. 'That's what I wanted to speak to you about.' He stared grimly ahead and she could see the silhouette of his profile and the way his throat worked. 'The thing is . . . ' His face twisted in a grimace and then settled into an expression of stoical resolve. 'We've never really talked about the end of the road, have we?'

The end of the road . . .

Slam.

'Do – do you mean the end of our relationship?'

Luke nodded. 'I'd say it's run its course, wouldn't you?'

She closed her eyes against the sudden wave of despair that

swamped her. Why hadn't she seen this coming?

Or had she known it was coming and simply refused to look?

In a nearby paddock curlews set up their mournful, soul-searing cry, while beside her, Luke sat in statue-still silence, waiting for her response.

She swallowed again, trying to ease the ache in her throat. 'So . . . you mean we won't be seeing each other any more?'

'Well, not like we have been.'

'I guess you'd probably still come to Townsville now and again.'

'Maybe. Not often.'

He turned to her now and there was just enough light for her to see the concern and determination in his beautiful green eyes. 'Sal, we always knew this was casual. Not leading anywhere. We had an agreement, didn't we?'

She flinched, and yet everything he said was true. Absolutely, terribly true.

Of course they had an agreement. She'd insisted on their no-strings relationship and she should have known Luke wouldn't hang around on the off-chance that she might change her mind.

Foolishly, she'd been so self-absorbed she'd left it too late to admit that her feelings for him had moved beyond casual. Even if she tried to back-pedal and confess how she felt now, Luke probably wouldn't believe her. And who could blame him? She'd only just begun to believe it herself.

'Sal?' Luke was waiting for her reply.

She couldn't bring herself to say, 'Yes, I agree it's over', but she managed to nod.

Luke made a soft sound that might have been a groan and rose quickly to his feet. He stood looking down at her, his face tormented, as if he wished he could take back everything he'd just said, as if he wanted to reassure her, wanted to haul her from the seat and into his arms.

Sally's urge to leap up and embrace him was huge. But before she could act on it, he turned abruptly and strode away. Into the night.

39

Dearest Kitty,

It's a dangerous thing to look back as I have been doing in these letters to you. It's especially dangerous to dwell too deeply on the twists and turns that our lives have taken.

Fate, if you believe in it, walks such a precarious tightrope. The wrong decisions are made despite the best of intentions. Words that should have been spoken are held back for fear of causing an upset.

I've been looking back, however, and thinking about you again . . . thinking in particular about the time we said goodbye at the hospital. I've been asking myself why I didn't take a leaf from that precious old poser Macarthur's book and promise you that I would return. Instead I gave you no hope, no hint that I planned to come back to Townsville.

Initially, there was the injury, of course – I couldn't bear to saddle a lively young woman with a blind man. By the time I knew for sure that I was going to be able to see again, so many months had elapsed.

Perhaps, if I'd remained in an Australian hospital it

would have been different, but once I was back in America,
I experienced a strange sense of disconnection. Perhaps
the blindness was part of it, but I felt cut off from the war
and from the whole experience of meeting you, as if I was
wandering in some kind of emotional wasteland.

Okay, I know that sounds over the top, but I've been
reading the fairytale Rapunzel to my granddaughter, you see.

I'm sure you know the Rapunzel story, Kitty. The lovely
girl is locked away in a tower and a prince discovers her when
he hears her beautiful singing. Eventually the witch throws him
out of the tower and he's blinded when he falls into bramble
bushes.

I've often thought of you as my Rapunzel, banished to that
outback homestead. I think I fell in love with you on that first
night when I heard you singing so beautifully to Bobby.

The fairytale has a happy ending, of course. After the
prince stumbles around in the wasteland he eventually comes
across Rapunzel, guided by the sound of her singing. By then
the poor girl's had his babies. Heaven help her, she's had twins,
and when the prince turns up, she falls into his arms, her tears
restore his sight and the little family lives happily ever after.

Not so for our real-life story, hey, Kitty?

My sight was restored by medical care and by long periods
of rest in faraway Boston. When I finally recovered, I was told
that I couldn't fly again, but I was made a flight instructor and
promoted to major.

The war rolled on and eventually I was sent back to the
Pacific on a tour of our various bases. My job was to help the
pilots adjust to the Lockheed P-38 Lightnings, which replaced
the inadequate Airacobras that Bobby and I flew.

But Kitty, even then, when I knew I'd be paying a visit to
Townsville, I didn't warn you I was coming. It was the middle

of 1943 and I'd been gone for a year. I suppose I was worried that you'd 'moved on', as they call it these days. If I'd written in advance, heralding my return, you might have felt obliged to welcome me, even if you had another guy. I didn't want to put you in an awkward position.

At least that's what I tell myself now. Too late . . .

Anyway, I returned to Townsville, which was swarming with more Yanks than ever, and I had an overwhelming sense of nostalgia mixed with soaring hope when I walked over the hill at the top of Denham Street and saw the sea and Magnetic Island.

I was remembering every detail of our weekend in that beach hut, as well as our meals in the Bluebird Cafe, our walks along the Strand, our conversations on the beach, our kisses at the water's edge.

By the time I walked to Mitchell Street and was knocking on the lattice door on Elsie's front verandah, I was desperate to see you.

I knew from Elsie's reaction as soon as she opened the door that my visit would not have a happy outcome. My sudden appearance clearly distressed her and I will never forget the immediate onslaught of loss that hit me, as if a block of concrete had been tied to my hopes. I could feel my heart sinking to the very depths.

Still, I went through the motions. 'How are you?' I asked Elsie. 'How's Geoff?'

I gave her a food parcel – I can't remember what was in it now, but she was very grateful. She said they were 'sick to the back teeth with the rationing'.

And then, almost fearfully, I asked, 'How's Kitty?'

Elsie had so much trouble telling me. Her eyes were so sad, her lips were trembling and for a horrified moment I thought something truly terrible had happened to you.

'Kitty's married,' she said at last.

Dearest girl, have you any idea how final and deathlike that word 'married' is?

'She was married two days ago,' Elsie said.

Two days.

Two days, Kitty!

Elsie was a little calmer then and she added details. 'Right now, she's away on her honeymoon. Just a few days at Paluma, up in the mountains.'

There's no need to carry on about how I felt. In retrospect, I took some small comfort from the fact that you didn't have your honeymoon on the island.

Elsie told me that you'd married an Australian, a boyfriend you'd known for years, and after a few careful questions, I was sure that he was the guy who'd been lost up in the islands. So I was glad he was safe.

But, damn it, he won you after all, Kitty.

Don't worry . . . I had to get that off my chest.

What I also want to tell you is this: I've lived a long and successful and, I'm very pleased to say, happy life. I chose a suitable wife primarily to please everyone at home, but I was lucky. I loved Rose. Not as much at first as perhaps she deserved, for she was a good, talented, sweet woman, but over the years my love for her grew deeper and stronger and our marriage was, ultimately, very rewarding.

In time, Kitty, you were just a sad, sweet dream that came to me in my dark moments. You've helped me through the midnight terrors that visit anyone who's been to war. So thank you, my darling girl.

I hope you've been as lucky as I have.

A tear slid down Laura's cheek and onto the letter and she sent a hasty, embarrassed glance to the passenger sitting beside her. Fortunately, the portly businessman had become engrossed in reading a report on his laptop almost as soon as they'd taken off from Sydney and he'd only looked up when lunch was served. He certainly hadn't noticed Laura's weepy moment.

She looked down at the wet spot on the paper and blotted it with her fingertip, wondering if it would leave a mark. Not that it mattered. Now that she was on her way to Italy, flying somewhere over Northern Australia at thirty thousand feet, she wouldn't be sharing this letter with anyone.

Perhaps, in time, she might show her father's letters to her family, and possibly to Jim Mathieson if he kept in touch as he'd promised . . . but she had abandoned her original plan to show the letters to Kitty.

For Laura, the big takeaway message from her journey to Moonlight Plains had been the value and complexity of secrets. She knew now that guarding judiciously chosen secrets was sometimes the wisest action.

Yes, it was easy to feel puzzled and angry about everything that her father had kept to himself for seventy years, but Kitty and Andy had kept an even bigger secret, and reading between the lines, Laura suspected that Kitty's friend Elsie had probably never told Kitty about Ed's return to Townsville. Like the others, she'd wisely decided that sometimes the truth could only cause more harm than good.

The astonishing thing was, Laura realised now, that she alone was privy to all sides of this story. Her father would never know about his son, and Kitty would never know that Ed Langley had come back to Townsville to court her.

She wondered if this knowledge had changed her. The whole ordeal of her divorce had been bad enough, but she felt as if she'd been through another emotional maelstrom since she'd opened the first letter all those months ago. Now, after Jim's revelations at Moonlight Plains, she felt as if her perceptions had been even further ripped apart.

It was hard to judge if or how this had changed her. Perhaps the art classes in Florence would help. She'd enrolled in advanced classes in oil painting that promised, among other things, to help her to express her subjectivity and her perception of situations and surroundings.

Laura smiled. She couldn't wait to see how the results of her recent journey would filter through to her art. In many ways, the timing couldn't have been better.

She was still smiling at the thought of Italy and the brand-new set of experiences that lay ahead of her, as she folded the pages along the old crease lines. She slipped the letter back into her purse, her fingers brushing the edge of a coin, the dollar Kitty had given her. A silver dollar from 1923.

Laura took it out to look at it again. So pretty, with the head of Liberty on one side and an American eagle on the other.

'That's a Peace dollar.' Her neighbour was suddenly alert and excited. His laptop forgotten, his eyes were practically bulging behind his spectacles.

'Do you know about coins?' Laura asked, holding out the dollar so he could see it better.

'Yes. These were specially minted in America after World War I to commemorate peace. Look here,' he said pointing. 'You can see the word "Peace" under the eagle.'

'Oh, wow. How neat. Are you a collector?'

'My father was. I've inherited his collection and I haven't decided what to do with it yet. These coins are getting rarer. I'm not sure how much they're worth.'

'Oh, it doesn't really matter,' Laura assured him. 'I won't be selling this. Its main value is sentimental.'

She had given Kitty her word that once she was back in the States, she would do her darnedest to track down the Kowalski family. Kitty had told her the whole story about Bobby Kowalski and his lucky dollar, and how it had remained lost until Luke's miraculous find. She knew it would mean a great deal to Kitty if the dollar found its way home.

Just then, the plane made one of those sudden stomach-dropping lurches, and to Laura's horror, the coin spilled from her outstretched palm. Her heart gave a terrified bound as she grabbed at thin air.

Oh God.

Not again.

'Oh, lucky catch.' Her neighbour was grinning broadly as Laura's fingers clasped around the coin. 'If that had rolled onto the floor and under these seats, you'd have had hell's own job trying to find it.'

'I know . . . I know.'

Laura's heart was still racing as she slipped the dollar back to safety and zipped up the inside pocket of her purse. She'd never been superstitious, but as she closed the purse with a reassuring snap and set it safely under the seat in front of her, she had an overwhelming prescience that her life was about to change again. This time, for the better.

40

The tourist cabins took Luke six weeks or thereabouts to complete. The work was straightforward and easy – his uncle didn't want anything fancy – so the job was nowhere near as interesting or satisfying as his project at Moonlight Plains. But what could a guy expect when he grabbed a quick job opportunity as a hasty escape?

At the time, he'd been sure that it was kinder and more sensible to make a clean break with Sally, far better than watching a great relationship fizzle out until it became stilted and awkward and painful.

Thing was . . . clean breaks were supposed to heal faster, and six weeks should have been ample time to get Sally out of his system, so it was damned annoying that he still thought about her all the time. It was even worse that he had no interest in dating anyone else.

A call from Mac towards the end of November included an invitation to Mac and Zoe's property, Coolabah Waters – if Luke was at a loose end, Mac could use a hand securing some of his sheds before the cyclone season. Luke knew he should be following up leads on bigger projects, but he still felt restless and unready to settle into something long-term.

So, when Sally's magazine arrived, he was working on Coolabah Waters and having a beer with Mac at the end of the day, out on the deck they'd both built overlooking the lagoons.

Zoe brought out the mail. 'There's something for you, Luke,' she said, setting a large, stiff cardboard envelope on the timber outdoor table. Her eyebrows lifted as she sent him a pointed glance. 'From Sally Piper.'

Luke did his best to appear nonchalant as he picked up the envelope and saw his name written in Sally's curly script. She'd sent it to Richmond, and then his uncle had crossed out that address and forwarded it on to Mullinjim, and finally, Bella had sent it here.

'I guess it's a copy of the magazine with Sally's article,' he said, and his gut felt strangely tight and nervous. He wasn't worried for himself, but he hoped for Sally's sake that the story had turned out well.

Perhaps Zoe and Mac both sensed that he was nervous, for neither of them plied him with questions. Mac paid studious attention to his own mail, while Zoe returned to the kitchen, where Callum was perched on a high stool at the bar eating his dinner. She liked to feed him early and settle him into bed before the adults ate.

Luke opened the envelope, and sure enough, inside were a magazine, a disk and a note. He read the note first.

Dear Luke,
So here it is. I think the spread looks great and the people at
My Country Home are pleased. There's talk of more work for
me, so that's great news. I hope you're happy with the story
and the photos and, of course, I also hope you're well and
thriving.

I've included a disk with all the photos I took over the
weeks at Moonlight Plains. I thought you might like them as a
record.

*Thanks again for letting me work on this project. I loved
every minute.*
Love,
Sally xx

Luke found himself mesmerised by those last two words. *Love, Sally
xx.* Of course, he knew it was probably the way she signed all her
letters and had no special significance, but the word *Love* seemed to
jump out at him and bounce around in his head.

He looked up to find Mac watching him with puzzled amusement. 'Well, are you going to take a gander at her story?'

'Yeah, course.' Luke folded the letter and slipped it back inside.
Then he drew out the magazine.

Moonlight Plains was on the front cover.

A painful rock jammed Luke's throat. He could remember when
Sally had taken that photo in the last week before the party. The
painters had only just left when she'd arrived from Townsville late
on a Friday afternoon. The sky was turning pink and mauve and the
sun cast a soft bronzed glow over the paddocks and trees.

'I've got to get a photo now,' she'd said, scrambling out of the
car and grabbing her camera. Her dark eyes had glowed with excitement. 'This is going to be *it*, Luke. The one I've been waiting for.'

She was right. It was a fabulous shot, totally worthy of its cover
spot. Across the bottom of the photo was a description: *Capturing
the Romance of the Past: The inspiring story of a forgotten homestead's restoration.*

'Wow,' said Mac, his attention caught. 'That looks amazing.'

'Yeah.' Luke gave a shaky laugh. 'It probably looks better than
it does in real life.'

'Doesn't matter. What's the story like?'

Luke turned the pages and quickly found it. Once again, the photos of the finished house were fabulous, especially in comparison

with the 'before' photos. There were also several photos of himself, including one where he was without a shirt.

The back of his neck grew hot and he knew his pulse accelerated as he scanned Sally's written words, reading quickly just to get the gist, aware that Mac was watching.

'Well, it reads pretty well,' he said, after a bit. 'Sally's a good writer.'

He didn't add that there was far more story about him than he'd expected. Zoe and Mac and the rest of the family would soon see that for themselves. He hoped he wasn't in for a grilling.

When he finished, he pushed the magazine across the table to Mac. Then he drained his beer and got to his feet, too restless to sit around while Mac read the story. 'Want another?' he asked.

'Sure,' Mac said without looking up.

Luke fetched two more beers from the kitchen fridge and hung around for a bit, chatting to Zoe and cheekily playful Callum. When he went back out onto the deck Mac was still reading. It was crazy to be so nervous, crazier to be so damn miserable.

'What do you think?' he asked as he set Mac's beer in front of him and resumed his seat.

'This is great.' Mac was grinning as he tapped the page. 'Sally really did the right thing by the old place, didn't she?'

'Yeah.' Luke stifled his urge to sigh and took a swift swig of beer.

'The story's as much about you as it is about the homestead,' Mac added and then he looked up from the magazine and narrowed his eyes at Luke. 'So, are you two still good friends?'

'No, we broke up,' Luke said emphatically.

'Oh?'

'What's with you? What do you mean . . . Oh?'

Mac shrugged. 'It's interesting to hear you've broken up with Sally. I guess that means you were more than friends.'

Bloody hell. He'd walked right into that one. 'You missed your calling,' Luke said through gritted teeth. 'You should have been a lawyer, trapping people with words.' And he took a long, deep, *angry* drag of his beer.

Mac leaned forward, his palms open on the table like a peace negotiator. 'Look, mate, we all saw the signs.'

'What signs?'

'Well, apart from the burning way you and Sally looked at each other, Sally worked her socks off at the party – like one of the family.' He gave a shrugging smile. 'Only a *very* good friend puts in that kind of effort.'

Great. So after all their subterfuge, they hadn't fooled anyone.

Luke stared moodily at his beer. 'It was only ever casual.' Then he added quickly, in case Mac tried to argue, 'We had a sort of no-strings agreement. Sally's still not over losing her husband.'

Instead of answering, Mac looked again at the magazine article, turning the page to a photo of Luke. Eventually, he said, 'And this husband died how long ago?'

'Couple of years or so.'

To Luke's relief, Mac didn't try to respond to this. He leaned back in his chair, drinking his beer and looking out at a flock of magpie geese flying homewards across the darkening sky.

A cool breeze drifted in, rippling the surface of the lagoon, and from inside the house came tempting smells of dinner cooking and Zoe's voice, warm and joyous, as she read a bedtime story to Callum.

'Listen, mate,' Mac said suddenly. 'If you're thinking you could never replace Sally's husband, I know that's not true.'

'You wouldn't know shit about this.' Luke stopped in mid-snarl as he remembered. 'Sorry, I almost forgot . . . about you and Lisa.'

Lisa had been Mac's fiancée, a city girl, and the poor guy had been mad about her. They were all set to marry when she'd panicked about living in the outback and had taken off one day, driving through a flooded creek. Mac had nearly gone crazy when she drowned.

'You might remember how hard I was on Zoe when she turned up,' Mac said. 'I'd decided that all city girls were the same. They simply couldn't cut it in the bush.'

As if on cue, Zoe appeared on the deck with young Callum laughing and squirming in her arms. 'Someone needs to say good-night to Daddy.' Her face, framed by dark curls, was alight with happiness.

Grinning, Mac rose and gave her a kiss before he took Callum from her, giving the boy a tickle and making him squeal. 'So what is it tonight? A helicopter into bed? Or a spaceship?'

'Helichopper!'

Even before Mac lifted his son high, zooming him through the air and making *whop-whop-whop* noises, the boy was squealing.

At the doorway, he turned and winked, and Luke had no trouble reading his silent message.

Look what I nearly missed out on, mate.

When Luke finally visited his grandmother for the first time since the party, she lost no time in bringing up the subject of Sally. 'Sally tells me that she's not seeing you any more.'

'Well, no.' Luke tried for a nonchalant shrug. 'It was never serious. We were only ever casual.'

'Why?'

He swallowed. 'That's how things are these days, Gran.'

'What nonsense.'

He might have tried to explain about his reluctance to live in the shadow of Sally's husband, but his grandmother fixed him with an especially stern frown and her grey eyes glittered with something akin to anger.

'I hope this has nothing to do with our conversation about your grandfather out at Moonlight Plains. You're not still worrying that Andy was my second choice.'

Luke could feel his jaw tightening and he shifted uneasily in his chair. Why couldn't they just reminisce about the party? Talk about the weather? Her health?

His grandmother leaned forward, fixing him with narrowed beady eyes. 'Tell me, Luke. Did you ever see me treat your granddad as second best?'

'Well, no, but —'

'Of course not, because he wasn't.' She settled back in her chair by the window with a sigh and shifted her unhappy gaze outside to a hedge of bright tropical shrubbery.

Luke thought how tiny and frail and exhausted she looked. He found it almost impossible to reconcile this fragile birdlike figure with the energetic, good-humoured dynamo who used to host their massive family gatherings without ever seeming to tire.

When she turned back to him, she smiled gently. 'I admit it's true that when I married Andy I was still in love with Ed and carrying Ed's baby, but I was fond of Andy. And very grateful.'

Fond? Grateful? Was that the best she could offer? Luke couldn't hide his dismay.

'I know it must be hard for you to understand,' she went on. 'But of course, those feelings changed as I grew to love Andy. How could I *not* love him? You know what a kind and caring man he was. Luke, you'd be doing your grandfather a huge disservice if you thought he was anything but the best husband I could have asked for.'

Now her eyes glistened and Luke felt like a heel. The last thing he'd wanted was to upset her. If only she hadn't started by asking about Sally. He'd been driving himself crazy enough with his own tortured arguments.

'It's like the old homestead,' his grandmother continued, now calmer. 'Is it second best now, simply because it's not the same as when it was built?'

'I don't think so. No.'

'But you had no hesitation about changing it from what it used to be. You were quite happy to pull down walls and change the way it looked and worked.'

'Yes, but —'

'You rebuilt the house for now, Luke, and for the future.' She leaned towards him again, her eyes bright and sharp once more in her delicate, wrinkled-creased face. 'You used your knowledge of the past, but you didn't leave it stuck the way it used to be.'

'Well, yes, but —'

'Just like a marriage.'

She glanced at the magazines he'd brought her and pointed to the top one with a full-page shot on the cover of a celebrity couple embracing. 'Young people these days have their heads filled with Hollywood and Valentine's Day, but romance alone can't sustain a couple through a lifetime. A good marriage doesn't just happen, you know. It's built by two people and it takes work, just like building a house. And however it starts in the beginning, if you work together with willing hearts, love – *the real thing* – grows.'

A wistful look softened her aged face. 'It grew for your grandfather and me, and you know that, Luke – you felt it between us, didn't you? Andy was not my second best. He became my rock and the most important person in my life.'

'Yeah, that – that's great, Gran. I didn't mean —' Luke had to swallow to try to shift the gravel in his throat. 'I guess I was reacting to the shock of learning about Jim and everything.'

His grandmother nodded. 'It was a difficult way to start a marriage,' she said softly. 'Just like the old homestead wasn't perfect when you started on it. But you and Sally made that old ruin into a beautiful home again. And it's in better condition now than it ever was.'

Luke was nodding thoughtfully, and he might have said more, if his throat wasn't still so uncomfortably tight.

'So don't talk to me about second best. And don't ever think of yourself as Sally's second best.'

He stiffened.

'That girl deserves better, and so do you.' His grandmother shooed him with a wave of her hand. 'Now, go away, darling. I've been talking too much and I'm tired.'

'Would you like me to help you onto the bed?'

'Yes, dear. Thank you.'

As always, he worried that his big hands might hurt her small, bony body, but she showed nothing but gratitude for his assistance. Bizarrely, as he settled her onto the bed, he could suddenly picture Sally at the age of ninety, with a loving family anxious to help her and with the wisdom of a long and happy life accumulated. A life that had only included him for a blink.

He'd never felt so wretched.

41

Sally was preparing her flat for Megan's bridal shower, and flowers were strewn all over her kitchen benches while she sorted out which ones best suited the various bottles she'd collected. Vivid pink dahlias in an old mint-sauce bottle. Fluffy bougainvillea blossoms in a honey jar.

It was all very 'crafty', as Sally wanted everything for the party to be pretty and girly – this was Megan's last hurrah as a single gal, after all. She'd even found a box of her nan's embroidered tablecloths stored away in her parents' spare room, and she was using these on the dining table, as well as embroidered linen napkins.

Linen, not paper. She'd asked her mother how to make starch, but Angela, who had a cleaning lady, had no idea.

'I'm sure there are instructions on the packet,' she'd said, and she was right.

Sally had washed, starched and ironed Nan's linen and now it looked crisp and gorgeous, lending her boring little flat just the right old-fashioned touch of quaintness.

Sally had ordered fancily decorated cupcakes, too, while Jane and Dimity were bringing savoury platters. The girls were having high tea and champagne cocktails and those silly, groan-worthy party games where everyone promptly gave the prizes to the bride.

The phone rang just as she had located a suitable bowl in which to float the apricot and white frangipani blossoms. Her hands were sticky as she pressed the answer button. 'Hello, Sally speaking.'

'Sally, it's Abigail from *My Country Home*. Sorry to ring you so late on a Friday, but I wanted to catch you before the weekend. Are you free to talk?'

'Yes.' Sally held her breath. Was she about to hear bad news about her story? Circulation for this month's issue had dropped dramatically? The cover photo hadn't grabbed?

'I've been talking to Charlotte, our editor,' said Abigail. 'She asked me to pass on the good news that our figures are looking stellar for this month's edition.'

'Oh.' Sally's relief was swift and sweet. 'That's great to hear.'

'And your webcam interview with the carpenter is going gang-busters on our website. We're so glad you offered it, Sally. That carpenter's so cute and sincere he's winning hearts all over the country. I guess you've seen all the comments?'

'Well, no, I haven't, actually.' Sally had been far too fragile to torture herself by watching the footage of Luke that she'd filmed in the week before the party. She knew it would only rouse too many memories, would stir up way too much pain.

Abigail laughed. 'So you haven't seen the number of women begging him to come and work on their homes?'

'No.' Sally felt sick.

'There've even been a couple of marriage proposals.'

Marriage? Sally clenched her teeth so tightly her jaw almost cracked.

'Anyway,' Abigail hurried on. 'Charlotte's hoping you'd like to do another story. Another renovation project. Actually, we'd like to offer you a retainer to write regular stories for us.'

Sally knew this was not the moment to be tongue-tied. For heaven's sake, this was her dream come true. It was what she'd hoped for when she'd first suggested the story to Luke.

Now her mind was spinning as she tried to think positively. It would help if she knew of another renovation on the go. It wasn't the sort of story you could pull out of thin air. And then there was the Luke thing.

She missed him so badly. She wasn't sure she had the heart to pour herself into a similar story that would keep reminding her of him. How could she ever drum up the same keen interest?

'I'd love to write more stories for you,' she said. 'But I'd – ah – have to do a bit of research to find a good project.'

'Yes, of course. I understand. Give it some thought, Sally, but just remember we'd love more stories like Moonlight Plains. We'll keep in touch, okay?'

'Yes, definitely.'

'Feel free to ring me any time if you want to talk over ideas.'

'I will, thank you. Thanks so much for the call.'

Sally disconnected and stood staring at the flowers still scattered around her kitchen. She knew she should be excited about this offer. She should be thrilled that her story was a success and they wanted more from her. A retainer, no less . . .

Meanwhile, women were ogling Luke on the internet and offering him marriage. How crazy was that?

She had to calm down. She couldn't think about any of it now. In less than an hour, her girlfriends would be arriving for the bridal shower. She had to focus. This was *Megan's* day.

She gave herself a little shake as she shepherded her thoughts. Right. Most of the flowers were in vases or bottles. The cupcakes were in the bakery boxes, safe for now in her bedroom, where she'd also stowed the party prizes. The champagne was on ice in the laundry tub and the crate of hired glasses was ready to be unstacked and set out. It was time for the best part of any party preparation, the finishing touches.

With a little skip of excitement, she hurried around placing the flowers on windowsills and bookshelves, on the coffee table, the dining table, the TV stand. Then she bundled up the stems and leaves and stashed them in the rubbish bin.

She was washing her hands at the sink when her dog Jess began to bark and a knock sounded on her door. She knew this had to be a girlfriend arriving early, and yet she tensed instinctively as terrifying memories rushed back. Another Friday evening . . . preparing a surprise party for Josh when the police knocked on this very same door . . .

Her heart took a sickening lurch and she had to clutch at the edge of the sink.

'Sally?' a male voice called.

Well, at least he knew her name, so it wasn't the police. And Jess's bark sounded happy. In fact, the voice sounded like —

But it couldn't be.

Hastily wiping her hands on her jeans, Sally forced herself to turn, to walk sedately across the kitchen and the living room. Bright sunlight hit the dusty grille on the flyscreen door, so she could only make out the outline of her caller. Tall, broad-shouldered. Disturbingly familiar.

She opened the door.

'G'day.'

Luke was wearing a blue chambray shirt and cream moleskin trousers and a lopsided, shy, sweet smile.

Sally's heart gave a foolish little swoon.

'Hi.' She wasn't sure what else to say, had no idea why he'd come. Jess leapt through the doorway, madly wagging her tail and making excited yips of welcome, but Sally wasn't inclined to invite an ex inside, so she stood holding the flyscreen door.

'I was in town,' Luke said, giving Jess's ears a quick scruff and then straightening. 'So, I thought I'd drop by.'

Why? Sally wanted to snap. Even if a guy didn't know he'd shattered your heart, he wasn't supposed to break up with you and then simply drop by.

The sun was beating down hard on their heads, making Sally squint. Luke dropped his gaze to his hands and she saw that he was holding some kind of wooden box.

'I brought this for you,' he said, holding the box out to her. 'Just a little something I thought you'd – well, a kind of thank-you present for doing the story and for helping with the party and – and everything.'

For the second time in a matter of moments, Sally was tongue-tied.

Luke looked nervous. 'I – uh – made it out of off-cuts of timber from Moonlight Plains. Cedar and kauri and a little silky oak. It might be useful for storing your jewellery or something.'

Her throat cramped on a sudden glut of tears. Luke was being thoughtful and sweet. He probably didn't know it, but his hand-made gift was almost exactly the same sort of thing Kitty's Andy used to make for her.

Just a little something I thought you'd like. Wasn't that what Andy used to say?

But there was one major difference. Kitty and Andy had been married, while Sally and Luke had gone their separate ways. Did Luke know this was killing her? Every time she saw this box she would think of him and she'd probably be as emotional as Kitty had been about a few rocks and a pond of water.

'Sally, are you okay? I'm sorry, I . . .'

Luke seemed as lost for words as she was. He was holding out the box, however, and she had to take it.

The soft honey tones of the timber glowed and it felt warm

and silky-smooth beneath her fingers. When she opened the lid she caught the woodsy scent she'd admired so much when she'd first visited Moonlight Plains.

She felt her mouth pull out of shape as she struggled not to cry. 'It's lovely. Thanks.'

'Sally, I was also hoping to speak to you.'

Oh, God, was she strong enough for a conversation?

'Well . . . okay,' she managed in a squeaky voice. 'I guess – um – come in.'

She was shaking as she backed into the flat and Luke followed, bringing a faint hint of aftershave as he closed the screen door carefully behind him. It was cooler inside, but Sally still felt flushed and nervous. So nervous.

She pointed to the lounge chairs, but Luke didn't seem to read this as an invitation to sit.

'I wanted to – to find out how you are,' he said, standing stiffly in the middle of her living room and filling it with his suntanned, outdoorsy maleness.

'I'm fine.' Although it depended on how you defined fine.

'Congratulations on the story, by the way. It's brilliant.'

'Thanks.'

His mouth tightened and he squared his shoulders as if whatever he had to say next was even more difficult than this initial awkwardness.

Anxiously, Sally gripped the box, clutching it tightly against her stomach.

Luke's green eyes flashed as he caught her gaze and held it. 'So, I'd like to know how you *really* are, Sal. Honestly. I need more than fine.'

She opened her mouth, and then quickly shut it. She couldn't lie, but she wasn't brave enough to tell Luke that these past few weeks had been miserable. It was a different kind of misery from the shocked grief that had followed Josh's death, but in its own way just as painful.

She needed to find exactly the right thing to say, the right words for both of them. She'd stuffed Luke around, playing the widow card, and if this was any kind of last chance she needed to get it right.

'In case you were wondering,' Luke said, sensing her reluctance, 'I've found it pretty damn hard since we split.' Then before she could react, he hurried on. 'So here's the thing. I want to scrap what I told you at Moonlight Plains. I still want you, Sal. I know you're not ready. I know you're still grieving, but I'm not prepared to walk away from what we had.'

Sally gasped. She couldn't believe Luke was offering her another chance; a very real chance for happiness.

'I'm not,' she said.

He frowned. 'Excuse me?'

'I'm not still grieving.' And before she lost her nerve, she launched into the speech she'd been practising in her head, hoping against hope. 'I'll never forget Josh, but I know I can't bring him back, and I want to focus on the future now.'

Luke's smile flickered briefly. 'When you say the future, do you mean *our* future?'

'Yes.' Most definitely. Absolutely. No doubt about it.

Time was measured by the thump of Sally's heartbeats as she and Luke stared at each other. It felt like an age before they moved, but when they did, they moved towards each other, and everything that had been difficult became wonderfully simple.

Luke took the box from her hand and dropped it onto a lounge chair and drew her close.

It was so good to feel his arms around her, strong and certain. Until this point, she'd felt lost in a maze, desperately trying to find her way out, but at last she had finally, *finally* opened the right door. She was home, safe.

Their kiss was quite possibly the sweetest kiss ever, and Sally could feel all her tension dissolving as happiness flowed into her, filling her from her toes up.

It was ages later when they found themselves on the sofa, touching close, but needing to talk.

Luke took Sally's hand in his and turned it over to expose her wrist, which looked pale and fragile compared with the hugeness of his.

'I'll play this any way you want,' he said. 'We can keep it casual.'

'No,' Sally said, emphatically shaking her head.

His eyes were intense now, demanding total honesty. 'You want to play for keeps?'

'I do.' She smiled, so happy to know for certain. 'I love you, Luke, and I've been so miserable without you.'

'Sal, you've no idea what this means.'

This time she was the one who started their kiss, but when Luke scooped her into his lap, things rapidly turned steamy.

Until a car door slammed outside. *Oh my God, the party.* How could she have forgotten?

'Sorry,' she muttered scrambling to her feet and smoothing down her T-shirt. 'I somehow forgot to mention that I'm actually about to throw a party.' She waved her hand at all the flowers. 'It's a bridal shower for Megan. And at least a dozen women are about to land on my doorstep.'

Luke sent a glance out her window. 'I think they're already here.'

'Yoo-hoo, Sally!' called Jane's voice.

Sally knew her face was bright red as she rushed once again to the door. Jane, Dimity and Megan were all there on her doorstep, a trio of young women in summery dresses as pretty as the cupcakes she'd ordered.

The trio spied Luke standing a few feet behind her, tucking in his shirt, and in unison their eyes widened and their mouths gaped.

Sally's blush deepened as she went through the introductions, followed by explanations that Luke had just dropped by unexpectedly, and then she realised that Megan was glaring at them. Her friend still hadn't forgiven Luke for breaking up with Sally.

'It's okay,' Sally muttered to Megan out of the side of her mouth.

Megan raised a doubtful eyebrow.

'Truly,' Sally whispered. 'We're fine.'

'You mean —' Megan gasped. 'Fine as in okay and back to normal? Or fine as in absolutely fabulous?'

Grinning, Sally slipped an arm around Luke. 'We're absolutely fabulous.'

Megan squealed. 'So you're not – don't tell me – engaged?'

Whoops. Sally shot a quick glance to Luke and saw that he was grinning as broadly as she was.

'Yes,' she said. 'Yes, we are.'

Next moment she was enveloped in an ecstatic hug.

'I'm so happy!' Megan squealed again, this time in her ear.

There were more hugs before Sally escaped with Luke to the footpath, while her friends headed for the kitchen.

'Sorry about that,' she told him.

'At least we have witnesses.' Luke slipped his arms around her waist. 'And Megan saved me from getting down on my knees.'

'Well, there's always time for that later.' Sally looked up at him with a playful smile.

'I can see you later? After this party?'

'I'm counting on it.'

The road stretched ahead, an undulating ribbon rippling through cattle-grazing country, heading south. Sally and Luke were in the front of the ute with Jess safely caged in the back, along with their luggage and Luke's tools.

They were off on an adventure: another restoration job in New South Wales at a sheep station near Inverell. The owners of the property had tracked Luke down after reading Sally's magazine story. They'd sent photos of their homestead and, after several phone calls, everyone was excited about this new venture.

Luke and Sally would be living in an old shepherd's hut, a very simple dwelling, but they didn't care. Everything about this was exciting for them. A new beginning.

'Did you know the name Inverell means a meeting place for swans?' Sally asked as they zipped down the highway.

Luke grinned. 'I'm glad you've started your research. You'll probably need to write more about the homestead this time and quite a bit less about the builder.'

'Most definitely. I don't want half the women in Australia ogling my man.'

She was smiling as she dropped her gaze to her engagement ring, a lovely coppery-gold tourmaline, so different from the traditional little diamond she'd left behind in Townsville. She'd had to store quite a bit of stuff with her parents, but luckily they hadn't minded in the least. They both adored Luke, and her mother had promised to spend more time at the nursing home with her own mother, Sally's gran, so Sally could leave without worrying on that score.

'Do you know my favourite moment of these past few weeks?' Sally asked Luke now.

'I can think of several highlights, but in most of them you were naked.'

She grinned. 'Well, yes, okay, that's very true, but I *also* loved it when we went to see Kitty to show her this ring.'

At the mention of Kitty, she could see the emotion flood Luke's face even though he was staring straight ahead at the road. He nodded. 'She was certainly happy, wasn't she?'

'I'm almost crying again just thinking about it. She was so teary and thrilled; it was like we'd fulfilled her final wish or something.'

'We have, Sal.' Luke shot her a shiny-eyed smile. 'I know we have.'

Acknowledgements

While this book continues my rural romance stories about the Fairburn family, the inclusion of Kitty's World War II story is a new direction for me, but it's a step I'd been looking forward to for quite some time. The urge to write about wartime Townsville has been quietly brewing since the city celebrated VP 50 – fifty years since victory in the Pacific.

In 1995 Townsville opened its arms to the hundreds of veteran American servicemen who returned to the place that held so many vivid, life-changing memories for them. Amazing stories circulated in the newspapers, on the radio and TV and, as I began to see the city where I lived in a very different light, I was captivated.

I've spoken to many people about the war years, but I would particularly like to thank Kay Ramm, who shared her experiences of living on a cattle station during the war. I'm also grateful for two very inspiring books – *The Morning Side of the Hill* by Marion Houldsworth and *A Soldier Remembers* by Herbert C. Jaffe.

When it came to writing Luke's story about restoring the old homestead, I was greatly aided by conversations with Louis Simon and Fiona Stewart, who are not only wonderful renovators but also great storytellers.

Of course, huge thanks go to my editors at Penguin, Belinda Byrne, Ali Watts and Arwen Summers, and proofreader Emma Dowden. Thanks to all of you for your belief and your encouragement and most of all for your wisdom. Thanks too to my wonderful first readers, my insightful and eternally patient husband Elliot Hannay and my brilliant, generous friend Anne Gracie.

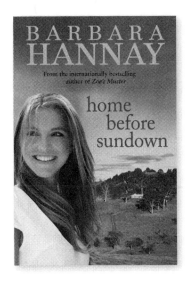

ALSO BY BARBARA HANNAY

home before sundown

Coming home can break your heart . . . or change your life.

For Bella Fairburn, a girl from the bush, her new life in Europe is a dream come true. But news of her beloved father's heart attack brings Bella rushing back to Australia along with her aunt Liz, an acclaimed musician who's been living in London for the past thirty years.

Coming home is fraught with emotional danger for both Bella and Liz. While Bella is confident she can deal with drought, bushfires and bogged cattle, she dreads facing her neighbour. Gabe Mitchell is the man she once hoped to marry, but he's also the man who broke her heart.

And for Liz, Mullinjim holds a painful secret that must never be revealed . . .

In the rugged beauty of the outback, new futures beckon, but Bella and Liz must first confront the heartaches of the past.

'An engaging story of joy, tragedy, romance and heartache set within the dusty landscape of the Australian outback.'

Book'd Out

'In beautiful, fluid prose, Hannay once again puts together all the ingredients for a real page turner.'

Toowoomba Chronicle

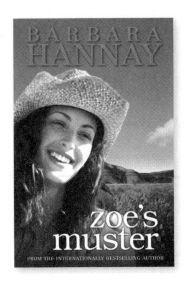

zoe's muster

When Zoe, black sheep of the Porter family, discovers that her biological father is a Far North Queensland cattleman, her deep desire to meet him takes her from her inner-city life to a job at remote Mullinjim Station. But Zoe is sworn to secrecy. Her mother, Claire, is afraid to confront the ghosts of her past.

Virginia Fairburn is happily married to Peter but she's always lived with the shadow of the other woman her husband loved and lost.

On the muster at Mullinjim, Zoe meets brooding cattleman Mac McKinnon. Every instinct tells Mac that Zoe is hiding something, and as the pressure to reveal her mother's secret builds, Zoe fears she must confide in him or burst. The truth has the potential to destroy two families. Or can it clear the way for new beginnings?

Set in the rugged outback of beautiful Far North Queensland, *Zoe's Muster* is a passionate love story from award-winning romance writer Barbara Hannay.

'Hard to put down . . . get your hands on a copy of this book and you will not be disappointed.'
Weekly Times

'An engaging story with appealing characters set in a wonderful landscape . . . Another fine example of the growing rural fiction genre.'
Book'd Out